He couldn't stop.

The whale-thing was chugging along behind him still, hemming him in. Bo had to get out. Bo had to get out, he had to get help. He had to come back for his sister and for the others, even the ones who cried too much. His throat was clenched around a sob as he hurled himself at the fence, remembering Ferris being dragged away by the whirlybirds. His limbs were shaking; the Parasite was vibrating him, like a battery in his stomach. He squeezed his eyes shut.

There was a shiver, a ripple, a strange pulse that passed through every inch of him, and he didn't feel the fence's tentacles wrapping him tight. He didn't feel anything until he collapsed onto the tarmac on the other side, scraping his left elbow raw. Bo's eyes flew open. He spun around, still on the ground, and stared at the fence. In the dead center of it was a jagged hole, punched straight through. The fence wriggled around it, fingering the hole like a wound.

By Rich Larson

THE VIOLET WARS

Annex

ANNEX

The Violet Wars: Book One

RICH LARSON

www.orbitbooks.net

Copyright © 2018 by Rich Larson
Excerpt from *Cypher* copyright © 2018 by Rich Larson
Excerpt from *One of Us* copyright © 2018 by Craig DiLouie
Excerpt from *Rosewater* copyright © 2016 by Tade Thompson

Author photograph by Micaela Cockburn
Cover design by Lisa Marie Pompilio
Cover illustration by Gregory Manchess
Cover copyright © 2018 by Hachette Book Group, Inc.

Orbit
Hachette Book Group
1290 Avenue of the Americas
New York, NY 10104
orbitbooks.net

First Edition: July 2018

Orbit is an imprint of Hachette Book Group.
The Orbit name and logo are trademarks of Little, Brown Book Group Limited.

The publisher is not responsible for websites (or their content) that are not owned by the publisher.

The Hachette Speakers Bureau provides a wide range of authors for speaking events. To find out more, go to www.hachettespeakersbureau.com or call (866) 376-6591.

Library of Congress Cataloging-in-Publication Data:

Names: Larson, Rich, 1992- author.
Title: Annex / Rich Larson.
Description: New York : Orbit, 2018. | Series: The Violet wars ; 1
Identifiers: LCCN 2017059882| ISBN 9780316416542 (paperback) |
    ISBN 9780316416559 (ebook)
Subjects: LCSH: Imaginary places—Fiction. | Oppression (Psychology)—Fiction. |
    Self-actualization (Psychology) in children—Fiction. | Liberty—Fiction. |
    Science fiction, Canadian. |
BISAC: FICTION / Science Fiction / Adventure. | GSAFD: Science fiction. |
    Fantasy fiction.
Classification: LCC PR9199.4.L375 A65 2018 | DDC 813/.6—dc23
LC record available at https://lccn.loc.gov/2017059882

ISBNs: 978-0-316-41654-2 (trade paperback), 978-0-316-41655-9 (ebook)

Printed in the United States of America

LSC-C

10 9 8 7 6 5 4 3 2 1

For Kit Reed (1932–2017), without whom this book would still be wandering

1

The pharmacy's sign was burnt out and the windows all smashed in—Violet had done one herself—but there were still three customers standing gamely in line. She stepped around them, shoes squealing on the broken glass, and headed for the counter. None of the three wasters noticed her butting in. They didn't notice much of anything, not their torn clothes or singed hair or bloody feet. The slick black clamps at the bases of their skulls saw to that. Violet tried not to look too closely at wasters. Peripherals only, was her rule. If she looked too closely, she was liable to see someone she recognized.

Of course, she made an exception for the pharmacist. "Oh, hi!" she said, feigning surprise. "I think you helped me last week, right?"

The pharmacist said nothing, moving his hands in the air a foot over from the register, his glazed-over eyes trained on something that wasn't there. His beard was hugely overgrown, but Violet had sort of a thing for the mountain man look. He was still tall and muscly, though in a wiry way now, because wasters forgot to eat more often than not. Still handsome.

"Well, if I'm an addict, you're my dealer, jerk," Violet said, cocking her hip and trying to flutter her eyelashes without looking like she'd detached a retina. She was getting better at it. Maybe she would try it on Wyatt soon.

The pharmacist said nothing, now pulling imaginary pill bottles out of an empty metal cupboard Violet had already ransacked. His vacant half smile didn't seem as charming today. Violet gave a sour shrug and tossed her duffel bag over the counter, then nimbly followed.

"That's our problem...Dennis," she said, leaning in to read the red plastic name tag stuck through his shirt. "You're a shitty communicator. We're not going to last."

Violet gave the pharmacist a consoling pat on the arm, then unzipped her duffel and set to work. Wyatt had told her to get antibiotics and painkillers, and since Violet knew her way around from last time, it didn't take her long to fill the bag with Tylenol-4s, ibuprofen, three rattling canisters of Cipro, and a bottle of liquid codeine. Wyatt was strict about who got the medicine ever since one of the younger Lost Boys made himself sick chugging cough syrup, and he never used it himself, never took a single pill, even though Violet knew the scar along his hips made him wince sometimes.

Violet wasn't interested in painkillers. She had more important drugs to look for. She rifled through the birth control until she found her estradiol—Estrofem this time—then emptied the tablets into her own private ziplock stash. She hunted down more Aldactone to top up her spiro supply.

She shook the plastic baggie, eyeing the candy-shop assortment of pills and counting days, then pincered a pale green Estrofem and swallowed it dry. Her Parasite rippled in response, whether with pleasure or revulsion, Violet never knew. She folded the baggie carefully into the bottom of her duffel bag with the other meds and dragged the zipper shut.

"Well, I *might* be free for coffee this weekend," Violet told the pharmacist, slinging the duffel over her bony shoulder. "But I can't give you my number because, you know, an alien invasion fried all the phones. No, I swear to God. Maybe next time, handsome."

She scooted across the counter and dropped down on the other side, brushing a slice of dark hair out of her face. The wasters ignored her on her way out, all of them still standing patiently in line.

Violet kept them in her peripherals.

2

Bo was hiding behind a powerjack, only meters from the fire door and the emergency exit sign glowing above it through the gloom. The Parasite in his stomach wriggled madly. He held his hand to the icy concrete floor; when the flesh of his palm was stinging cold, he pressed it against his stomach. That helped soothe it a bit.

The electricity had gone out earlier that day, dropping the grimy corridors and sleeping rooms into darkness, and Bo wasn't going to waste his chance. He'd snuck out of his bed while a boy named James was wailing and weeping loud enough to make the whirlybird drift over to him with its sleep-inducing syringe. A few of the other kids had watched Bo slip away, but he'd put a fierce finger to his lips and none of them had seemed particularly interested anyway. Most of them drank the water.

His older sister, Lia, was the one who'd realized that they put something in the water that made you feel dull and happy, and that it was better to collect drips off pipes in the bathroom. She was thirteen to Bo's eleven and she usually did the thinking. But she was gone now.

So Bo had found his way through the dark corridor alone,

running one hand along the pitted concrete wall and its retro-fitted wires, making his way toward the emergency exit that led outside. Now he was waiting for the last group of kids to go from supper to bed, trying to breathe slowly and keep the Parasite in check.

A familiar whine filled the air, then a whirlybird emerged from the corridor. It was as big around the middle as Bo and drifted along at head height, like a balloon, except made of slick rubbery flesh and gleaming black metal and other things he couldn't guess at. A tangle of spidery multi-jointed arms dangled down from its underbelly, flexing slowly in the air, and there was a bright acid-yellow lantern set into the top of its carapace that illuminated the kids plodding behind it.

As always, Bo scanned their faces. Everyone's eyes were turned to deep dark shadows by the sickly yellow glow, and everyone was stepping slow and dreamy-like. For a moment he fooled himself into thinking he saw Lia near the back of the file, faking the effects of the water, because there was no way she'd started drinking it, but it was a different black girl. Shorter, and lighter-skinned.

He knew Lia was in some other facility. They'd been split up weeks ago. But it didn't stop him from looking.

The whirlybird floated past and Bo imagined himself spring-ing at it, seizing one of its trailing limbs, smashing it against the floor, and stomping until it cracked open. The Parasite in his stomach stirred at the thought. But his wrists and hands were still crisscrossed with feather-white scars from the first and last time he'd tried that.

Instead, he waited until the glow of the whirlybird receded into the dark and the last of the kids got swallowed up in the shadows.

Bo was alone. His heart hammered his ribs and the Parasite gave another twitch. He levered himself upright, crept out from behind the powerjack. Three surreal strides and he was at the door, hands gripping the bar.

A girl named Ferris had tried to open it before, and the wailing of the alarm had drawn the whirlybirds in an instant. But with the electricity out, there would be no alarm and no fifteen-second delay on the crash bar. Bo still made himself pause to listen, to be sure there wasn't a whirlybird drifting on the other side of the paint-flaking metal. He heard nothing except the toddlers who'd been crying ever since the lights went out. With a tight feeling in his throat, Bo pushed.

The door swung open with a clunk and a screech, and cold clean air rushed into his lungs like the first breath after a storm. He'd been in the chemical-smelling warehouse for so long he'd forgotten how fresh air tasted. Bo gasped at it.

He took a shaky step forward, only just remembering to catch the door before it slammed behind him. He tried to focus. He was in a long narrow alley, garbage whipping around his feet and graffiti marching along the soot-stained walls. Bo knew, dimly, that the warehouses they'd been put in were near the docks. The briny sea-smell confirmed that much. He was far, far from their old neighborhood, and he didn't know if it even existed anymore.

Bo looked up. The dusk sky seemed impossibly wide after months of fluorescent-lit ceilings, but it wasn't empty. Unfurling over the city like an enormous black umbrella, all moving spars and flanges, was the ship. It didn't look like a spaceship to Bo, not how he'd seen them in movies. It didn't look like it should even be able to fly.

But it drifted there overhead, light as air. Bo remembered it spitting a rain of sizzling blue bombs down on the city, burning the park behind their house to white ash, toppling the skyscrapers downtown. And up there with the ship, wheeling slow circles, Bo saw the mechanical whale-like things that had snatched up him and his sister and all the other kids and taken them to the warehouses. Remembering it put a shock of sweat in his armpits, and his stomach gave a fearful churn. The Parasite churned with it.

Bo started down the alley at a trot before the panic could paralyze him. He didn't know where to go, but he knew he needed to put distance between himself and the warehouse. As much distance as possible. Then he would find somewhere to hide. Find something to eat—real food, not the gray glue they ate in the warehouses. He had been fantasizing about pepperoni pizza lately, or, even better, his mom's cooking, the things she made for special occasions: *shinkafa da wake*, with oily onions and the spicy *yaji* powder that made Lia's eyes water so bad, and fried plantains.

That made him think of his mom again, so he buried the memory, as he had for months now, and picked up his pace to a jog. The Parasite throbbed in his stomach and he felt a static charge under his skin, making the hairs stand up from the nape of his neck. That happened more often lately, and always when Bo was angry or frightened or excited. He imagined himself smashing a whirlybird out of the air right as it went to jab his sister with the syringe, and her thanking him, and admitting that if he had his shoes on he was faster than her now. He pictured himself opening the doors and all the other kids streaming out of the warehouse.

A harsh yellow light froze him to the spot. Shielding his watering eyes, Bo looked up and saw the silhouette of a whale-thing descending through the dark sky. He took an experimental step to the left. The beam of light tracked him. The whale-thing was close enough that he could hear its awful chugging sound, half like an engine, half like a dying animal trying to breathe. Bo was never going inside one again.

He ran.

After four months in the warehouse, four months of plodding slowly behind the whirlybirds because anything quicker than a walk agitated them, Bo felt slow. His breath hitched early behind his chest and he had an unfamiliar ache in his shoulder. But as the whale-thing dropped lower, its chugging sound loud in his ears, adrenaline plowed through all of that and he found his rhythm, flying across the pavement, pumping hard.

Fastest in his grade, faster than Lia. He said it in his head like a chant. Faster than anybody.

Bo tore down the alley with a wild shout, halfway between a laugh and a scream. His battered Lottos, tread long gone, slapped hard to the ground. He could feel his heart shooting through his throat, and the Parasite was writhing and crackling in his belly. The static again, putting his hair on end. He could feel the huge shape of the whale-thing surging over him. Its acid-yellow light strobed the alley, slapping his shadow on each wall of it, moving its blurry black limbs in sync with his. Bo raced them.

Faster than his own shadow.

He blew out the end of the alley and across the cracked tarmac of a parking lot, seeing the yellow-stenciled lines and trying to take one space with each stride. Impossibly, he could feel the whale-thing falling back, slowing down. Its hot air was no longer pounding on his back. Bo didn't let himself slow down, because Lia said you were always meant to pick a spot beyond the finish line and make that your finish line.

The fence seemed to erupt from nowhere. Bo's eyes widened, but it was too late to stop. He hurtled toward it, more certain with each footfall that he wasn't going to be able to scale it. It wasn't the chain-link that he used to scramble up and down gecko-quick. It wasn't metal at all, more like a woven tangle of vines, or maybe veins, every part of it pulsing. A few of the tendrils stretched out toward him, sensing him. Ready to snatch him and hold him and give him back to the warehouse.

He couldn't stop. The whale-thing was still chugging along behind him, hemming him in. Bo had to get out. Bo had to get out, he had to get help. He had to come back for his sister and for the others, even the ones who cried too much. His throat was clenched around a sob as he hurled himself at the fence, remembering Ferris being dragged away by the whirlybirds. His limbs were shaking; the Parasite was vibrating him, like a battery in his stomach. He squeezed his eyes shut.

There was a shiver, a ripple, a strange pulse that passed through every inch of him, and he didn't feel the fence's tentacles wrapping him tight. He didn't feel anything until he collapsed onto the tarmac on the other side, scraping his left elbow raw. Bo's eyes flew open. He spun around, still on the ground, and stared at the fence. In the dead center of it was a jagged hole, punched straight through. The fence wriggled around it, fingering the hole like a wound.

Bo clambered to his feet, panting. He wiped the ooze of blood off his elbow, nearly relishing the sting of it—he hadn't been properly scraped up for months. Then he put his hand on his stomach. The static was gone, like it had never been at all, and the Parasite felt suddenly heavy, no longer twitching or moving. Had he done that? Had he made the hole?

The whale-thing was stopped on the other side of it, and it didn't have a face but he got the sense it was as surprised as he was. Bo gave an instinctive glance around for grown-ups, even though he knew he wouldn't see any, then flipped it the bird. The whale-thing didn't respond, still hovering in place. Then a strange moaning noise came from inside of it. Bo watched as the whale-thing's underbelly peeled open. Something slimed and dark started unfolding itself, then dropped to the paving with a thick wet slap. It was human-shaped.

Bo felt a tiny trickle of piss finally squeeze out down his leg. The human shape moaned again, and that was enough to give Bo his second wind. He turned and ran again, the cut on his elbow singing in the cold night air, the Parasite sitting like lead in his gut. But he was out of the warehouse, and he wasn't going to let them take him again, not ever. When he came back, it would be to get Lia, and the others, and to smash every last whirlybird in the place.

It was the only way to be sure he got the one that had pinned him down that first day and injected the Parasite right through his belly button.

Bo made it his new pact as he jogged, deeper and deeper, into the dark and ruined city.

Violet was heading to Safeway to pick up some groceries, walking down a silent street under a cloudy gray sky. Gray as the day the ship came down, scorching the city with the electric blue pulses Wyatt said were exhaust from its engines. There'd been no sun since. Just gray, a hazy emulsion that looked close to rain but never gave it up. Violet didn't mind the new weather. Sun burned her and rain made everything too wet.

She walked down the middle of the street instead of the side-walk, weaving through the stalled-out cars. Some had wasters sitting inside, imagining themselves driving off to work, but most of the cars didn't work anyway. Their chips were fried. The ones that did work were useless, what with the roads so clogged and nobody really knowing how to drive besides.

The intersection ahead was stoppered up with the splintered geometry of a crash, a three-car pile-up that had happened during the big panic when the ship came down. Violet didn't want to walk around it, so she clambered up onto the accordion-scrunched hood of an SUV. The soles of her Skechers popped little dents in the aluminum. She tried to ignore the dead-thing smell that wafted from the backseat.

On the other side of the wreck, she faced a corner liquor store, half of it black and crumbled from an electrical fire, and then beyond it her destination: the Safeway where she'd shopped with her mom four months and a lifetime ago. The parking lot was strewn with garbage, picked at by a flock of dirty gulls, and wasters shuffled slowly around it with grocery bags that Violet knew were sometimes full, sometimes empty. Some of them were pushing squeaky shopping carts across the ruptured tarmac.

But one of the carts wasn't being pushed by a waster. Violet narrowed her eyes. It was a boy, maybe ten or eleven, skinny frame swallowed in an oversized hoodie. She watched him roll his sleeves up to his elbows, one of which was swatched with Technicolor Band-Aids, and start wrestling with the cart again. He'd picked one with sticky wheels, but it had alright stuff in it: a sleeping bag, a trussed-up Styrofoam mattress, canned food, and bottled water. Usually kids fresh out of the ware-house were too dopey to do much more than wander around all shell-shocked.

Violet swapped the duffel to her other shoulder and cut across the culvert of yellowed grass to the parking lot pavement. By the time she was close to him, the boy had snatched an empty cart from one of the wasters and was dumping everything from his own into the replacement.

"Hey," Violet said. "Those Winnie the Pooh Band-Aids?"

The boy looked up, startled. The hood fell back off his head and Violet could see his face still had a bit of chub to it, the kiddie kind, but his eyes were sharp. A little bloodshot from crying, but focused. His black hair reminded her of a ball of steel wool, and she could see a comb mostly buried in the tangle. He yanked his sleeve down over the yellow patchwork on his elbow and stared back at her for a moment, mouth working for words.

"You're not a zombie," he finally said, in a voice that was a little closer to cracking than she'd expected from someone his size. It made her extra conscious of her own.

"Nobody's a zombie," Violet said, as the waster he'd swapped carts with stumbled past. "They don't eat brains or anything. Just wander around being useless. We call them wasters."

"Where'd you come from?" the boy asked.

Violet peeled the stretchy fabric of her shirt up off her stomach, showing him the rust-red Parasite under her pale skin. The boy immediately stuck his hand to his own belly. His face twitched.

"Same as you, Pooh Bear," Violet said, tugging her shirt back down. "You thought you were the only one who got out?"

The boy frowned. "Is everyone else . . . Is all the grown-ups . . ." He tapped the back of his head, where the clamps went in.

"Everyone over sixteen," Violet said. "Or around there." She reached over and yanked the sleeping bag and a single bottle of water out from the cart. "What's your name?" she asked.

"Bo," the boy said. "Bo Rabiu."

"Violet." She stuffed the sleeping bag into his arms and tossed the bottle on top with a slosh. Getting groceries could wait. "Alright, Bo, time to get out of the streets," she said. "The othermothers are going to start coming through soon."

"What?"

"The o-ther mo-thers," Violet enunciated. "You'll see one soon enough. For now, we're going to a safe spot, alright? A hideout. So you can meet Wyatt."

Bo tucked the sleeping bag under his arm and tossed the water bottle up and down with his other hand. "Who's he?" he asked suspiciously.

"He's a jerk," Violet said. "Let's go."

She set off back out of the parking lot, mapping the way back to the theater in her mind's eye. She didn't bother to check if Bo was following. They always did.

3

Bo slipped into the wake of the dark-haired girl named Violet as she weaved through the shuffling dim-eyed adults. It made Bo feel sick looking at them, seeing the shiny black piece of metal that dug into the backs of their heads and made the veins in their necks bulge. One man in a shredded business suit stopped abruptly on the sidewalk, reaching into his pocket to pull out an invisible phone. Bo nearly plowed into him, jerking away at the last second. He didn't quite manage to hide his shudder.

Violet stopped, shooting him a look over her shoulder. "Don't be scared of them," she said in her slightly scratchy voice. "They don't do anything."

"Not scared," Bo said reflexively, watching the businessman turn away, mouthing a conversation. "They stink real bad. That's all."

Violet bent to snatch something up off the sidewalk. It was an old cracked iPhone. She flashed Bo a smile, and for a moment he thought she was going to go up and put it into the businessman's empty fingers. Instead, she juggled it once in her hand, then hurled it at the back of the man's head. His neck snapped forward. Then he steadied himself, continuing his pantomimed phone call with a tiny trickle of carmine running down his scalp where the cracked screen had cut him.

"They're like NPCs," Violet said. Her smile didn't crinkle her eyes. "Think of them like that. Not like people."

"They are, though," Bo said. "People." He'd already had a horrible thought. He'd thought of going back to his burned house and finding his mother was alive but wandering through it with her eyes filmed over, smiling all empty-like. He didn't know which option would be worse: dead or a zombie. There was a reason he'd decided to get supplies first.

"Not anymore," Violet said in an icy voice. "Clamp's in the head, better off dead. Got it?"

Bo glanced away, pretending to tend to his elbow. Violet had already decided which was worse. He couldn't think about his mom yet, anyway. He had to think about Lia. If he was going to rescue her from the warehouses, he was going to need help. At the very least, he was going to need to know what had happened on the outside during the four months he'd been locked away. Violet seemed like she knew those things.

As for the othermothers, whatever they were, Bo still remembered the slimy silhouette dumped from the belly of the whale-thing, and it still made him shiver.

"Got it," he said.

Violet gave him a skeptical look, one eyebrow cocked high, then turned and hurried on. Bo followed. She was taking him into the oldest part of the downtown, past an ancient hotel where his mom had told him to be careful of strangers and stepping on needles. The sidewalks were narrower and crooked, with a blackish moss seeping through the cracks. One waster they passed was knocking her fist against a graffiti-splashed brick wall, over and over, like she thought it was a door. Her knuckles were a mess of raw meat.

"They look happier than they used to," Violet said, catching him off guard. "The wasters who hang around here. Happier than before they got clamped."

"What do they see?" Bo asked.

"Dunno," Violet said. "Not us." She gave a vague wave around the street. "Something nicer than this, I bet. Lots nicer."

They came to a halt in front of an old theater Bo remembered passing on the bus once, maybe twice. It had been closed for years. The signage had more blank white spaces than it did black letters, making it look like a wide gappy grin, and the few movie posters that hadn't been snatched were curled and yellow inside their glass slots. Most of the globe lights around them had been smashed. Up on the top of the building, Bo saw the name of the place, Garneau Cinema, painted in dark red letters that were peeling like scabs.

The door had been boarded over with a two-by-four, but Violet skipped up and yanked it open, showing the plywood to be nailed on only one side. The inside looked dark, dark as the warehouse, and Bo smelled dust and mothballs and what might have been old popcorn grease.

"Why not the IMAX theater?" Bo asked, hesitating on the threshold. "They have those comfy seats. Memory foam seats."

"Be full of wasters pretending to watch movies, wouldn't it," Violet said. "Come on in. You know Peter Pan?"

"Sort of," Bo said.

"This is Neverland," Violet said. "Come meet the Lost Boys."

"Who are you, then?" Bo asked. "You, uh, Tinkerbell?"

"Fuck you," Violet said, flashing that smile again that was both pretty and scary. It was better than the dull grins of the drugged-up warehouse kids or the wasters. That counted for something.

Bo stepped into the musty entryway, and she eased the door shut behind him. The dark gave him a nervous drop in his stomach, and the Parasite gave a sluggish twitch. He was half relieved, half disappointed that it was finally moving again. He'd thought maybe it was dead after whatever had happened with the fence.

Violet switched on a bulky black-and-yellow flashlight, thumping it a few times with the heel of her hand. In the stark beam Bo saw the interior of the theater was floored with cigarette-scorched carpeting. The wallpaper had water stains.

But there weren't any whirlybirds. He licked his dry lips and followed Violet past the abandoned ticket booth and concession stand, where the smell of ancient cooking grease still hung off a defunct popcorn machine. Through a set of faux-oak doors thrown wide open, Bo saw the blank movie screen, half-illuminated by mismatched lamps. Violet led the way in, switching off her flashlight. Stripes of exit lighting still glowed faintly on the floor.

The theater had velvet red seats, some of them with armrests torn away or their cushions slashed open, and some of them had kids splayed on them. Bo had a sudden thought: Maybe his sister was already here. Lia'd always been smarter than him. Maybe the power outage had affected all the warehouses, or maybe she'd gotten out before that, somehow. Bo looked hopefully over the ten or so kids, most of them clustered in a group near the front, others scattered.

None of them looked older than Violet, who Bo had pegged for fifteen—the carefully drawn makeup around her eyes made it harder to tell. And none of them were his sister.

Bo sank a bit. Some of the kids gave him curious looks as he followed Violet along the aisle, but most of them kept their attention fixed toward the front, where a tall and bony boy maybe Violet's age, maybe a bit older, was seated on the edge of the stage. He had a messy blond head and gray eyes, and Violet was fixing her hair all of a sudden.

"...at least a block away before you start heading back here," the boy was saying, splayed back with one leg dangling off the edge, swinging slow like a pendulum. "We don't want mothers following us back, right? So we have to be careful, right?"

"Right," came the reply, a dozen intent mutters.

"Elliot knows, don't you, El?" the older boy said, flicking a look to one of the kids in the front, a slightly younger brown-haired boy hunched on the edge of his seat.

"I know," Elliot said solemnly, and the older boy, who Bo could guess by now was Wyatt, gave him an affirming nod in return. As Wyatt's gray eyes traveled back over the theater seats, they caught on Bo and Violet. He smiled, bright and white, how Bo had seen mostly in movies.

"All the under-tens, you go everywhere in doubles when there's othermothers out," Wyatt continued. "From now on. And what if the mother stops and squats and squeezes her glands? What's she doing?"

"Pheromones," the kids chanted, in unison this time. Bo sideways-saw Violet forming the word on her pink lips.

"So what do we do?" Wyatt asked. "Elliot?"

"If a mother drops 'mones, don't breathe through your nose," the boy named Elliot recited, wiping at his own with the neck of his oversized orange T-shirt.

"Right," Wyatt said. "Breathe through your mouth and get

away from there quick, or you'll be following her right back to the warehouses."

A collective shiver went through some of the kids, and Bo took a second look to note their slightly distended stomachs. One pale boy had no shirt on, and he could see the rust-colored tendrils splayed around his belly button like a flower. Bo's own Parasite gave a wriggle of recognition. He didn't recall any of their faces from the four months he'd been inside, but he didn't know how many warehouses there were either.

"That's it," Wyatt said. "Everyone clear out so I can talk with Vi and our new recruit, alright?" He paused. "What's it take to be a Lost Boy?"

"Guts," the kids chorused.

Wyatt nodded, then they all slid off their seats and started filing past. Most of them shot looks at Bo on the way, some friendly, some not. Bo had been new before. He met the gazes cool and calm, how Lia had told him to do, not too friendly but not too mean. Bo remembered getting the bus together to their first day at a new school, in a new country, back when they both had their accents still.

You can just look at the spot between their eyes, if it's hard, she'd advised. *Shouldn't need to, though.*

Why? Bo'd asked, sticking his head against the cold glass window.

You're cooler than them. Then she'd jabbed him under the ribs, right where he hated it. *Not as cool as me, though.*

As for the kids here, Bo estimated he was older than half of them, even if he was only taller than a handful. But he'd been small before too. He was probably faster than any of them, except maybe Wyatt, who was approaching now on long lanky legs.

"Hey, Vi," he said, warm all at once as he turned to her, putting a hand just above her elbow. "Found something more interesting than food, I see."

"Yeah," Violet said. "He was there foraging. He's fresh out the warehouse."

"Yeah?" Wyatt turned to Bo again with a renewed interest. "Fresh out the warehouse? There hasn't been any new kids out in a month." His gaze felt like a laser scanner. "How'd you get over the wormy wall?"

The Parasite squirmed in Bo's stomach and he remembered the storm of static and the impossible hole it had sliced through the living fence—the wormy wall. He debated whether Wyatt would believe him or not.

"I didn't," Bo said. "Didn't go over it. I went through. With my Parasite."

It was the first time he'd said it that way: *my* Parasite, not *the* Parasite. It didn't feel as strange in his mouth as he'd thought it might.

Wyatt's brow furrowed. "How?" He shot a glance over to Violet, who shrugged, lips pursed.

"It just happened," Bo said. "One of the whale-things was chasing me. Right over me, blowing air on me. I got, you know, the twitches. And then the static. I was running at the fence—at the wall—and I felt shakes all through me. Like, vibrating."

Wyatt was rapt, and Bo realized even Violet was frowning intently.

"I shut my eyes," he continued, standing up a bit straighter, speaking a bit louder. "And the static was really big, like, making my hairs all stand up, and I thought I was going to smack into the wall. But I went through it instead. And when I looked back, there was this chunk missing. This hole." He stretched his arms out to approximate the circumference. "Bigger than that. Like it just got punched out with a...a...you know."

"Hole punch," Violet supplied.

"Yeah," Bo said. He mimed the motion. "Pop." He looked at Wyatt, daring him to disagree. "That's what happened."

Wyatt raised his chin, narrowed his eyes. "What's your name?"

"Bo," Bo said. "Bo Rabiu."

"I believe you, Bo." Wyatt's mouth curled into a smile. He turned to Violet. "Show him a shift, Vi."

Violet looked startled, brushing her hair back behind her ear. "I'm not amped up," she said. "And it's early."

"Just a little one," Wyatt said. "Come on. You're best at it."

Violet didn't show it on her face, but the tips of her ears were flushed, and the way she looked at Wyatt when Wyatt wasn't looking reminded Bo of the boys he teased his sister about. She slid her hand under her shirt, splaying her fingers across her stomach. The outline of her hand through the fabric, long skinny digits, looked like a spider.

"That seat on the end," she said, nodding to one of the dilapidated chairs. Bo looked at it, unsure what he was watching for. Violet's hand clenched tight under her shirt and Bo felt a faint static charge whispering around the room. His own Parasite tingled in response. Violet's face was screwed up, focused on the chair, and Wyatt gave her an encouraging nod.

The chair wasn't there. Bo blinked. The plush red seat, one armrest, and a thin slice of the seat beside it, had disappeared entirely. Bo's eyes leapt around the empty space where it should have been, uncomprehending.

Suddenly the static stopped and the chair was back in its place, Coke stains and all, as if it had never moved. Bo saw

Violet shoot Wyatt a pleased look, but Wyatt was already speaking.

"That's a shift," he said, with a hint of eagerness in his voice. "That's what you did on accident. You moved a bit of the wall out of the way and ran through the gap before it came back."

Bo looked at Violet, who was breathing hard, like she'd just run, then back to the seat she'd shifted away. But that wasn't what he'd done to the wall. He hadn't shifted it for just a moment. He'd bored a hole right through.

"Can everyone do it?" he asked.

"A few of us," Wyatt said. "With practice. Takes work."

"Can you?"

Wyatt gave a wry smile. "Not me."

"Why not?" Bo asked.

In answer, Wyatt tugged his red shirt up. But instead of the dim silhouette of the Parasite, there was something else entirely: a ripple of jagged scar tissue, salmon-pink, crossing him from hip to hip.

"First thing I did when I got out," Wyatt said darkly. "I hated the little monster. I hate the fuckers who put them in us."

Bo stared at the scar, transfixed. Better than the whirlybird's marks on his wrists. Better than any of his scars, from any fall or fight.

"I hate them too," he said. "I hate the fuckers." He tried to make the curse come out smooth.

"They made us their experiments, right?" Wyatt said, leaning forward as he tugged his shirt back down. "But it's going to backfire on them. They gave us our weapon. We're going to learn to use it. Use the Parasite."

"Then what?" Bo asked, feeling his Parasite wriggling, his heart pumping. Use it.

"Chase them back where they came from," Wyatt said. "Or kill them all here. You've got a strong one, if it took you through the wormy wall on your first go. If you've never shifted anything before. Maybe the strongest yet. But having a strong one's not enough."

Bo looked from Wyatt to Violet, both of them standing stock-still, both of them with cold hard eyes fixed on him. "Guts," he said. "Right?"

Neither of them cracked a smile.

"The grown-ups, they let themselves get rounded up and clamped," Wyatt said. "They were scared. Now they're wasters. The kids in the warehouses, the ones who drink the water and follow the whirlybird and think if they're good, nothing bad will happen to them. Nothing worse." Wyatt nearly snarled. "They're scared too. If you're going to be a Lost Boy, you can't be like them. You need guts. Are you brave, Bo?"

Chase them back, or kill them all here. Bo's heart hammered in his chest. Get his sister out, free the others.

"I'm brave," he said. "I'll show you I'm brave."

"You'll have to," Wyatt said. "If you want to be a Lost Boy, you have to kill your othermother first."

4

want you with him for it."

Violet looked up. She'd been reorganizing the drug cabinet, a black Ikea shelf Bree and Elliot had put together, slotting the painkillers and antibiotics in neat rows. She used to think nobody could sneak up on her, but that was before she met Wyatt. Wyatt, with his silent step and slate-gray eyes. He was standing over her now with arms crossed.

"With the new kid?" Violet asked, trying not to let her gaze linger too long on his biceps flexed all taut. "It's Jon's turn to do the mother hunt."

"I want you to do it," Wyatt said. "Nobody's gotten out since the wormy wall went up. If he's telling the truth? If he actually shifted the wormy wall enough to get through? That's something special."

Violet felt a strange twist of jealousy in her stomach; maybe it was only her Parasite on the move. She glanced behind her to where Bo was eating, spooning cold ravioli out of a tin, jaws working slow and careful after four months of warehouse nutrient gel. He had a tough-kid act, how most of the escapees did, but that didn't mean he wouldn't freeze up at the critical moment. Just bumping into that waster on the street had shaken him.

Of course, the first time Violet saw the clamped adults up close, their ragged clothes and pierced skulls, she'd hid behind the dumpster of the 7-Eleven and nearly pissed herself right there.

"You want me to do it for him?" she asked. "If he's too soft?" She said it knowing it would put a twist on Wyatt's perfect face.

"No," Wyatt said, after a beat. "He has to do it himself, like everyone else. Every Lost Boy kills their mother. Just make sure he gets that far, right? Make sure things go smooth."

He touched her shoulder in a way that still made heat creep through her skin. Flashed his white smile. Violet tried not to smile back too big. Wyatt headed off, leaving her with the small imprints of his fingers on her flesh, and she wished she was as smooth around him as she was around Dennis the pharmacist. She finished up with the medicine cabinet, double-checked for the aluminum baseball bat in her duffel bag, then walked over to where Bo was cleaning out the can with one finger.

"Let's go, Pooh Bear," she said.

Bo licked red sauce off his knuckle, frowning up at her. "Bo," he corrected. "That girl over there said I could sleep first. Sleep a night, if I want."

"I say we're getting it over with today, because I have other shit to do. Don't you want to be a Lost Boy?"

She watched his gaze travel over to Wyatt, how most kids' did. Wyatt was stretched back in one of the theater seats, reading Sun Tzu again or else one of the military history books he'd taken from Chapters. He read twice as fast as Violet, and she'd always been decent at it.

"Yeah," Bo said. "I wanna."

"Then let's go find her," Violet said. She checked and saw

one of his shoe soles was peeling off, wagging against the floor. "We can get you new runners first," she said. "Don't want you tripping over those."

Bo's dark eyes lit up. "Foot Locker," he said. "The one in the mall."

"Sure," Violet said. "I think they got a sale on today."

A smile ghosted over Bo's face, just for a second. That was good. Some of the kids never smiled again. Violet adjusted the sit of the duffel on her shoulder and cocked her head toward the exit. Bo stood up from the duct-taped table, wiping his hands on the seat of his pants. The other Lost Boys who'd been eating looked up at him and saluted. Violet couldn't remember when that had started—nobody had saluted when she and Wyatt set off to kill her first othermother.

"Good luck, Bo," Gilly, the youngest, said solemnly.

"Thanks," Bo said, then looked around at the others, maybe trying to decide whether to salute back or not. "Be right back."

Cocky of him. Violet sort of liked it.

Bo knew the exact shoes he wanted. He'd known since before the ship came down, when he went through the mall on his way back from school and stopped and stared at them, wishing his feet were growing faster or that he hadn't wasted his eleventh birthday asking for PlayStation games. He knew they'd make him aggressively agile, like the Nike ad with the cyborgs, even though he didn't like cyborgs so much anymore because they were too close to wasters.

He was thinking about the shoes when the girl or boy named Violet reached back and pinched his arm to stop him. Girl or boy, because he wasn't quite sure now. Violet was really pretty, puffy lips like a fashion model, sooty lashes, but her voice was different from Lia's or any of the older girls Bo knew. He'd decided it wasn't that important.

"There's one," Violet said. "Look."

They'd been heading to the mall by the backway, hopping a fence and crossing the empty railroad track, crunching on gravel. As they entered through the derelict parkade, Violet had pulled him behind a concrete pillar. Bo peered around the edge of it now. He could see the food court entrance. The grass was overgrown and tangled yellow, but apart from that it looked nearly normal. A few wasters were shuffling around the outside; the sliding doors didn't open for the sensor anymore.

But Violet hadn't meant for him to see more wasters. Bo blinked as what he'd taken at a glance as a spindly tree suddenly turned and started to walk. The thing, which he knew had to be an othermother, towered over the wasters, taking slow and delicate steps. From the waist up it looked like a person—it was even wearing a floral-printed shirt, from what Bo could see. But its legs were long metal stilts, jointed like a praying mantis, and when they lifted off the ground the feet were clawed clubs.

Bo felt his mouth go dry and his throat go tight. He remembered the slimy figure that dropped out of the whale-thing, and wondered how they gave it the skeletal metal legs. The othermother was making a warbling, trilling sound, indistinct. It took Bo a second to realize she was calling someone's name, over and over.

"Gilly! Gilly! Gilly!" The othermother's voice was high and syrupy and she never paused to breathe. "Gilly! Gilly! Gilly!"

"Why would they do that?" Bo asked, swallowing bile. "It's not actually... That's not really her mom, is it?"

"No," Violet said casually. "They grow them. Whole batches of them. Like, cloning type thing." She shrugged. "The aliens don't think how we do, Wyatt says. Not yet, anyway. So to them, sending our moms to come get us, you know, it makes sense." She gave her no-eyes smile again. "Gross, right?"

"Yeah," Bo said. "Gross." But it wasn't just disgust making him feel sick; it was fear too, and his Parasite could tell. He hoped Violet couldn't. He was going to have to get near to one of those things. He was going to have to kill it.

"We'll sneak around it," Violet said. "No use getting the wrong one all riled up. Then I'll pick up a few things while you grab your shoes, alright?"

Bo tried to visualize the shoes again, the deep green with dayglow orange slashes and laces. Sitting on the untouched shelf, waiting just for him. It didn't help any. The Parasite in his stomach curled over and over.

Once Violet had retrieved Bo and his new shoes from the Foot Locker, she took him up to the top of the parkade for a better vantage point. The sky overhead was still a thick nuclear gray and unlikely to change. Violet sat on the hood of a battered white Nissan while Bo watched from the edge, his elbows hooked over the concrete railing.

The othermothers were easy enough to spot, stalking the streets on their long skinny legs, calling in high grating voices. At least a half dozen passed under the parkade, but Bo shook his head after each, until Violet began to suspect he was lying. She pictured Wyatt waiting in the theater and wondered how long it would take for him to start worrying just a little.

She thumbed absently through the new underwear she'd gotten from the La Senza with a shattered front window and dismembered mannequins. Bo's whisper a minute later was so faint she almost didn't hear it:

"That's her."

Violet slid down off the hood, going to the edge and splaying her fingers on the barrier to steady herself as she peered over.

From the waist up, Bo's othermother looked mostly human. Her hair was glistening wet, like she'd stepped out of the shower, and it was the same black as Bo's but less tightly curled. It clung to her over-long neck, not quite hiding the bony nodes of her vertebrae, and plastered over a bulging forehead. She had slim shoulders, a trim waist; the cornflower-blue summer dress looked nice on her, even if it wasn't appropriate to the season. They hadn't done her fingers quite right. The digits looked more like the tines of a fork.

Below the waist was nowhere near human. Under the hemline of the dress, her legs were the usual long insect-jointed stilts, mostly metal but with swathes of raw-pink flesh and a hard, shiny sort of keratin.

The mother picked daintily through a gaggle of wasters, looming over them as she started to trill. "Boniface honey Boniface honey Boniface honey!"

"Boniface, huh." Violet saw the numb kind of terror sneaking into Bo's eyes and tried to quell it. "That's worse than Pooh Bear."

Bo shook himself. He was shaking all over, actually, and Violet felt the strange, hot impulse to wrap herself around him, bury her face in his hair, and tell him it wasn't real, it wasn't real, none of this was real. She'd done that for a few of the younger ones and sworn them not to tell.

"Time to see what you're made of, Bo," she said. "This goes over your head. And stays there." Violet peeled apart a pair of panty hose and handed one over. "It helps keep her guessing. If she gets a clean lock on your face, she'll lunge. Like I said, they're quicker than you think. And if she starts wafting pheromones…"

"If a mother drops 'mones, don't breath through your nose," Bo chanted back to her, pulling the fabric over his head. It made his face warped and shiny, like a burn victim.

"Yeah," Violet said. "Or else you'll be following her right back to the warehouses."

"Never going back there." Bo's face was hard under the nylon.

Violet couldn't say good luck, because Wyatt said luck didn't exist. "It's a nice dress," she said instead. "She must have been really pretty."

Bo's throat bobbed. "Yeah."

"But that's not her," Violet enunciated. She nodded her chin toward the exit. "So go."

Bo went, scampering down the double flight of chipped concrete steps. The panty hose over his head caught his hot breath and held it. His Parasite quivered. Violet had told him, while they waited, that the Parasites ate chemicals. She'd told him adrenaline was their favorite. Bo knew he was full up of it, his limbs all jangling how they'd be before a race. He told himself this was a race, or maybe more like tag, or Marco Polo. He pushed the door open and walked out into the street.

The othermother was turned away. He would have to see her face sooner or later, but even just the blue dress put an ache behind his nose and mouth. His mom had worn it last summer, when she packed them into a friend's borrowed car and drove them, barefoot, windows down, to the pale-gray beach outside the city. Him and Lia had stuck their arms out the windows, trying to make them ribbon in the wind and sniffing for the sea.

They'd played rock-paper-scissors for the radio—Lia liked
Top 40; Bo liked music without words in it. Lia nearly always
picked scissors, and Bo nearly always beat her.

Get out of my head, Bo, she'd growled, as Bo gleefully knocked
his fist over her two fingers.

Get out, Boniface, his mom had agreed. *It's dangerous, there's
nothing in there but scissors.*

Lia'd pursed her lips how she did when she was angry, but
laughed a second later. The three of them hadn't really fought
once that whole drive, that whole day.

The othermother still hadn't noticed him.

"Hey!" he tried to shout, but it came out choked and quiet.
He sucked in a breath. "Hey!"

Violet had briefed him on getting their attention, on dangling them, on ins and outs. The othermother's waist split and
rotated with an awful grinding noise and suddenly she was
staring down at him, smiling curiously.

"Boniface, is that you?" Her voice tumbled over the syllables like bad text-to-speech. "Shoes off at the door, honey. Put
them on the shelf."

Her legs realigned, stomping a neat circle, then folded down
with a series of clicks as she crouched. Bo felt like his insides
were thick black tar. Up close, her face was rubbery, like a
porpoise he'd seen at the aquarium, and the proportions were
wrong, her mouth too wide and gashed into her face. Her eyes
looked like black pigment inked onto the skin.

"Boniface, is that you? Shoes off at the door, honey. Boniface, is that you?" The othermother cocked her head to one
side, peering at him.

Bo turned away, sucked in air again. He stared down at his
pristine Nikes he'd taken while Violet tried on underwear two

stores over, and realized he didn't even want them anymore. He hoped they'd still make him aggressively agile.

"It's me," he said. "Come on, then." He was mustering up a curse, something Violet would hear and know that he wasn't fooled by the othermother, that he was tough and ready and had the guts to be a Lost Boy. But he'd never sworn in front of his mom, not even when he tore his toenail off at the swimming pool, and he still couldn't.

Bo started to walk, and the othermother stalked a hesitant step after him.

"Come home for dinner. Dinner's at six. Boniface, is that you?"

Bo felt saline pricking his eyes, but he knew as long as he didn't wipe them Violet wouldn't be able to tell he was crying.

Baiting an othermother was stop-and-go stuff, laborious, but it looked like Bo was getting the hang of it. Violet watched him lure her in close, sometimes too close, and then dart nimbly away each time she reached with her tine fingers, leading her ever closer to the parkade ramp. If the othermother was getting frustrated she made no sign of it. Still cooing and chirping. Othermothers were patient.

Violet remembered her first. Standing with Wyatt in the middle of the abandoned plaza, a stiff wind whipping their hair and clothes. She watched and waited while he unzipped his black duffel and set to sharpening the Cutco butcher knife. When the othermother came wailing for Ivan, Violet knew Wyatt knew about her, but there was no distaste, no embarrassment, no confusion on his face. Not even curiosity. That was when Violet started loving him, or at least lusting him.

Nothing ever shook Wyatt. Hardly anything could startle him. Violet had seen him flinch only once, when she had her fingernails long and was feeling daring and ran them down the back of his arm. The cloudburst fear in his eyes, so brief she almost missed it, was something she'd recognized. She knew Wyatt had scars besides the one on his stomach, and that made her want him more. It made her think, in a small stupid way, that they were perfect for each other.

Down below, there was a problem. Violet frowned. At the mouth of the parkade ramp, the othermother had come to a dead halt, planted stubborn despite Bo's coaxing. Violet hadn't seen that before. The mother rotated her waist, spinning and scanning, and Violet ducked instinctively. Othermothers were not supposed to get suspicious.

Violet craned over the edge again and saw the mother swaying, indecisive. Bo was shouting. Pleading, almost. Then, incredibly, the othermother turned and began stalking away. Bo looked as stunned as Violet felt, his small shoulders imploded, his hands dangling slack. He looked up. Violet waved, motioning him to come back up, but Bo shook his head.

She realized what he was going to do a moment before he ripped the panty hose off his face.

Bo let the stifling nylon flutter down to the street as he jogged after the othermother, heart jackhammering his ribs. "Hey!" he shouted. "Hey! Look at me!"

The othermother swiveled her waist without breaking stride, then froze all at once. She lurched into a clacking crouch. "Boniface, is that you? I missed you! Honey. I missed you!" Her head cocked one way and then the other, twisting on the long veiny neck, and Bo looked her right in the eye. She smiled with teeth that were two long white chunks in her gums and—

Lunged.

Bo dove right, then scrambled to his feet as the othermother gathered herself again, leaning back on her haunches like an accordion. She sprang, shrieking through the air, grasping for him with hands that looked more like hooks now, like metal claws. Bo took off. This was not Marco Polo.

He pelted for the parkade and the othermother pelted after him, head bobbing, brushing a waster aside with one swinging arm. She gained, and gained, and Bo's muscles were searing. He'd spent too many months getting fattened up like a cow, maybe he wasn't the fastest in his grade anymore, maybe he wasn't fast enough to—

One last push onto the ramp, and a breath behind him the othermother slammed into the hanging bar that said LOW CLEARANCE: 2.8 METERS. Bo scrambled backward, watching her thrash against the tangled chain.

"It's your sister's birthday," she said. "Come home for dinner. Honey. I missed you!"

She pulled free, but Bo was already off and running.

Bo shot up the top of the ramp with the othermother millimeters behind. Violet stepped from the corner and blindsided the spindly leg as it came down. The aluminum baseball bat made a bone-deep crack and the othermother went sprawling, skidding across the tarmac and leaving a wet smear under herself. The cornflower-blue dress was the same rubbery flesh as the rest of her. Violet felt a slight urge to vomit.

Instead, she set to work on the other leg, smashing the joint to pulp, working with methodical blows while the othermother writhed and chirped. One of her shoulders had come dislocated in the fall and she waggled the boneless arm in Bo's direction. Bo was getting to his feet, breathing hard and fast, tears tracking down his face in a torrent. Violet spared him a glance but didn't stop with the bat until she was sure the othermother wouldn't be able to stand. A black fluid like engine grease was leaking from the shattered limbs.

"Boniface, give your mom a hug," the othermother trilled. "It's your sister's birthday. I know you love her deep down. Deep deep down. Come home for dinner. Dinner's at six."

Tears were still rolling down Bo's face, but he picked a jagged rock off the concrete all the same. His mouth was set. Violet watched, intent. Bo stared at the rock in his hand, unmoving, for a beat and then another. The othermother writhed.

"We can cover her face," Violet offered.

Bo looked up. "They never really hurt us," he said thickly. "In the warehouses."

"They care about what they put inside you," Violet said, dropping the bat with a tinny clang. "Not you. Never think they care about you, Bo."

"But they know about her," Bo said. His face worked. "My sister. She's still in the warehouse." He stared at the rock again. "It's not her birthday. Her birthday's in summer."

"Boniface, honey, Boniface, honey, Boniface. Honey!"

"They won't hurt her," Violet said, trying to sound certain. "They don't think how we do." She halfway wanted to take the rock out of Bo's hand and send him away, tell him that she would finish it. But every Lost Boy had to kill their other-mother. Wyatt would know if she did it for him. He always knew those things.

Violet watched Bo's face. She knew that something broke and slid once you killed your first othermother, that something shifted like cartilage inside you. It slipped a little more for the next one, and a little more for the next one after that, until there was just a hollow. Some days, Violet wished she hadn't let Wyatt hand her the knife.

Bo cocked his arm.

Violet stopped him. "You said you used the Parasite to escape," she said. "To get through the fence." She nodded at the othermother. "Show me."

"Can't," Bo said. "Can't decide when it happens."

"You're pumped full of fight-or-flight chemicals right now," Violet said. "Try." She plucked the rock out of his fingers and tossed it aside. "Focus on it hard. Focus on how much you want it to, you know, to shift. You have to really want it."

Bo shook himself, then took a breath. Through his thin shirt, Violet could see his Parasite pulsate. He screwed up his eyes, staring at the broken othermother, and suddenly Violet's hair was standing on end, wreathed in static. She took a step backward.

The othermother started to shimmer, to ripple, and then all at once she was gone. Vanished, leaving only the stains on the tarmac.

"Holy shit." Violet walked forward, gingerly prodded her foot into the place the fallen othermother had sprawled. "Holy shit." She paused. "I can't do that," she said. "Nobody can. I can shift things for a bit, but I can't flat-out disappear stuff."

"Didn't know I could either," Bo said. His voice was still numb.

Violet tried to inject some enthusiasm into her next words. "She's gone. That means you're in, Bo. You're a Lost Boy."

"What will they do?" Bo asked.

"Normally one of the flying pods comes and picks up the dead one," Violet said, looking at the empty space again. "Then maybe a week later, they send another. And another after that."

She stuck the aluminum bat back into her bag and slung it over her shoulders. "Eventually it gets so you don't even recognize her."

Bo said nothing, staring out at the ruined city. Violet could guess he was thinking of the docks where the warehouses squatted like black coffins. He turned back and his face crumpled all at once.

"I shouldn't have left without her," he choked. "Mom said to stay together. But I left. It's because we made a deal, me and Lia both agreed on it, but I didn't think..." His voice broke then pitched up, thin and desperate. "We have to get her out. We have to get her out *now*."

Violet tried to assess. Bo was nearly hyperventilating, his scrawny chest heaving. There was usually some panic on the mother hunt, but this was different. Guilt and fear were written all over his screwed-up face. Scared for his sister, even more scared to be without her. Ashamed he'd left her behind.

Violet was an only child, but she knew all about guilt and fear. She felt the first one now as she leaned in close, putting her hand on Bo's shoulder. "Wyatt will have a plan," she whispered. "He's always got one." She turned him toward the exit ramp. "We'll get your sister out by summer. Before her birthday."

Aside from Wyatt, Violet could lie to anyone. Bo wasn't the only Lost Boy who'd left someone behind in the warehouse, but for all Wyatt's talk, Violet knew the Lost Boys weren't saviors. Just survivors.

5

Bo's head was a blur. He followed Violet back to the run-down theater on automatic. When they came in, and she nodded to Wyatt, all the other kids made a ragged line to hug him one by one. He had his arms slack at his sides and he didn't look them in the face. Gilly, the little girl with eyes the color of a Sprite bottle, hugged longer than most, in a way that might have made Bo peel her off if he hadn't been thinking of her floral-printed othermother taking jerky birdlike steps and singing her name.

Wyatt was last in line. He wrapped him in a tight hug, then stepped back. "Bo. Look at me."

Bo blinked hard, to be sure the tears were all gone. He looked.

"You're one of us now," Wyatt said, serious but kind-eyed. "You're family." He pulled him in again with one long arm, so their foreheads pressed together. "It gets easier," he said quietly. "My first was tough too." He gave a half smile. His hand trailed on Bo's arm for a moment, just above the elbow, before it vanished.

With the line finished, some of the kids drifted away, but

some stayed. They asked about which warehouse he'd been in, how he'd gotten out. Bo didn't know the answer to the first question, and barely knew the answer to the second. He explained about the power outage and how he'd run through the wormy wall. His mouth moved on autopilot.

Once he might have bragged, but he still had the image stamped hard behind his eyes of his mother—no, his othermother— writhing on the concrete while Violet dismantled her legs. All of these kids had seen that, and they hadn't made her just disappear. They'd used the rock. Bo kept thinking about the weight of it in his hand. Maybe he wouldn't have had the guts to use it.

Some of the younger kids pushed little gifts into his hands: chocolate bars, smooth stones, one tiny plastic dinosaur. Some of the older kids, in hushed voices, asked about certain names. Mostly Bo shook his head, and even when he recognized a name, there was nothing to say. They were alive, they were drinking the water, they were following the whirlybird to food and to bed and to food and to bed. Bo asked them about Lia, but none of them remembered meeting her. One girl, Bree, asked about Ferris.

"She's twelve," Bree said. "Same height as me. Blonde hair. Talks fast."

"Yeah," Bo said. "I know her. She was in my group."

Bree sucked in a breath. "She's my cousin. We were sup- posed to find each other. Get out and find each other."

"She tried," Bo said. He told her how Ferris had tried to escape through the emergency door, how the whirlybirds had taken her away. Bree bit her lip while she listened. She didn't cry, but she walked away with an empty kind of look.

Bo had lost all track of time, but when Violet offered to show him his bed, he went. The lobby was scattered with sleeping bags and nests of pillows, some of them on their own, most of them clumped in groups. A few had little makeshift curtains around them using broomsticks and blankets. It all looked a million times better than the thin orderly cots of the warehouse.

When Bo came to the sleeping bag he'd taken from the camping store, he found it built up with fleece blankets and pillows with no cases. He sank down onto it and closed his eyes.

"Night," Violet's scratchy voice said.

She was gone when Bo opened his eyes again. He wormed his way into the sleeping bag and stared up at the shadowy ceiling. The othermother was still stuck in his head, the way her mouth hadn't moved properly when she said *Boniface, honey, it's your sister's birthday*. Lia was still stuck in the warehouses, still catching water drops off the pipes, still looking for a way out. And his real mother, Bo didn't want to think about.

But Wyatt would have a plan, Violet had said. Wyatt, who'd cut out his own Parasite with a butcher knife and lived to tell the tale. Wyatt, who said they had a weapon now. Bo had a weapon now. He focused hard and tried to coax the static again, the tingling storm that had made the mother disappear. Bone weary, he was asleep before he could elicit so much as a twitch.

He slipped in and out of dreams, sometimes half waking when other kids made their way to bed. They had low whispery conversations. He heard the slither of nylon shells as some kids rearranged themselves, dragging their beds together. It was the dead of the night when Bo came awake again. Everyone was sleeping, breathing deep and even, except for one boy peeling off his baggy orange shirt. Bo recognized his skinny face and floppy brown hair and remembered his name was Elliot.

Elliot was slow with the shirt, careful, and when it came up over his head Bo saw, in the dim glow of the battery lamps, angry red marks on his back. He drifted to sleep again, wondering what sort of whirlybird could have made them.

Up on the roof of the theater, Violet and Wyatt sat on the dented electrical box. Violet swung one leg, near enough to graze Wyatt's if he wanted them to graze, as they stared out over the shadowed city. There were no streetlamps anymore, and no lights in windows. The streets were a blackout maze. The only illumination came from the ship. At night its underbelly peeled open, exposing pale yellow tubing that reminded Violet of glowing veins. The flying pods swarmed to the light, maybe feeding off it somehow, maybe just drawn to it how insects were.

Sort of spooky, Violet thought. Sort of romantic. But Wyatt hadn't so much as looked at her. She patted the flashlight and the fresh batteries in her pocket, about to give up and leave, when he finally broke the quiet.

"So it didn't come back at all," he said.

Violet made a face he couldn't see in the dark. She didn't want to talk about Bo and the othermother again. "No," she said. "Straight vanished. Didn't come back. We waited."

"Where'd he shift it to, I wonder," Wyatt murmured.

"It's late," Violet said, standing up, making the batteries clack.

Wyatt looked at her, sharply. "You going to bed?"

"No," Violet said, pulling out her flashlight. Wyatt never asked her where she sometimes went at night, the same way he didn't ask her about the pills she took or anything else. She was glad for that. So long as he never asked, she never had to try lying to him. He could always tell when she was lying.

She lingered for just a second, in case Wyatt was going to tell her to stay, the way he sometimes did in her head.

"Alright," he said. "Goodnight."

"Night."

Violet left down the fire escape, making it clatter and sway. The rungs' flaking paint crackled under her palms. She used to get vertigo climbing, a queasy helium feeling in her stomach, but ever since the Parasite went in she hadn't noticed it. One good thing they'd done for her. As soon as her shoes touched the pavement, she set off on a familiar route.

It was safer at night than it used to be. Before the aliens, Violet was always jumpy after midnight, walking quick and focused, trying not to be seen. She used to wish she could make everyone else disappear, so she could walk how she wanted, dress how she wanted, talk how she wanted. Now that everyone was gone, she took graffitied alleyways and hopped over fences and didn't duck her head for anyone. The wasters who were still awake, no matter how close she got to them, their bloodshot eyes slid right off.

She came up on a small brown house through the overgrown backyard, clambering the fence with her hands wrapped in her sleeves to avoid splinters. The dandelions were thick around the porch. The backdoor was bright red—her mom had painted it one summer for no reason her dad could figure out, but she'd done it with a fierce kind of pride, glowering at the paintbrush, wearing a sleeveless old T-shirt and a rag tying back her hair. Violet liked it more than she'd let on.

She pulled open the unlocked door and stepped inside, raking the shadows away with her flashlight. The living room still had its lingering smell of cheap beer and cats who were now long gone; she didn't know where to. Her dad's lolling head was visible over the back of the chair parked in front of the dead television. If it weren't for the clamp glinting in her flashlight's beam, it would've looked normal, just him near passing out.

Violet thought of all the times she'd stared at his dark head silhouetted against the bright plasma screen, at the beer bottles lined up at his feet like a firing squad, and wished that his liver would give out or that he'd choke on his own vomit. Even now that the bruises were long gone, she still felt sick and anxious and angry looking at him. It made the Parasite flex in her stomach.

She scanned the floor for broken glass or dropped knives, anything dangerous to a waster, then checked for spoiled food. All the wasters had some sort of survival programming, she knew that much. They managed to stay hydrated and eat enough to function. But sometimes they tried to eat rotting food and got sick, or hurt themselves and didn't disinfect it. She'd already seen dead wasters in the street and figured there would be more and more as time went on.

Wyatt would be angry if he could see her doing this. She could hear him in her ear: *Clamp's in the head, better off dead.*

Violet ghosted down the hall, past her old bedroom, past the mold-smelling bathroom. She trailed her fingertips along the edge of a family photo, leaving it crooked. It didn't really have her in it, anyway. It had Ivan, dark hair cropped short like his dad's, puffing out his chest, not quite smiling.

At the end of the hall: her parents' bedroom, door cracked open. She took a step inside, flashlight off. As her eyes adjusted to the gloom she could see the shape of her mom wrapped up in the sheets, twisting them around her legs how she always did, but her chest was rising and falling too fast to actually be asleep. She didn't know if the wasters ever really slept, or if they only pretended like how they pretended to talk on the phone, or watch the TV, or buy drugs at the pharmacy.

But her chest was rising and falling, and that meant she was still alive. Violet turned around and slipped back down the hallway, back through the living room, back out the door. She was stepping off the porch when a mewling noise startled her. Perched on one of the sunken fence posts, bony tail looping side to side, was Anise.

"Anise," Violet said, grinning. "You little anus. Come here, Anise."

She crouched, rubbed her fingers together, tried a bit of a whistle. Anise's ear flicked around like a satellite dish. She didn't move. Violet bit her lip. Anise was their oldest cat, and their smartest, and she always came when Violet called. For a second she imagined a tiny cat-sized clamp on the nape of Anise's furry neck.

"Come here, Anise, come here," Violet repeated.

Anise made a graceful pirouette and disappeared back over the fence. Violet had what felt like hard plastic in her throat. She wanted to cry, like she hadn't cried yet over her mom, or her aunt, or all the dead people, and it was because their stupid cat didn't recognize her anymore. Maybe she'd been on the hormones long enough that she smelled different.

Violet swung herself over the fence and headed back toward the theater. She didn't cry.

6

The buzzing whine of the whirlybird jerked Bo awake. He kept his eyes squeezed shut, wishing he could slip back into the dream or nightmare where he'd escaped the warehouse and met the other kids and killed the thing that was not his mother. He tried to burrow deeper into his cot and realized it wasn't a cot. The unfamiliar fabric of the sleeping bag rustled underneath him, and the sound of the whirlybird wasn't quite right either. He winched his eyes open.

Bree, the girl with nearly buzzed hair, the one who was cousins with Ferris, was standing over him with an electric toothbrush tugging her cheek back off pink gums. She switched it off, spitting a glob of toothpaste and saliva into the plastic Coke cup in her hand.

"Wyatt wants to talk to you when you're awake," she said. "He's outside."

Bo rolled over once she was gone and sat upright. All the other makeshift beds were empty. Sitting in a pool of blankets, he felt the last twenty-four hours crash over him. Sprinting away from the whale-thing, shifting a hole in the wormy wall, wandering the abandoned city. Meeting Violet, and then Wyatt and the others, and then going to find his shoes and the othermother. All of that had been real. The othermother's singsong voice ran through his head: *It's your sister's birthday, come home for dinner.*

He got to his feet. The lobby of the theater was empty, apart from Bree slouching away toward what had to be bathrooms. He took stock of his surroundings again. The carpet was rough under his bare feet, a faded pattern of black and yellow like a caterpillar he'd seen once on the sidewalk. The off-white walls had been scribbled on with Sharpies and spray-painted in colorful swathes of green and purple. When he stretched a crick out of his neck, he saw a chandelier dangling from the ceiling. The bulbs looked plastic.

Bo could hear people inside the theater auditorium, but he passed the double doors, making his way toward the exit instead. Past the concession stand and the ticket booth, the main door was open, letting in faint morning light filtered through the gray clouds. He stepped outside and the air smelled clean and sharp. On the sidewalk, Wyatt was putting a bike together, working at the seatpost with a small wrench.

"Hey, Bo," he said. "First sleep go okay?"

"Yeah," Bo said. "Fine." He paused, looking around. A second bike, larger, red, was leaned up against the theater wall, but he didn't see Violet or anyone else. "Where is everybody?" he asked.

"There's a forage group out getting food and batteries," Wyatt said. "And a scout group. Violet and Jon should be back soon. I sent them to the wormy wall. See if that hole you tore in it is sealed up yet." He stood, easing the bike he'd been working on upright. "You have any nightmares?" he asked.

"No," Bo said quickly. He wasn't sure, of course. Dreams and nightmares and real life were all blurred lately. But he didn't want to look soft. He wasn't one of the kids back in the warehouse, sobbing through the night. He was a Lost Boy.

"Good," Wyatt said, wiping his hands on a bit of rag. "Violet told me about your sister last night. She was in the same warehouse as you?"

"They split us up," Bo said.

Wyatt grimaced. "Yeah," he said. "It's like herding cattle to them, Bo. They don't give a shit." He rolled the bike back and forth, watching the chain for catches. "You're not the only one who had to leave family behind."

"You have siblings?" Bo asked.

"No," Wyatt said. "I don't. I always wanted a brother, right? But my parents didn't. Here." He swung the bike over to Bo. "This is yours."

Bo wrapped his fingers around the rubber-gripped handlebar. The bike's aluminum frame was on the large side for him, but the tires had good thick tread still on them and he liked the bright blue-and-silver paint job.

"Thanks," he said.

"You're welcome." Wyatt went to the red bike and started tightening its spokes. "You want to get your sister out, right?"

Bo nodded.

"Since they put the wormy wall up, nobody's escaped," Wyatt said. "Just you. We don't go near it anymore." He looked up from the spoke wrench and gave a white grin. "Maybe if we had a tank, or something. That's what I always thought."

"Why aren't there tanks?" Bo asked. "Tanks and soldiers and planes. And stuff. Where are they all?" He clenched his teeth, trying to dredge up the thought he hadn't dared speak yet. "Or is it like this everywhere?" he finally said. "The whole world? Did we already lose?"

"Yeah, that's the big question, Bo," Wyatt said. "Internet doesn't work. Phones don't work. Cars don't work. Everything's fucked."

"Someone could go to the highway," Bo said, swiveling the handlebars. "Start biking to the next town. Try to find other people. Find out what happened."

"We've tried," Wyatt said. "It's not as easy to leave as you'd think. That's where we're heading, once Violet's back." He twisted the last spoke tight and straightened up, wiping his hands on the rag. His smile was hard for Bo to read. "A little field trip," he said. "To the end of the world."

Violet and Jon went as close as they dared to the wormy wall, stashing their bikes with a tangle of drainage pipes and then sneaking around the corner of the crumbling brick apartments nearest to the alien structure. Violet hadn't been expecting to see anything where Bo said he'd escaped—shifting didn't leave marks—but she was surprised. The stretch of wormy wall was marked with a long zigzagged wound, stitched shut by interlocking tendrils but still visible to the eye, colored an off-putting pink like raw meat.

"Guess he really did take a chunk out of it," Violet said.

Jon pushed his thick black hair out of his face and didn't reply. He rarely did. The bike ride over had been dead quiet, but Jon was built like a brick and quick on his feet, and there weren't many people Violet would prefer to have along on a trip this close to the warehouses. She trusted Jon. He'd been late to escape, but he was fifteen, putting him third after Violet in seniority. She knew from experience that most fifteen-year-olds with his thick shoulders and thin wisp of moustache, the ones who got their growth early, were idiots drunk off their own testosterone. She didn't blame them. It was chemistry.

But Jon was gentle, especially with the under-tens, and sometimes at night he talked a foreign language in his sleep in a voice that always sounded on the verge of tears. She wasn't sure where he was from, with his wide cheekbones and narrow eyes, and he never said. He didn't have any accent during the day.

Violet returned her attention to the wormy wall. In a spot farther down, the tendrils were starting to whip back and forth, quicker than normal. She nudged Jon's elbow. They both peered at the wall, and both of them flinched a bit when an othermother's head popped over the top of it. Violet watched as the rest of the othermother rose slowly over the barrier, conducted along by the tendrils, passed gently down the other side of it like crowd-surfing.

The othermother was stiff as a plank, arms straight at her sides and long legs locked together, and when the tendrils set her down she didn't move. Violet recognized the cornflower-blue dress. They were already replacing the one Bo had vanished.

"That was quick," Violet said. "Let's go before it starts sniffing around." She made toward the bikes, and this time it was Jon who nudged. Violet turned back to see the wall was in motion again. A second othermother, identical to the first, glided up and over it to stand stock-still beside her twin. Then a third. Then a fourth. For a moment Violet thought they might keep churning over the wall forever, a cartoon assembly line on loop, but after the sixth they stopped.

Six othermothers, lined up like toy soldiers, swaying slightly on their long skeletal legs as a stiff breeze came through. Violet had seen plenty of things in the past four months, but the sight still sent ice down her spine. The othermothers waited without moving, eyes unblinking. Violet and Jon were frozen too, waiting to see what would happen.

On some inaudible cue, all six othermothers came to life at once. Their necks started swiveling, too elastic to be real, and Violet shrank back instinctively, pressing herself flat to the brick. Jon didn't say anything, but she could feel him tense up. The othermothers started forward, already cooing Bo's name. It might have been her imagination, but Violet thought the way they walked was slightly different. Longer, more liquid strides. More like predators.

As the first wave stalked past them, the wormy wall began to ripple and wave again. The process started over. Six more othermothers, all of them in cornflower blue, being lowered into place one at a time. Violet had never seen so many. It was fucking scary.

The othermothers were still coming as Violet and Jon slid along the apartment wall, keeping low until they were around the corner. She yanked her bike off the drainpipe with trembly hands.

"They want him back bad," Jon said, swinging onto his seat.

When Jon did speak, he had a way of saying what Violet didn't want to. Even if she was thinking it.

"Tough," she said, trying to inject her usual bravado. "He's ours now."

She kicked off, and then they pedaled hard and fast until the othermothers' trilling voices faded away.

It was Bo's first time leaving the city by the west, taking the curving bypass around the industrial park. There were three of them: Wyatt leading, Violet after, and then Bo bringing up the rear. The older kid, Jon, had stayed behind. Him and Violet had had a quick hushed talk with Wyatt while Bo pretended to be focused on hopping up and off the curb. Then Jon had wheeled his bike back into the theater while the rest of them set off.

At first the ride was exhilarating. Bo'd never been able to ride on the road here except in residential areas—too much traffic. But now, following Wyatt's lead, they swerved back and forth from sidewalk to street, weaving around stalled cars and shambling wasters. The bypass itself was near empty, and the downhill slant meant all three of them picked up good speed. With the bike rattling under him and the airflow slapping back his clothes, Bo felt better than he had in a long time. His mouth kept flexing back into a grin without him meaning it. He could focus on the tarmac, and his feet on the pedals and his grip on the handlebars, and nothing else really mattered.

Eventually the downhill turned uphill, though, and before long, even with the sun hidden by thick dark clouds, he felt a slime of sweat on his back. They had to go down into the ditch to get around an overturned semi, and burrs from the long grass stuck to his socks, scratching his ankles. The burrs, the sweat, and the burn in his legs were distracting enough that Bo didn't notice the creeping fog for another few minutes.

The pale gray vapor roiled around their moving tires the way car exhaust did in winter, and it was thickening as they pedaled. Mist prickled on Bo's hot skin and pressed at his eyes. Wyatt and Violet had slowed down; he did the same. The fog bank loomed in front of them, more opaque than any Bo had seen before. It reminded him of stories his mom used to tell about a huge dust storm, during Harmattan season, back in

Niger when she was a little girl. How the whole sky was blotted out and she couldn't see her hand in front of her face.

Just before they were swallowed up completely, Wyatt braked to a halt.

"Stop here," he called. His voice was flat and strange sounding in the fog. Bo rolled even with him. Violet was leaning back on her seat, face blank. She hadn't said more than a few words to him today. She hadn't smiled at him either. When Bo remembered her warm hand on his shoulder, how she'd talked to him after he disappeared the othermother, he felt almost tricked. His Parasite squirmed again.

"We can keep walking, can't we?" Bo said, looking to Wyatt instead. "Won't get lost if we just follow the road. Is it far?"

"We're already here," Wyatt said. He unzipped his backpack and pulled out a water bottle, taking a swig before he passed it along to Violet. Violet wiped the top with her sleeve, then she drank too. Bo wasn't ready for her to toss it to him but he managed to catch it without falling off his bike.

"This is the end of the world?" Bo asked flatly, waiting for some kind of joke. He dismounted.

"Yeah," Wyatt said. "Start walking."

Bo gripped the water bottle hard. Were they teasing him, or something worse? His heart sped up again, and a million wild thoughts whirled through his head. Maybe Violet had the metal bat in Wyatt's backpack, and she was going to break his bicycle, and maybe his legs, and leave him out here in the fog. Maybe they'd decided he wasn't a Lost Boy after all. He looked from Wyatt, who had an intent, almost eager look on his face, to Violet. She cracked half a smile at last.

"It's alright," she said. "We've all tried it. Just walk, and—"

Wyatt shot her a look. She fell quiet with a shrug, but the

smile stayed. Bo tried to mimic the shrug, tried to pretend he didn't care about whatever game they were playing with him, and slowly turned into the fog. He didn't hear them leaving behind his back, or whispering, or anything else. They were only watching.

Bo started to walk, wheeling the bike along with him just in case. The fog was so thick he couldn't see anything but white. He counted out ten steps before he stopped, looking back to see if even a glimpse of Wyatt and Violet was still visible.

They were right behind him, standing with their bikes, pretending they hadn't snuck along behind his back. Bo gave a hesitant grin, but neither of them laughed at the trick. Wyatt only nodded, brow still furrowed, for him to continue. Bo took another step, and another, but when he turned around again Wyatt and Violet were in the same position. They hadn't moved, and neither had he.

A strange shiver went down Bo's back. He dropped the bike and set down the water bottle and started walking backward, keeping them in view the whole time, but the distance between them never changed. He turned and tried to run, lengthening his stride. He pounded away into the fog, sure at any second he would fall into the ditch, or ram up on a stalled car, or something.

"Weird, right?" Wyatt said over his shoulder.

Bo slowed to a stop and turned around, swallowing his spit. "So we can't get out."

"No," Wyatt said. "We've tried this way, and we've tried going north too."

Bo stared into the fog. It was like coming to the end of a video-game map, walking out into the ocean forever but really just grinding against the skybox, marching in place against invisible walls. Maybe it was like a game to them. Maybe they wanted to keep everyone inbounds.

"We can't get through," Wyatt said. "But maybe you can. With your Parasite."

Bo put his hand to his stomach, trying to remember how he'd done it the day before, up on the parkade roof. It was blurry. He'd stared at the othermother and wanted it gone, wanted it somewhere else. He'd been scared and sad and furious. Then the static storm had welled up out of him, the Parasite vibrated him head to toe, and the othermother was gone.

"I haven't gotten to see it yet," Wyatt said, grinning his white grin. "Show me something, Bo."

Now he wanted the fog gone. He wanted the invisible walls gone. He wanted to get out, and get help. Help for Lia. His Parasite flexed and he felt a small crackle of static.

"Alright," Bo said. "I'll try."

The ride back was quiet. True to his word, Bo had tried. He'd tried until he was sweaty and shaking and Violet wished Wyatt would just give up and tell him to stop. Nothing had happened, though. The charge in the air had made her hair stand up again, which pissed her off because she'd been having a good hair day, but Bo couldn't step any farther than the rest of them. Eventually Wyatt had let him give it up.

"It was worth a shot, right?" he'd said, but with disappointment radiating off him.

Bo had nodded, looking tired and frustrated, and then they'd left.

Now, coming up on the overturned semitruck again, Violet wondered if it was impossible to leave the city because there was nothing left outside of it. Maybe it really was the end of the world, and the aliens had destroyed everything except for one tiny soap bubble with all of them drifting around inside of it. Or maybe none of this was real at all, and she had a black clamp sitting on the back of her skull. Violet reached up and ran a hand over her neck. She remembered her hair was a mess.

She started to slow down for the detour into the grassy ditch, and Wyatt did the same. He was still expressionless, cold and polite and detached how he got when he was angry with something. Violet knew it would pass, but she could tell it was making Bo anxious. She was thinking she might need to say something to him when he pumped past her. She caught a flash of his face, teeth clenched and bared.

"Bo!" she shouted. He didn't slow down. He pedaled harder, zooming along the yellow center line, picking up more speed as the flipped semi loomed, jackknifed across the road. Bo was tearing toward it like an idiot; if he didn't brake now he would smash into the box. Violet waited for the rubber squeal, for him to skid, to bail and hit the tarmac. She hoped he wouldn't break anything. Nobody knew how to do a good splint.

She realized what he was trying to do a split second before the air started to ripple. A tidal wave of distortion jumped forward, with Bo and his bicycle at the crest of it, warping the road and the semi and the sky in a way that ached her eyes. Then the box of the truck was gone, sheared away whole. Bo coasted through the empty space. No handlebars, for good measure.

"Jesus," Violet said. She looked to Wyatt.

"Next best thing," Wyatt said. His smile was back in place. "They're the ones who are going to need to go for help. Not us."

Bo circled back around, gliding through the gap again. His skinny chest was heaving, but his face was a mix of little-kid elated and grown-up smug. Wyatt slung an arm around his shoulders the way he never did with Violet, shaking his head in disbelief. She felt a small stab of jealousy. But she also thought, for the first time, that maybe Wyatt was right, that maybe a bunch of scared messed-up kids hiding in a movie theater could actually drive the aliens away. Maybe Bo was the key.

7

Pedaling back to the theater, Bo felt like Superman. The first time he'd shifted, it had been an accident. The second time, weeping and angry, up on the parkade with the maimed othermother, it had felt like a fluke. When he'd tried and tried but couldn't break through the end of the world, he'd been scared that maybe the vanishing was something he couldn't direct. Maybe the Parasite would never do it again.

Then he'd made the truck trailer disappear. Focusing hard how Violet said, wanting it as bad as he knew how, he'd felt the Parasite like a ball of electricity in his stomach, growing and swelling as he got closer to the crash, and when it all reached a sizzling pitch, he'd released it. The memory of it was still fresh: coasting through the empty space, the air hissing and oddly cold. And then the looks on Violet's and Wyatt's faces.

He was still charged with excitement as he rolled his bike inside and saw the other Lost Boys back from foraging. It faltered a little when they shot him funny looks.

"There's othermothers all over the downtown," Bree said, sounding faintly accusing. "And they're all yours. Alberto almost got nabbed by the 7-Eleven."

The last part was directed more toward Wyatt, who was leaning his bike up against the water-stained wall.

"I didn't, though," piped up a younger boy, grinning broadly as he stacked cans on one of the cobbled-together shelves. "I didn't get nabbed. I went in its blind spot."

Wyatt gave a permissive smile, then his face turned serious. "There's going to be a lot of othermothers out hunting Bo," he said. "Because Bo's got something special. Bree, go get Jon for me."

Bo couldn't help but grin.

The warm proud feeling in his chest stayed there all day, and Violet must have told someone about the disappearing, because when they ate dinner together everyone sidled up to ask about it.

"I can do it too," said the green-eyed girl, Gilly. She was the youngest, barely eight, and she never stopped moving, usually around Bree like a satellite. She chewed the skin between her thumb and forefinger. "Violet's the best at it, but mine's active too. Like hers and Q and Jenna's."

"You can't shift anything bigger than a pop can," Bree snorted, giving the smaller girl a not-unfriendly shove. "And it comes back. When he did the mother, it didn't come back."

Gilly's eyes went wide, and when Bo came back with seconds—after the warehouse, even food from cans tasted delicious—she had wormed her way in to sit by him. As the evening went on, Bo matched names to everyone else.

Second youngest to Gilly were the two boys who'd escaped with her when their group's whirlybird malfunctioned, named Saif and Alberto. Saif was quiet, dark-eyed, brown-skinned. He said he was nine and a half.

Alberto was louder, cute the way kids in advertisements are

cute, all ruddy cheeks and wavy hair. He was always grinning a slightly confused grin, and said he was nine and three quarters but didn't know his months very well. There was a battered soccer ball glued to his foot, even at the table, and the only time Bo saw his grin falter was when someone pointed out that all his favorite players probably had clamps in their heads now.

The two boys had gone to the same elementary, according to Gilly, but had never spoken except for when Alberto teased Saif about his gappy teeth. Now both of them grudgingly admitted to being best friends.

Jenna and Quentin were eleven and twelve, both tall for their ages and pale-skinned. Bo could tell without asking that they were sister and brother, and it made his throat ache. They seemed to keep mostly to themselves, sometimes smirking to each other in a secretive way that Bree mocked whenever she could.

Bree was twelve but seemed older with her close-cropped brown hair and acne marks on her cheeks. She talked older too. She'd been in a foster place before the ship came down, and said she beat the shit out of a whirlybird with her bare hands when she escaped.

That made Elliot snort into his food, though he didn't argue. Elliot was thirteen, but small, especially next to Jon, who was fifteen and big. Jon's facial features reminded Bo of the family that ran the Nepalese restaurant near his family's old apartment.

Wyatt had been the first out of the warehouses, everyone agreed on that, and Quentin and Jenna had been there from nearly the beginning too. After that the order was muddled. Some kids didn't like to talk about the warehouses at all, acting like they'd always been on the outside, always been Lost Boys.

Others had spent a long time on their own, hiding in

basements or attics, before they finally ventured out and Wyatt found them. Bo could sense that some of the kids were not quite *right*, in that they would stop speaking suddenly and not start again, or twitch at any unexpected sound, shy off from touch. But Bo knew he wasn't the same as he was before the warehouses either.

And maybe that was why they seemed to take him in so easily. There was something deeper inside the theater than being in the same class or on the same team or even good friends. There was a kind of respect that each of them had earned from the others. Everyone had gotten out of the warehouses, and even if some of them had been more lucky than brave or smart, they'd all done the other thing too. They'd all killed the othermother. They all had guts, from wide-eyed Gilly to twitchy Elliot.

Maybe more guts than Bo had—the thought gnawed at him again. He hadn't had to feel the bone, or whatever was inside the othermother's rubbery body, give way under the rock. He'd done it clean, and maybe easy.

He wondered what Lia would have done. Lia was tough. She'd gotten into five fights, which was two and a half more than Bo. But up on the parkade hadn't been like a fight. It had been more like when he was little, back in Niamey, and Lia had found him and the neighbor boy crouched in the sand jabbing at an injured grasshopper with twigs.

That's not funny, Bo, she'd said, with a catch in her voice. *What if some big bug did that to you?*

He'd stomped on it then, feeling ashamed, even though he knew there were no bugs big enough to do that to him. He figured Lia would have used the rock on the othermother, but only to put it out of its misery.

Later on, when the sky outside was dark and Bo was play-ing cards with Quentin and Bree and the younger kids, Wyatt came over to the circle. He'd been speaking with Jon and Vio-let again, all three of them off in the corner.

"Come up on the roof, Bo," he said. "Show you something."

Gilly and Alberto and Saif all watched with wide-eyed awe as Bo got to his feet. Even Quentin had something like envy on his thin lips. Bree just swiped his cards up and shuffled them back into the stack. Bo looked over on instinct to where Violet was sitting, but she only gave him a distracted nod. Her face seemed a bit pale.

Just him and Wyatt, then. He couldn't help but feel another swell of pride.

He followed the older boy up through a cramped back stairwell that had a sticky-looking puddle of what looked like orange Fanta in the corner. He took a long step to clear it and his hamstring ached a good ache, the kind he hadn't had in a long time, from the running away and then the bike ride to the end of the world. Wyatt pushed through a rusty metal door with a broken lock and they were outside. There was only a small wedge of flat roof, with an electrical box and a metal pipe Bo thought must be some kind of chimney, or air intake, or something. The surface was pebbly under his new shoes' treads.

Above them, filling up a whole corner of the dark sky, was the huge jagged shape of the alien ship. Sometimes it looked so big Bo thought it was the size of the city itself, a reflection floating up there in the gloom.

"It opens up every night at 10:17," Wyatt said. He pulled a silvery watch out of his pocket and peered at it. "Got a few minutes."

Bo stared up at the dark ship. He imagined vanishing it, balling up the static inside his Parasite until his whole body was trembling, then letting it tear up into the sky like a tsunami. But the ship was far away, and the ship was big. Too big. He knew the Parasite had limits, the way he knew his own arms and legs had limits.

"You think we've seen them yet, Bo?" Wyatt asked.

"Seen what?" Bo said.

"The aliens," Wyatt said, waving an arm upward. "The actual aliens. Think about it. What were the whirlybirds like, back at the warehouse? Were they smart?"

"No," Bo said. He paused. "They'd run into each other, sometimes. Sometimes get caught on things. Glitches, we said."

"And what about the othermothers?" Wyatt asked. "How are they?"

"Stupid," Bo said.

"Stupid as shit," Wyatt agreed. "They don't really talk. They repeat. They repeat things they know we've heard." He narrowed his eyes. "I think they scanned our brains when we were sleeping, right? They pulled out our dreams. That's how they know what the mothers should look like, what they should say. Or at least, they think they know."

"They're just drones," Bo said. "The othermothers and the whirlybirds. They're all drones."

It wasn't a new thought. Some of the Lost Boys had talked about it over dinner, said that either the flesh-and-mech machines were being piloted by someone up in the ship or else had crude AI of their own. Elliot used to build his own camera drones, back before the invasion. He seemed to know what he was talking about.

"Yeah," Wyatt said. "They don't even see each other. They're like wasters."

He pointed up to the ship. On cue, the harsh black surface started to peel open, exposing luminous yellow conduits that looped and crisscrossed each other. The whale-things that circled the warehouses started to ascend, drawn to it like moths.

"The pods, though," Wyatt said, peering up at them. "They're different, right? Listen. They speak to each other."

Bo listened. As the pods drifted into the light, there were bursts of a mournful droning noise that reminded him of bagpipes. He'd heard it some nights in the warehouses but had never known what it was. He observed as one pod would make a noise, and then a different pod, and then the first again. Wyatt was right. They were speaking.

"You think the real aliens are inside them?" Bo asked, watching the hulking shapes cluster around the light, silhouetted. The droning sound put his teeth on edge.

"No," Wyatt said. "I think those are their bodies. Machine and meat all mixed up, same way the othermothers and the whirlybirds are. But I know the pods are smart, Bo. If they weren't, why would they get close to each other to talk?"

Bo remembered the pod that had chased him through the alley, up to the wormy wall. He remembered how it had stopped and hovered when he tore through to the other side, seeming so surprised, and how it waited only a second before it pumped out what he knew now had been his first othermother. The pod had already known who he was when it was chasing him.

"We haven't been sitting on our asses out here," Wyatt said. "We've been learning. You should always know your enemy, Bo, so you know how to hurt them better. We can't just keep fucking with their tools." Wyatt's voice was calm, matter-of-fact. "We have to catch a pod. That's what I've been working toward."

"How?" Bo asked, remembering what Violet had said. Wyatt would have a plan. He always had one.

"We're going to set a trap," Wyatt said. "And now we have the perfect bait for it. That's you, Bo. They want you back. They pumped out a dozen new mothers today just to look for you."

Bo stared up at the pods, watching their small fins shutter up and down, watching how they brushed up against each other. He'd been hating the aliens so much without really knowing what to hate. Fantasizing about smashing whirlybirds back in the warehouse. Getting that sick kind of rage when he remembered the ugly parody of his mom stalking around on its metal insect legs.

Now he knew what to hate, and it was the thing that had taken him and Lia away from their blazing house in the first place. Sometimes he still dreamed about being inside the pod, the smell of smoke cut away suddenly by ammonia, feeling the suffocating grit and slime pressing at his mouth, his nose. He always woke up grasping for his sister's slippery hand.

"Are we going to kill it when we catch it?" Bo asked before he could stop himself.

Wyatt's movie-star grin gleamed in the dark. "When we're done with it, yeah."

About a block away from the pharmacy, Violet ducked over an iron-grilled trash can and threw up. Nobody put bags in them anymore, so the splatter came out the bottom and caught her shoes, steaming a bit in the cold morning air. Violet grimaced, holding onto the rim as the nausea hit again. Her Parasite flexed, her ribs heaved, and she got only drool.

She'd known starting out that self-medication had its risks, but up until now everything had gone smoothly. She'd been careful. After a year of trawling forums she had all the brands and dosages cemented in her head, and she'd always had a knack for chemistry besides. It was the one class she'd liked at school. Seeing things react, seeing things change. She'd never had more than a few bouts of mild nausea.

But now she'd just vomited all night and all morning, and felt absolutely miserable. Violet crouched down, keeping a hand on the trash can to steady herself, and thumbed puke off the toes of her sneakers while she contemplated the situation. Maybe she'd somehow lost track of dosages and taken too much. Maybe it was food poisoning that everyone else had somehow avoided.

Or maybe it was the Parasite's fault. Violet rose wobbly to her feet, sucking in a deep breath. She didn't know how having an alien creature in her gut might change her body chemistry, but she was sure it did, and lately she felt, in a crazy paranoid way, like the Parasite knew what she was doing. Knew, and didn't like it. Maybe they'd promised it a male host with only traces of estrogen and an incoming spike of androgen and testosterone.

She drew her finger along the curve of her stomach, pretending it was the tip of a knife and trying to imagine how it must have felt for Wyatt. He'd told her about it only once, how there had still been a few working gas lines when he got out and he'd boiled everything in a pot to sterilize it. How he'd packed ice around his hips and belly and sharpened the Cutco knife until it was scalpel sharp.

Even thinking about the story made her shudder. She started to walk toward the pharmacy again, spitting the vomit taste out of her mouth every few meters. She would never be able to cut out her Parasite. She would never be able to change other things either. There weren't plastic surgeons anymore. Sometimes knowing that made her want to scream.

The aliens coming had been like a fairy tale at first. A twisted scary dark one, but that was the best kind anyway. She'd escaped from the warehouses in the first month, when everything was still chaos, and she'd hidden in a gas station overnight. When she crawled out the next morning, it was a brand-new world. Her father couldn't hit her; her mother couldn't cry. She didn't have to be an invisible boy. She could be an invisible girl instead.

After a few heady days of freedom and shoplifting, she'd even found a prince. Wyatt, with his beautiful gray eyes and perfect fucking bone structure. It had been terrifying and elating to introduce herself as Violet for the first time. He'd accepted it without so much as blinking. He'd asked if she was brave, and if she wanted to join the Lost Boys. He didn't care what was between her legs. She'd gotten herself out of the warehouse, she was quick and smart and she had guts, and that was enough. Before, Wyatt had trusted her more than any of the other kids.

But now she was supposed to be showing Bo the ropes, and instead she was throwing up on her shoes. Yesterday's stunt with the trailer had cemented Bo's role in the plan. She only had three days to get him up to speed before they went after the pod, and Wyatt thought she'd be best at it, said Lost Boys always liked whoever brought them in first the best. She'd countered that Bo wasn't a fucking baby bird, which made Wyatt laugh but not change his mind.

Violet yanked the pharmacy door open and stepped inside. She was hoping it was a bad reaction to the Estrofem that was causing the problem, and that a brand switch would fix it. As a temporary measure, she needed Tums. She grabbed it on her way past the line, noticing there were only two wasters in it now. She wondered, grimly, if the third one had died.

"Probably died," she said aloud. "Right, Dillon?"

The pharmacist was still smiling blandly, searching up a pre-scription on a dead screen. Violet let herself through the little door, not feeling up to bouncing over the counter, and went to the birth control. She glanced over her shoulder while she rummaged.

"Long time no see," she said. "So, are you always smiling like that? Or just when I come in?"

The pharmacist didn't respond.

Violet dumped out her remaining Estrofem and plucked the Estrace out of the cupboard instead. For the first time she took notice of the small printed numbers showing its expiration date. Ages away, but she still felt a lump in her throat. She'd known, in the back of her mind, that all medications expired. Even if she scoured every pharmacy in the city and raided houses to go through medicine cabinets, on a long enough timeline all of it would turn useless anyway. No surgeons, no drug manufactur-ers. Eventually the testosterone would come back.

And if Bo really was the next best thing to a savior, if they somehow did manage to beat back the aliens and maybe even free the wasters, what then? She would have to go back to real-ity. Go back to having a mother and father who wanted a son. She would lose Wyatt, obviously—there would be pretty girls lining up for him. He would be the one who saved everybody. Him and Bo.

"Dennis," she said, catching sight of the name tag again. "Sorry. Look, you're the lucky one, Dennis. You have the chillest workday of your life, over and over. I have real shit to worry about."

The nausea hit fast, and before she could make a run for the bathroom, or uncap the Tums, she threw up again right in front of him. In any other universe, it would have been mortifying. The pharmacist kept smiling, and Violet left without cleaning up.

For the next three days, while the other Lost Boys worked on the pod trap, Bo learned everything he could from Violet about the aliens. One of the first lessons was how othermothers' one blind spot was right underneath them, between their clicking insect legs. When Bree claimed that they had a kind of stinger tucked up there like a big needly cock, the tips of Violet's ears went red and she told her to shut the fuck up.

"That's a myth," she elaborated. On their next scouting trip she demonstrated, distracting an othermother with a hurled bottle and then sliding underneath. Bo had joined her, darting out from behind a dumpster, and then they crouched there for a full ten-count, grinning adrenal grins at each other while the othermother swiveled and chirped and swiveled again. He confirmed for Bree later that there was no stinger, just smooth blue-pigmented flesh.

The streets were teeming with othermothers during the day now, and most of them were in cornflower blue, but Bo had learned not to look at their faces or listen to what they were saying. It was easy enough to avoid them by ducking into low doorways or finding any sort of stairs—their lanky legs had trouble with both. He kept a medical mask in his pocket for the rare occasions he was spotted and recognized and they started wafting their sickly sweet-smelling pheromones.

Bo saw what happened to the ones they killed, and sometimes to dead wasters. A pod would come to the site, pick up the body with big raspy pincers, and fly it away. Violet explained that it was recycling them to make new ones, which made Bo's joints feel loose and watery, thinking how the othermothers were made at least partly of human meat. It was important to know, though, because that was how Wyatt said they would lure a pod away from the warehouses in the first place.

Violet was a good teacher, but often impatient, and when he asked a question she thought was stupid she had a scornful look that let him know. Even so, the evening after he scraped his shin climbing a fire escape with her, he found a big stack of Dora the Explorer Band-Aids waiting by his bed.

He used plain ones from the medicine shelf, but kept the ones from Violet too.

8

Violet didn't usually pay attention to the calendar Elliot kept scrawled on the wall of the lobby, but now they were only a day away from the square he'd lassoed with black and red Sharpies. The spot was picked out, the weapons were ready, and Wyatt seemed to have full confidence in Bo playing the bait. Violet wasn't feeling sick anymore—the brand switch seemed to have worked—but she did feel nervous.

Up until now, there had been a kind of equilibrium. Lost Boys escaped, the aliens sent othermothers. Lost Boys killed the othermothers, the aliens sent replacements. Up until now, what happened outside the warehouses hadn't seemed to matter all that much to them. But now there were more othermothers out than she'd ever seen, all of them looking for Bo, and the Lost Boys were about to provoke their enemy in a big, big way.

As she crept through the dark lobby, Violet glanced over to the corner where her little protégé usually slept. He hadn't shifted anything big since the semi—Wyatt's orders, in case the Parasite only had so much juice in it—but she'd seen him practice little ones, sitting cross-legged on his mattress and zapping drifting beetles or crumpled pop cans out of existence while Gilly watched in awe. He could be distractible and over-eager when they were out in the city, not paying close enough attention to his surroundings, but when he shifted things he had a dead-serious focus.

Maybe he'd gone and shifted himself too, because his bed was empty.

"Where're you going?"

Violet jumped—she hated that, how she was still jumpy even now that there was nobody to be scared of. Bo was standing against the peeling wall, rubbing at his eyes with the heel of his hand. Violet switched the grocery bag she was carrying to her other shoulder.

"Go to sleep, Pooh Bear," she said. "Tomorrow's the big day." She walked past him into the entryway, but she could hear him padding along softly behind her. She turned.

"I can't sleep tonight," Bo said. The sullen way he said it, the way his shoulders were slumped, made him look like a little kid again. He still was, really. Eleven was too young for all this shit. Maybe fifteen was too. Maybe any age.

"I'll give you a pill," Violet said. "Knocks you out good and you don't dream."

"I'm not having nightmares," Bo said, scowling away into the darkness. "I'm just thinking."

"About the plan?" Violet asked.

"No. About my mom."

"That's even worse," Violet said flatly. "Take a pill. Come on, I'll show you which bottle."

"Where do you go at night sometimes?" Bo asked. His face flickered to sly. "I thought maybe you and Wyatt go meet up somewhere, but he's sleeping on the stage."

"You just been sneaking around watching everybody sleep?" Violet asked, glad the dark hid her flush. Bo just shrugged and stood there looking sad. Thinking about his mom. She rocked foot to foot, debating. "You can come one time," she said. "But it's a secret. That means you don't tell Wyatt either."

"Wyatt doesn't know?" Bo sounded actually puzzled at the idea of Wyatt not knowing something, like Wyatt was supposed to be omniscient. It did seem that way sometimes, Violet knew.

"You promise?" she asked. "Swear on your sister?"

Bo's face went serious, so much so that Violet almost felt bad for saying it. "Alright," he said. "I swear."

Violet looked at him for another minute to make sure. He didn't have a good face for lying. Didn't have a good anything for lying. When he said something he either meant it with every bit of his body or with none of it. Right now he meant it.

"Let's go, then," Violet said. She turned and led the way outside. The cold air slipped between her lips. She'd worried, in the beginning, about the weather changing. About winter, and how the Lost Boys would keep warm, never mind all the wasters freezing to death. But it was the same day every day, cool and cloudy gray, and the same night every night. Chilly, but not enough for frost.

Up above them, the pods were starting to make their droning noise. The ship's underside gave off its pale yellow glow, making her think of bioluminescence, like it was the stomach of some huge dark deep-sea creature.

Violet switched her flashlight on and motioned the way. She'd thought maybe the trip would feel less lonely with Bo along, but he was uncharacteristically quiet as he followed her along the avenue, past the bombed-out liquor store, through a parking lot. Violet didn't feel much like talking either. They cut diagonally across a park, through rows of twisty trees. The branches waved and trembled, reminding her a bit of an other-mother's grasping hands.

"I came here before," Bo suddenly said, breaking the silence. They were passing a playground, the skeletal silhouette of a swing set, a climbing frame, poles and bars.

Violet looked over at him. "I did too, a few times. Instead of going home after school. There's some real fucking creepers around, though."

"Didn't have your bat?" Bo asked, grinning a bit.

"It was my dad's back then," Violet said. "I hate baseball. Boring as shit."

She led the way across the dark street, then into the grassy alley that ran between peeling blue fences. She stopped at hers and hopped it. Bo came over nimbly, and then they were both standing in her backyard. Violet had the brief giddy thought that she was bringing a friend home, how she hadn't done since grade school. Her mom would've been thrilled.

"Your house?" Bo guessed.

"Yeah," Violet said. "I like to come back. Check up on it. And..." She paused, debating. She could tell Bo to wait and he would wait. She could go in and make sure her parents were still alive and keep it her secret, her one secret from Wyatt and the Lost Boys and everybody. But she'd kept secrets all her life, and she was getting sick of them. If she could tell anyone, she felt like she could tell Bo, who had sworn on his sister. "My parents are in there," she said. "They're alive. Clamped, but alive. I check on them."

"What?" Bo demanded. His voice was ragged and she knew at once she'd made a mistake.

"Just in case," Violet said, watching his face. He wasn't a liar. He was angry, his brows knit with it, his mouth twisted.

"You said they're not people anymore," he said. "Clamp's in the head, better off dead. You said that. You told me that."

"We all say that," Violet said, but she felt a hot wave of shame. She tried to turn it into something more comfortable—anger, mostly at herself. She shouldn't have brought him. He was going to tell Wyatt and ruin everything. Wyatt would be pissed. Wyatt wouldn't trust her anymore.

"Wyatt says we're a family," Bo said, like he'd read her mind. His voice was screwed back tight against tears. "The Lost Boys, that's our new family. We have to forget about the ones that are gone. Clamp's in the head, better off dead."

"Bo—" Violet didn't know what to say, and she was cut off anyway.

"Clamp's in the head, better off dead," Bo chanted, sticking his hands over his ears. "Clamp's in the head, better off dead." He stalked past her, to the front gate, and swung himself over. She knew he was heading back to the theater. Back to tell Wyatt. She stood stock-still for a second, then followed after, feeling numb, unsure if she should try to stop him or not. She lifted the hinge on the gate and let herself out with a long creak.

Bo had stopped short at the end of the gravel driveway, staring down the street. There was a reason Violet always came through the backway. Her street had come through relatively unscathed, but the rest of the neighborhood, the Wally's, the elementary school, the storage units and apartments, were mostly blackened rubble. The ship's fizzing blue exhaust had come down heavy here, and electrical fires had done the rest.

Before Violet could say anything, Bo set off running. She watched him tearing down the scorch-marked sidewalk for a moment before she went after him. The pods in the sky had stopped their droning. The only sound in the night was their feet slapping the concrete. Violet hadn't realized how quick he was until now, chasing him. He had a smooth gliding gait that seemed too long for his legs, and he was nimble, avoiding the divots and ruptures that pocked the road. Violet gave up on catching him and just tried to keep him in sight, her heart thudding hard and her breath loud in her ears.

When he finally stopped, it was at the burnt-out husk of what Violet vaguely thought had been a duplex. She could see a few twists of blackened rebar from the foundation, some barely standing framework that looked ready to turn to powder at a touch. Bo stood upright at the edge of the ruin, breathing even, not winded from the run. But as she listened she could hear a sobbing whine building in his throat. She tried not to look for the telltale shape of bones in burned fabric.

"Last place I saw her," Bo said. "Last place I saw her. She told us to get out, and she was right behind us."

"Your mom?" Violet asked, soft.

"Then the pod picked us up," Bo said. "And I thought maybe it was trying to save us from the fire. I thought maybe another one had picked up Mom too." He rubbed his eyes fiercely, kneading them with his knuckles until Violet wanted to tug them away, sure he'd bruise himself. "Stupid," he said. "Stupid, stupid."

Violet felt ashamed again, ashamed that she'd brought him here, that she'd reminded him. There was a reason Lost Boys didn't talk about their old family. There was a reason they had to kill the othermother. She reached forward and put her hand on Bo's shoulder.

He jerked away.

"I hate the fuckers," he said, turning to her with teeth clenched, tears sliding down his cheeks. "I hate them, hate them, hate them, hate them—"

Violet pulled him into a sort of hug. It was badly angled and she didn't know what to do with her hands, but a beat later Bo hugged her back, hard. They stood clung together like that for what might have been a long time. Violet wasn't sure. Eventually Bo pulled away, wiping his face on his sleeve, partly just to hide it, maybe.

"We were neighbors, almost," she said, just to be saying something.

"Don't you cry anymore?" Bo asked, one last bit of anger in his voice. Then he gave a shuddery sigh. "We were new here," he said. "Had an apartment before. She was excited about this place, like...really happy, really excited for it. When we got the place, she called our grandparents and talked all in Hausa with them for an hour. Long distance. They don't know how to Skype."

"Talked in what?" Violet asked, because it seemed important to ask.

"Hausa." Bo swallowed. "From Niger. I know a little bit. She wanted me to learn more. I only know the greeting you say in the morning. *Ina kwana, lahiya lau. Ina gajiya, ba gajiya.*"

"What's it mean?" Violet asked, because that seemed important too.

Bo screwed up his face, thinking. "Like, how did you sleep? Good. Are you tired? No." He shrugged. "Then at the end, she says *to, madalla.* And I think that's like, good. Okay. Everything's fine." Bo shook his head. "It's not, though," he said, quiet.

Violet put her hand on his shoulder again, and this time he didn't flinch away. "Yeah, Bo," she said. "I know."

9

The next morning, the morning of what they had all started calling the mission, Bree dug out a battery-powered set of clippers. Bo saw her at work when he came back from the bathroom. She sat cross-legged on the lobby floor, looking down into a cracked Hello Kitty–stickered mirror, and moved the electric razor with deft swipes until she was surrounded by a dusting of shorn hair. Gilly, darting around behind her, was already sporting the same haircut and a mad grin.

"What d'you think, Bo?" she asked. "Like soldiers, isn't it?"

"Sure," Bo said offhand, then, when her face fell a little: "Sure, you look cool."

Gilly's grin got even wider and her cheeks went pink. "Bree can do yours too," she said. "Can't you, Bree?"

From the floor, Bree clacked the clippers off and on in affirmative. Bo dug a hand into his hair. He'd been able to find the shampoo his mom used to buy for him, but he had to lean over the drain in the bathroom floor and dump bottled water over his head to rinse it out. The knots and tangles were past combing and pushed out his hood when he tried to pull it tight. The shaved head made Bree look older too. Tougher.

Everyone was waiting for Violet and Wyatt to come back. They were out watching the wormy wall, waiting for the first wave of othermothers to exit. Then it would be time to hunt.

"Yeah, okay," Bo said. "Might have to use scissors on it first."

"Got those too," Bree said. She stood up, brushing loose hair off her neck and face, and motioned to the spot she'd vacated. "Have a seat in the barber chair."

Bo sat as still as he could while Bree hacked away, and by the time she'd finished there was a queue forming, first Saif and Alberto, then Jon, then even Elliot and his thick brown mop. When he was buzzed clean, Bo helped sweep the fluffy piles of his hair away, then went to the bathroom mirror. He ran his hands over his scalp and the stubble prickled his palms. His reflection in the mirror looked harsher than it used to, and it wasn't only the haircut either. He hadn't noticed that his cheeks were starting to slim down. His eyes were different too, darker underneath.

He liked it. Bo bared his teeth at the mirror, then came back out. Bree was working on Alberto, shaking his dark curls out of the guard. The air inside the theater was thick and buzzing with excitement, and it ramped up each time a Lost Boy stood up, head shorn. Bo could feel his heart beating quicker than normal and goose bumps on his arms. The adrenaline was infectious, like every bit of touch or eye contact was more meaningful than it had ever been. Bo's Parasite was moving, and he knew everyone else's was too. It was partly the knowing that charged his skin with static.

People started to cheer for whoever it was getting shorn, and once the last girl, Jenna, was done, they started the rhymes. Bo knew some of them already, like the whirlybird one: *I eat firsts, seconds, thirds, whirlybirds can eat my turds.* That was from back in the warehouses. Bo chanted loud as anyone. Quiet Saif had a new one, one that caught and carried and made Bo's spine tingle. *The othermother's not my mother, I done killed one I'll kill another.*

He knew, by the math, that the othermothers they used for the first bait would probably be wearing his mom's cornflower-blue dress. But it wasn't his mom, and he couldn't let himself think it was. He had the second bait to worry about. So Bo chanted along with the rest, letting the excitement course through him, until Gilly, who'd been watching outside the door, ran up to tell him Wyatt and Violet were coming.

"They're coming!" Bo shouted. "Shut up!"

To his surprise, mostly everyone did. They respected him. They knew what he could do with the crackling Parasite in his stomach. Feeling like he was on the crest of a wave, like he could do anything at all, Bo raised his arm.

"In a line," he ordered. "Everybody in line."

When Wyatt and Violet stepped into the lobby, all the Lost Boys, heads shaved, eyes forward, were standing in a row. Violet had been on the verge of saying something, but her mouth shuttered closed when she saw them. She looked worried for a second, nearly scared, but Bo spared her only a glance before he looked to Wyatt.

Wyatt was grinning a fierce grin, eyes bright. He walked slowly down the row, and when he passed Bo he gave him a nod, and Bo gave it back. At the end of the line, Wyatt turned.

"Where do I get mine done like that?" he asked.

Gilly couldn't hold back her cheer, and then Bree was getting out the clippers again as Wyatt peeled off his shirt. He sat stock-still while she sheared the blond locks away from his head, only moving his eyes, scanning back and forth while his Lost Boys all got geared up. Some had knives, some had found police batons; the others, Bo included, had makeshift black-jacks tied off by Elliot's tight knots. Elliot had made the hooks too, and fastened them all to the bungee cords. Jon was helping spool them and pack them into the backpack.

Bo looked for Violet and realized she was skulking in the shadows by the door, her face stony, nostrils flared. They hadn't spoken since they came back last night. He caught her eye and hesitantly raised his hand, miming the clippers. He could guess why she didn't want to, but it felt important that everybody do it, so they were all the same. All Lost Boys.

She gave half a shake of her head, looking angry and almost pained. But Bo didn't have time to worry about her as Wyatt stood up, brushing the last bits of hair off his wiry shoulders. Everyone went quiet without needing an order.

"Most of the othermothers are heading downtown," Wyatt said. "Remember, we want to get them isolated first. Pick one, lead it off, take it out. We want three bodies fast, so we're doing three groups. Me, Jon, and Violet leading."

Bo rocked on the balls of his feet while Wyatt divvied every-one up, and a minute later he followed Wyatt out of the theater, swinging the blackjack back and forth, feeling the Parasite sparking in his belly. He was reciting the rhyme in his head:

Done killed one, I'll kill another.

"Boniface, is that you, honey? Boniface, honey, is that you? Boniface, is that—"

Violet reversed her bat, smashing the knob down into the othermother's bobbing throat. Something crunched inward and the syrupy voice jittered to a halt. She wiped the bat off with the hem of her tunic, leaving a dark smear. She didn't care about stains today. She was pissed.

"Take a leg each," she ordered. "Hold it by the first joint."

Saif and Alberto scurried to comply, wrestling for a second to see who would take the one leaking fluid. They were both bouncy on their feet, all wired up like the last time she caught them playing potions, which meant dumping a half dozen energy drinks into a big plastic cup and swilling it until their hearts beat hummingbird-fast. They weren't as smart as Gilly. Everything was still a game to them, hunting othermothers included.

Violet and Alberto had done the dirty work and Saif had done the baiting, since he was nearly dark enough to pass for Bo. Of course, everyone looked more or less the same now, thanks to Bree's little stunt. Like a bunch of fucking space monkeys. Violet was sure, with a burning clarity, that she'd done it to barb her. Bree knew Violet wouldn't shave her head, even if the other girls did.

That wasn't the only thing either. While she'd been out with Wyatt, he'd asked her where she'd gone last night. She'd said nowhere important, and he'd dropped it, but it still put a squirmy fear in her. She hated it when she disappointed Wyatt. It stung all over.

Violet stowed the bat and seized the othermother's rubbery wrists. "Up on three, guys," she said. She gave them the three-count, then they all lifted in tandem. Violet knew that dead bodies were supposed to be heavy, but the othermother was light. She briefly wondered if they had honeycombed bones, like birds, or maybe no bones at all. Then she remembered how pissed she was and jerked her head forward.

They'd done the othermother near a dumpster outside the Safeway, meaning they didn't have far to go to the meet point. A few times they heard the sound of another othermother approaching and had to either detour around or duck into an alley to avoid being spotted, but when they got to the fountain, Violet felt a small bit of satisfaction seeing they were the first to arrive. They dragged the othermother up to the lip of the fountain and heaved her over. She splashed into the scummy water, bobbing the plastic refuse around.

"We're first," Alberto beamed, running his dirty hands over Saif's head.

"Yeah, well, this was the easy part," Violet said, flipping the othermother's dangling arm over the edge with the rest of her. "Don't get too excited, my little skinheads."

Three othermothers drifted around the fountain, limp limbs knocking against each other. Bo rubbed absently at the little pink scar on his elbow, the one from when he first escaped the warehouse. He was perched a ways off from the fountain, on top of an empty electrical van, watching the sky and waiting. Wyatt had picked the plaza because it was a wide empty space. The pods didn't like maneuvering in cramped quarters. Here there was the fountain, a bare island of cobblestone, and mostly empty streets surrounding it. Nowhere to hide, nothing to make it suspicious.

Bo stretched his legs and his arms, then flexed his knuckles until they cracked. He'd been watching and waiting for over an hour. He was getting restless. He stared up again into the cloudy gray sky, squinting hard. And suddenly, there it was: three or four times the size of the porpoises he'd seen in the aquarium, floating through the air, steering itself with serrated fins. A pod.

Bo slipped down off the van, swinging himself into the open back and out of sight. He didn't see its descent, but he heard the familiar chugging noise, the mixture of dying motor and gasping animal. It set his teeth on edge. Then the pod dropped low over the fountain and he had a good look at it. The outside was part inky-black flesh and part something else, something hard and plastic-looking. Bundles of wire and glowing electronics clung to it in patches. The fins were metal and sharp.

It loomed over the fountain, and from its underbelly Bo saw two spidery pincers unfold. Slowly, delicately, the pod picked the first othermother out of the dirty water, dripping on the stone. Bo watched it envelop the ragdoll corpse, sucking it back into its belly. He felt a flare of anger knowing they would use it to grow another, and another, and another. His Parasite caught the emotion and crackled. He wondered, briefly, if he could vanish the pod from here. If he could make the static ripple far enough to rip the pod right out of existence.

But that wasn't the mission. Bo waited instead, waited as the pod reached for its second corpse, reeled it in slowly. Wyatt had said to wait. Minutes ticked by. Bo clenched and unclenched his hands. Waited. Waited. When the pod was finishing with the last corpse, intent on its work, Bo knew it was time. He slapped at his face, letting the pain pump his adrenals—Violet had shown him that trick, and not gently. His Parasite surged. He almost hoped he would need it.

The pod was full of sodden bodies now. Wyatt had said it would be slow, sluggish even. Wyatt was always right. Bo slipped out of the van and paced three cautious steps toward the fountain, judging distance. He'd baited plenty of othermothers over the past few days. He had the timing for it. But as far as he knew, nobody had ever baited a pod before. Bo watched it drift in place. He wondered, briefly, if it might be the same pod that had chased him when he first escaped the warehouse. He wondered if aliens knew what a rematch was.

Bo licked his lips and whistled loud. The pod revolved in a slow circle until its blunt nose was facing him. Bo peered at it, trying to distinguish features. It didn't seem to have any eyes, but that went with what Wyatt had said too, that they used sonar like dolphins. Its head was a smooth blank curve. Bo took a big step backward, keeping his eyes locked on the pod.

He remembered the one that had swooped down on him outside the warehouse with its blinding lights, the one that had picked him off the sidewalk in front of his burning house, how terrified he'd been both times. Out here low to the ground, in daylight, instead of circling in a dark sky, it didn't look as frightening. It looked out of place. Almost like a cartoon, all clumsy and swollen.

Bo took another step backward, and the pod drifted slowly toward him. No different from an othermother. Easier, maybe. He took another step. The pod followed, chugging and wheezing, still hovering only a few feet off the ground. Bo turned and kept walking, checking over his shoulder every so often, drawing closer and closer to the alley Wyatt had picked out, recognizable by the old rusted water tank on the one rooftop. He felt almost giddy. Almost wanted to laugh.

Then, as he looked over his shoulder, there was a whirring and a bright yellow light flashed in his eyes. Bo blinked hard, chasing spots away. He saw a miniature image of his half-turned profile slide across the pod's black skin like a hologram. The pod hovered in place, as if it was thinking, almost, considering its options.

Bo rubbed his eyes. "Yeah," he said. "It's me."

There was a scraping noise, and from the underside of the pod's featureless head Bo saw a spiny projection slide into view, a spiky proboscis-looking thing with a gleaming sharp hook at its end.

"Shit," Bo said, and he took off down the alley.

It was a strange déjà vu, like he was breaking out of the warehouse all over again, but this time there was a plan and a destination and he knew what he was running toward. He dug in, found his rhythm. Stretched his stride. It felt springy and pure, better now with the new shoes, better now that he was eating real food and drinking all the water he wanted.

This time the pod had to stay low to keep him in sight, because the Lost Boys had crisscrossed the top of the alley with heavy wires, strung roof to roof, and draped tarps over the top. He crossed over into their shadow. The pavement pounded away under his feet, all of it swept clean of debris, nothing left that might trip him up. At the end of the alley he could see the twin dumpsters they'd pushed into a blockade. He put on an extra burst of speed.

Bo could hear the pod chugging along behind him, picture its sharp proboscis level to his shoulder blades. His Parasite was thumping in beat with his heart, crackling and nearly sparking. Hot greasy-smelling air blasted over his shaved head in waves like an animal's panting breath; the pod was closing the gap, close, closer—

Wyatt stepped out from behind one of the dumpsters, spear gun held up against his shoulder, gray eyes narrowed to slits of concentration. Bo dove to the ground.

It was Jenna's idea to put an old spongy mattress down to break the fall, and he was briefly grateful to her as he hit it and rolled. He saw the glint of the pod's proboscis whistle past his face, then the rest of it, its smooth black underbelly skimming inches over him. The blast of air shut his eyes for him, but he heard the dull pneumatic *chunk* of Wyatt firing.

He scrambled up from under the pod's now-thrashing tail, back the other way. More Lost Boys were out from behind the dumpsters now, swinging the hooks Elliot had made so sharp. Bo took another step backward, not daring take his eyes off the scene. The pod was trying to turn around, but the alley was too narrow, even when it tucked its metal fins up against its sides. Wyatt had guessed right. He was clutching tight to the spear gun in both hands as the line unspooled, hissing into the air. The dart had stuck deep, buried in the pod's ink-black flesh, and Bo could see something luminous and yellow leaking out of the wound.

Quentin was the first to hurl his hook, but it slapped against the pod's side and bounced off. Jon went next and struck true, sinking it into the skin around its left fin. Bree's dragged an oozing gouge along the pod's back but slipped out. Jenna's bounced.

The pod was thrashing wildly, making a horrible keening drone that Bo could feel in his jawbone. He stared, transfixed, as it twisted Wyatt's dart free with a wet *pop*. It wasn't sluggish-seeming anymore. It was strong, terrifyingly strong. Wyatt loaded the spear gun again, cursing, and Jon slid on his feet trying to keep hold of his cord. Bo was frozen.

Cold metal slapped into his hand. He looked up and saw Violet.

"Get in close," she said. "Don't throw it. Get close."

She had a hook of her own clenched in white knuckles, and she took off toward the pod as it slammed its tail end against the stone wall, raising a cloud of dust and grime. Saif and

Alberto were right behind her, howling with fright and excitement. Bo watched in frames as Violet darted in, back out, then finally underneath the twisting pod. She drove the hook into its underbelly with more force than Bo thought she could get from her skinny arms.

The pod wailed, an ear-splitting sound that seemed to shake the whole alley. Saif struck next, planting his hook under its fin and then hurling himself out of the way. Alberto missed, but by then the other Lost Boys had seen what Violet had done. Bree came from the other side, taking a flying leap off the top of the dumpster, and stuck her hook into the pod's arching back. Yellow fluid splattered into the air.

Bo gripped his hook, heart hammering hard, Parasite thrumming. He went in on the next opening. The pod jerked sideways, nearly taking him off his feet, but as he hopped backward he managed to stick it. The pod gave another wail, quieter this time. Bo scrambled backward, snatching the cord up off the alley floor, holding it in both sweaty hands.

Wyatt had reloaded and he shot again. This time it hit the pod in the head, or where its head should have been, shearing deep. There were a half dozen hooks in it now. All of the Lost Boys were holding the cord, some doubled up, everyone straining and sliding. Bo had wrapped his around his arms, pulling down hard as he could while the pod writhed.

"Hold it!" Wyatt called. "Quentin, help out on Saif's. Hold it!"

Slowly, slowly, the pod's struggles slowed. The tugs became weaker. Across from him, Bo could see Gilly and Alberto doubled up on a cord, pulling with all their might. Gilly grinned at him and he tried to grin back. The pod stopped all at once, hovering in place, no more twisting. A second ticked past.

Another. Everyone shot looks to Wyatt, questioning, ready to celebrate. The pod wasn't droning now, and even its breathing was modulated, quiet. Hesitant smiles appeared. Bo's heart started to slow. Even Wyatt had a look of triumph on his face. Bo took a deep shuddering breath and let his grip slacken.

The cord leapt out of his hands like a startled snake as the pod shot straight upward. Bo lunged for the cord but it slithered out of reach; he saw half the other Lost Boys doing the same, trying to grab hold again. He managed to get his fingers around it an instant before the pod surged again, climbing higher. He dug in his heels. The cord slid and burned his palms, and in the corner of his eye he saw Bree lose her hold, then Violet, then Quentin.

The pod climbed until it struck up against the wires they'd strung along the roof of the alley, and Bo was nearly yanked off his feet before he lost hold. He fell on his tailbone with a jarring thud, watching the cord spring away. The loosed bungees danced wildly under the pod's wounded belly; Saif was still somehow clinging to his, kicking his legs a foot off the ground.

Only Jon's was still taut. He'd crouched low against the corner of the dumpster, using it as leverage so he wouldn't be pulled off the ground. Wyatt and Jenna were bracing him from behind. Jenna had a vein blue and throbbing on her pale forehead. Wyatt's teeth were gritted. But Bo saw, with a lurch in his stomach, that they were slipping. The pod was pulling away, slowly, inexorably, straining against the wires above it. One of them ripped free from the ledge of the roof with a terrific crack and shower of dust. Tarps slipped and toppled to the floor of the alley. The pod was getting away.

Some of the Lost Boys were running to help hold Jon's cord, others to grab at Saif's dangling shins, but Bo's eyes climbed higher, through the gap left by the fallen tarp. They zeroed in on the water tank. It was big around as two of him, flecked with rust, and he couldn't imagine it was full, but the metal looked heavy on its own. Bo let the fear in his stomach feed his Parasite. He felt it sparking.

This wasn't like vanishing the othermother or the box, where he'd focused on the whole of it, the shape of it. He didn't want to vanish the water tank at all. What he wanted was to vanish the two spindly metal legs that propped it up on the near side. He stood stock-still, staring hard at the first of the legs, coaxing the static through his body. He dimly felt someone tug his arm, someone trying to get him to help pull Saif. He shook them off.

Jon's hook came free with a rending sound, tearing a chunk of flesh and circuitry with it. The pod gave a reverberating drone of pain, or maybe triumph, because Saif had fallen with a thump and now the only thing keeping it in the alley was the flimsy mesh of wire and tarp. Bo tried to concentrate on the leg, only the leg, as the pod strained upward. The hairs on the nape of his neck stuck straight up and he released the static, not all of it, just enough.

The air rippled like a mirage and the metal leg was gone. Some of the wall was too, the bricks sheared neatly in half, but Bo'd already refocused on the second leg. It was creaking, buckling slightly without its partner. The pod snapped another wire, making a gap big enough to fit through if it could twist its back half. It started wriggling its nose through the space, pointed up at the thick gray sky, giving another long drone. Now or never.

Bo sent his second surge of static, taking out the buckled leg and half the water tank too, in a spray of foamy rust-colored water. The heavy metal tore away from its last leg and plunged downward just as the pod slipped free. Bo watched with caught breath as the tank slammed into the top of the pod with a dull *crack*. The pod dropped a full foot before it caught itself; the broken tank crashed to the floor of the alley, sending reverberations through Bo's shoe soles.

He could see a dent where the metal had hit the pod, and the creature seemed to be reeling. It sank down, down, then finally settled on the wreckage of the tank. The labored breathing was loud in Bo's ears, nearly as loud as his heart. As he watched, the pod's fins retracted and its body went limp. He couldn't tell if it was dying or only stunned, but he felt a white-hot triumph in his chest. They'd done it. They'd pulled a pod out of the sky. Proved they weren't invincible.

No, even better: *He'd* done it. Bo had a grin spreading across his face and couldn't stop it, especially when Bree started a new chant.

"Bo! Bo! Bo! Bo!"

The Lost Boys streamed around him, slapping him on the back, hugging him around the middle, pounding his chest. Jon heaved him up high in the air. Then they were all pushing him onto the back of the collapsed pod, still electric with excitement. Bo's shoes sank slightly into the jet-black flesh. He leaned down and put his hand on its heaving surface.

"That was for my mom," he said, quiet so the Lost Boys wouldn't hear. "And the next one's for Lia."

He straightened up, took one step, then another, then stood on the arch of its back and raised his arms in a victory V. The chant got even louder. Bo's grin was so big it felt like it would split his jaw.

"Bo! Bo! Bo!"

He looked for Violet in the chaos but didn't see her, and then his gaze fell on Wyatt, standing apart from the mob. His lips were fixed in a smile. Bo gave him a fierce nod, and he nodded back, but there was a look in his eyes Bo didn't quite recognize. He turned back to the cheering Lost Boys instead.

10

The pod was still buoyant enough to be dragged easily, so they made good time to a storage unit two blocks off the theater. Violet's heart was still pumping hard from the excitement. It was contagious, all the grinning and whooping and cheering. She nearly forgot about being pissed off. Violet still remembered the pod that had carried her to the warehouses, how terrified she'd been in its liquid cocoon. The Lost Boys all remembered, she figured.

It felt good to get one back. Violet didn't even stop Alberto running and bouncing off the pod's spongy tail end as they hauled it along.

She knew Wyatt had picked the storage unit carefully. It was close enough to make a quick trip back and forth from the theater, but not too close. If the pod, even with its mangled circuitry and torn flesh, could still communicate with the others, there wouldn't be a vengeful fleet of them converging on the Lost Boys' hideout. That was important.

The interior of the storage unit was dark and stank like gasoline. The pod still seemed dazed when they manhandled it in, but as the metal shuttered down, Violet saw a strange shiver go through its body. She didn't know anything about alien anatomy. She didn't know if the pods even felt emotions how people felt them. But she hoped, savagely, that it was scared. It deserved to be the scared one for once.

Wyatt posted Elliot and Quentin to first watch—both of them nodded gravely, stuck out their chests like pigeons as they spotted up outside the unit. The rest of the Lost Boys headed back toward the theater in shifts, splitting into smaller groups and taking winding routes. Wyatt wanted to take no chances, in case the ship was watching them somehow. Violet was one of the last to leave.

The mood in the theater was subdued, at first, like everyone was waiting for retribution, maybe a swarm of whirlybirds or jets of blue fire. They all sat in the theater, playing cards on autopilot or retelling, in hushed voices, the story of how they'd taken the pod down. Wyatt went up to the roof a few times, to check on the ship, and Violet didn't try to follow him.

Eventually though, as the sky went dark and the aliens showed no sign of responding, the victory sank in all over again. Wyatt came down off the rooftop with a calm smile on his face, like everything was under control. He settled in next to Violet and his hand brushed her knee but she figured it was an accident. It still made her thrill a little, made her hope he'd already forgotten about her disappearing in the night.

Now the retellings got louder, more exaggerated, until Saif had been dangling twenty feet off the ground and Bo had dropped a full-sized water tower on the pod's head. At some point Jenna and Bree went down into the basement and brought back a crate of pop that was cold as you could get without refrigeration or ice. The younger kids were excited by it, even though they could swipe whatever they wanted from convenience stores now.

Them and Bree started re-enacting the pod hunt, arguing over who would be the pod, who would be Bo, who would be the falling water tank. Wyatt laughed and Violet couldn't help cracking a grin when Bree puffed her cheeks to imitate the pod's wailing drone. For a moment she caught eyes with Bo, who was laughing too, smiling, loud. It was hard to think he was the boy who'd cried for so long last night. He waved his plastic bottle in her direction, nearly sloshing orange pop onto his shirt.

Someone nudged her arm. Violet turned and saw Jon, quiet Jon, grinning and red-cheeked. He passed her a heavy glass bottle with exaggerated slyness. She recognized the label and knew it was expensive, one of the vodkas they stuck behind glass in the liquor store. Normally Violet didn't drink. She'd cleaned up too much puke and smelled too much alcohol in her dad's sweat. But the corner of Wyatt's mouth tugged up in a smile, like he was daring her, and that was enough.

"Cheers," Violet said. She swigged. It might have been expensive, but it still tasted like shit. Not too much burn, though. She didn't even cough. Jon took it back with an approving nod, then passed it to an eager Bree, who nearly spat it right back out. Violet laughed, maybe a little meaner than usual, but Bree laughed too. Wyatt drank deep when it came to him, and then he called Bo over. Bo had been the pod in the latest re-enactment, and had to pry Saif off him before he bounced over.

They passed the vodka around clockwise—Bo took only a few swigs before he started passing it off, but he stayed in the circle, grinning wide. Violet suspected Bree had her lips closed, but that only meant more for the rest of them. She had a warm feeling in her belly now, and a flushed feeling in her face. Her Parasite didn't seem to like it, giving an odd ripple, but fuck the Parasite. They'd caught a pod. She needed to celebrate.

Normally Violet didn't drink, but normally Wyatt didn't either. This wasn't a normal night.

Bo was trying to concentrate on the card game, but he kept getting distracted and Gilly had to nudge him every time it was his turn. Whatever Jon and Wyatt and Violet were drinking had spun his head a bit. He felt warm, though, and happy, and every time he did play it seemed really intentional, like his hand was moving the card so smooth and so perfect.

"Gotta pee," he realized. It had snuck up on him somehow.

"One, two, three, Bo's gotta pee," said Saif, who was trying to rhyme everything now. Bo hopped up to his feet. On his way by he gave Saif a little cuff on the head, the friendly kind. He liked Saif. He liked everyone. They were a family, how Wyatt had said.

Bo wanted to take a piss from the edge of the roof. It seemed like a good idea, a really good one. He crossed the dim lobby to the stairwell, liking the feel of the carpet under his sock feet, the texture of the ripped-up spots. The rusty metal door to the stairwell was swung open. Bo skipped through, dodging the coagulated puddle on muscle memory, and scrambled up the stairs, nearly to the top before he noticed voices leaking through the second door.

Violet's voice. Wyatt's voice. If Jon was up there, he was being quiet like usual. Bo hesitated on the top step, wavering a bit back and forth. They could be making strategies, something they didn't want him eavesdropping on. But maybe they were talking about how Bo had really pulled it off, really saved the day for them, and didn't he deserve to know the strategies too?

Bo stuck his face up to the crack in the door. The cold air made his eyes water a bit and he blinked. Violet and Wyatt were sitting with their backs to him, right on the very edge of the roof. Bo remembered his plan and his bladder gave a twinge. He had a creeping suspicion of what might be going on, what older kids might actually do instead of just talk about. Violet and Wyatt were speaking in low, slurred murmury voices. The suspicion was confirmed when Violet leaned over and suddenly they were kissing, Wyatt's fingers tangling her hair.

Bo looked away, feeling a bit embarrassed to have seen it, knowing immediately it was a secret. He supposed it made sense. Violet was pretty. Wyatt was handsome. It made sense they liked each other. Wyatt was good too, and sometimes strict but usually kind. He would understand about Violet's parents if she explained it to him. Maybe Bo would tell her that in the morning.

Bo slipped back down the stairs as quiet as he could, then ran flat-out to get into the bathroom before he pissed himself.

11

The storage unit door hauled open with a rattle and clank. The smell of old gasoline spills and something else, something strange and chemical Bo had never smelled before, wafted out. It made his head ache. Back in the shadows, the pod was rolled over on its side, flesh pumping up and down, its raspy breathing echoing in the enclosed space. Bo tried hard to dredge up the feeling of victory from the day before, but he mostly felt ill and tired.

It was early still, the same pale gray morning as always, but Wyatt didn't seem sluggish at all. Even after last night. He had dark circles under his eyes, but his steps had been springy all the way from the theater and there was a grin stretched tight across his mouth. He'd shaken Bo awake with both hands, telling him only that they were going to see the pod.

Now Quentin and Elliot, who'd taken turns sleeping in a green camo tent set up against the storage unit, were stumbling red-eyed back to the theater. Bo felt vaguely bad that they'd missed the party, but he didn't feel very good in the aftermath, so maybe they were lucky.

Now it was just Bo and Wyatt and the pod. Wyatt took a

step inside and Bo followed, standing at the edge of the unit. The pod was a hulking shadow and he didn't want to go farther. He remembered something his mom had said, ages ago, about wounded animals being the most dangerous. And this wasn't an animal either. It knew what was going on.

"How's it feel, Bo?" Wyatt asked. "We really did it."

"Yeah," Bo said. "Did it." He met Wyatt's hard gray gaze as long as he could. The grin was still on his face, but it seemed different in the dark. He was almost relieved when Wyatt redirected his attention to the pod. It took up the whole back half of the storage unit. Once his eyes adjusted to the gloom, Bo looked for yesterday's puncture marks on its back but didn't see them. The pod's skin was smooth gleaming black again, other than the gash torn by Jon's hook. That one was sealed over with a thin yellow membrane, or scab, Bo supposed, if the yellow stuff was its blood.

"Heals fast," Wyatt muttered. "That's good."

Bo didn't know why that was good; his head was still muddled. But then the scraping sound of a knife shivered his teeth and he realized why. Wyatt was sharpening the knife with casual precision, the same look he'd had while tightening the spokes on his bike. Bo remembered back to the rooftop conversation—*when we're done with it,* Wyatt had said. But somehow Bo never pictured it like this, all dark and foul smelling and with just the two of them.

"We have to know our enemy, right?" Wyatt said. "So the first thing is establishing communication. Doesn't have eyes. Can't really see any organs on it, can you?"

"No," Bo said, wishing it was still last night and he was still on top of the world.

"I still think it echolocates," Wyatt said, thoughtful. "Maybe we can find out later. But we know it's got nerves, and there's something all things with nerves understand. Right?"

"Right," Bo said faintly.

Wyatt looked down the length of the knife like a chef. He nodded. Bo watched, feeling numb, as Wyatt approached the prone pod. He searched over it, then raised the knife. Even before it came down, Bo knew the spot he'd picked, the spot that made the most sense. He clenched his teeth as Wyatt dragged the razor edge of the blade through the yellow patch of healing membrane. The pod shook, and a low drone bounced a thousand times around the cramped storage unit, putting goose bumps on Bo's skin. When Wyatt looked up, there was a sort of flush on his cheeks.

"Good," he said. "First contact."

The pod shied away from the knife, rolling upright. Facing them, it flashed its yellow light again, but it seemed dimmer this time, even in the dark. Bo saw, again, miniature versions of himself, and now of Wyatt, trickling over the pod's skin. The chugging noise intensified and it managed to lift itself an inch off the floor of the unit. Wyatt took a step backward, clutching the knife and frowning.

From the pod's underbelly, a multi-jointed metal arm telescoped outward, clicking and clacking. It was the same pincer Bo had seen it use to pick up the othermothers, but now there was something else in its grip. A glossy black sphere, maybe the size of a baseball. Bo thought of Violet's bat and wished she was here with them, or that she was here with Wyatt instead of him.

The pod set the sphere down on the floor of the unit. Wyatt looked at it for a moment, his face blank, then kicked it away. It clanged against the back wall. A strange shudder ran through the pod again. The arm disappeared and reappeared. A new black sphere, identical to the first. Bo thought of the other-mothers that came one after another after another. They didn't think how people did, Violet had said. Not yet.

Wyatt darted in and slashed the knife into the pod's yellow scab, eliciting another moan. The sphere clattered to the floor, rolling, and Bo saw that the underside of it was different. An eye-sized red circle with something liquid-looking inside. He thought he saw tiny things floating in it, like a petri dish under infrared light, before Wyatt picked it up and hurled it at the pod. The black sphere bounced, banged against the wall.

"Could be trying to talk to us," Wyatt said casually. "But we're not going to talk until we establish the relationship. Between us and it. As in we've got the power, it's got nothing. Like that." He gave the side of the pod a kick. "You ready for a go, Bo?"

Bo's mouth was dry as sand. His violent little fantasies of punishing the pod had been so different, no smell in them, no sick feeling. This wasn't like the whirlybirds or the othermo-thers. It could think, and it could feel. He tried to get the hate back. The hate that had let him drive his hook in deep yester-day when they ambushed it in the alley. Maybe this was the pod that had taken him and Lia to the warehouse in the first place. Maybe this pod was the reason for everything.

Wyatt placed the handle of the knife in his hand and gave him a reassuring touch on his arm, just above the elbow. Bo's legs felt like sloshing water and it was hard to grip the knife. He took a step forward. The pod was reaching into itself again, producing another black sphere, identical to the first two. It didn't think how people did, because it wasn't one. Bo hovered the knife over its wound. Fresh yellow was leaking out, gleam-ing in the dark.

"Right there," Wyatt said gently. "Right where it hurts."

Bo thought of his sister trapped in the warehouse, of all the stumbling wasters with clamps in their skulls, all the dead people incinerated when the ship first came down. He remembered the pod swallowing him up and taking him away from his mom forever. He felt a sob working its way up from his belly, felt the Parasite start to thrum.

He drove the knife into the pod's flesh and his sob came out as a snarl. Then he was stabbing it over and over, twisting and gouging, feeling the pod shake and groan under the blade. It tried to turn away, hide its wound against the wall. Bo dragged it back and started again. When he was finally done, the yellow fluid had drenched his fingers and spattered the roof of the unit, glowing up there like constellations. The pod was heaving and twitching. Bo was panting. He distantly felt Wyatt peel the knife out of his hand.

"It's alright, Bo," his voice was saying. "Relax, Bo. Relax."

Bo saw the yellow stains on his hands and tucked them under his armpits. His breathing slowly subsided. He still felt sick, maybe even worse. But for a heady instant when he'd had the knife, it'd been different. He'd been strong. Savage. Untouchable.

"You really liked that," Wyatt said. "I can tell. Loved it, even."

Bo looked up.

"So do I," Wyatt said. "I love that feeling. Damage, right? That's what it is. The feeling when you *damage*." His gray eyes flicked cold over the pod. "They deserve it," he added.

Bo watched, feeling nearly hypnotized, as Wyatt washed off the knife with a water bottle and bit of rag.

"A lot of the others wouldn't like this," Wyatt said. "They've got some guts, or they wouldn't be Lost Boys. But if Gilly knew what we were doing in here..." He gave a wave of his arm to encompass the storage unit. "I mean, fuck, if she saw you like this? She'd be scared, right?"

Bo could picture it, her big green eyes wide and teary. It gave him another hot pulse of shame. Violet wouldn't like it either, he knew. Or Saif. Or Jon. Or Bree, even if she'd try to pretend she did.

"You and me are different, I think," Wyatt said. "We want it more." He offered the wet rag, and Bo took it automatically, wiping his hands. "That makes us special," Wyatt went on. "You and me. I don't want there to be any secrets between us, Bo."

"No," Bo said. But this storage unit, what they'd been doing to the pod—Bo wanted that to be a secret. Between them, from the others.

"We're special, and that gives us more responsibility," Wyatt said. "To protect the others. Make the tough decisions. Do the tough things. We have to keep the other Lost Boys safe, even if it means being hard on them. Right?"

Bo didn't feel special anymore. Not in a good way. "Right," he said. He wanted to get out of the storage unit, out of the shadows and the sickly smell. If Gilly could see him like this. If Lia could see him like this. He remembered back to the injured grasshopper and old guilt came back.

"Now that things are in motion, it's more important than ever," Wyatt said. "Now that we've got one of theirs. Things are going to heat up. It's a war, right? We can't have any distractions. We can't have anyone straying."

"Right," Bo repeated.

"Good," Wyatt said, taking the rag back. "I've been wondering about something. Night before last. Before we caught the pod. Where did Violet and you go?" He wrapped the knife up in the rag and then put it into his bag, out of sight, like Bo had never had it in his hand at all. "I'm worried about her, Bo," he said, gray eyes clear and earnest. "And I don't want any secrets between us."

Violet woke up in the afternoon with a seriously skull-pulping headache. She'd never been hungover before, to her knowledge, but she knew she was now, and had to get up in stages. First, sitting upright and swilling her cottonmouth away with the water bottle she kept beside her mattress. Second, clutching her head and grimacing for a while. Third, staggering off for a shower.

Even though she felt terrible, a big idiot smile kept slipping onto her face. Sure, it was only some kissing and they'd both been drunk. But just remembering back to it made her feel flushed and tingling all over, and the big idiot smile wouldn't go away. People did things drunk that they'd thought about doing sober—she knew that much from her dad. Sometimes bad things, sometimes good ones. Like making out on the roof.

Still, she was a bit relieved when Jenna told her, on her way back from the bathroom, that Bo and Wyatt were gone to the pod. She needed time to get a hold of the smiling thing, and think of something smooth and unconcerned to say to Wyatt without her ears going red. It was stupid to be worrying about it anyway. Wyatt was already focused on learning about the pod, probably coming up with big plans to topple the ship out of the sky and save the world, or some such shit.

Bo came back in the afternoon, but he didn't talk to her, or to anyone, really. He only said that Wyatt was still studying the pod, gave her a strange look, then disappeared into the theater auditorium to practice his shifting. Curiosity was seething under her skin like an itch, a little bit about the pod but mostly about Wyatt. She commiserated with Jenna about the loss of her hair for as long as she could stand it, then volunteered for a forage that nobody really needed and set off.

Sneaking along behind an othermother and smashing the last few windows of her favorite rock target, an old place with panes that shattered like sugar brittle, cleared her head. As she headed back to the theater with a mismatch of cans and boxes, she decided she would act like nothing had happened at all, like she didn't even remember it. Then she saw Wyatt walking into the entry, unslinging his backpack, and the big idiot smile was back like it had never left.

"Hey," she said. "Long day at the office?" Stupid thing to say—her ears were heating up already.

Wyatt turned. "Hey, Vi," he said, glancing at the bag in her hands. "Forage go smooth?"

"Smooth, yeah," Violet said.

She didn't know what she'd been expecting, some secret sexy look to pass between them, or a second-too-long hug, or something, but he only smiled and cocked his head for her to go in first.

"Going to talk to everyone in the theater," he said. "Want to round them up?"

Violet rounded them up, interrupting the evening card game with a little less patience than usual, grabbing Alberto and Saif off the roof and sending Saif to get Quentin out of the bathroom. She knew Wyatt was right to act like nothing had happened at all, like he didn't even remember it. Same thing she was doing. She just fucking hated it, that was all. When every-one was in the theater, squeezed up in the front rows, she sat two back.

Wyatt swung himself up on the stage, and everyone went quiet. "This whole time, they've been fucking with us," he said. Nobody had to ask who he meant. "Treating us like lab rats," he continued. "They locked us up and drugged us and put the Parasites in us. But now we finally have a card to play. We have one of them. And we can make the rest of them understand, for the first time, that we are not to be fucked with." Wyatt's eyes were hard as granite. "We have a way to send them a message."

His words bounced around the theater, and everywhere Violet looked she saw teeth bared, eyes fixed, shaved heads nodding. She even felt it herself a bit, the adrenaline ache in her chest. Wyatt always had a way with words.

"We've got one of them now," he repeated. "And we couldn't have pulled this off without every single Lost Boy here. Who made the trap? Who sharpened the hooks and tied the cords? Who held the pod long enough for Bo to drop a tank on its big ugly head? We needed everyone, right? Everyone."

Wyatt paused, scanning the room.

"I need all of you," he said. "You're my family. I killed my othermother, remember? We all did. We can't go back to how it was. We can't make the wasters human again. This is our family now."

Violet felt a dart of ice up the back of her neck. He wasn't looking at her. He was looking at everyone but her.

"And it's more important than ever that we keep each other safe," Wyatt continued. "That we don't endanger our family. When we do things that endanger the family, there's a consequence." His eyes traveled up and down the row and landed on Elliot. "Elliot knows, don't you, El?"

Elliot's cheeks went red. He nodded.

Violet's heart started to pound. Her Parasite flexed.

"No one person is more important than the all of us, right?" Wyatt said. "Even if it's someone who should know better. Someone who should be a better example."

He finally looked right at her, and Violet felt like she was crashing into cold water. Other heads started to turn. Gilly, eyes wide and hurt. Bree, boiling over with righteous fury. Bo, feigning anguish even though he'd been the one who snaked on her. Bo had told Wyatt. Bo had betrayed her. Violet felt a hot sick feeling in the pit of her. She stared at him until he looked away, shaking his head. Her hands were clenched hard enough to draw crescents of blood off her palms.

"Violet's been taking care of a pair of wasters," Wyatt said flatly. "She's been sneaking back to her old house at night." He blinked hard, looking off to the side for a moment, then back to her. "Aren't we enough for you, Vi?"

Violet tried to hold her anger, tried to bore it right through the back of Bo's shaved head. But she felt it slipping into fear, and the worst one, shame. Wyatt jerked his head, motioning for her. Feeling dazed, Violet got up. Her legs were trembling underneath her. She walked up to the edge of the stage, feeling the collected gaze on her back like a tightening vise. An eternity later she was standing in front of him. His stormy gray eyes were full of pity.

"They don't love you," Wyatt said, low enough that only Violet could hear. "We do."

Violet realized she was ready to cry. It was building behind her eyes and sinuses like a mudslide. Maybe he was right. Maybe they'd only ever loved Ivan, or the idea of him. And even if the Lost Boys won, there would be no going back to how things were. Not for anyone, and especially not for her.

Wyatt put his hand on her arm, just above the elbow, warm, firm, forgiving. Violet took a shaky breath. She was ready to apologize to him, to everyone. Maybe she was even ready to forget the parents who couldn't see her and never had. Wyatt loved her. That was way more than enough.

"Take your shirt off, Vi," Wyatt said.

Violet stared, disbelieving.

"Your shirt," Wyatt repeated.

Violet saw the length of electrical cord wrapped around his free hand. She traced up his lean arm, his perfect shoulder, to his unconcerned face. The theater was graveyard quiet, but Violet's ears were roaring. She thought of all the times she'd imagined slowly undressing in front of him, seesawing her jeans down her hips, letting him help pull her shirt up over her head. All those stupid little fantasies. She thought of the feel of his lips on hers.

"Are you fucking kidding me?" she choked.

"Consequences, Vi," Wyatt said calmly, and she saw it creeping behind his eyes, the dark thing she knew came from sadness, from trauma. From the same kind of hurt she had. But Wyatt had done something different with his. She knew, with ice-cold clarity, that he was going to enjoy this. He was going to enjoy beating her like he'd enjoyed kissing her.

Wyatt's grip on her arm tightened, hard enough to mark her skin. She stared at his hand. The fury came back in a white-hot flume. This, after the rooftop. This, maybe because of the rooftop.

"Let go of me," she said.

Everyone was silent. Jon wasn't here; he'd been sent off to watch the pod—Wyatt would have planned it that way. Jon was the only one who might have stood up to him. Violet stared at Wyatt's hand, focusing on the shape of it, the muscle and tendon. Her teeth were clenched tight. Then, as he started to speak again, she *shifted* it.

There was a sharp wet crack and blood flicked into the air as mist. For a split second Wyatt's face was drained white and there was nothing but raw meat and jagged bone where his forearm ended. Then his hand was back, but hanging crooked and swollen with pooled blood. It slid limply off her arm and she pulled away, feeling nauseous. Neither of them moved. Wyatt's face was pale with shock as he slumped to one knee. None of the things she wanted to scream at him made it past her lips.

She turned and saw Gilly clutching tight to Bo's arm, staring at her like she was an alien, or something new and worse. Bo looked shocked as the rest, mouth open, no sound coming out. Violet wanted to ask why he'd snaked. Why he'd wrecked everything for her. It had been so stupid to take him along with her. She couldn't form the words, so she started to walk. The Lost Boys watched her as she stumbled up the aisle, all of them frozen in place. She seized her jacket with shaking hands.

"Bo!"

The sound of Wyatt's voice made Violet look back, even knowing she shouldn't. He was standing upright again, his wrecked hand dangling at one side. His face was contorted but his next order came perfectly clear:

"Don't let him leave."

Him. The one little word carved Violet open and scooped her hollow. She swayed there for a second, staring back in shock, unwilling to believe it. But Wyatt's lips were tugged back off a savage smile and she knew she'd heard right.

Violet didn't wait for Bo to shake Gilly off and come after her like a good little Lost Boy, to club her with a blackjack or vanish her in a rush of static. She ran, out of the theater, out into the night.

12

The first breath of cold night air seared her lungs. Her heart pounded; her Parasite shuddered. She didn't know if anyone was following her. She didn't hear them but she didn't stop either, not until she was off the ave, through the park, and finally bent double outside the small brown house with a gravel drive. Her shoulders heaved. She was sobbing, gasping for breath. Wyatt's final words were still chasing circles in her head. She'd come here on automatic, not knowing where else to go. But there was nothing for her here.

She put her shaking hand on the doorknob and turned it. Inside was pitch dark. She didn't have her flashlight, so she picked her way carefully through the entryway, kicking aside a pair of old shoes. As her eyes adjusted she saw her mom washing dishes in the dark, or at least going through the motions, head bent over the sink, scrubbing a dry plate with a dry sponge. It was sad and stupid and put another sob in Violet's throat. She took a step forward, unsure what she wanted. To rip the plate out of her mom's hands and smash it over her head. To wrap around her from behind and hug her and tell her everything that had happened.

Then she saw it. Crouched off to the side of the counter,

statue-still, head twisted toward the sink on a long flexible neck. Her othermother's warped face was only inches from her real mom's, eyes wide and unblinking. Studying her. Violet's anguished noise caught hard in her chest. The othermother's head swiveled toward the sound.

Violet's fingers curled for the bat she didn't have. The othermother stared at her, and she felt fear sweat under her arms. She realized it was the silence that was most frightening—she'd never heard an othermother silent. It was eerie. Violet swallowed, trying to slow her heart, calm her Parasite. She needed a weapon. The kitchen knives were across the counter, out of reach. The empty beer bottles were in the living room. Othermothers were clumsy in tight spaces, but still fast, and there was no way she was getting past it.

The smart thing would be to leave. To shut the door behind her and start working on a hiding spot, on food, on somewhere new to sleep where the othermothers and the Lost Boys wouldn't find her. More pills too; the ones in her jacket would last only a few days. But Violet couldn't bring herself to leave her mom with this horrible doppelgänger watching her, maybe for the whole night. Not daring to turn her back, she crouch-walked backward until she could grope the spare key out from under the ratty welcome mat. She clenched it between her knuckles.

The othermother lurched forward, making Violet jump, then stopped in place. Violet's heart thumped hard. Her othermother extended one spiny hand, and Violet saw there was something clutched inside.

"A letter came for you today," she warbled. "Isn't that nice?"

She opened her hand, revealing a dull black orb.

"A letter came for you today, Violet," the othermother said. "I have to get going, though. Isn't that nice?"

Slowly, delicately, she set the orb down on the floor. Then she straightened up, legs flexing and clacking, head pressed up against the ceiling. Violet tensed as the othermother came closer, but she didn't reach for her with her long sharp fingers. Instead she shuffled past, ducked to fit through the door, and left.

Violet let the key drop from her fist. A breath she didn't know she'd been holding came out as half sob, half sigh. Her heartbeat slowed, and for a long minute the only sound was her mom scraping the dry sponge rhythmically against a metal bowl. Violet looked at the black orb on the floor and realized with a jolt that the othermother hadn't called her Ivan. She'd called her Violet.

She took a slow step toward the orb. Nothing happened. She plucked it off the floor. The metal, or whatever it was, was smooth and warm in her clammy palm. There was a pulse to it too, like a heartbeat. Violet hefted it up and down in her hand, thinking how maybe it was a ticking bomb and that it was a few moments from exploding in a mass of shrapnel. At this point, though, getting blown up didn't seem like the worst thing in the world.

The orb wasn't smooth solid black all over. Her thumb found a concave, and when she held it up to her face she saw a small circular window of red glass or maybe plastic. Things were swimming inside, tiny things that looked like bacteria through an electron microscope. Violet realized there was a rubbery ring around the red circle. She was supposed to press her eye up against it.

Maybe it would shoot a needle through her eye and blind her, or maybe suction her eyeball out of its socket entirely. Maybe not. *A letter came for you,* the othermother had said. Violet looked at her real mother one last time, blinking away saline, then put her eye up against the red window.

⋆　　⋆　　⋆

"You understand why I had to do that, right?" Wyatt asked softly. His wrecked hand was wrapped in bandages, but Bo could see slivers of puffy purple flesh through the gaps. They were sitting in the theater auditorium alone, everyone else sent out to the lobby.

Bo kept looking at the hand. He didn't know what to say. Kept thinking back to what he'd seen on the rooftop, or thought he'd seen. And then farther back, to the first day he'd met the Lost Boys. Elliot, twitchy Elliot, who'd waited for everyone else to be asleep before he took his shirt off. Bo remembered the vivid red marks he'd thought were maybe a dream.

He didn't understand. Not at all. "What did Elliot do?" he asked.

Wyatt's face didn't even flicker. "The same thing," he said. "Endangered our family. He was trying to take people's clamps out. Figure out how to deactivate them. The wasters aren't human anymore, and they won't ever be. Clamp's in the head, better off dead."

"What happened?" Bo asked, still feeling numb, numb.

"To the wasters?" Wyatt asked. "The ones he practiced on? They died. Or seized up frozen and *then* died. He unplugged their brains." Wyatt's voice was harsh. "I could have made him do his parents. Made him show everyone there's no way to bring the wasters back. But I didn't. I was nice to him, right? I took him aside. Private. And gave him his lesson."

Bo looked at the unspooled electrical cord on the stage and nearly wanted to laugh. "She didn't make me go with her," he said. "You should beat me too."

Wyatt shrugged. "You didn't know where you were going," he said. "Violet did. And she'd been going for months. She had a delusion. You know what a delusion is?"

Bo hesitated. "When you're crazy."

Something close to a snarl rolled over Wyatt's face, almost too quick to catch. "It's a false belief," he said. "One that fucks up your life, and other people's lives too. Believing you can be loyal to the living and the dead at the same time, that's a delusion. The wasters are gone. That's that, right? They're gone. We have to focus on the living. That's us. The Lost Boys."

"You kissed her," Bo finally said, feeling his breath come high and fast how it did before he cried. "I saw you on the roof. I thought. You loved her."

"You little sneak," Wyatt said, with an easy white grin, then turned serious. "I did, Bo. I love everyone who's part of my family. But if someone decides they don't want to be one of us, that they don't want to be a Lost Boy, then how can I still? Violet decided. Not me." Bo watched as Wyatt's bandaged hand moved onto his shoulder to sit there like a spider. "Violet picked dead people over you or me. Picked them over your sister too. Over Lia."

Bo gave a start. He hadn't heard her name out loud in a long time. He hadn't thought Wyatt even knew it. It cut through the fog in his head and gave him some kind of clarity again.

"That's who we need to focus on," Wyatt said, slowly nodding. "Forget about Violet. Violet made the wrong choice, and the consequences are going to catch up eventually. With or without our help."

Lia was more important than any waster. More important than Violet, even. Their mom had made them promise to always look out for each other, even when they hated each other, but he hadn't. Bo was with the Lost Boys, and his sister was rotting in the warehouse.

"We're going to free her?" Bo asked. Wyatt had been right

about other things. Maybe he was right about Violet, about her delusion. Stopping her from going to her old house night after night, maybe that was the right thing to do. For her own good. And if Violet had taken the punishment, maybe Wyatt wouldn't have hit her hard. Maybe he barely would have hit her at all.

"This is a war, Bo," Wyatt said. "We're going to need soldiers, right? And we'll find them in the warehouses."

Bo wanted to feel happy. He wanted to feel like Violet wasn't important, not the way the war was, not the way Lia was. But his Parasite wouldn't stop sliding around no matter what he did, and Wyatt's hand on his shoulder felt heavy as lead.

"There's going to be more tough things," Wyatt said. "More tough decisions. That's why we're here, Bo. We can make those." His gray eyes drilled hard into Bo's. "So you understand now? Why I had to do that? Are you with me, Bo?"

The electrical cord, the gloomy storage unit, the red marks on Elliot's back—Wyatt would have hit hard. He was more dangerous than any whirlybird or othermother or flying pod. Bo knew it with a cold hollow feeling in his chest. Something had changed Wyatt even more than the invasion had changed the Lost Boys, and it was Wyatt's word that came back to Bo's mind now: *damage.*

But Wyatt was going to help him free Lia, and that was more important than anything.

"Yeah," Bo said. "I get it. I'm with you."

Violet woke up to sunshine streaming through her bedroom window and Anise tiptoeing across her stomach. She plucked her off quickly enough to avoid the claws digging in, setting her down beside the pillow. Anise's bottlebrush tail stiffened, then curled as Violet petted her.

"So you do remember me, you little shit," she said.

Anise gave a rumbling purr, and then something else started to purr from outside. Violet frowned, reaching across herself to scissor two blinds farther apart with her fingers. The sunlight was brighter than she'd seen it in a long time. It took a second of squinting to see her dad with the electric mower, pushing up along the fence to get the dandelions.

Everything was wrong. Her dad wasn't walking like a waster—he was taking smooth even steps, straight-backed, making tiny adjustments with the mower. The mower shouldn't have been working because there was no electricity. The grass was soft dewy green. The sun was shining through the clouds.

Violet scrambled off the bed, making Anise hiss and jump. She yanked the blinds all the way up to look closer. Her dad seemed taller, and his hair was dark and full with no gray in it, how he looked in old photos from when she was a kid. There was no clamp gleaming at the nape of his sunburned neck. When he turned back toward the house and saw her at the window, he waved.

Violet felt her heart drop. He could see her. Stranger still, he was smiling at her, giving a crooked grin as he backhanded the sweat off his forehead. Her dad didn't smile at her. Hadn't for years. By the time she dazedly raised her arm to wave back, he was mowing again. As she pulled back from the window, her faint reflection jolted her. With a giddy feeling in her stomach, a feeling like helium that could float her away if she wasn't careful, Violet threw herself over to the mirror.

It was her. It was more her than she'd ever been. The thick nose she'd inherited from her dad, the one she tried to thin with makeup when she could, was gone. It was small and straight now, like her mom's, and the shape of her face had subtly changed too. Higher brows, higher cheekbones. Thinner jaw. She was fucking beautiful.

Violet peeled off her shirt. The rest of her had changed too. Her shoulders were narrower, and the puffy flesh filling her bra cups was more than three months of hormones could account for, and her sharp hips had widened. She touched her stomach. Nothing but pale smooth skin, no Parasite and no scar either, like it had never been inside her at all. And when she reached lower, the other thing was gone too.

"This isn't real," she whispered. But she didn't move.

"Violet!" Her mom's voice, from the kitchen, warm and rich and nothing like the othermother. "Violet, are you up?"

She had never called her Violet. Not once. Violet didn't reply, half because she wanted to hear it again, half because she wanted to stand in front of the mirror forever.

"Violet? I heard you get out of bed, don't you dare get back in. It's practically noon."

With the helium feeling tugging her along, Violet took one last look in the mirror and then stepped out into the hallway. She remembered the shirt in her hand and pulled it on as she entered the kitchen. When the fabric slid off her face, she saw her mom at the table. She looked like she did in Polaroids, with flyaway blonde hair and a ruddy color to her skin. Younger, prettier. No puffy bloodshot eyes from crying or smoking up in the basement, where she thought Violet couldn't smell it.

"This isn't real," Violet said again.

Her mom was sitting at the table with a dog-eared sketchbook Violet hadn't seen for years and years. There was a jumble of wooden shapes and blocks set up in the middle for a still life. She glanced up and gave Violet a faint smile, then returned to the sketchbook, working it with a charcoal pencil.

"No," she admitted. "Not how you think of real."

Everything in the kitchen shivered and flickered, like a glitch in a game, and for a brief moment Violet felt herself standing on the dusty linoleum, still clutching the black orb to her eye. Then she was back inside. Sunlight. Gleaming clean sink. Air freshener wafting lavender to her nose. Everything clean and beautiful and perfect.

"We can make it more real," her mom said, scratching thoughtfully against the paper. "How you think of real. It will take a little more time. It will take a little more of your mind. We are beginning to process data from the other simulations. Already we understand you better."

Violet looked at the drying dishes in the rack and realized there were no empty beer bottles beside them. She went to the fridge, ignoring her mom-not-mom, and yanked it open. Where her dad usually kept his Heineken, there was a nonsensical row of plastic water bottles. She nearly laughed.

"This is so fucked," she breathed. "This is . . ." She whirled back to the table. "Is this what they see?" she demanded. "Is this how it is for everyone?"

"Better, for them," her mom said. "We can make yours better too. More real. How you think of real." She held up the sketchpad and studied it, then feathered in a carefully chosen new line. "It will be like the sky."

"The sky?" Violet repeated.

Her mom tapped her chin, leaving a smudge of charcoal, eyes rolled up how they always did when she was trying to remember something. Then she smiled. "Like heaven," she said.

Violet pictured a whirlybird drilling into her skull, sealing in the clamp. She thought of herself and her family stumbling around the dark house, smiling at nothing. It was sick and horrifying and it made her heart ache with longing. Because on the inside, it would be bright. It would be a mom who still painted in the summer and a dad who still loved her and she would be Violet because Ivan had never even existed. She caught sight of her reflection in the kitchen window and it split her.

"Why did you come here?" she asked bitterly. "Who the fuck are you?"

But she realized she didn't even care about those answers anymore. It was just something to ask before she asked the real question.

"We came because it was necessary," her mom said. "We are strangers. How you think of strangers."

"Yeah, well, kids aren't supposed to talk to strangers," Violet muttered, looking past her reflection, watching her dad maneuver the mower around an apple tree that had died ages ago. She turned back to the table. "What do you want me to do?" she finally asked. "I know I don't get this heaven shit for free."

In answer, her mom turned the sketchbook to face her. It was a beautiful and frightening thicket of gray and black and bleached-bone white. Violet could see the dark swoop of the ship up in grayscale sky, the jagged silhouettes of ruins. In the foreground, she saw the shadowy tangled mass of the wormy wall. In front of it, two figures, the taller one guiding the shorter by the arm. Violet recognized her face in sharp profile, poking out from her curtain of black hair. She already knew before she looked at the second figure who it was.

Short and skinny and dark-skinned, with a face that seemed gaunter now that his head was shaved, no longer a little kid's face. And drifting over Bo, its underbelly peeling open, reaching for him with long pincer-tipped arms, was the pod that would take him back to the warehouses.

Everything in the kitchen shivered and flickered and was gone. Violet found herself sitting on the linoleum, the orb clutched hard in her fist. It wasn't warm anymore. It felt cold and heavy as pewter as she turned it, over and over, in hands that wouldn't stop trembling.

13

The days after Violet left were quiet. Nobody was supposed to talk about it, but everyone did, about whether or not she would come back, about what would happen if she did. Jenna had puffy eyes the first morning from crying, and the next one Bo saw that someone had left a letter on Violet's bed. It was a sheet of printer paper, markered with shaky oversize script Bo thought was Arabic, and had two tiny plastic dinosaurs taped to it. Later he saw Saif knuckling his eyes in the stairwell with Alberto rubbing his back and grinning in a more worried way than usual.

Bo had thought Jon would be angry—it had seemed like him and Violet were friends, good ones—but if he was, Bo couldn't detect it in his blank face. Most of the Lost Boys were like that. Maybe there had been too many upsetting things before this one, and now the scar tissue was too thick. Nearly everyone agreed that Violet should have taken her punishment, and then everything would have been fine, but nobody looked at Elliot when they said that.

As for Bo, he felt hot guilt crash over him every time he passed Violet's empty mattress or heard someone whisper her name. He'd sworn on his sister not to tell anyone where they'd gone that night. But inside the dark storage unit, with the rasping knife and shuddering pod and Wyatt's soft voice in his ear, it had seemed like he was always going to tell. Like there had never been any other choice.

He hadn't known what Wyatt would do. Wyatt had said he was worried about her, and Bo had believed it. Every time he remembered the kiss he'd seen on the rooftop, he felt confused and angry all over again. And he knew, in his gut, that it wasn't something he would understand when he was older. Wyatt didn't have a Parasite, but he did have something else. Something bad that he knew how to hide. It scared Bo to wonder if he had the same thing now.

Wyatt had spent all of yesterday at the pod, only coming back near midnight, smiling a weary smile and saying vague things about learning weaknesses, making plans. He was at the pod again today, and Bo was glad. He didn't want to be around Wyatt. He didn't want to be around anybody. But when he went on a forage to get out of the theater, Quentin volunteered to go with him. It took Bo a while to realize Wyatt had probably ordered it. He sulked around kicking rocks and picking food stores at random while Quentin followed him like a pale gangly shadow. He thought about taking off running, knowing Quentin wouldn't be able to catch him, and maybe trying to find Violet and apologize to her.

But he didn't know where she was, and he didn't want to piss Wyatt off again. The important thing was that Wyatt was making plans. The important thing was that they'd get Lia out before summer, before her birthday, at least, because the seasons didn't seem to be changing anymore. They would rescue her just like Violet had said.

By the time they were back to the theater, Bo had stopped scowling at Quentin and both of them were gnawing on a spicy beef jerky he'd found in the back of the supermarket, far away from the spoiled meat. He reasoned Quentin was just doing what Wyatt told him, same as everyone did. Bo was putting Violet out of his mind, planning to join the evening card game loud and laughing, until he saw a small sliver of yellow stuck up beside the doors.

He peeled the Winnie the Pooh Band-Aid off the brick while Quentin's head was turned. Farther down along the wall, he saw two more placed higher up, forming an arrow that pointed around the corner of the theater. Maybe it would be better if he ignored it. Maybe if he tried hard enough, he could forget how tight and fierce Violet had hugged him while they stood outside his burned-down house.

"You need a leak, Q?" Bo asked. He knew only a few things about Quentin. One was that he was shy in the bathroom.

Quentin shook his head.

"I'm going to go in the alley," Bo said. "Bathroom smells funny today." He held out the bulging grocery bag. "Can you stash my stuff for me?" he asked.

Quentin chewed thoughtfully on the jerky, debating, then reached out and took it. "I'll wait for you," he said, sheepish. "Wyatt said nobody's supposed to go solo outside the hideout. Not just the under-tens."

Bo nodded. His heart sped a bit as they approached the alley and his Parasite noticed, giving a little ripple. Quentin carefully turned his back, as if Bo was going to take a dump or take off his clothes or something, and Bo started down the alley, searching the sooty wall for another Band-Aid. He pulled his track pants down his hips as loudly as possible.

Then he saw it: a folded-over newspaper on the ground, with a cartoon-covered Band-Aid sticking out of it like a bookmark. Bo cleared his throat, set his feet, and snatched up the paper. He heard Quentin shifting around behind him, making the grocery bag rustle. Bo tucked the paper in his waistband and stood there for a while, trying to coax something out of his bladder. He whistled a few notes through his dry lips.

"You done?" Quentin finally asked.

"Can't go when I know someone's behind me," Bo said, working his pants back up. The paper slid against his waistband.

"Me either," Quentin said, looking apologetic. "Go in the bathroom, I guess."

"Yeah," Bo said. He took the grocery bag back and followed Quentin into the theater, feeling a bit of sweat on his palms, a bit of static off his Parasite.

Violet yanked the orb away from her face and hurled it across the room. It smashed an old picture frame off the mantle, bounced to the floor, rolled. She glared at it. She'd been trying for hours, ever since she got back from leaving the note for Bo at the theater. But no matter how long she stared, she didn't see anything but glowing red. No more perfect house, perfect family, perfect reflection in the mirror.

"Let me see it again," she said thickly. "I need to see it again to decide, alright?"

Nobody answered. Her mom was gone to bed; her dad was slumped in the chair, staring intently at the blank television. With a jolt, she realized the sky outside had darkened. She'd lost track of time. The analog clock in the kitchen ticked toward midnight. Nearly time to go.

She could guess why the orb didn't work anymore. They

already knew what she'd decided. Even so, she snatched it up off the floor on her way out and slid it into the pocket of her jacket.

Bo waited until he was sure everyone was asleep, then waited a little longer. Then he levered himself up off his bed, quiet as he could, and crept toward the door. The note Violet had left him in the alleyway was crumpled deep in his pocket. It was brief. Six words. *Midnight. Fountain. I need your help.*

The lobby was dark but Bo knew where everyone slept: He recognized them by their shapes and snores as he snuck past. Gilly always started a mattress-length away from Bree and wriggled closer to her in the night; Elliot hid under a big cocoon of fleece blankets; Jon murmured in a language Bo had never heard before.

He felt a tug of guilt as he slipped out the door, into the entryway. Like he was betraying them. But he would come back once he'd helped Violet with whatever it was she needed. He would help Violet, apologize to her, and maybe that would make up for what he'd done at least a little. Then he would come back and follow Wyatt's plan.

The main door gave a bone-deep creak when he eased it open. He grimaced, froze to listen. Someone back in the lobby rolled over in their sheets. Jenna's telltale snores, which always seemed too big for her body, stuttered to a stop. Bo held his breath. It wasn't strange for a Lost Boy to get up in the night, stare at the ceiling, go off to piss or cry in private. Nearly everyone had bad dreams. But Bo didn't want anyone asking him where he was going, and if Wyatt had made that new rule just for him, like he suspected, they might try to stop him.

Jenna took a deep gaspy breath and started to snore again.

Bo pushed the door open just a little bit more, enough to slide through sideways, and then he was out of the theater. Cold air slipped over his shaved skull and widened his eyes. It felt good. Clean. He sucked in a deep breath of his own, letting it hollow out his chest. Nothing had felt clean since his visit to the storage unit, even after he'd scrubbed the yellow fluid off his forearms and used seven whole bottles of water for his shower.

But now he was going to set things right, at least a little. The cold breeze nipped harder at the tips of his ears and he pulled his hood tight, setting off down the sidewalk.

"What are you doing, Bo?"

Bo's heart stopped. Slouching out of the alley, hands in his pockets, was Wyatt. Quentin fidgeted behind him, guilty-looking. Wyatt gave a slow disappointed shake of his head. With the shadows half hiding his face, blacking his eye sockets, he suddenly looked more frightening than any waster.

"Couldn't sleep," Bo said. He paused. "I'll go try again."

Wyatt laughed, a warm laugh that gave Bo an odd feeling of relief. Quentin's lips twitched a confused smile, and that made Bo start laughing too. The fear and the exhaustion and all the other chemicals made him almost giddy. He'd been caught, but he'd tried his best to meet with Violet. And if he got the electrical cord in the morning, that would even things out another way.

He was turning back toward the theater doors when Wyatt crossed to him in two quick steps and put the knife up under his chin.

Bo's heart hammered, his Parasite roiled, he felt adrenaline crash through him cold and—

"None of that," Wyatt said. "Deep breaths, Bo. I don't want you to go disappearing anybody." He spun him around, yanked his hood off; Bo felt the cold pinprick of the knife move to the base of his neck. "I don't want to feel any static, Bo. None. Breathe slow. If your Parasite keeps twitching, I'm going to kill you."

Bo was shivering all over; his joints felt like sloshing water. He hyperventilated. Remembering the storage unit, the way Wyatt had jabbed and twisted, knowing it wasn't some bluff. His Parasite crackled. Maybe if he was quick. But he'd never vanished a person before, never even thought of it. Didn't know if he could.

The tip of the knife wormed into the skin of his neck.

"Relax, Bo," Wyatt said. "Just relax. I know it's tough. Think about something else, right? Think about a happy memory."

Bo wanted to scream. Quentin was nervously circling, surprise all over his face, but Bo knew he wouldn't help him over Wyatt. Quentin had been a Lost Boy from the start. Bo wanted to scream, but slowly, slowly, he brought his breathing under control. He shut his eyes tight and thought about the summer, about him and Lia and his mom in the car with the windows down. Sea smells. Rock-paper-scissors for the radio dial. Gas station slushies that stained their mouths red.

"Good job," Wyatt said softly. "Let's walk now. Keep breathing."

Bo walked with Wyatt tight behind him. After a few missteps they were in sync, so the knife was resting light on Bo's shoulder, flashing in the corner of his eye. Quentin trailed after them silently. Bo tried to stay in the car. He tried to breathe even. He was watching his feet, but his subconscious must have known where they were headed, because when they finally stopped and he looked up at the sealed storage unit, he wasn't surprised.

"Open it up, Q," Wyatt said, moving the knife back to Bo's neck. "You remember the combo, right?"

Quentin didn't answer, but he went to the combination lock and started twisting it back and forth. The first try he was too shaky and missed the catch. He had to wipe his hands and start over, but Wyatt didn't seem to mind.

"Remember when you said you were with me, Bo?" he asked.

"Yeah," Bo choked, not daring to nod his head even a centimeter.

"You're a bad liar."

The storage unit rattled open. Wyatt prodded the small of Bo's back, and they stepped up into the dark.

14

The smell had gotten worse, cloying and chemical. It made Bo's eyes water. His Parasite was moving again, his heart was beating fast, but he couldn't help either. The pod's breathing was a raspy echo that filled his whole head. Was this a punishment? Was he going to have to sit locked in the dark with it until the morning?

"Could you hold this for me, Q?" Wyatt said. "If he tries to get away, or if you feel the static, you go up and under and twist. That's how soldiers do it. Shuts the brain right off."

Bo stayed perfectly still as Quentin took the knife, letting Wyatt rummage in his pocket with his good hand. He knew Quentin was twitchy. Wyatt held up a lighter and flicked it with his thumb. There was a *click-whoosh* and the flame bloomed in the enclosed space, throwing their shadows against the metal wall. The pod seemed to flinch.

"I've been finding some things out," Wyatt said conversationally. "One thing they really don't like is fire. Makes sense, right? They must be full of gases to float like that. I bet if you lit one up it would blow like a firework. Or a propane tank. Boom."

He waved the lighter and the pod shrank backward, pressing itself to the wall. Bo saw rivulets running down its black sides, puddles of something shiny underneath it.

"It's scared," Wyatt said, with a bit of a smile. "It knows its place now, right? Knows to respect me." He turned back. "You respect me, Bo?"

Bo knew there were no answers that would make Wyatt forget the whole thing, that would get him out safely. He clenched his teeth and focused. On keeping the Parasite calm, on ignoring the knife hovering behind his head, ignoring Quentin's jumpy hands.

"I don't think you do," Wyatt said. "That's my gut feeling." He crouched down, groping in the corner of the unit, and straightened up with a battery lamp. "You're too special, right?" he said, putting the lighter away. "You and your Parasite. You don't think you have to take orders." He switched the lamp on and bathed the storage unit with bright white fluorescence.

Bo's stomach dropped as he saw the whole back of the pod crisscrossed with scars.

"It doesn't heal so fast anymore," Wyatt said. "It's dying." He turned and hauled the door of the unit shut behind them, closing them in, and Bo knew for certain this wasn't a punishment. It was something worse. "Needs to go up to the ship and get a proper refueling," Wyatt continued. "It used those three dead othermothers for a makeshift. That was messy." He reached into his pocket again and came out with a dull black sphere, tossing it up and down. "We have a bit of an understanding now. This is how they communicate. I've been talking to it."

"You said we were going to kill it," Bo said. The scars made him feel sick, worse knowing some of them were maybe his.

"More fun this way," Wyatt said, with a conspirator smile. "Remember? Two of a kind, right?"

Anger flared in Bo's chest. "No."

"No?"

Bo worked hard to tamp the Parasite down. "No," he said. "You're different from me."

"Yeah, sure," Wyatt said. "The difference is I'm at peace with it. I make the most of it. You're wasting it." His nostrils flared. "You don't deserve that Parasite. That power."

Through the stink of the dying pod, Bo could smell Quentin's sharp scared sweat. He startled when he felt the tiny hairs on his arms rise. He'd kept his Parasite down—the static was coming off Quentin's. Quentin's was active too. That was why he was sweating scared: He knew he wouldn't be able to tell if the static was from Bo's or his own. Wyatt wouldn't have thought of that. Wyatt didn't have a Parasite.

"I made a deal," Wyatt said, looking at the black sphere in his unbandaged hand. "I'm going to let the pod go. Let it live. But before I do, it's going to take out your Parasite and put it into me."

Bright white light, like an operating room would have. Bo's heart went double time and the static swirled around his Parasite, but Quentin's was surging too, almost crackling. Bo heard him wipe his free hand on his shirt. Heard his feet shuffling nervously against the floor. Wyatt hadn't noticed anything yet. He was watching the pod intently, holding the black sphere out toward it.

Vanish the knife. That was Bo's first thought, but it was behind him, clutched in Quentin's slippery hand, and he needed to see it to vanish it. His eyes slid to Wyatt. Bo had vanished the othermother, rippled it right out of existence. This would be like that. He was standing still. Not a moving target. Bo felt the static starting to storm. Whatever he did he would have to do it soon, before Quentin panicked, before he spoke up or maybe just shoved the knife through his skull.

Bo thought about the look on Violet's face when she'd run out of the theater. What Wyatt was planning to do now, cut him open and tear out his Parasite. He focused, letting the rage and the fear and the fight-or-flight build, build and build until he shook from it. The pod was drifting slowly forward, its underbelly peeling open. Quentin was swallowing spit, about to speak. Bo focused; the static lashed up and down his body.

Wyatt would do the same to him.

As Quentin formed the first word, as Wyatt finally felt the static and turned toward him, Bo released it in a tight focused punch, eyes fixed on the lamplight.

Black. Bo dove to the floor, bowled hard into Quentin's legs, felt his shoulder smack shinbone. Quentin gave a surprised shout as he toppled back. The knife clattered and Bo tried to triangulate it from the sound, kicking for it. His foot caught the handle, making it spin and skitter away. Then Bo was scrambling up and over Quentin in the dark, groping for the door, smashing his fingers against the latch. He flung it open just as a hand clamped his ankle from behind.

Bo was ripped off balance and toppled forward, out of the storage unit, barely managing to break the fall with his hands. The concrete scraped his palms raw but he didn't even feel it, already twisting to his feet, ready to run, ready to—

Wyatt's knee drove hard into his back and collapsed him. Bo's wind was knocked out of him as Wyatt flipped him over, pinned him to the paving. The cold flat of the knife pressed up under Bo's jaw. He stopped thrashing.

"Man, Bo." Wyatt laughed. "That was close."

He wriggled backward so he was straddling Bo's legs, dead weight trapping him to the concrete. Bo was flat on his back, not daring to sit up, not with the blade resting on his bobbing throat. He tried to coax his Parasite again, but it was heavy and sluggish now, spent. He hadn't held any static back. He'd wasted it. Wyatt reached down with his bandaged hand and clumsily worked Bo's hoodie upward. The night air cooled the sweat on his stomach. His Parasite gave a slow ripple.

"Fuck it," Wyatt breathed. "Maybe I'll just cut it out now. You might survive, right? Might not." He prodded Bo's exposed abdomen.

Bo couldn't turn his head but in the corner of his eye he sideways-saw Quentin standing on the lip of the storage unit, rooted to the spot. "Q!" he croaked. "He'll kill me. Help me, Q, he's crazy, he's—"

Wyatt swooped over him, clamped his bandaged hand over his mouth; it stank like stale sweat and copper. "Don't," he hissed. "Don't you dare. Don't you dare say that." Wyatt's face was a snarl and Bo knew he was going to die. He tried to bite but the bandage was thick. He tensed himself for one last struggle. Maybe he'd be able to snap up and get his hands on Wyatt's face after the first slash, before the pain set in, before he bled out. Do one last bit of damage.

Then Wyatt sucked a deep breath through his nostrils and let it out his mouth. The knife steadied.

"Man, I hate that word," he whispered. "Crazy." Something in his voice had changed. He sounded, for the first time, uncertain. Almost anxious. He leaned even closer. "No secrets between us, Bo. They say confession is good for the soul, right? You want to know something?" His whisper was hot in Bo's ear. "I didn't cut out my own Parasite. I never had one. I did the scar for show and it's shallower than it looks." Before Bo could process the words, he yanked Bo's waistband downward, widening the swathe of skin. "They never gave me one," Wyatt continued, the words spilling out faster now, like he was desperate to get rid of them. "They never took me to the warehouse. Wasn't my age either. It's where they found me. Nobody in the ward got taken away. Didn't get clamped either."

Bo looked to Quentin again, but Quentin had sunk to a crouch, his eyes squeezed shut. Bo knew he was hearing things the other Lost Boys had never heard. He knew it was because he wouldn't be able to pass them on.

"I think they were curious, at first," Wyatt whispered. "About the hospital. But once they understood what it was, the whirlybirds went through and they just...put them all down. All the kids. Needle to the neck." Bo felt the tip of the knife trace around his belly button. He didn't dare breathe. "They would have done me too if I hadn't got away. As if I was one of them, right? One of those pathetic little shits desperate for someone to *fix* them, to take all their little pills and be a good little zombie. They were wasters already, those kids. Right?"

Bo's Parasite gave another weak pulse. The static built; slipped away, hovering just beyond his reach. He was going to die. Knowing it felt how falling felt. He could see a slice of dark sky up past Wyatt's shoulder and for some reason wished there were stars, even though he'd never cared about stars that much before.

"And the whirlybirds thought I was one of them," Wyatt said, louder now, caught up in the memory. "They didn't want anything to do with me. With me! Like I wasn't good enough for them. Like I didn't even deserve a Parasite." He shook his head, gave half a laugh. "I deserve it more than you do," he said. "I'll make the most of it."

His hand tightened on the handle of the knife; Bo saw his tendons moving.

"Decided I'm going to do your throat first, Bo," Wyatt said. "To make the next bit easier. The pressure drop should knock you right out. Then just a minute or two of bleeding. No pain or anything."

Bo readied himself for the last try, to jackknife off the pavement and hit some part, any part, of Wyatt. But he was also trying to remember the exact smell of the salty air blowing through the open windows, the exact sound of his mom's voice singing and his sister's voice telling her to stop.

A brick smashed into the side of Wyatt's face.

Bo flinched backward as hot blood flicked onto his cheek. The uncontrolled knife slashed through the hood bunched up under his ear, splitting the fabric, then Wyatt was toppling one way and Bo rolled the other, legs finally freed. He hauled himself upright, head rushing, heart hammering. No time to look for Quentin or thank him or tell him to get another brick. Wyatt was on hands and knees, spitting blood and drool onto the pavement. The fallen knife glinted near his foot.

Bo laid out for it, but a hand snatched it up and away. His fingers curled on air and he looked up.

"I thought we were meeting at the fountain," Violet said. Her face was ash-pale, frightened-looking, but when she wrapped her fingers around the knife handle her hand was steady. Relief washed over Bo. Violet hurled the knife off into the dark; he didn't hear it land but he knew it was gone. He shut his eyes, breathing into his arm, feeling the cold pavement on his knee, his hips, his elbow. Alive, alive, alive.

When he opened his eyes, Violet was picking up the brick again, carefully so the blood didn't touch her. He watched her walk slowly to where Wyatt was trying to get up.

Violet stopped in front of him and waited, cradling the brick in both hands. Wyatt had sunk back to his knees, heaving, drooling. When he finally looked up, half his face was already dark and swollen. He smiled. His lip split even further.

"Couldn't stay away, could you, Vi?" he slurred. "Missed me too much." He lay back on the concrete with a groan.

"I hate you," Violet whispered.

Wyatt looked up. "No, you don't," he said, blood leaking dark through his grin. "I bet you wish you did, though." He tried to spit; most of it ran down his chin, streaked his neck. "Good throw. You were always a good throw. Remember how we used to go to that old house and pick windows? That was fun, right?"

"Shut up," Violet breathed, lifting the brick. "Just shut up for once." She was still shaking from the adrenaline, from seeing him hunched over Bo with the knife. Her heart was beating dangerously fast; the Parasite seethed in her stomach. She lifted the brick higher, higher. She could do it. All she had to do was smash it downward, and Wyatt would shut up.

"Even if you did kill me, Vi, you're only going to meet me over and over again." Wyatt smiled through a mouthful of blood. "I'm your type."

The brick was heavy. Her hands were slick from sweat.

"You're going to die now," she said, slowly, evenly, enunciating every word.

Wyatt's eyes went wide, and there was something in them she had only ever seen once before: fear.

She smashed the brick into the pavement an inch from his head. Stone chips flew and he flinched back with a yelp; one of the shards stung her shin. But she wasn't looking at Wyatt anymore. He'd believed her. She'd made him believe her.

She stepped over him, heading back toward Bo. Then a metallic *chunk* and a gurgling gasp split the quiet. She spun to see Quentin standing on the lip of the storage unit, up on tiptoe, and as she watched he jerked higher still, somehow hovering in the air. His face contorted. His mouth stretched, impossibly wide, around a scream that wasn't coming. Violet looked down to his chest and saw something sharp and gleaming sprouting from between his ribs.

Her stomach heaved.

The dark shape of the pod shifted behind Quentin, then its hooked proboscis retracted with a long loud sucking sound. Quentin fell boneless, like a rag doll, and smacked against the concrete. The pod drifted in the doorway, a weak yellow light from its head rolling over the scene. Then it hurtled out of the unit like a bullet.

Violet dove out of the way, but it wasn't aiming for her. She heard a strangled shout of surprise as she rolled upright, saw the pod wrapping Bo in its mechanical arms. Then he was gone, swallowed up in the pod's underbelly. Violet stumbled forward; Wyatt grabbed for her ankle and she gave him a solid kick in the side.

The pod was going to take Bo back to the warehouses. But

she couldn't think about that. She had to think about her perfect house, perfect family, perfect reflection. She heard a muffled scream from inside the pod's belly that made her sicker than any pill ever had.

"I helped, didn't I?" she said, voice raw and odd-sounding in her own ears. "You didn't want Bo dead. You wanted him alive."

Slowly, almost gingerly, the pod started to rise. The chugging noise grew louder, drowning out Bo's screams.

"I helped!" Violet shouted, sobbing, but the pod ignored her. It had Bo. It had Bo without needing her help, and it was going to leave her here in the dark with Wyatt, who was laughing now, gasping and laughing and rolling on the concrete. Bo was going back to the warehouses, all for nothing.

Violet hurled herself at the door of the storage unit, groping for handholds, jamming the toes of her shoes into the slats. She heaved herself up and over the top, her Parasite sparking, muscles thrumming, fueled with her panic. The pod was still rising, slow and weary. Violet scrambled to one end of the unit's roof, wiping her hands on her shirt. Her Parasite charged the fabric with static and she saw sparks.

She ran and flung herself off the end of the roof just as the pod drew level. The impact jarred her, rattling her ribs. She slipped half a foot before she could find purchase. The pod's skin wasn't smooth anymore; it was ridged and rippled with scar tissue and she dug in with her fingers where she could. The pod lurched and shivered under her, but kept rising, picking up speed.

Violet had a wild dizzy glimpse of the scene below, of the receding roof of the storage unit, of Quentin's limp body spread-eagled on the concrete, of Wyatt lying back with his hands behind his head, still bleeding and laughing.

The pod rose higher, higher. Wind whipped her hair around her face, nearly plucked one hand away from its hold. Cold air burned her bare skin and roared in her ears. The city was a mass of indistinct shadows below her. If she slipped she was dead. She knew her hands would go numb soon. Her lips had already.

Up above her, she saw the ship, saw its lights peeled open. She realized they weren't going to the warehouses, and just as she realized it, her cold fingers started to slide. The pod was secreting its hot yellow fluid again, turning slick. She dug in as deep as she could, trying to make her fingers into hooks, but she was losing hold. She couldn't hear anything over the wind. She wondered if Bo was still screaming inside the pod.

Her left hand lost purchase and she swung from just her right, slamming against the belly of the pod, scrabbling for a new hold. Her heart stopped. She wondered if Bo could feel her clinging to the outside and if he would feel it if she dropped away. Then she focused hard on her pumping Parasite, on the slick black hide of the pod. The static started to build.

Her right hand slipped, her gut lurched, and she shifted. The pod's black skin flickered for just a heartbeat, barely enough for her to swing inside. Darkness sealed around her. For a frenzied moment she wondered if she'd gotten into the underbelly or if she'd gone too high, if she was going to suffocate in its flesh and metal body, but then the warm gelatin flooded her nostrils and she felt another occupant kicking and twisting alongside her, sending ripples through the cocoon.

Violet tamped down her drowning reflex, tried to remind herself that the gelatin was breathable. Her heart was still going like a jackhammer. She'd been in a pod before. They all had. But nobody had ever been to the ship.

Through the warm sliding liquid, she felt a hand clamp to hers and cling hard. She squeezed back. Bo didn't know what she'd been planning to do, was maybe still planning to do, and he wasn't going to find out. Violet could lie to anyone now.

15

The pod's warm gelatin was slowly sluicing away. Bo realized it when he jammed the stinging heel of his hand up against the curved roof of its belly and felt a pocket of cold air. He tugged Violet's wrist, to get her attention, then rotated himself so he could push his face up against the roof. He gasped. The air tasted like tin, but it was air, and a thousand times better than forcing the porous gel into his lungs to breathe. There was enough space for his mouth and nose, and a few gurgling seconds later for the whole top half of his head if he jammed up hard against the roof.

Violet burst up out of the gel beside him and raked in a long breath.

"Are you alright?" Bo coughed.

"Yeah," Violet coughed back. "You?"

The events of the night were a nightmare jumble in Bo's head: Wyatt straddling him with the knife, Violet standing over Wyatt with the stained brick, Quentin hoisted into the air, impaled, the pod rushing at him in a black blur. He'd lost himself for a little while when the pod swallowed him up. He'd thought Lia was inside it with him. He'd thought they were being swooped off the sidewalk outside their burning house.

But then he'd felt someone hanging on the outside, slamming against it, then there'd been a sudden surge of static and the someone was inside with him. The hand he reached out to touch was too big for Lia's, too smooth and soft for Wyatt's, and he knew it was Violet. Violet trying to save him one more time.

"Thank you," Bo said, struggling to link his thoughts to words. "You threw the brick. I thought—I thought it was Quentin at first. But—"

"Don't think about Quentin," Violet said, and he felt her shudder ripple through the gel.

Bo tried not to, but he knew it would be one of the things he saw at night. For now he needed to relax. To focus. He took a deep shaky breath of metallic-tasting air.

"The pod's leaking," he said. "Maybe you broke something when you shifted in. Or maybe it's on purpose."

"Could be dumping weight," Violet said. "Like a sinking boat. Getting rid of ballast, or whatever."

Bo fell silent, and from the way Violet did too he could guess they were both thinking the same thing. Both picturing the pod's underbelly peeling open entirely and the two of them free-falling with a shower of gelatin. The chugging sound from the pod's engine, or lungs, or whatever it had, seemed to grow louder, sending vibrations through the gel.

"We keep going up," Bo said. "We haven't gone sideways any. Not that I can feel, anyway."

"It isn't going to the warehouses," Violet said. Her voice was small and tinny in the enclosed space. "It's going to the ship."

The ship. Bo saw it in his mind's eye, drifting over the city like a jagged black cloudbank, and alongside his fear he felt a small thrill of excitement. It was cut short as the pod gave a sudden lurch. The chugging sound started to sputter, then pitched up, turning shrill and whiny.

"If it can make it there, I guess," Violet added.

More of the gelatin was sluicing away, leaving Bo's neck bare, then his shoulders. He was curled up in a crouch, bobbing slightly with the motion of the pod. Goose bumps prickled over his exposed skin and he nearly wanted to burrow back down into the warm gritty fluid. He could hear Violet's teeth chattering in the dark.

"It won't drop us," he muttered. He was almost sure of that. They wanted him, or at least they wanted his Parasite.

Violet made a noncommittal noise in her throat.

Bo thought about how the pod had been locked for days in the storage unit, scored with wounds from Wyatt's knife, starved for fuel. Maybe it was desperate. Maybe even if it wanted to bring him back alive, it would choose dropping them and surviving over dropping itself.

"I'm sorry I told Wyatt," he said. He felt Violet turn and look at him in the dark. He wished he could see her face, even though sometimes that wasn't any help with Violet.

She was silent for a second, then: "It's not going to drop us."

Bo shook his head. "I know," he said, not knowing. "But I shouldn't have told Wyatt. I swore I wouldn't. I'm sorry, is all."

Maybe it was better that he couldn't see her. The dark meant he didn't have to know if she was staring at him how she'd done in the theater, so furious it hurt. He heard her open her mouth.

The pod slammed into something, rattling his bones, flinging him up against the hard ceiling. Violet bounced too; he heard her curse and her flailing leg smacked against his back. They tumbled back into the hip-high gel with a thick splash. Bo's head throbbed and purple blots swam across his eyes. Violet was disentangling herself, swearing again through a mouthful of gelatin. Through his ringing ears Bo realized that the pod's chugging noise had stopped. They had stopped moving.

For a moment both of them were still and silent. The pod rocked slightly, back and forth, but they weren't floating. They were resting on something solid.

"We're not inside the ship," Violet said. "Listen."

Bo put his ear up against a swathe of wrinkly flesh. He could feel palpitations running through the pod, could hear the sound of labored organs, maybe, pumping the yellow fluid around its body. But beyond that, from the outside, he heard the whistle and roar of strong wind. The pod rocked again and Bo fell into Violet.

"How's that Parasite feeling, Pooh Bear?" she asked, jerking him upright. Her voice had a nervous edge. "Think you better bust us out of here."

Bo wiped a glob of gel away from his eye. "Where are we, then?" he asked, his heart clamoring. Violet didn't reply. His Parasite was only just starting to move again, curling gently in on itself. He put both hands against the curved roof and took a steadying breath. His nerves felt raw and stretched, but maybe there was just enough adrenaline left for the Parasite to feed on.

The static flared. Bo felt a bit of relief. He still remembered what Wyatt had said when he'd first arrived about not wasting it, about it running out of charge like a battery. He hadn't paid much attention, but that was before he'd had Wyatt sitting on his legs with a knife to his throat and the static not coming no matter how hard he tried. He needed to be more careful with it. Smaller bursts, holding back a reserve, and only using it when he needed to.

The pod gave another violent lurch; Violet lunged to one side to steady it.

He needed to use it now. Bo couldn't see to focus, but he could feel the smooth metal under his fingers. He let the static go slow, painfully slow, trickling out of his Parasite and up through his body. It vibrated out from his cold hands and he felt the roof dissolve. He pushed up farther into the gap he'd made, feeling pulsing flesh and machinery around him, something warm dripping onto his shoulders, and let more static out.

The pod gave a low moan and Bo realized he was killing it, burrowing through it like a worm. There was a stab of guilt, but only until he remembered Quentin. He poured more static on, and the moaning grew loud and then cut away all at once. The pod gave a final shudder and went still. Bo gave one last surge of static. Suddenly cold air was whistling through the gap and he could see a vast black shape above them, illuminated by a familiar yellow glow.

"What do you see?" Violet asked from underneath him.

"Hold on," Bo said. "I'll stick my head out."

He wriggled up the tunnel he'd carved away, trying not to catch himself on the splintery bits sticking out—wire or bone, he wasn't sure. Tendrils of steam whisked past him up through the gap, carrying the same chemical smell from the storage unit, more pungent than ever. It hugged to the back of his throat and he tried not to breathe until he had his head outside.

Cold wind sliced across his face and watered his eyes. He blinked hard. He couldn't see sky, only the ship, too big and too close to understand its dizzying architecture, all the slowly shifting struts and revolving cylinders. Bo pulled himself all the way out and the wind nearly buffeted him over. He wind-milled his balance back, his heart in his throat, and crouched down against the pod's black skin. Slowly, slowly, he craned to look over the edge of its body.

They were resting on a strut like the ones up above them. The massive spar jutted down from the ship horizontal enough for the pod to have run itself onto the end and collapse there without sliding off. But the wind was tugging them back and forth, and if the strut started to move at all, like the others, they would slip. Right off the end.

Bo stuck his head back into the pod and nearly banged foreheads with Violet. Both of them recoiled.

"Come on," he said. "We're sitting on the end of this big spike, but the wind's going to—"

There was a jolt, a creak, and the pod started to roll backward. Violet's eyes went wide, she flung up her hand; Bo seized it with both of his and heaved, ignoring the pain in his scraped-up palms. She burst out of the gap and they toppled back in a tangle of limbs just as the pod reached its tipping point. Bo landed on his butt, slammed his tailbone against the hard cold surface of the spar. Violet landed half on top of him. Both of them watched, panting, as the pod slipped off the end. With all the gas escaped from its punctured body, it plummeted out of sight like a stone.

"Holy shit," Violet exhaled.

"Holy shit," Bo agreed.

She squirmed off him and they lay on their stomachs for a moment, catching their breath. The wind was whipping Bo's hood up against his face and he let it. He didn't want to look off the edge of the spar. He'd never liked heights, not even the diving board. This was nearly as high as an airplane, he was sure. It was cold enough to frost his breath.

His hood whipped away again, and he looked up. He wished he hadn't. Backlit by the ship's eerie glow, drifting side by side, two pods were slowly converging on them. He glanced over to Violet, but she'd already seen them. Her jaw was clenched tight.

"What should we do?" Bo asked. "Violet?"

Violet was still watching the pods approach, not looking at him. She ran her tongue over her teeth. "Maybe we should let them take us," she finally said. "Better than falling."

Bo shook his head fiercely. "No," he said. "No, I'm not going in one of them again. Not ever." He looked up the spar with a queasy feeling in his stomach. It was long, but it stretched up and away into the ship at an angle gentle enough to walk, or at least crawl. "Let's go up it," he said. "Maybe there's a way inside at the top."

Violet clenched her teeth again, still watching the pods.

"Come on," Bo said, getting carefully to his feet, bracing himself against the wind. "We got to try," he pleaded. "Come on, Violet."

Violet shook herself. "Alright," she said, finally turning to look at him. "Let's try."

She let Bo go first; he was smaller and if he slipped she might be able to catch him. And this way he wouldn't see her take a last look at the pods to wonder if she'd made the right choice. They were still floating toward them, unhurried, droning in short bagpipe bursts. Maybe they had a whirlybird ready and waiting for her, to put the clamp in her head. She'd forget all about Wyatt. Maybe she'd go to the pharmacy and meet Daniel the pharmacist, except he'd actually talk back and they'd actually get that coffee. She would have to forget Bo too or she would feel guilty forever.

But now wasn't the time to give him up. Bo would have tried to climb it with or without her, and if she'd tried to stop him they both would have ended up falling off. She watched him scramble along the spar, using hands and feet, nimbler than he'd been climbing fire escapes.

Violet felt an ache in her throat that was getting to be way too common, thinking about that and then about the theater and her corner mattress and the other kids. Saif and Alberto. Jon. Jenna. It was hard to remind herself that they didn't want her. That they'd all just been waiting on an excuse to drive her away, and Wyatt had given it to them.

Bo turned and looked at her over his shoulder, gave a serious-faced thumbs-up. "I think I see a way in," he hollered.

Violet returned the thumbs-up and a savage gust of wind nearly ripped her other hand away. She hunkered lower against the spar.

Wyatt had given them the excuse, but Bo had given it to Wyatt first. He'd betrayed her, so there was no reason she should feel guilty giving him up. Besides, they never really hurt kids in the warehouses. Bo had admitted that himself. And if she hadn't found him in the Safeway lot, he would be back there already.

Violet clenched her teeth and returned her full attention to the spar. Wind was blowing her hair all around her face and for a brief second she wished she'd had her head shaved like Bo's, all smooth and aerodynamic. The black metal was cold enough to sting under her palms, but it was rougher than the pod's slick side, easier to cling to. As the wind grew stronger, Bo flattened himself out and Violet followed suit. They shimmied along on their stomachs for the last stretch; her Parasite squirmed at the pressure, then the wind's howl dampened and they were at the juncture where the spar met the ship.

She saw what Bo had seen: a triangular gap, illuminated by the yellow glow of the ship's underbelly. It looked wide enough to fit through with a bit of effort.

"Made it," Bo said, his voice shakier than she would have thought. "Beat those fuckers." He pointed his chin back toward the pods. They were drifting near the end of the spar. Violet wondered if they'd even spotted them. Maybe they'd only seen the dead pod fall. She was dressed dark and so was Bo, and they wouldn't stand out much against the black surface.

"Don't swear so much," Violet said. "It sounds funny when you do it."

Bo gave a rueful shrug, looking a bit sheepish, then turned and wriggled through the gap before Violet could tell him to wait. She'd read stories about people trying to stow away in landing gear and getting crushed by the moving parts, but judging by Bo's triumphant *ha!* a moment later, he was safely uncrushed on the other side.

Violet cricked her neck, glad for once that she had so much experience hiding in tiny spaces. She stuck her head through first, then worked her left shoulder, then the right, then twisted the rest of her body in after. The wind cut out entirely. The sudden silence made her ears ring as she palmed herself up and looked around. They were inside some kind of pipe. The walls and floor and ceiling were all curved, but it wasn't the same hard metal as the spar. Her shoes squished into it a bit. Lighting was dim, provided by streaks and swatches of faintly glowing yellow against the black surface.

"A pod wouldn't fit in here," she realized. She could brush her head against the ceiling on tiptoe, and it was nowhere wide enough.

"Good," Bo said.

"Yeah," Violet said absently, studying the streaks on the ceiling. They weren't nearly as bright as the yellow light where the pods went to fuel at night, but maybe it was all the same stuff. Fuel in a pipe, blood in an artery. Maybe the ship was alive the same way the pods were. In any case, there was enough of it to see by.

"Should walk," Bo said. "Get away from the hole, in case they come try to stick their heads through. Or send a whirly."

"Yeah."

They rock-paper-scissored to pick a direction. Violet won with just two rocks because Bo was too stubborn to try paper, and they started to walk. The air was warm and the roar of the wind was replaced by a low, constant hum. She could feel all the adrenaline draining out of her body, replaced by what felt like lead.

Before long, just putting one foot in front of the next was taking all of Violet's concentration. Every part of her body was aching. Her shoulder, from wrenching up the brick and hurling it all in one desperate motion. Her ribs, from throwing herself onto the pod. Her hands worst, from the clinging and the climbing. She could feel all the tendons in them throbbing. They looked a little swollen too.

The pipe branched off over and over again, into smaller passages only wide enough to crawl through. Violet thought of veins again. They didn't want to get stuck in one, so they stayed in the main pipe, even as it began to curve. She'd lost all sense of direction and wasn't sure if they were heading farther into the ship or still along the outside of it. It was hard to care. She was exhausted and the floor seemed to be getting softer. The air was so warm.

The pipe was warped and gnarled in places, with little

pockets protruding out to the sides like air bubbles. The next time they came up on one, they stopped and crawled into it in a wordless agreement. Violet groaned as she sank down onto the soft floor. Bo collapsed beside her. She massaged her shoulder, about to suggest one of them keep watch, and probably it should be Bo, because she was the one who hadn't slept for three days straight, not since she'd run from the theater. But he was already asleep, face digging into the floor. With the drool at the corner of his mouth he looked more like a little kid again.

Violet dug out her plastic baggie and swallowed her last couple pills. Then she lay down, tucking her head into her elbow. The instant before sleep washed her away, she felt a trembling warmth against her side. The orb. She'd forgotten. But she couldn't use it with Bo here. She wrapped her fingers clumsily around it and hoped she would dream the dream they'd shown her.

16

"Left or right?" Bo asked, kneading his eyes.

He'd slept until he woke up hungry, an empty churning made worse by his Parasite wriggling back against it in response. Violet had already been awake, sitting with her arms wrapped around her knees, and he'd guessed from her grimace that she was experiencing the same thing. He'd inspected his scraped-up palms, relieved to find they were already less tender. Then, because there was nothing else to do, they'd kept walking.

Now they were at a split, the corridor forking off in two directions. Bo felt a growing frustration. They had gotten away from Wyatt, and they had gotten away from the pod, but now what? They were stuck wandering around up on the ship with no way to get off it. If the pod had taken them to the warehouses, at least he would be closer to Lia. Maybe he would have even had a chance to break her out. He knew how to use his Parasite now, knew better than anyone.

But it wasn't any use up here. Here, all they could do was pick left or right.

Violet gave a tight shrug. "Right," she said in a half whisper.

She'd barely spoken since they got up. Bo guessed she was worried. Sometimes he caught her giving him a strange look from the corner of her eye.

They went right. Before long the corridor started to slant downward, and it seemed to be narrowing too. Bo sped up a bit as the gradient changed. At least this was different. He wanted to get out of the thick warm air. He was sure he'd be able to think better, and maybe think of a way to get off the ship.

He dug his heels in as the floor suddenly dropped out of sight. Violet nearly bowled him over from behind before he braced himself against the gnarled wall. The slope had turned to a ninety-degree drop. He peered over the edge and found himself looking down into a long dark hall. Everything seemed to be made of the same black metal, except for a massive vat directly under them. It was clear and it was full of rippling luminescent yellow liquid.

Violet bellied out beside him. "It's not that high," she said hoarsely. "We could jump."

"Into the yellow stuff?" Bo asked, gritting his teeth. He felt a familiar helium sensation in his forehead. It was higher than the high-diving board.

"Softer than the floor." Violet paused. "You swim, right?"

"Yeah," Bo said. "In water."

"It's not acid or anything," Violet said. "I've touched it. Had it all over my hands when I was trying to hold on to the pod."

Bo had an unbidden flash of the storage unit, of plunging the knife into the pod's wound, the spatter on his hands and wrists. He shoved the image away.

"Okay," he said. "I got first."

He straightened up on the lip and looked down. Suddenly he had a memory of the swimming pool in Niamey, from back before they left Africa. There had been a cement diving board coated in flaking white paint, nothing like the floppy green ones at the pool here, and because he'd been six years old it had seemed incredibly high. He'd stood shivering on the edge for ages until Lia coaxed him off.

But in the past four months he'd done scarier things. He'd killed othermothers and run from pods and had a knife put under his throat. Bo touched his hand against his Parasite, feeling almost reassured by the ripple, then jumped.

Cold air gusted his clothes and whistled in his ears; he locked his legs and shut his eyes just before he hit the surface. It was hotter than he'd expected. Not enough to scald him, but enough to make him claw his way back up to the surface as quickly as he could. He splashed his way over to the side of the vat and clung there. His heartbeat had settled by the time Violet dropped down beside him, then both of them clambered over the edge and slopped out.

Bo tried to get purchase on the outside of the vat, but he was slippery and the side was smooth and he landed badly, sending a sharp shock of pain up his already-sore tailbone. Violet stuck hers, crouching low and then straightening up to wring out her hair. Bo got slowly to his feet. They were both drenched, sopping a puddle onto the metallic black floor. Violet blew a spray through her pursed lips.

"Looks like we got peed on by a radioactive elephant," she said.

Bo wiped at his face. "Maybe we'll get superpowers," he said.

She looked at him for a second, then at his stomach where his shirt covered the Parasite, and burst out laughing. Bo tried to stay straight-faced serious how Violet did for jokes, but he cracked. First he just grinned, but then he was laughing too, hard enough to toss his head back and see a whirlybird drifting right above them.

He grabbed Violet's shoulder, felt his Parasite rushing, the static sparking, ready to vanish it before it could swoop down on them with its needle or its claw.

But the whirlybird wasn't drifting. It was fixed to a rack that stretched the length of the hall, something he hadn't been able to see from their vantage point inside the pipe. Its limbs were folded up under its flesh-and-metal shell. Inactive. Bo exhaled, let his Parasite calm down. The static trickled away.

"Spares," Violet said, looking up at them. There were more racks above it, all of them lined with the compacted whirly-birds. Hundreds of them, Bo thought.

"I always wanted to smash one of these," he blurted. "The whole time I was in the warehouse. I always wanted to wreck one. Especially the one that did my Parasite."

"Me too," Violet said. She gave a little shudder and he could tell that she was thinking back to the same place, to the whirly-bird hovering over her and unslinging its big scraping needle, to the feel of a tiny squirming *thing* burrowing through her belly button. The not knowing had been the worst part, Bo remembered. Not knowing if it was going to kill him or do something worse, the foreign thing that was suddenly part of him.

He peered up at the whirlybird. He recognized the big nee-dle, and the smaller one it used on kids to put them to sleep. He'd never had a chance to look at its tools up close. The claw that had scarred his arms, all those months ago when he tried to grab one on the way to supper, was folded up. Tucked beside it, he saw a tiny drill. He thought of the wasters and could guess what it was meant for.

"Why would they clamp people at all?" Bo swallowed. "Why not just kill them?"

Violet was quiet for a moment. "Nobody likes to think they're the bad guy, Bo." She looked at the whirlybird when she said it, not at him.

Bo stared at the needle again. "Wyatt told me something," he said slowly. "Before you showed up. He said they didn't clamp anyone in the hospital. They killed them all. He said they put them down. Like animals."

Violet stiffened. "Lied a lot," she said. "Wyatt lied a lot."

"Yeah," Bo said. "I guess."

They wandered down the empty hall, staring up at the rows and rows of whirlybirds and not speaking.

The ship didn't have any doors, so far as Violet could tell. It seemed like one hall led to the next led to the next, all connected by vaguely keyhole-shaped archways. Sometimes the rooms were high-vaulted like cathedrals, all spikes and flanges up the walls, and other times they were low and crammed with humming, shifting machinery Violet couldn't even begin to guess purposes for. Sometimes there were silvery pyramids and sometimes there were more of the cylindrical vats, bubbling full of their yellow fuel.

So far as Violet could tell, the ship was also empty. She kept waiting to round the corner on a group of pods, or hear the whine of a whirlybird, or even see the spidery silhouette of an othermother stalking the corridors with them. But it was just them, wandering lost.

There was a reason she hadn't been speaking much. Her voice had broken earlier that morning, just for half a sentence, slipping past her with a bray that she knew sounded a thousand times worse in her head. Bo hadn't seemed to notice it. But it put a thick black fear in her belly, worse than anything she'd felt over the last few topsy-turvy days.

It took her back to nights in her bathroom at home, back before the ship came down, back before she was taking spiro. She used to lock herself in for hours, scour her body with tweezers, shaking and red-faced as she found the hairs she hated, so much thicker and coarser and darker than they should be.

If the deal was still there for the taking, she wouldn't have to feel that fear ever again. The orb was warm and waiting in her pocket; she'd taken a spare second to wrap it up tightly in a sock before she jumped into the vat. She hadn't looked at it yet—Bo'd woken up only a moment after she did—but it wouldn't be hard to pretend she needed a piss and sneak away to some corner. Maybe it would give her directions to follow or show her where to take Bo.

Then Bo would go to the warehouses, and she would never need to hunt for hormones again. She would be how she'd always been meant to be. She would plug herself into a beautiful dream and forget Bo ever existed. Forget him, forget Wyatt, definitely forget Ivan. *Like heaven,* they'd said.

Bo's stomach gave a noisy rumble that cut through her thoughts. "Think there's food anywhere up here?" he asked. "Like the stuff the whirlybirds fed us. Right now I'd eat that."

"Doubt it," Violet said. "We can start looking." They were in another hall, this one low-ceilinged and lined with little alcoves on each side, like storage rooms. Bo broke off to check the right side; Violet took the left. The little rooms were all identical and all empty, until one up ahead caught her eye.

The second-to-last storage room had a door, or something like it. A fizzing red screen seemed to ripple back and forth in front of it, stretching wall to wall and floor to ceiling, boxing it off. The red screen was translucent enough, but she couldn't see anything behind it but shadows.

As Bo came up to join her, she bunched the sleeve of her shirt into a knot and reached out with the very tip of it. Sparks flew, and when she pulled it back from the screen it was singed. She blew away the little wisp of smoke. Turned to Bo.

"Guess we're not allowed in that one," she said.

"Or maybe he's not allowed out," Bo said.

Violet spun back, following Bo's gaze, and nearly jumped. There was a tall bony man sitting cross-legged on the floor, where she was sure there'd been nothing but shadow a second ago. He was dressed all in black with an old-fashioned looking bowler hat on his head, and his hands, resting on his knees, were pale and spidery. His eyes were shut behind bruise-colored lids.

Not storage rooms. Cells.

"Why would they have a waster locked up here?" Bo murmured, peering at the man. "He must be clamped, right? All the grown-ups got clamped, you said." His voice was excited.

"All the ones on the ground," Violet said. The man was gaunt like a waster, but his clothes were immaculate, and something else about him, about the way he was sitting so still, made her think he wasn't one. "Maybe they kept a few free," she said. "For experiments. Maybe they tried to put Parasites in some adults too."

"Should try to find out," Bo said. "Shout something at him. See if he's a waster or not."

"You shout something at him," Violet said.

Bo stuck out his fist and bounced it up and down, giving her a challenging look. "Best of five."

"You're only going to lose again," she said, grudgingly putting her own fist in. Rock-rock-scissors this time around, she figured. Bo was predictable like that.

"Hello, children."

This time Violet did jump, and Bo flinched back almost as badly. The man was standing up against the fizzing red screen with his nose nearly touching it. He'd moved as quick and quiet as a cat; Violet hadn't heard a single footstep. She put a hand to her rippling Parasite and tried to steady her breathing. This man wasn't a waster. He was staring right at them, wearing a smile that seemed too wide for his mouth.

"Let me out, please."

Violet's first instinct was to back away, back away, run. Everything about the man was off, from his stretched-out smile to his strange toneless voice. But there was no way of knowing how long he'd been stuck up here on the ship by himself. Maybe it was stir-crazy, not crazy-crazy.

"Let me out, please, children," the man said again.

"Who are you?" Violet asked. "How'd you get here?"

"I am a prisoner," he said. "They caught me. I was careless." His face twisted into an exaggerated frown.

"Did you never have a clamp?" Bo asked. "The thing they stick on the back of your head. To make you a waster. Did they never try to give you one?"

The man was silent for a long minute. His black eyes flicked from Violet to Bo and back again. "No," he said slowly. "They never tried to give me the thing they stick on the back of your head."

For a moment, even through the red blur, she could tell something wasn't right with his eyes. They were too large, too dark, all pupil. She blinked and they were normal again.

"How long have you been up here?" Bo asked.

Violet didn't wait for the answer. She grabbed Bo by the arm and jerked her head back the way they'd come. He gave her a questioning look, but followed. The man didn't call after them, only stood, hands at his sides, watching until they were around the corner.

"That's not a real person," Violet said in a low voice. "No way is that a real person."

Bo gritted his teeth. "Moves funny," he admitted. "And how he talks. It's weird." He shot a glance over his shoulder, like the black-clad man might have followed them out of his cell. "You think he's like the othermothers? Like, a better version?"

"Why would they put him in a cell, then?"

"To trick us." Bo's eyes were shiny, a little frantic-looking. "They think we'll trust him right away. Automatic. Because he's the first grown-up we've seen in forever who's not a waster."

"That's a lot of work for a trick," Violet said. "They stuck him there just in case we walked by, or what?" She felt the weight of the orb in her pocket. "They would have to know we're on the ship," she said. "Also exactly where we are on the ship."

"So what is he, then?" Bo asked, sticking both hands on his head, looking unsettled.

"Ask him."

"You ask him."

They went back around the corner one rock and two scissors later. Violet half expected to see the cell empty again, but the man was standing there how they left him.

"Oh, hello again," he said. "Will you let me out now?"

Bo gave her a look. Violet scissored her two fingers together as a reminder of who'd won. She was glad it wasn't her asking, just in case the man broke down in tears. Just in case she'd imagined the big black eyes, and forgotten how weird some adults could be, and he was just an eccentric dresser who'd been losing his mind up here on the ship for the past four months.

"We know you're not human," Bo said. "So what are you?"

The man's eyes winched wide and he put his hands up, palms out, innocent. Then his stretched smile came back, and Violet saw something starting to wriggle out of his face, just above his cheekbone. What looked like a minuscule beetle burrowed out from his skin and clung there. She was narrowing her eyes to peer closer at it when the rest of his face burst into a mass of scuttling black metal.

Violet recoiled; Bo yelped. The black metal rippled from the man's face down the rest of his body, his suit jacket and long legs and pale hands all turning into a writhing, vaguely human-shaped tower of gleaming machinery. It slid back and forth in front of the red screen like a shadow come to life, slithering up the wall, across the ceiling, back to the floor.

Then all at once it was the man again, legs and arms and body and head. The bowler hat was last, black blots of machine trickling up his face to form its brim. He stomped down on a stray bit that nearly scurried away, and when he lifted his foot, Violet saw only the smooth black sole of his shoe.

"I am a saboteur," the man said. "I was careless. Now I am a prisoner."

Violet had seen a lot of shocking things, but it still took her a moment to regain her bearings. She did not like things that scuttled.

Bo was quicker to recover. "So you're not one of them," he said eagerly. "You're not on their side."

"No," the man said. "I am not on their side. I sabotaged them." He lifted his hat, exposing unfinished black skull, and gave a modest bow.

"You didn't sabotage them very hard," Violet said dryly. "They're still running everything. And you're stuck in a little box."

"I did sabotage them very hard," the man said, narrowing his dark eyes. "I destroyed all of the keys. Will you let me out now?"

Violet swapped looks with Bo.

"What keys?" Bo demanded. "To fly the ship?"

The man gave him a long look. "Keys open doors," he said. "I destroyed the keys that would have opened the door. They would have opened the door to bring the other ships through. Hundreds of ships. Instead, they are alone. I sabotaged them."

"Wait." Violet nearly put her hand against the blurry red screen before she remembered and yanked it back. "They're alone? This is the only ship?"

She thought back to the end of the world, to the thick prickling fog that wouldn't let them leave. She'd supposed that everything else had been destroyed, all the other cities and countries and continents, or else that all of them were trapped in their own gray day with their own black ship drifting in the sky, their own warehouses and pods and whirlybirds. Everyone stuck in the same scary dark fairy tale.

"Of course," the man said. "They were only sent to open the door."

"But they can't," Bo said. "They can't bring any more ships, because you destroyed the keys, right?"

The man stooped down slightly to Bo's eye level. "I like you," he said. "When you let me out, I will be your friend. I destroyed the keys. Yes." His black gaze flicked down to Bo's stomach, then to hers. She felt her Parasite wriggle. "But, as you know, they are growing new keys now."

17

Back around the corner, but only because Violet insisted on it. Bo knew what they needed to do. They needed to let the man in black out of his cell.

"He can be our ally," Bo said, bouncing up and down on the balls of his feet. "He can help us beat them. You see how quick he moved? Across the ceiling like that?" He scurried his hand through the air to demonstrate. "Like a . . . Like a *mijin kunama*."

"A what?"

"A special kind of spider," Bo said. The ugly, lightning-fast spider that he remembered speeding across the cement floor of their old house in Niamey, the one his mom sometimes joked was the reason they immigrated.

"Regular old cockroaches do that too," Violet said. "The ceiling thing." She had her arms folded, her back stiff. She looked worried.

But Bo was electric from excitement. The ship was the only ship, meaning the rest of the world was still alright. Even better, the gaunt man was on their side, and he knew what the Parasites were really for. He knew everything they'd wondered about for four months.

"We have to let him out," Bo said. "I bet he knows a way off the ship. Like, a lifeboat or something. How a ship ship would have."

"We should leave him where he is," Violet said. "He gives me the creeps. Doesn't he give you the creeps?"

"He knows things," Bo insisted. "Knows more than we do, anyway. About them, about the ship, about the Parasites."

"How do you know anything he's saying is actually true?" Violet demanded. "He just wants us to let him out. It could all be bullshit." She rubbed her arms. "The second he's out, he could turn into that black stuff again and smother us."

Bo shook his head. "He's not on their side—"

"Doesn't mean he's on ours."

"—or they wouldn't have put him in a cell," Bo finished. "You said that. Before, you said that."

"What if they locked him up for a good reason?" Violet demanded. "Maybe whatever he is is even worse than they are."

"I hope he is," Bo said fiercely. "It's a war, right? The enemy of my enemy is my friend." He was starting to feel angry, feel it in his chest and his Parasite. They needed all the help they could get. Violet knew that. They needed the gaunt man.

Violet looked at him and her eyes were colder than they had been in a long time, like they'd been back when she first found him in the parking lot.

"You get that from Wyatt?" she asked. "Sounds just like him."

Bo felt himself flush hot. What might have been regret flickered through Violet's face, but only for a split second before she set her jaw. She was right—it was from Wyatt. Wyatt, who could justify anything, whether it was torturing the pod or cutting Bo's Parasite out of his stomach. Wyatt, who said they were two of a kind.

But this wasn't like that.

Bo took a breath. "We don't have to trust him all the way," he said. "We can be careful. We can ask him some questions first. But I'm letting him out."

"Fine," Violet said. She looked like she was going to say something else too, then just shook her head. They went back to the prisoner. He was still standing, so close to the red screen it looked like he was in danger of toppling into it. Bo had a feeling he didn't lose his balance easily.

"Oh, hello again," the man said. This time there was some sarcasm to it.

"Before we decide about helping you, we want to know some things," Bo said, making his voice cool and firm how Lia did when she wasn't going to take no for an answer. "Who are you? And who are the other aliens? The ones who own the ship."

"I am a saboteur. When you let me out, I will be your friend. Was that unclear?" The man leaned even closer, his waxy pale face almost brushing the red screen. Bo checked his feet; there was no way he should be able to lean so far without falling, but his polished black shoes were still somehow anchored to the floor. "The ones who own the ship will never be your friends. They are conniving. Do you know what *conniving* means, children? They are conniving and bad and their dead metal stinks." He tapped a long bony finger against his nostril. "We were their slaves once. They will make you their slaves now."

Bo immediately pictured the wasters wandering through the ruined city. That was what the aliens wanted: a whole world of sleepwalking slaves. He had heard enough.

"If we let you go, will you help us off the ship?" he asked.

The gaunt man gave his not-quite-right smile. "I will fly you off the ship." His arms and shoulders burst outward in gleaming black ropes, then twisted together into massive moth-like wings, beating up and down. "I am very tired of the ship," he said. "I want better lighting." The wings collapsed back into his body, tendrils sucked back in to re-form his black sleeves.

Bo's heart pounded. He shot Violet a triumphant look, but she didn't return it. "And will you help us free the other kids?" he demanded. "The ones with the new keys put in them."

"The new keys cannot stay where they are," the man said. "Or they will be used to open the door. I will help you move them."

"Alright," Bo said, clenching his fist at his side, tamping down his grin. "We're going to let you out. What do we call you?"

"What do you call me?"

"Yeah." Bo stuck his hand on his chest. "Like, I'm Bo. That's Violet. What's your name?"

The man didn't respond for a moment, his face perfectly blank. "You can call me Gloom," he finally said. "In your manner of naming, we are all called Gloom."

"Pleasure," Violet said. "Let's get Mr. Gloomy out of here and get going." She had both her hands bundled tight in her pockets. She looked anxious. Bo wanted to tell her that it was alright, and that if Gloom tried to attack them, he would use his Parasite to vanish him. But three conferences around the corner was maybe too many. A whirlybird might come to check the cell soon.

"How do we open it?" Bo asked.

Gloom put his spidery pale hand against his middle, where a Parasite would sit. "With the four of you, I am sure you can think of a way," he said.

Violet stepped back with an *all-yours* wave. Bo studied the sparking red screen. It didn't look solid, like the kind of thing he could vanish. It reminded him more of the fog at the end of the world. He took a step to the right to see it lengthwise. On the inside of the doorway, there was a vertical row of bulbs. Projectors, maybe—the more he looked, the more it seemed like the red screen was a wave bouncing back and forth across the space. When he finally managed to coax the static out of his Parasite, he aimed it at the black frame.

It wasn't as focused a hole as he'd done boring through the pod. More of a wide gash, like something had taken a bite out of the metal. But it worked: Steam twirled out of the sliced circuitry and a second later the red screen jittered and died.

Gloom stepped through the empty space, and Bo felt just a hint of trepidation. He'd held some of the static back, enough for another burst. The gaunt man seemed taller now, looming over the top of them—he'd forgotten how tall adults could be. Not that Gloom was even a human.

His big pale hand jerked forward and Bo stepped back instinctively before he realized it was poised to shake. He threw a look to Violet, half hoping she had her Parasite ready too, just in case. She'd taken Wyatt's hand off her. She could take Gloom's off him.

Bo swallowed, then put his hand into Gloom's and shook. It didn't feel like real skin. It was too smooth and too cold.

"We are friends now," Gloom said, smiling widely. "My motes will taste your genes to remember you."

"Your what?"

"My motes. My body."

Gloom's hand burst into a rustling black blob that enveloped Bo's, swirling all around it like a thousand tiny bugs. Bo gritted his teeth and held still. Gloom's hand re-formed an instant later and pulled away. He held it out toward Violet next.

"I'm good," she said. Her hands stayed in her pockets.

"You can be my second friend," Gloom wheedled.

"Tempting." Violet's voice was terse. "Let's go, Bo."

Bo was still wiping his hand on his shirt, trying to get rid of the phantom feel of Gloom's motes scurrying over his skin, as the gaunt man turned back to him.

"Your key is tuned," he said. "Much better-tuned than the other keys they have brought to the ship. Congratulations."

Bo's hand froze. "What other keys?" he demanded. "You mean there's other kids on the ship? Like us?"

"Yes," Gloom said. "Would you like me to show you?"

Bo looked to Violet, but before either of them could speak a bone-deep vibration shook through them. At first he thought it was his Parasite, or hers, but there was no static with it. Just the vibration, rippling past them into the walls and up the ceiling. It came again and he braced himself as it passed under his feet. He realized it was moving out in concentric circles from the center of the empty cell.

"We should not stay here," Gloom said. "They know I have escaped. Follow me."

He dissolved back into shadow and flowed, like quicksilver, across the floor of the hall. At the doorway he stopped, forming a rustling black pillar, and waited for them. Bo followed, heart pounding, and glanced back to make sure Violet was following too. The vibration shook them again, and in the distance he heard the soft whine of whirlybirds coming to life.

18

Gloom was fast, so fast Violet couldn't imagine how he'd been caught in the first place. Sometimes he was the flowing black mass of machinery, others he was the tall skinny man, but he was always moving. Scuttling along the ceiling and surfing the wall, or else running bent double with his lanky arms making short chopping motions like an animatronic gone wrong. Bo bounced along gamely behind him and Violet could barely keep pace.

He really was creepy as fuck, with his stretched-out smiles and gleaming black eyes, and he made things about a hundred times more complicated. There was no chance she could sneak away to use the orb now. And if what Gloom had said about the ship was true, if it really was the only ship, then maybe she wasn't as cornered as she'd thought.

Maybe there was a way to get past the end of the world, to get out of the city, to start over in the real world. She could leave Wyatt to his war and Bo to his own version of it. Escape.

"Stand against the wall, please, children," Gloom said, his face appearing through a cloud of swirling black motes. "Now."

They'd been running through another dark hall, this one dotted with circular pits in the floor. Violet had looked down into one and seen a writhing mass of tendrils—same thing as the wormy wall, being grown under a pale purple light.

Bo shimmied back flat against the wall; Violet did the same, glad to catch her breath, and a moment later she heard what Gloom had already. It didn't have the same wheezy edge as it did outside the ship, but she recognized the chugging sound of a pod approaching. Maybe more than one. Her palms went clammy as Gloom stretched himself thin and started to web across them like a blanket. Bo gave her a nudge on the hip, maybe remembering what she'd said about it smothering them, maybe trying to be reassuring.

The motes slithered across their bodies like a million little bugs. Violet hated bugs. She closed her eyes briefly as they covered her head. When she opened them she realized the camouflage was thin enough to see through and porous enough to breathe through, but also somehow soundproof—the noise of the pods was muffled.

She tried to slow her heart and lungs as the aliens drifted into the hall. They had harnesses of some kind slung from under their bellies; she couldn't tell if it was flesh or machine. Tubes were coiled around each other and a thick blue mist leaked from what might have been a nozzle. A slight ripple went through Gloom's distended body at the sight.

"That is how they caught me." His voice came through the motes in a tinny whisper. "It is a gas that freezes. Do you understand freezing, children?"

"Bo," Bo muttered through clenched-sounding teeth. "And Violet. Yeah, we know what freezing is."

The pods floated toward them and for a moment Violet thought of breaking away, getting their attention. But maybe they would douse her with the freezing fog before they bothered using their yellow flash to recognize her. Her hand went to the orb in her pocket and tightened around it. The pods passed by them, close enough to reach out and touch, then continued into the next hall. Violet felt Bo exhale a long breath. She let herself slump back against the wall.

Gloom started to peel back, away from Bo, then from her, and in the split second when it was only her face still covered she felt the motes crawl up her temple and into her ear.

"What do you have in your pocket, Violet?"

She stiffened, but the motes were already gone and Gloom was standing in front of them again, his hat resettling on his head. The tinny whisper had been faint, so faint she could nearly pretend she'd imagined it. But she knew she hadn't.

"We are getting close, Bo and Violet," Gloom said. "Please move quietly." His black stare lingered on her for a moment too long. Violet's heart hammered. Did he know what the orb was? Had he recognized the shape of it when he slid across her? Her Parasite gave a nervous wriggle.

But Gloom said nothing else as they crept along at a more cautious pace, pausing several more times to hide against walls or corners as whirlybirds whined past. Bo had a fierce sort of grin on his face whenever she checked. This was exciting for him. Violet only felt sick and trembly all over.

Gloom led them down a grate into a small winding tunnel lined with sharp edges and twists of circuitry. They had to go on hands and knees. Even being as careful as she could, Violet managed to scrape the skin off her knee. She barely felt the sting. Too many other things to worry about. Tetanus didn't make even the bottom of the list.

As they crawled along, small black blots dropped down off the ceiling onto Gloom's shoulders, sinking into his coat.

"You waited for me," he crooned. "Hello, my motes." He twisted around so he was crabwalking backward at uncanny speed. "I lost a portion of myself when I was being chased," he explained. "They burrowed this passage trying to root me out. So they could pump the gas that freezes through the ship's infrastructure. Now we are using it to escape from them. Do you know irony, children?"

Bo shot her a look over his shoulder, like he was expecting something.

"No," Violet said. "But it sounds fucking fascinating."

"I learned of many things before our enemy disabled your primitive machine mind, your information net," Gloom said. "Some were fascinating, yes." He came to an abrupt halt. "We are below the other keys now. The other keys in the other children. I will look to see if the room is empty." He dug two fingers into his eye socket and pulled; his eye came out as a gleaming ball of motes. He tossed it upward and Violet watched it slither through a crack in the ceiling.

"He's right," Bo said. "There's more Parasites up there. Active ones. You feel them?" He put his hand on his stomach, and Violet saw a steady ripple going through his abdomen. "I always feel them," he muttered, looking up at the tunnel ceiling.

She shook her head—she only ever felt her own Parasite. But she knew Bo's was different. Stronger. That was why they wanted him so bad.

Bo was clenching and unclenching his fists as he turned to Gloom. "Why are some of the kids here, and not in the warehouses?" he asked.

Violet knew what he was thinking. It was written all over his face. He thought his sister might be up here. She felt a churn of guilt.

"The keys are not being grown in ideal conditions," Gloom said. "The enemy is desperate. They used as many viable hosts as they could, hoping at least a handful would have compatible genes to turn the key. Do you understand genes, Bo?"

"Not really," Bo said. "So why are some of the keys here? I mean, kids."

"The best keys have been moved here to be tuned," Gloom said. "That is why they brought you up here. Your key might already be capable of opening the door."

"I'm not opening any door for them," Bo said darkly. "I'd cut it out first."

Violet thought of the scar across Wyatt's hips and flushed. She would never forget about Wyatt if they didn't give her a clamp. He'd be lurking around in the back of her head forever, even if she managed to somehow escape past the end of the world.

The motes dropped back down from the ceiling and scurried over Gloom's face, back into their hollow dark socket. "Empty," he said. "Bo, would you make a hole, please?"

Bo was crouched, rocking back and forth on his heels. "We have to look," he said. "Right? Even if she's not here, maybe we can rescue the others."

Violet nodded, not trusting herself to speak. She scooted backward so Bo could position himself. He slapped at his face, shook himself. The static came quick. She felt her hair stand straight up as he put his hands against the roof of the tunnel. The metal and wire ate away into nothing, and Gloom swept up through the hole in a rush of motes. Bo levered himself up after. Violet followed last.

The room was smaller than the last few they'd been through, and the far side was lined with tanks full of an aquamarine and faintly luminescent liquid. Violet knew what had to be inside them, but it still gave her a jolt to see the drifting silhouettes. She stepped shakily to the nearest tank. A boy, maybe Saif's age or not even, was bobbing up and down in the liquid. His eyes were shut and tubes kept him tethered in place, snaking into his limbs and down his throat. Violet wanted to gag just looking at it.

"It is simpler to keep the hosts sedated at this point," Gloom said in her ear. "To ensure the chemical balance."

Violet's gaze traveled to Bo, who was sliding from tank to tank, eyes wide, searching. This was what they would do to Bo, and once they used his Parasite to open the door, it really would be the end of the world. But she wouldn't have to know about it. The thought slipped into her like a morphine needle. It would be the end of the world that had never liked her much anyway, and she would never have to know.

"Do not touch the tanks," Gloom said, louder than usual. "They will know if you touch the tanks."

Bo jerked his hand away from the last tank in the row. He looked over with a sunken expression on his face. "She's not here," he said, in a voice that was biting back a sob.

Violet looked up and down the row at the three drifting kids. There was a fourth tank perpendicular to the others. Empty, but judging by the tubes waving inside, and the droplets of liquid splattered around the outside, it had once been occupied. She opened her mouth.

The high-pitched whine of a whirlybird cut the silence. Her eyes flicked toward the doorway.

Gloom had heard it too. "Back into the hole, please," he whispered.

Bo didn't move for a second, still looking dazed, defeated.

Gloom turned back into shadow and swirled around his legs, nudging him back toward the hole he'd made in the floor. Bo shook himself, slipped down into it. Violet folded herself in beside him and Gloom swept over them, concealing the hole, just as the whirlybird entered the room.

It wasn't alone. One of its multi-jointed arms was guiding what looked like a massive hovering embryo sac, veined with circuitry and lights, and for a moment Violet could see a figure balled up inside it. Then it passed over their hiding spot and out of sight. She heard a whirring noise, then a slimy *pop* and dull splash. Another whirr, and then the whirlybird and the deflated sac floated past again, almost directly over them.

It was barely out of the room before Bo struggled up past Gloom, or through him, and ran to the fourth tank. He made a noise Violet had never heard him make before, not when he baited his first othermother and not inside the pod either. She levered herself out of the floor.

The girl adrift in the tank was long-legged, dark-skinned, and there was something so familiar in the shape of her face that Violet knew, without seeing Bo's tortured expression, that they'd found his sister. Her eyes were shut under long lashes and Violet could see her chest moving with each long, slow breath from the tube in her throat.

Bo sank to a crouch in front of the tank, clutching his head in his hands, moaning in a way that made Violet's stomach churn, made her Parasite twitch and flex. Gloom was standing awkwardly beside him, looking from Bo to the tank and back again. His pale slack face was uncomprehending. A small part of Violet remembered what Gloom had said about touching the tanks.

She took a step backward. Gloom didn't notice, neither did

Bo. All she had to do was reach out and touch one of the tanks, Gloom had said, and it would trigger an alarm. The whirlybird would be back in an instant, and maybe the pods with their freezing gas. Violet pictured it in her head. She would swipe her hand along the tank and then go to Bo, and hug him, and when the alarm went off all she had to do was hold him there while Gloom slithered back down the hole.

Bo might not even struggle. He looked nearly paralyzed.

She reached her hand out, fingers splayed inches from the smooth surface of the tank with the little boy inside. They would come and take Bo, and she would only have to show them the black orb. Then she could go back to the perfect house with the perfect family and be the perfect Violet.

She looked at Bo one last time, at his crumpled shoulders. She could see his face reflected in his sister's tank. See his expression. It made him look older than any kid had a right to. No simulation pulled from her dreams and memories could ever get that expression right. There was too much love in it. She didn't think she'd ever seen that much.

Violet curled her fingers back into her fist. The orb was heating up again in her pocket but now she wanted to grab it out and hurl it away. If she looked inside it, if she saw the dream, she might not be able to turn it down again.

Violet took a trembling breath. A step forward. "How do we get her out?" she asked.

19

"How do we get her out?"

Violet's words broke through the fog in Bo's head and he slowly stood up. He didn't look at Lia. He'd always imagined getting to the warehouses and finding her waiting for him on her cot, still sharp, still ready, scolding him for taking so long. Maybe with the other kids already prepared to escape, a plan already in motion, something he interrupted on accident. She was the one who'd found out about the drinking water. She was the one who'd told him to take the chance when he had it.

She shouldn't have been the one floating in that tank like a human puppet, with the tubes squirming into every part of her, naked and drugged to sleep.

"Yeah," Bo said, wiping his face. "How, Gloom?"

Gloom flitted back and forth in a swirling mass of motes, then re-formed in front of them. He rolled his hat between his long pale fingers. "I did say we would move the keys," he said. "But that might not be possible. It might be better to destroy them here."

Bo stepped between Gloom and his sister and the static surged so hard from his Parasite, it flew blue sparks down his arms.

"Without killing the hosts," Gloom amended, putting his hands up, palms out. His hat flowed up his arm and back onto his head. "I can use a single mote for each. The entry wound will be very small. Working simultaneously, if I am quick, I can destroy the keys before our enemy arrives." He gave a stiff little nod, looking pleased with his plan. "I am always quick," he added. "I am a saboteur."

"You can kill the Parasites without it hurting the host at all?" Violet demanded.

"Yes, yes," Gloom said. "The key needs a host. The host does not need a key. Although keys can be very useful." He gave Bo a pointed look.

Bo looked back hard, trying to gauge if Gloom was telling the truth. Motes were scurrying down his long lanky legs, spreading out, one to each tank.

"Wait," Violet said. "If they come back and find all the Parasites dead, what'll they do with the kids?"

Gloom had a blank look on his face. "I do not know," he said, but his toneless voice put goose bumps on Bo's arms. The motes fanned out, finding their targets.

"They'll kill them," Bo realized. "That's what they do when kids aren't useful. They put them down." He looked at the mote creeping toward his sister's tank. "Stop it," he said.

"We cannot let them have these keys, Bo and Violet," Gloom said. "They will open the door."

Bo let out a focused wave of static. The mote vanished, taking a small chunk of floor with it. Gloom's face twitched, maybe in surprise, maybe something like pain; the other motes stopped where they were. Then Gloom's mouth twisted into an unnatural snarl, his teeth bared.

"I'll do the rest of you too," Bo said, forcing bravado into his voice. "You're not as fast as you think you are."

"I am exactly as fast as I think I am," Gloom said. His face turned instantly blank again, and Bo couldn't decide if it was more or less frightening. "We cannot take all of these children off the ship. It is impossible. Even if they were awake and their bodies were not atrophied."

"We'll come back for them," Bo said. "We'll make a plan." He swallowed. "But we have to bring one with us. We have to bring Lia." He looked to Violet for support.

"Can you fly three of us off the ship?" she asked. She finally looked like herself again, standing up straight and alert. Bo felt a grateful ache in his throat. Violet understood. She knew he couldn't leave without Lia.

"Maybe," Gloom said, his eyes flicking between them. "Three is heavy." The too-wide smile split his face again. "Maybe Violet would like to stay behind. Would you like to stay behind, Violet?"

"She's not staying behind," Bo said tersely. "Nobody is. Can you carry three of us or not?"

Gloom stared at the tank. Bo followed his gaze automatically and felt another punch to his gut seeing Lia adrift inside. He made himself keep looking, even though he felt sick and ashamed doing it. He needed to look, and remember, and punish the ones who'd put her in there.

Punish. That made him remember Wyatt's electrical cord, and he felt sick and ashamed for another reason. The important thing was to get Lia out. He needed to focus on that, only that, not revenge.

"I can carry three of you," Gloom said at last. "And we will come back for the others? You will make a plan?"

"Yeah," Bo said. "We'll make a plan. A good one." He looked to Violet. She was watching Gloom closely, distrustfully. He didn't blame her.

Gloom's black eyes narrowed. "Are you known as great tacticians, Bo and Violet?"

"The very best," Violet said dryly. "They throw parades."

"You do know irony," Gloom said, not sounding pleased.

"We freed you, remember?" Bo said. "We trusted you. Now you trust us back."

Gloom stared at him for a long moment, and Bo had the sense that his gleaming black eyes were boring tunnels into him. "Very well," he said. "I trust you back, Bo."

Bo felt a rush of relief. "So we can't touch the outside," he said, before Gloom could change his mind. "What if I vanish the glass?"

"The liquid will escape," Gloom said. "They will know if a certain percentage of the liquid escapes. There are sensors." He peered at the tank. "And without the liquid to suspend her, the cables may damage her flesh."

Bo had the image of Lia's limp body jerking in the empty space like someone dangling from the gallows. He shuddered.

"I will have to untether her," Gloom said. "That will take time."

"Will they know if you're inside the tank?" Violet asked. "Or at least some of you." She folded her arms. "I can shift a bit of the glass. Just a flicker, then it's back. If you're fast enough you can slip inside. A little of the water, or whatever, the liquid, will get out. But not much."

"I am fast," Gloom said. "I am a—"

"Saboteur," Bo guessed.

Gloom nodded. "A fast one."

"Alright," Violet said firmly. "I get you in, you untether her. Bo gets the both of you out. We're back in the tunnel before anyone shows up."

Bo nodded, swallowing another lump in his throat. Gloom nodded too, then he turned back into motes and took up position in front of the tank. Violet stepped up beside him, narrowing her eyes. Bo remembered back to the first day he met her, back to the theater, where she'd shifted the chair. Her static was fainter than he remembered it, or maybe it was his that was stronger and he'd gotten used to it. Even so, he felt the hairs on his arms floating.

"That spot level with you," Violet said, drawing a circle in the air with her finger. "Ready?"

"Yes," Gloom whispered.

Violet took a deep breath. "Go."

Static crackled as Gloom sprang through the air in a gleaming black blur. Liquid spat out of the tank in a saline spray that caught Bo in the face, then the glass was sealed shut again and Gloom was swirling around behind it like a cloud of ink. Some of his motes had been blown back by the jet of escaping liquid; when Bo wiped his face he saw them scuttling agitated circles around his feet.

"It worked," Violet said, triumphant. They watched as Gloom slithered up and down Lia's arms, freeing the tubes that hooked into her skin. Bo's own throat clenched as Gloom worked the breathing tube out. It seemed to go on forever. He squeezed his thumb inside his fist watching. Finally the last of the tube slid free and air bubbles started to leak out of his sister's lips.

Gloom's head re-formed beside Lia's and he gave a nod. There were no bubbles coming out of his mouth.

Bo flattened one hand over his stomach, feeling his Parasite. The static swelled. He needed to be perfect. He couldn't overshoot and risk hitting Lia. Or Gloom. And he couldn't leave jagged edges that might cut them on the way through, though he didn't think Gloom could be cut. He felt Violet's steady hand on his shoulder. He inhaled. Exhaled.

Let go.

The static rippled out and suddenly all the tank's blue liquid was gushing out as a wave, crashing into foam against the floor. Lia and Gloom spilled out with it and nearly bowled Bo over. He grabbed for Lia's arm and caught it. Gloom slid a little farther along the floor, sopping up his lost motes, then got to his feet. A familiar vibration was starting to move through the room, but Bo hardly noticed it.

"How long will she be asleep?" he asked, looking at Lia's closed eyes, trying to not look at the rest of her, her nakedness and the purple bruises where the tubes had been inside her. He struggled out of his soaking hoodie and draped it over her.

"Too long," Gloom said. "I will carry her. We have to hurry."

The vibration rattled through the floor. Gloom turned into shadow again, wrapping around Lia's prone body like webbing until she was fully cocooned. Bo checked to be sure her chest was rising and falling. He didn't understand how Gloom was going to move her until a thousand tiny legs sprouted from underneath, raising Lia's stiff body an inch off the floor. They scuttled her past him and down into the hole like an oversized black slug. It looked wrong, and weird, but it obviously worked. Bo hurried after; Violet had already climbed down.

The contents of the tank were still dripping into the tunnel, making it dangerously slick, but Gloom set off at speed and Bo

didn't dare lose sight of his sister again. He and Violet scrambled along as quickly as they could, slipping around, sometimes
banging a head or shoulder against the wall but never stopping.
From above them Bo could feel the alarm's vibration moving
through the ship. There was no way a pod would fit down here,
but a whirlybird would, and the thought of one floating along
behind them with its claw outstretched was another reason to
keep pace.

"We are close to a cargo elevator," came Gloom's disembodied voice. "Rarely used. It will take us to the hull."

"Then we fly?" Bo grunted.

"Yes," Gloom said, then skittered to a halt. "Here. Stop here.
You will need to make another hole, please."

Bo crouched, panting. His knees and wrists were aching
from the long crawl. Violet was massaging a bruise on her
elbow.

"You got enough juice left?" she asked worriedly. "Mine's
dead weight right now."

"I've got enough," Bo said, but he knew it would be a near
thing. His Parasite felt numb and sluggish, spent from freeing
Gloom, from boring through the floor, from vanishing the
tank's glass. It took longer than he liked to dredge up the static.
No sparks and nothing but a weak ripple from the Parasite in
his stomach.

He put his hands up against the roof of the tunnel, and
pushed out every last bit of static he had. The metal ate away
slowly under his fingertips, like something decomposing. He
focused. Focused. There was a strange hissing noise and the
air in the tunnel seemed to be cooling. But he couldn't think
about that. Couldn't think about Lia, couldn't think about anything except the vanish. By the time he finally broke through,

his forehead was drenched in sweat. He'd made a smaller opening than the last time, a tight fit, but they were through.

Bo broke into a relieved grin, and Violet did the same, but it fell away as she looked back down the tunnel. He followed her gaze. A thick blue fog was creeping slowly toward them. Bo saw frost furring the metal nearest it.

"Hurry, children," Gloom said, his voice edged with something that sounded, for the first time, like fear. "Lift us through."

Bo took Lia's shoulders, trying to be as gentle as possible, and Violet took her feet. The motes parted around his hands to give him better grip. His sister's skin was dry now. They pushed her upward, Gloom's motes forming tendrils to get purchase against the sides, and she was through. Violet clambered up next, quick as a gecko. Bo threw one last look back at the fog and realized he could see his breath steaming, could feel the sudden cold on his bare skin. He hauled himself up and out.

Another hall, this one high-vaulted and filled with rows of towering black pillars. Facing them was a massive metal platform shaped like an Aztec pyramid. It looked nothing like the elevator he'd been envisioning, but Gloom was already carrying Lia toward it.

"We are nearly out, Bo and Violet," he said. "We are nearly in the sunshine." He made an inhuman warbling noise that had to be happiness. Bo gave Violet another weary grin as they stumped along behind him, sore all over from hurrying through the cramped tunnel. Nearly out, and Lia with them. Bo felt triumph flaring in his chest. They had Lia. They had an ally. Nearly out.

A sharp high-pitched whine filled his ears and the whirlybirds seemed to come from everywhere at once, streaming from behind the pillars, descending from the vaulted ceiling.

Their claws and needles glinted, extended. Drifting into view behind them, fanning out to block the elevator, were four pods harnessed with the gas guns. The freezing fog was wafting into the air.

Bo's heart dropped.

Gloom stopped short and Bo heard Violet swear from behind him. He reached down for the static but his nerves felt raw and his Parasite wasn't moving.

"No," Gloom hissed. "They are not going to catch me and keep me in the dark again. They are not going to freeze me again. No, no." His motes swirled up and away from Lia's prone body, unwrapping her.

"Wait!" Bo shouted. "Gloom!"

But Gloom was already streaming away, and Lia's body thudded to the floor defenseless as the whirlybirds zeroed in on her.

20

Violet wished she had her bat. But it was back in the theater in her bag—she hadn't dared sneak all the way inside to retrieve it—and with the sheer number of whirlybirds zooming toward them she didn't know how much good it would do anyway.

Gloom was a blur, darting toward the platform, dodging around the whirlys or bursting through them to rearrange himself midair on the other side. The pods were trying to track him with their nozzles. Bo was racing the nearest whirlybird to his sister, who'd been left splayed out on the floor, all limbs.

And Violet was standing here doing nothing. She sprang after Bo, two long strides to get to him and his sister, then pulled him down just as the first whirlybird swooped in at them from the side. Its claw grazed his shoulder blade; she heard the fabric of his shirt tear. A second whirlybird was bearing down on them and the first was coming back around for another go.

"Drag her," Violet panted. "Have to try to get to the elevator. Pods are looking at Gloom, not us." She hooked Lia's underarm and Bo, eyes wide and frantic, took the other. They made it only a step before the whirlybirds were on them again.

Violet swung blind with her fist and connected with a part that wasn't sharp, knocking the first whirly off course, but the second slipped under her flailing arm, its syringe aimed for Bo's neck, and—

Something black and gleaming erupted from it like a geyser and the whirlybird spun wild, crashing to the floor beside them. The syringe flew past Violet's face an inch from her eyeball. There wasn't time for a thank-you. Gloom was already off again, springing away, searching for a gap as the pods closed ranks. One fired; she saw the gas jet out in a frosty plume and glance Gloom in midair. There was a horrible grinding shriek and part of him seemed to shatter, dropping instantly to the floor in dead disparate motes.

Bo was slinging his sister onto his back, bent nearly double. "Can't do a vanish," he choked. "Parasite's tired. Can't do anything."

Violet's eyes landed on the carcass of the whirlybird Gloom had downed, still hemorrhaging sparks. She jammed her shoe against its joint and yanked an arm free. It wasn't heavy enough to swing, not really, but it was better than nothing.

Bo stumped forward, pulling his sister's slack arms tight around his neck. Violet followed, waving the stiff whirlybird arm back and forth, trying to keep the others off them. The whirlybirds were stupid, moving at straight angles, never feinting or swerving, always aiming at Bo and Lia, but they were endless. Violet jabbed, retreated, jabbed again. One got through and caught hold of Lia's arm before she managed to batter it off. Blood oozed out of the gash, slower than it should have, more like syrup. Violet only had a millisecond to wince at that before the next whirly swooped at them.

Through the swarm, she saw that Gloom, or at least most of

him, had gotten past the pods. He was swirling up the base of the platform. She heard the sound of machinery coming to life, humming and whirring. The platform started, slowly, to rise. Violet felt a tight panic in her chest. Gloom was getting out no matter what, spooked by the gas, scared to go back to the cell. He was getting out whether the rest of them did or not.

Then the platform jerked to a halt. Maybe malfunctioning, or maybe Gloom was giving them a chance.

"Let me carry her," Violet ordered. Bo hesitated for a split second, then slipped Lia off his back and helped move her onto Violet's. She straightened up, caught her balance, and they ran. The whirlybirds had mostly stopped; they were turning away, distracted. Violet didn't understand why until she saw that Gloom had flattened himself onto one of the pod's backs, clinging there like a second skin, and the other three pods were circling it, reluctant to use the freezing gas and hit one of their own. The whirlybirds were going to peel him off.

The platform started to rise again, creaking and grinding. Violet broke into a sprint, off-balance, nearly spilling on every step. Bo was running along beside her, his jaw clenched hard. Eyes forward. Eyes on the platform. They hurtled under the distracted pods and up the wide cubic steps, and Violet finally did trip, sprawling forward, but Bo was there to yank her upright again. He vaulted up onto the platform, then splayed out on his belly, reaching down for his sister. Violet boosted her up with a hard shoulder. Bo pulled her the rest of the way, then Violet sprang herself.

Bo snapped to her hand with both of his, straining as the platform ground its way upward, and Violet realized they were going to make it. She wormed her elbows onto the edge, then her ribs, then all of her, rolling over to lie flat on the metal. Her ears roared; her heart pounded. The Parasite in her stomach was awake again, feeding off the rush.

She heaved herself upright just in time to see the three pods fire on the fourth, three jets of the icy blue gas lancing into the air. Gloom sprang away, snapping through the space like a black snake, and slapped against the edge of the platform. He wriggled up, over, and burst into a living cloud of motes again. She saw flashes of his suit and his pale hands, like he was trying to re-form his human shape but couldn't quite manage it.

"The controls, the controls," he rasped. "More speed."

He splashed over to the corner of the platform where exposed circuitry was fizzing sparks, past Bo, who was holding tight to Lia. The platform lurched and Violet lost her balance, thumped down to her hands and knees. She looked up. They were heading toward a square-shaped opening in the roof, but the pods were rising with them, staying level. She saw the nozzles take aim.

"Gloom!" she hollered.

In jerky film, the jet of gas flung out toward him and he burst around it, letting it pass through a perfectly parted gap in his motes.

And strike Bo instead. Bo dropped, sprawling forward and losing his grip on his sister's arm just as the platform gave another sharp lurch. Violet was jerked off balance, and as she tumbled back she saw Lia's body ragdoll up and over her brother's. Bo reached, but slow, clumsy, and Lia slipped over the edge. Violet threw herself forward on her stomach.

Lia was plummeting away from the platform, limp limbs flailing, but just as Violet braced to see the impact, a pod snatched her out of the air. The platform accelerated. Violet pulled back from the edge an instant before they hurtled through the ceiling, into the shaft, slamming into the grooves, leaving the pods and the whirlybirds and Bo's sister all behind.

Bo struggled upright with a howl torn out of his belly. His shirt tugged at his skin, frozen to it, and he felt a burning sensation all up and down his back, like touching a metal door handle in winter but a thousand times worse, but it didn't matter because Lia was gone. He'd seen the pod grab her. She would go back into the tank. They would put the tubes in her again and put her back to sleep and she wouldn't know he had ever been there.

"We have to go back down," he gasped. "Gloom, we have to go back down, take us back down..." They were still shooting upward like a rocket, climbing toward a dim gray square of light. Bo crawled to the corner where Gloom was crouched, human-shaped again, his long skinny hand buried in the peeled-open circuitry of the controls. "We have to go back," he snarled. "You have to take us back down, we have to get her back—"

"No," Gloom said flatly.

Bo threw himself at him, raining blows on his chest, grabbing for his arm, but his hands sank deep and then Gloom was slipping around him, through his fingers, re-forming on the other corner of the platform. Violet was sitting there panting for breath, her hands clenched to her sides. She said something Bo couldn't hear. He lunged for the gash in the metal where Gloom had stuck his fingers, thinking maybe he could stop the platform, maybe he could turn them around.

Spidery hands yanked him back by the shoulders; he felt his skin tear. He gave a scream that was half pain, half fury. Lia, Lia, Lia, tumbling over the edge and out of sight and he'd reached but couldn't grab her. He wrestled against Gloom's grip.

"We are not going back down," Gloom hissed. "We are lucky

to escape at all. They were waiting for us. They knew where we were."

Bo kept twisting, kept fighting, until finally he gave up on freeing himself and was only slamming his fists against the metal platform, over and over, skinning his knuckles raw. Finally he stopped that too, and sat there with his whole body heaving around a sob. The platform had decelerated but they were still moving steadily upward. Away from Lia.

"We're coming back for her," Violet said in his ear. "We had to come back anyway. For the other kids. She'll be fine, Bo. The pod caught her." Her hand touched his back, then darted away when he flinched and settled on his bare arm instead. Bo sucked in a trembling breath. Another. She was right. They'd always planned to come back. But he still felt like his chest was speared through.

Gloom released him at last and drew himself up to his full height, then higher, his limbs becoming impossibly long and spindly. He loomed over them like a shadow. His dark eyes were fixed on Violet.

"How did they know, Violet?" His voice was soft but clear, clipped and dangerous. "How did they know where we were emerging from the tunnel? Did you tell them?"

Bo choked out a laugh at the absurdity, but he felt Violet stiffen beside him. Her hand left his forearm.

"What do you have in your pocket, Violet?" Gloom asked. "I thought it smelled like them. But my senses were so full of their dank dead metal." His face twisted into exaggerated rage. "I should have tasted it. I should have made sure."

Bo looked up at her, to share her confusion, but his eyes were drawn to her jacket instead. She had her hand clenched hard around something inside her left pocket. Bo got slowly to his feet, facing her, as she pulled out a black baseball–sized sphere. He had seen those before. He knew what it was. He swallowed.

"Why do you have that?" he asked. His mind was already cycling through the possibilities; he grasped at the one he wanted to believe. "That's the one Wyatt dropped," he said. "In the storage unit. You picked it up?"

He was willing her to say yes, say she'd grabbed it not knowing what it was and forgotten she had it with her. He remembered the pod pulling the identical spheres out over and over. *How they communicate,* Wyatt had said.

Violet slowly shook her head. "They gave it to me," she said in a strangled whisper. "The night I left. They were waiting for me at my house. They gave it to me then."

I made a deal, Wyatt had said, tossing the black sphere up and down.

"Why?" Bo demanded, almost snarled the word. He could feel new tears smarting his eyes. Blinked them back hard.

"They wanted me to bring you to them," Violet said shakily. "But—"

"You liar." Bo felt fresh rage pour through him like gasoline. His skin flushed with it; his Parasite twitched to life too little too late. "You said you needed my help. Your note. You said you needed my help, you liar, liar, *liar.*"

The last word was a shout and the static made his clothing crackle, made sparks halo around his head. He didn't need it now. He'd needed it down there, with the pods and the whirlys.

"You're the one who's like Wyatt. Not me. You're a liar like him. Making people do what you want." He searched for a way to hurt her, for words that would make her feel how he was feeling. He bared his teeth. "No wonder you loved him so much."

Violet flinched back like he'd slapped her. Her nostrils flared. "Oh, no," she snapped. "No, you don't get to talk. You're the reason all this happened. You swore you wouldn't tell anyone. Remember? You swore on your *sister.*"

Bo felt a surge of guilt; he shoved it aside. "So you were going to just switch sides? Give me to the aliens to make things even?"

"I didn't bring you here," Violet shouted. "The pod did. It brought us both. Who saved you from Wyatt, huh? Who helped get your sister out of that tank? I should have fucking handed you over. You know what they were going to give me?"

"Why do you still have it, then?" Bo demanded, pointing at the sphere in her fist. "That's how they knew. That's how they tracked us, I bet. I bet they can see where it is and—"

"They were going to give me my family back!" Violet screamed. She was shaking, her ears were bright red. "I was going to get my family back. But better. They were going to give me my life back, but better. I was going to be a perfect fucking girl with perfect fucking parents and everything I fuck-ing wanted. I was going to be a waster." All the energy seemed to leave her body at once and she slumped to the floor of the platform. "But I decided to get you your family instead," she said heavily. "Your real one. What's left of it."

Bo thought of Violet sneaking out of the theater, night after night, going to spend hours in her old house with her parents, who couldn't speak or even see her. He thought of Lia, who he'd sworn on, being put back in the tank. He sank down too, sitting with his arms wrapped around his knees. His shirt pulled against his back and seared but the pain was almost wel-come now. He felt like he deserved it.

Gloom was standing off to the side, looking at both of them, his expression blank and unreadable again. The platform kept rising.

The dim gray square above them widened and widened, until Bo could hear the howl of the wind across the top of the shaft and see the cloudy gray sky. He didn't speak, and neither did Violet, and neither did Gloom. He thought the elevator might keep rising forever and they would all be stuck sitting there, saying nothing, but at last the platform ground to a halt a meter from the top of the shaft. Wind whistled over them. Bo knew they needed to move. Knew more pods had to be coming after them. But standing up and walking away would mean leaving Lia behind all over again.

Gloom turned his face skyward. "Where is the sun?" he asked, breaking the silence.

Violet ignored him. Bo looked up. "What do you mean?" he said dully. "It's cloudy. It's been cloudy for months."

"I need more light," Gloom said. His voice was fearful. "I thought there would be more light. Do you understand photovores, Bo?"

Violet finally raised her head. "Can you fly us still?" she asked.

Gloom's face twisted. "Maybe one," he said. "Maybe one of you."

Violet snorted. She didn't look surprised. She looked like she was nearly going to laugh. "Then go, Bo," she said.

"Bullshit," Bo said fiercely, surprising himself. "Both of us go or neither of us. You want me to leave you behind so you can hate me."

"You're the one who got the perfect Parasite, remember?" Violet said. "If they get you, they bring their other ships and they do this to the rest of the world. I don't hate people that much." She blinked. "And you I don't hate at all. I don't blame you for telling Wyatt. What happened would have happened eventually. No matter what."

Bo looked down at the space between his feet and took a ragged breath. "You're not like Wyatt," he said slowly. "You're nothing like him. You're... You're like my other sister."

"Like, your othersister?" Violet said. She tried to smile. "Pooh Bear, honey, Pooh Bear, honey." She put on a shrill voice for it but it turned thick with a sob.

The floor of the platform shook; Gloom slithered up and out, onto the hull of the ship. "They regained control of the elevator," he said. "Hurry, please."

Bo got shakily to his feet, still looking at Violet. "No," he said, feeling hot tears in his eyes. "I don't mean that. I mean—"

"I know, Bo," Violet said, tired-sounding. "Just go, okay?"

The platform started to sink.

"I am coming back," he choked. "For you and Lia and everyone."

"Alright," Violet said, wiping her nose with her sleeve. "Now go."

Bo took a running leap up the wall and Gloom caught him under his arms, hauled him over the edge. Then Violet was sinking out of sight, down into the shadows, and even with Gloom swirling all around him Bo felt as alone as he'd ever felt. He stood up.

21

The hull of the ship was an enormous black plain, burnished smooth in places, pitted and scarred in others. Bo was small as an insect by comparison. They were near the edge of it, a sheer cliff dropping away. Gloom slithered toward it, craned over to look, slithered back.

"From here," he said, re-forming, cracking his long fingers. "We will jump from here."

"You said you can fly," Bo said automatically.

"I can fly," Gloom said. "We will jump, and then we will fly." He paused, grave-looking. "I know it is difficult to leave motes behind. I feel like less than myself. Is that how you feel?"

"Yeah," Bo said, rubbing his eyes. "I guess, yeah. A lot like that."

Gloom looked at him for a moment but said nothing else. He jerked his head and walked over to the edge. Bo followed, taking slow, bracing steps against the gusting wind. He flattened himself down to stick his head out over the drop. The dizziness hit him instantly.

Spinning out underneath him, too tiny to be real, he saw what was left of the city. The stalled cars on the roads looked like toys. The burned-down buildings were smudges of charcoal. He tried to see something he recognized, to make sense of the scale, but had to pull back before he could. His stomach had already plunged off the edge, dropping, dropping. Bo scooted another foot backward and took a deep breath.

Higher than the high-diving board. A hundred times higher. But Lia was counting on him, and now Violet was too.

"The elevator," Gloom said urgently.

Bo got to his feet and looked back the way they'd come, hoping, irrationally, to see Violet clambering up out of the shaft. The pods came instead. Only two of them, though. Maybe Violet was inside one of them. Maybe Lia. Bo's Parasite surged and for a moment he wanted to stay, to fight, but he knew he would lose in the end.

"Okay," he said. "Let's do it."

Gloom nodded and turned into the motes again, flowing up Bo's arms, wrapping around his midsection, feeling like cold sand where they touched his bare skin. Bo clenched his teeth as they hugged tight to his back. The pain across his shoulder blades had dulled to a steady throb but spiked again as the motes rasped against his shirt. He thought he knew what he would find when he peeled the fabric away later, the skin all shiny and purple. He'd seen photos of frostbite.

The pods were drifting closer now, unhurried. Maybe they didn't know that Gloom could fly. Bo figured they would now, as the motes finished enveloping his torso and two massive wings sprouted. Gloom had shown them off in the cell, but they seemed bigger now, stretching out to either side of him, skinned a smooth featureless black. They caught the wind and nearly blew Bo off his feet before they sucked back into Gloom's body.

"I will extend after you dive," Gloom's voice echoed in his ear. "When we are clear of the ship."

Bo wished he hadn't used the word *dive*. He shot a glance back at the pods, still coming, still unhurried, then went to the edge. He felt slow-rising bubbles of fear making their way up from his gut. His legs were suddenly shaky, like all the bone had gone out of them, and his heart was pounding. He remembered what he'd said to Violet, about trusting Gloom all the way, or actually about not trusting him.

He had to trust Gloom all the way now. Bo flexed his knees, swung his arms. He tried to imagine a swimming pool down below, with Lia doing her casual backstroke and shouting for him to hurry up, jump, just jump already. He remembered how she'd jeered at first and then softened. *I'll give you a countdown,* she'd said. *We'll count together from three.*

The pods were still coming slowly. Maybe they didn't think he was going to do it. Maybe they were right.

Do I go on the one or the zero? he'd shouted down to her, trying to delay it a little longer.

The zero, she'd said. *But we don't say the zero. Ready?*

The pods didn't know that people were so crazy they jumped from high-up places for fun, and they jumped from even higher ones if their lives depended on it.

"Ready?" Bo muttered.

"Yes," Gloom said. "Are you?"

Bo didn't trust himself to say anything else without throwing up. The count was already going in his head. He turned back to the pods one last time to flip them the bird, hoping they remembered the gesture. Then he ate the space in three quick strides and dove off the edge of the ship.

Down.

The ruined city rushed up at him impossibly fast, air collapsing away beneath him. He felt the speed bending his spine, yanking back his eyelids, ballooning his cheeks. He knew he was screaming but he couldn't hear it over the roar in his ears. He could only feel it in his vibrating chest.

Gloom's wings snapped out, jarring him as they caught wind. Bo's bones shook with it. He knew he was still falling but it felt like they'd jerked to a halt, suspended in the air. He turned his scream into a triumphant whoop as they started to bank in a wide looping circle. Gloom's huge moth wings beat once. Twice. Bo swallowed his spit and tried to unclench his fists. He'd nearly punctured his palms with his nails.

Looking down still dizzied him, but he could make out the city below. He recognized the downtown from the skyscrapers that hadn't toppled. He tried to find the ave, the brick-and-metal roof of the theater, wondering if anyone was up there to see him flying.

A sudden lurch snapped his head back; his teeth slammed shut and he nearly bit the tip of his tongue off. He craned his aching neck to the side. What he saw made his fists clench up again. Gloom's outstretched wing was trembling, pocked with tiny holes. More and more of them started to open and the air shrieked through; Bo could see individual motes in the wing tremble and come apart from the others.

"I lost so many motes." Gloom's voice was a panicked groan in Bo's ear. "And there is not enough sunlight. It is possible this was careless. Sometimes I am careless."

Bo's breath stuck to his ribs. "Don't drop me," he said. "Please don't drop me."

"I am your friend, Bo," Gloom said, sounding hurt. "I will not drop you." A ripple went through his wings. "You might still die, though," he added. "When we hit the ground. We are falling too fast."

"Aim for water," Bo said, his mind racing. "If you can, aim us for the docks. Set us down in the water."

"The wind is carrying us," Gloom said. His voice was strained. "I cannot aim. I am concentrating very hard on not falling apart."

Bo looked down and wished he hadn't. The city was hurling up at them and they were heading down into the center of it, nowhere near the sea. "Can you make a parachute?" he demanded. "Do you know what parachutes are?"

Gloom said nothing, but slowly, slowly, his wings curled upward and melded over Bo's head in a loop, re-forming into a single piece. It buffered them; Bo felt another teeth-rattling jerk as they shed some speed. But they were still dropping. Quickly.

Bo remembered his mom reading some story about a window-washer who fell from the top floor of a hotel and lived. The man had realized he was going to die, and accepted it, and had been so relaxed that when he hit the asphalt he bounced like rubber. Bo tried to relax his muscles, but every part of him was tight with terror.

There was a rending noise and he looked up to see a wide gash tear through the parachute. Wind snagged the rip and suddenly they were somersaulting, spinning wild. Everything was a blur. In the corner of his eye Bo saw Gloom's parachute dissolve to waving black tendrils, felt them slithering over him. It was a free fall now. He saw a snatch of the ship far above them, then the ground rushing up at them. He knew he was going to die, but all he could think about was Lia in the tank, and how maybe now Violet was in the one beside her.

A flash of twisted rebar, blackened cement, his shattered

reflection in a broken glass window as they plunged past a half-torched skyscraper. Bo knew he was going to die, and then Gloom was wrapping all around him, cocooning him, sealing over his eyes so all he saw was black. All he could hear was his hammering heart.

22

Violet woke up to sunshine streaming through her bedroom window. For a moment she was adrift, disembodied, but then she felt her sunk-in-the-middle mattress under her and sheets twined around her legs. She rolled over and sank her face into her pillow, breathing the familiar smell in deep. She ran her hands down her body and her breath caught. It was *right*, again. It put an ache in her throat.

"Not real," she mumbled into the pillow. "Not real."

She'd been caught. She remembered that. Remembered the long agonizing ride back down the elevator shaft and the whirlybird who'd been waiting for her with its syringe glinting, dripping sedative. Now she could be anywhere. Inside a pod, inside a tank. Inside her head, that much she knew for sure.

"Violet!" called her mom's voice. "Are you up?"

For a moment she wondered what would happen if she just stayed in the bed. But wherever she was, they hadn't killed her. It would have been easy to impale her how they'd done to Quentin and dump her body off the ship. She was still alive. They had her plugged into their illusion again. That meant they wanted to talk, and she figured she didn't want to piss them off any more than she already had helping Bo escape.

She got up, intentionally ignoring the mirror. Instead she slipped out the door, toward the kitchen. In the hallway she saw photos of herself as a little girl, photos that had never existed. There was one of her and her mom and her dad at some beach, all smiling and sunburned. Had those been there the first time? Had she missed them?

In the kitchen, the younger, prettier, happier version of her mom was sitting at the table. She had no sketchbook this time. Her hands were folded on top of each other on the wood.

"Hello, Violet," she said.

"Hi," Violet said. She nearly called her Mom, but it stuck in her mouth. This wasn't her mom. It was just as much a photo as the ones in the hallway frames.

"Why did you renege?" her not-mom asked. "We thought you wanted this." She waved a hand to encompass her house, her body, her life. "We were willing to make heaven for you. In exchange we wanted what grows in Bo."

Violet gave a start hearing her say Bo instead of Boniface, how the othermothers did, but of course this was all happening inside her head. Maybe she was clamped already. Maybe she was down on the ground, wandering, smiling.

"I went back on it because this is all bullshit," Violet said quietly. "How I think of bullshit."

"We do not need what grows in Bo any longer," her not-mom said, lacing her fingers together, smiling kindly. "Another key is nearly ready. Perhaps two. But you freed our ancient enemy, and that cannot be excused."

"He doesn't seem that scary," Violet said.

"We would have made heaven for you, Violet," her not-mom said, no longer smiling. "We can make hell too."

Violet felt a hot, sick fear run through her at the words. Before she could say anything else, before she could argue or plead, the bright clean kitchen flickered and fell away.

"Bo. Bo. Bo. Bo. Bo."

Bo wrenched his eyes open, ready for impact, ready to slam and splatter against the paving. The scream caught in his throat as he realized he wasn't falling. He was lying on his stomach on solid ground. He found himself in pieces, his cheek resting against his forearm, his hip pressed into what felt like loose dirt. Dry grass tickled his belly. His shirt was off. He was on the ground. He was alive.

"Are you going to stay awake this time, Bo?" came Gloom's voice in his ear.

"What happened?" Bo asked, or tried to ask. His tongue was thick and dry. He could sideways-see Gloom's immaculate black shoes and pant legs.

"Your body is not so fragile as it looks," Gloom said, crouching beside him. "Congratulations. You survived the fall. You are intact. Barely damaged."

Bo licked his lips. "You wrapped me up," he said hoarsely. Memories were swimming back up through his aching head. "Before we hit."

"Yes," Gloom said. "I tried to cushion your delicate animal spine and skull."

"My spine's not delicate," Bo muttered. He got up to his hands and knees and retched, his head spinning again. Gloom's words came back. "Barely damaged," he echoed. "What's that mean, barely damaged?" He felt numb through his whole body and had a sudden fear that there was a rib sticking out of his chest, or his shin was snapped in two. Gloom came apart all the time. He might not even understand injuries.

"Contusions," Gloom said.

Bo grimaced. "What?"

"That is a word that means bruising."

"What about my head?" Bo asked. "I got knocked out when we hit?"

"Your brain collided with the inside of your delicate animal skull," Gloom said.

"Concussion," Bo said. The nausea welled up again. His Parasite was awake and whipping around. He tried to calm it, putting a hand to his stomach. "My shirt?" he asked thickly. "Oh. My back?"

"The freezing gas is more dangerous to me than it is to you," Gloom said. "There was no permanent damage and there were no burst blood vessels. I looked."

Bo's head was starting to clear. He could still feel where the jet of gas had raked across his back, but it was muted now, more pins-and-needles tingling than an actual burn. The rest of him was sore and aching, and he was ravenously hungry. The gray sky made it hard to tell, but he guessed it was afternoon already.

His stomach gave a loud gurgle.

"I found food for you," Gloom said. "It is sealed. You requested that, the last time you were speaking." His long pale hand reached down into view and set a tin on the ground. Bo grabbed it and yanked it open so quick he nearly cut his thumb on the edge. It was tinned peaches. He scooped the contents into his mouth with two fingers, then drizzled the syrup onto his tongue. His stomach gurgled even louder.

"I assume you need to eat in order to repair the damage to your body," Gloom said, setting down a second tin.

"I told you to get this?" Bo asked. He rocked back into sitting position to wolf down the second tin. He licked his thumb and fingers, getting every last bit of the juice.

"You seemed lucid at the time," Gloom said. He was still standing, staring down at him. "A host saw me when I was looking for the food. A child. I think I frightened him."

Bo wasn't listening. He leaned over as his stomach heaved and at least half the peaches came back up in a yellow-orange mush. He spat.

"Is that how you typically eat?" Gloom asked. "You refine and regurgitate it first?"

Bo shook his head, clutching his stomach. His Parasite twitched. When the nausea had passed, he shakily stood up, walked a few feet away from the vomit, and sat again. He realized they were on a lawn. The house behind them was open, the front door creaking back and forth on its hinges, and he figured it was where Gloom had gotten the food from. He wondered if there were wasters inside.

"Water," he said. "Was there water in there?"

Gloom held out a capped bottle. "You asked that before too."

It was lukewarm and tasted like plastic, but it was better than nothing. Bo drank it slowly until his thirst was quenched and his stomach soothed. Gloom watched him intently, expectantly. As Bo's thoughts sharpened, he felt a creeping dread. They had escaped from the ship, but Lia was still up there and they'd lost Violet too. And if Gloom couldn't fly, how were they ever going to get back aboard? He kept sipping the water, to make it last, to give him time to think.

But he didn't have a plan. He'd never had a plan, not really. Just stupid little fantasies that skipped to him already halfway through rescuing everyone.

"You said this ship is the only ship," he muttered, grasping for threads to tie together. "So if the rest of the world is okay, why hasn't anyone come to help us? Is it the mist?"

"Your city is being contained," Gloom said. "That is why the sky does not change. That is why there is not enough sunlight."

"And you can't get past the end of the world either?" Bo asked. "I mean, through the container?"

Gloom gave a rueful shrug that reminded him of Violet. Maybe he'd copied it off her. "Perhaps I could," he said. "But only if there was more sunlight. Do you know paradoxes, Bo?"

"No," Bo said. "I don't know plans either." He ballooned his cheeks around a long sigh. "You got ideas?" he asked. "For getting the other keys?"

"I am a saboteur," Gloom said, his voice flat and accusing. "I react and improvise. I do not have enough motes for complex strategy."

He stared at him with his shiny black eyes and said nothing else. For a moment Bo wanted to scream at him how he was only a kid, and everything was getting too big. The keys, the door, the other ships waiting to come through and end the world. Then he remembered what he'd told Gloom up on the ship. About trusting them. About coming back with a plan.

"I bet you wish you killed all the ones in all the tanks," he said heavily. "And then mine and Violet's too. Right?"

"Perhaps," Gloom said.

Bo was twisting the empty plastic bottle in his hands, crumpling it. He stopped. Looked from the bottle to the scattered tins. Something Gloom had said earlier floated back to the surface.

"What did you say about a kid?" he asked. "When you were looking for food. Someone saw you?"

"Yes," Gloom said. "I think I frightened him."

One of the Lost Boys. Bo wondered who it had been. Jon never looked frightened. Maybe Elliot out foraging, or maybe Gloom had thought Bree was a boy. Everything that had happened aboard the ship had driven the other Lost Boys out of his head entirely.

"Are there many free children?" Gloom asked. "Did they escape?"

"Yeah, some," Bo said, feeling a new kind of dread now as he realized his best, maybe his only, option. And he wasn't trying to decide whether or not to do it either. He was only trying to decide how.

He rubbed his neck where he could still almost feel the ghost of a knife. It would be different, this time. He knew what he was getting into. He had Gloom to back him up.

"Yeah, there's some," Bo repeated. "And there's one who makes plans. Who's always got one."

Gloom leaned forward, his face switching over to look intrigued. "Is he known as a great tactician?" he asked. "Is he the one who sent you to the ship?"

"Sort of," Bo said, with an icy ball growing in his stomach, his Parasite flexing at the memory. "Yeah. Sort of. He was trying to kill me."

"You have very untrustworthy friends, Bo," Gloom said. "You are lucky to have met me."

Bo grimaced. "Right."

23

Something prodded the back of Violet's knee, making her whole leg buckle. She spun around. It was Stephen Fletcher, grinning his wolfish grin.

"Why are you walking funny?" he asked.

Violet ignored him, looking around. Mustard-yellow floors, dull gray lockers scribbled over with Sharpie, humming fluorescents tubed along the ceiling. Junior high school.

"Really?" she muttered.

"You walk like you have a cock up your ass," Stephen Fletcher said. Still small and beady-eyed and vicious, just like she remembered him. But junior high seemed like a lifetime ago. So did high school. So did everything before the ship came down.

She dropped the binder from her arms. Loose-leaf and a few splintery black pens spilled out on the yellow floor. She turned and headed down the empty hallway, dimly aware of Stephen Fletcher trailing after her, still running his mouth. Hell was a bit of a moving target, she figured. It definitely didn't involve her school bullies anymore.

Still, she was hoping there might be a way out of the illusion.

She'd never tried it when she was in her perfect house. She hadn't even opened the front door. Better to be looking for an escape than sitting around while simulated assholes tried to lower her self-esteem.

On cue, a shove between her shoulder blades sent her stumbling into a bulletin board. "Faggot," Stephen said. "You faggot."

Violet took a deep breath. In, out. She picked one of the thumbtacks out of the cork, sagging one corner of a sign-up sheet. Then she spun around, grabbed Stephen's wrist, and shoved the point of the tack into his open palm. She ground it deep with the heel of her hand for good measure. He wailed.

She set off back down the hall, opening doors at random. Some of them had normal-looking classrooms behind them; others had only a white haze, sometimes with a narrow slice of floor, wall, desk. The ones she'd never been inside, maybe. Stephen trailed after her, whining about his hand and telling a teacher, but they seemed to be the only ones in the school. She stomped on his foot a few times to slow him down.

She knew he wasn't real, but it was still a little disturbing how easy she found hurting him. Violence came almost naturally to her, now that she'd killed a dozen othermothers. Now that she'd spent so long listening to Wyatt.

When they came to the front doors of the school, she shoved them open and stepped through. Rather than the street outside, there was an endless white plain, everything blank. It ached her eyes like fresh snow in sunlight. They hadn't bothered to finish the level.

"You can't leave," Stephen said, grating in her ear.

"I have a sick note," she said. "Piss off." She took a tentative step and found invisible flooring supporting her. She walked out into the void, somehow feeling no vertigo.

"You cannot leave, because there is nowhere to go," Stephen said, not sounding like Stephen anymore.

Violet kept walking, plunging into the blank space. She wondered if it was like the fog, if she would end up walking in place forever, but then everything flickered dark.

Gel creeping down her throat, gagging her. Warm pressure on her skin. Floating, suspended, weightless. Everything black. She tried to force her eyes open, tried to—

Violet blinked, back in the white space. She set off again, determined, pushing at the boundary. She knew it wasn't real. If she knew it wasn't real, she could make herself wake up, and maybe she could even get out. She tried to picture the reality. Tried to picture herself inside the pod.

They were walking toward the theater, or at least Bo hoped they were. Gloom had crashed down in a part of the city he didn't know well. Lots of newer houses, some empty lots. Bo figured so long as they were walking toward the city center, they would hit the ave. Whoever Gloom had seen foraging must have been on a bike, because it was turning out to be a long, long walk.

Bo's head was feeling better and he'd eaten again, finding a new shirt on the same detour. The gnawing feeling in his stomach was now nervousness, not hunger. He didn't know what the Lost Boys would do when he showed up with Gloom. He didn't know what Wyatt had told them.

"Are you shorter?" Bo asked, looking over at his companion. He wanted something to fill the silence. Gloom's steps didn't make any sound, so it was more like walking with a shadow than a person. They'd only seen a few wasters out, and no other-mothers, which was strange.

"You look a little shorter," he pressed. "Than before, on the ship."

"I lost many motes," Gloom said dourly. "I am smaller."

"You can get them back when we get Lia and Violet," Bo suggested.

Gloom gave a resigned shrug. "Some of them. Maybe."

"Sorry I vanished that one," Bo said, remembering back to the tank room, remembering Gloom's shocked then angry face when the single mote disappeared.

"It is very far away," Gloom said. "I can barely feel it."

His baleful tone made Bo think he didn't want to discuss it any further, but Bo's curiosity was piqued and it was better than thinking about what might happen when they got to the theater.

"What do you mean it's far away?" he asked.

"It is in another cluster of stars," Gloom said. "It is where the other ships are waiting for the door to be opened."

Bo stopped walking. It was bizarre to think about, that he'd never really been *vanishing* things at all. He'd been sending them away to some other dimension, or some other galaxy, or something. The image popped into his head of the other-mother he'd disappeared, now floating around somewhere in outer space, covered in ice, maybe with its skull exploded from the vacuum. He'd seen that on a movie, he was pretty sure. So, if he vanished a person...

Bo winced.

"But you can still feel it?" he asked, starting to walk again. "It's still, you know, alive?"

"You have a very narrow definition of alive and not alive," Gloom said. "But yes. I can still feel it. Motes are always drawn to their own. Do you know quantum entanglement, Bo?"

"No," Bo said. He rubbed his head, feeling the prickle of growing hair. "If I can send things over there, why can't they send the ships here already?" he asked, voicing the question that had been bubbling up in the back of his mind. "Don't they have Parasites on the other side? Keys? Why fly the one ship here at all?"

"There must be a key on this side to open the door," Gloom said. He looked pained. "You understand," he said slowly, "that it is not a door like the doors you have on your houses?"

Bo snorted. "I figured, yeah."

"It is not wood," Gloom said. "It does not have a doorknob."

"I know," Bo said sourly. "It's like a portal. Like a black hole, or something. Something with a lot of"—he paused—"physics shit," he finished, thinking of how Violet would put it. They started down an alley that looked halfway familiar.

"Yes," Gloom said, with a serious nod. "Your key is tuned, but each time you send matter through the door, it seals shut immediately after. If they caught you, they would have put you into a machine. The machine would have amplified and sustained the energy of your key. The door would have been held open, and the ships on the other side would have come through."

"Maybe you should have sabotaged that machine," Bo said, aiming a kick at an empty pop can.

Gloom bristled, the motes of his shoulders jumping out and back in. "Are you a saboteur, Bo?" he asked. "Are you known among your people as a—"

"Hey, look." Bo had recognized the corner of an office building he knew was on the ave. "I know where we are," he said. "We'll be at the theater soon." The momentary relief turned quickly back to nerves. He glanced over at Gloom. "Do you have to look like that?" he asked.

"I do not have to look like anything," Gloom said.

They emerged from the alley, on a street Bo now realized was only a couple of blocks off the theater.

"Creepy, I mean," he clarified. "You look like a bogeyman."

Gloom's face turned into a pantomime of confusion. "I thought this shape would be comforting to you," he said. "Children are comforted by adults who appear taller and more capable than them." He paused, then turned back into a seething shadow. "I could look like Violet, if you want."

Bo watched with a queasy fascination as the motes re-formed into a perfect replica of his friend, clad in the exact same clothes, standing with the exact same posture, hands in her pockets.

"Or I could look like the sleeping girl," Gloom said, as Violet's face dissolved into a swirl of black motes. Lia's face started to emerge, eyes shut like they'd been in the tank, and Bo felt his stomach drop.

"No!" he said. "No. Don't look like her."

Violet's face reformed, looking quizzical. "Very well," Gloom said. "Should I look like Violet? Is it better if your friends think that I am Violet?"

Bo gave a pained shrug. "They'll know it's not her as soon as you talk," he said. "You don't sound anything like her. Just. Just look how you want."

Gloom turned back into his usual gaunt self, adjusting his black hat. "I suppose it is too late for disguises," he said. "I think those two hosts have been watching us." He pointed one spidery finger.

Bo turned just in time to see a small blurred figure duck out from behind a rusting car and hurtle at his midsection.

"Bo!" Gilly hollered. "You're not dead, Bo!" Her skinny arms were wrapped so tightly around him he could barely pry her off. "He's not dead, Bree!" she beamed, as Bree stepped out more cautiously from behind the SUV.

"Hey, Gilly," Bo said, grinning despite himself. "Hey, Bree."

It felt like he'd been gone a much longer time than he really had. So much had happened since they brought down the pod, since Violet ran out of the theater, since Wyatt tried to slice him open and they'd been carried off to the ship. He'd actually missed Gilly. He'd missed the other Lost Boys too.

"Hey, Bo," Bree said. She wasn't smiling. Her eyes were fixed on Gloom. "Who's this guy?"

Gloom swept his hat off his head and gave a deep bow. "I am called Gloom," he said.

Bo could see down into the jagged black crown of his skull and realized it was mostly hollow. He hoped Bree didn't have the same view. She looked almost ready to grab Gilly and bolt.

"He's on our side," Bo said. "He was a prisoner up on the ship. We freed him."

"Who's we?" Bree asked, squinting at him. "Get over here, Gills."

"But it's Bo," Gilly said, still hanging onto his arm, swinging it back and forth, grinning wide.

"He looks like Bo," Bree said. "That thing looked like Violet a minute ago. Get over here, *now*."

Gilly's grin slid off her face, and a second later her fingers slid off his arm. She scooted back over to where Bree was standing. She watched him now with her forehead creased, her lips pursed. Bo felt an ache in his chest. He hadn't known what kind of welcome to expect, but he'd thought they'd at least know it was him.

"It is me," Bo croaked. "Come on, Bree. You shaved my head the morning we caught the pod."

"Second after me," Gilly said quietly. Bree said nothing, but her frown deepened.

"You're cousins with Ferris," Bo said desperately, looking to Gloom as if he could back him up. Gloom stared back blankly. "She tried to get out the fire door," Bo said. "I told you. Remember?"

"Wyatt says they've been in our heads," Bree said, addressing Gilly, not him. "Maybe they did it again. Took Bo's memories and put them in a fake."

Bo felt a flare of anger. "It's me," he snapped. "I didn't jump off the ship and walk this whole way so you can be a..." He mustered up a cuss. "Be a fucking idiot," he finished.

Bree clapped her hands over Gilly's ears, but did it with a hint of a smile at the corner of her mouth. "You get mad like Bo," she admitted, as Gilly wrestled away. "You said you jumped off the ship?"

"Yeah," Bo said. He nodded over to Gloom. "Gloom made me a parachute."

"That's cool," Gilly blurted. "That's cool, isn't it, Bree?"

"Yeah, that's pretty cool," Bree said grudgingly. "Alright. You better come talk with Wyatt."

Bo inhaled. Looked to Gloom. He'd already told him that Wyatt wasn't to be trusted, no matter what he said. He'd told him that if Wyatt went for the knife, if he attacked Bo or anyone else, Gloom had full license to wrap him up and smother him.

Even with all that, Bo could feel a slow, cold fear eating holes in him as the four of them set off toward the theater.

24

The blank white space turned to pebbly tarmac underneath her feet, and Violet nearly pitched over the edge of the theater roof before a hand steadied her from behind.

"Easy, Vi."

She froze. It was Wyatt. Of course it was Wyatt. She turned around and saw him smiling his perfect smile, a little bleary from the drinking. The sweat-and-vodka smell of him, how close he was standing to her, his hand on her skin—all of it still sent a thrill down her spine just how it had in real life. She could feel herself flushing and hated it.

"How drunk are you?" he asked, all caring and concerned, his brow slightly creased.

"Shut up," Violet said.

Wyatt smirked, then leaned in and kissed her. It cut her at the knees. His fingers got knotted up in her hair and she was kissing him back, hard, thinking it might not be so bad to let the simulation run, to just let whatever happened happen.

She yanked back. "You're not real," she said. "Not even in real life."

Wyatt wiped his mouth. "You're really drunk, Vi," he said, shaking his head, grinning. "Come on. Let's sit down."

He eased down onto edge of the roof, swinging his legs. He patted the space beside him. Looked up at her innocently. She stared down at him and shook her head. Her legs were still trembling, but she was angry now, angry at him and at herself.

"I can't believe I thought I loved you," she said. "Can't believe I didn't realize."

"You realized," the simulated Wyatt said. "That's why you loved me so much. I'm really, really messed up."

Violet remembered what the real Wyatt had said before, when she was standing over him with a blood-smeared brick. *I'm your type. You're only going to meet me over and over again.* Maybe that was the hell they'd decided on: meeting Wyatt over and over again.

"And I'm the best you'll get," Wyatt said, rolling his neck side to side. "Someone like you, you won't really get a lot of choices, right? That's life, Vi." He smiled up at her. "Want me to fuck you now? Would that help you feel like a real girl?"

Violet planted both hands in Wyatt's back and pushed. He went over the edge laughing, the way he'd laughed when the escaping pod started up into the sky. She waited for the wet thud but it never came. Violet peered over the edge, blood still rushing in her ears, her heart still pounding. It was a white void again. No Wyatt, no anything.

She closed her smarting eyes, trying to focus on the image of herself in the pod. She tried to feel like she was weightless. Maybe the free fall would help. With every nerve in her body shrieking against it, she let herself tip backward and plunge off the edge of the rooftop.

*   *   *

Gilly had run ahead, so when they arrived at the theater the Lost Boys were standing outside on the street. Bo stared, uncertain. They were lined up like soldiers, hands at their sides, chins out, not speaking or moving their heads. Standing off the end of the line, perpendicular to the others, was Wyatt. Half his face was a mass of bruises. His lips peeled back off his teeth in a grin, but Bo knew now that was just as dangerous as a scowl.

"Tell the man in black to stay where he is," Wyatt said.

Bo turned to Bree, but she was already sliding away, joining the file. He clenched his teeth. "You're fast, Gloom," he said under his breath. "Really fast."

"I am," Gloom said. "Thank you. Is that the one with plans?"

"You might have to move really fast in a second," Bo muttered. "I don't know what's going on. What'll happen." He swallowed, glancing down at Wyatt again. "Just wait here for now, okay?"

Gloom nodded. Bo wiped his sweating palms on his pants, then walked forward. What had Wyatt told them? He had a sudden image of them all leaping at him, frenzied, pulling blackjacks out of their sleeves and beating him down. Wyatt could make people believe anything. He could make them do what he wanted.

But at the near end of the line, Alberto and Saif were almost wriggling from excitement, beaming at him as he approached. Gilly was trying her best to stand still and straight-faced, giving Alberto a nudge under the ribs. Bo realized he was mouthing his name. He grinned and mouthed *Alberto* back to him, then fixed his eyes on Wyatt again.

Wyatt lifted his fist in the air. "Bo came back," he said.

"They couldn't keep him away from his family. From us. Bo's too strong. Bo's too smart. Bo's a Lost Boy. Bo!"

"Bo!" the other kids shouted, like they'd done after he brought the pod down all those lifetimes ago. "Bo, Bo, Bo, Bo!"

Bo felt confusion and relief at the same time, catching his breath in his chest. He looked back at Gloom and shook his head just slightly. Then the Lost Boys broke out of the line to surround him, hugging him, rubbing his stubbly head, pushing him. The ones who didn't like to touch so much just hovered around the outside, grinning and laughing.

Bo had the wild thought that maybe the brick had rattled Wyatt's brain, made him lose memory. Maybe he didn't remember what all had happened that night in the storage unit. Maybe he'd forgotten his mad plan to take Bo's Parasite for himself. Maybe everything would be simple.

Bo was wrapped in a bear hug and looking over Jon's broad shoulder when he saw Wyatt's face go cold and blank again. His steel-gray eyes locked onto Bo's and he gave a slight, almost imperceptible shake of his head. Ice ran down Bo's back.

"Alright, alright, give us some space," Wyatt said, suddenly jovial again. "He'll tell us all about how he escaped tonight, right? We'll have a little party for him." His gaze flicked to Gloom. "But for now, me and Bo and Bo's prisoner are going to have a talk."

Bo nodded. Wyatt always had a plan. He was always scheming.

Nothing was going to be simple.

Violet landed on clean kitchen tiles. The impact was muted, like she'd fallen off a stool instead of off a rooftop. She sat up. Back to the perfect house, everything lit with sunshine, everything swept and tidy and lavender-smelling. She went to wipe the last of the tears off her face and found they were gone.

Her not-mom stepped carefully over her, carrying a steaming pot over to the table. "Time to eat!" she called. "Hey! It's on the table."

Violet heard a door open. She looked down the hallway and saw her dad, her not-dad, coming out of the bedroom, doing up the last button of his plaid red shirt. His dark hair was slicked back with no gray in it, still damp from the shower. He was whistling.

She scooted backward as he passed through the kitchen, but his eyes never landed on her. He went to the cupboard, then the fridge, and started filling drinking glasses with water. Her not-mom came over to give him a peck on the cheek and show him something on her phone, something that was making her laugh. Violet watched, feeling a lump in her throat. They looked happy, the way she sometimes thought she remembered them. Or maybe she'd only ever imagined them that way.

"Ivan!" her not-dad shouted, setting the glasses down on the table. There were three of them. "Get your ass up here!"

The words sent a spike of fear through Violet's body, but her not-dad wasn't angry, and he wasn't looking at her. Violet heard someone thumping up the stairs from the basement, then her breath caught in her chest. Slouching to the table, smiling ruefully, one earbud trailing from her ear—it was her, but it wasn't. Taller, broader. There was a dusting of moustache over her lip. Her hair was cut short. Her face had no makeup, and it wasn't smooth-skinned from the estrogen. Seemed heavier, more angular.

She felt sick. Then sicker, as her doppelgänger slid into her seat at the table. It wasn't her. It was Ivan the way they'd always wanted Ivan to be. She watched, with a tight kind of panic rising up her body, as her dad slugged Ivan in the arm, but softly, not meant to bruise. Ivan returned it, grinning. Her mom reached across the table to show the clip on her phone to Ivan too, while her dad started dishing food onto their plates. Everyone laughing, everyone smiling.

Violet got to her feet. It wasn't real. She knew it wasn't real. They were showing her this to torture her. Her fists balled tight at her sides. She wanted to smash them on the table, dump the pot onto Ivan's lap, grab a knife, and—

They were happy. Ivan was happy, the way Violet never had been. Trembling, she backed away, then started down the hall, letting their conversation fade. She opened the door to her bedroom. There was a warm-up jacket she didn't recognize tossed over the chair. A few medals dangling off a hook in the wall. Ivan how her dad had wanted him. Something moved behind her and she turned around.

"Do you get it?" Ivan asked her, his hands stuffed in his pockets. "They would've been this happy, if you could have just been fucking normal. Everyone would have been happy." His voice was deep, almost as deep as her dad's.

"This isn't real," Violet said shakily.

"Yeah, I know," Ivan said. "But it could have been. Dad wouldn't have started drinking himself to death. Mom wouldn't cry herself to sleep every night wondering if it was something she did, something she did when you were little. All that shit, that's all on you."

"Shut up," Violet whispered. "Shut up. You're only in my head."

"I'm going to help you, though," Ivan said, stepping forward. "I'm going to fix you." He reached forward and grabbed her forearm; she yanked it back.

"Stay away," she said, but Ivan didn't try to touch her again. The skin where his fingers had brushed her was itching. Blistering. She rubbed at it, not daring to take her eyes off her doppelgänger, but he just gave a sad sort of shrug and walked out of the bedroom, closing the door behind him.

Violet looked down. Hair was sprouting out of her arms: not the fuzz she was used to, but dark and wiry like the stuff her dad grew on his. She felt the fear like cold black ice in her stomach. Of course they would do this to her. They were in her head. They were in her hell.

She didn't want to look in the mirror, but suddenly it was in front of her and she couldn't drag her eyes away. Something between a sob and a scream got stuck in her throat. She couldn't breathe. Her shoulders were thickening with muscle, her chest widening, flattening.

"No," she choked. "No, no, no—"

Her voice broke on the last one, braying and dropping. She could feel more body hair creeping up her legs, trailing down her belly, and the thing she sometimes hated even more than she hated her Parasite was growing and thickening against her thigh. Everything she'd worked so hard for, all her hours of careful research, all her months of hunting pills and fighting nausea and adjusting dosages, was being ripped away.

"Not real," she groaned, her new voice loud and wrong in her ears. "It's not real."

But even if it wasn't real, they could keep her here forever. They could keep her here so long she'd forget what *real* even meant.

Violet started to scream.

25

Wyatt told Bo he didn't want Gloom inside the theater yet, so they went to a café patio around the corner from it. Two of the bubbled glass tables were still standing. One was occupied by a pair of wasters, both of them women, curling their hands around invisible mugs and bobbing their heads in pantomimed conversation. They had swollen bloody feet and were stick-thin. Bo figured the one of them was sick with a fever; she had sweat pouring down into her blank eyes and her gesticulating hands kept shaking.

The free table was short a chair, so Wyatt slid it out from under her. She fell and something gave a dull crack that made Bo wince. Wyatt didn't look. He dragged the chair over to the free table and the three of them sat down. Bo stayed on the very edge of the plastic. His Parasite was crackling and this time, if it came to it, he thought he would be able to vanish Wyatt. Even if that meant him spinning through space as a frozen corpse.

"We didn't leave things in a great place," Wyatt said, laying his hands palms down on the table. "But I don't hold grudges, Bo. That's what weak people do." He smiled, and it made Bo almost boil over. "You and me, we aren't weak people, right?"

"What did you tell the others?" Bo snapped. "What did you tell them happened?"

Wyatt had moved his gaze to Gloom, studying him. "I told them the truth," he said. "Violet was trying to free the pod. Why else would she have been sneaking around there, right? We tried to stop her. The pod got away and took you and her with it." His eyes flicked back to Bo. "All the Lost Boys were really getting to like you, Bo. So I made you sound really good. Made you a bit of a martyr. I didn't know you'd be back."

"I'm back," Bo said. "And I'm not scared of you either." He knew in his gut it wasn't true. He remembered a story his mom had told him once, about a farmer who made a deal with the devil. He couldn't remember the ending.

"Why would you be?" Wyatt asked, frowning. "We're all on the same side, right? Your friend here too, you said."

"I am called Gloom," Gloom said. "I am a saboteur." He didn't bow this time.

Bo tried to rein in his breathing. Calm his Parasite down. He needed to focus on the important thing, not on Wyatt's lies. He needed to focus on Lia and Violet.

"Gloom was being held prisoner on the ship," he said evenly. "We freed him, and he told us what's going on. He told us what the Parasites are for."

Wyatt's eyes gleamed for a split second. "I'd be really interested to hear that."

Jointly, Bo and Gloom explained about the keys, and the door, and the ships waiting on the other side to come through and do to the rest of the world what had been done to their city. They explained the machine, and the kids in the tanks who needed to be rescued before their Parasites were tuned enough to open the door.

"If the door opens, a hundred ships come through," Bo finished. "And then we're all screwed. They won't need to grow any more Parasites. They won't let the Lost Boys keep running around. Everyone will be dead, or else clamped. Gloom said they'll make us slaves."

"Clamp's in the head, better off dead," Wyatt said blandly, staring up at the sky over Bo's head, pensive. Bo tried not to look at the table beside them. For a long moment the only sound was the fallen waster scritching around on the concrete, still holding up her imaginary drink.

"So, what, you think we just have to get the kids off the ship?" Wyatt finally said, sounding annoyed. "Then they just bring another batch up from the warehouses and start...tuning those." He looked to Gloom. "How long can they keep us contained?" he asked. "With the fog. We can't get out of the city, obviously nobody can get in. How long can they do that?"

"A long time," Gloom said. "A year, perhaps."

"Then anything we do is just delaying them," Wyatt said. "Unless you have ships too. Are your people sending ships to help us out, or what?"

Gloom slowly shook his head. "I was the only measure taken," he said. "Our war is fought on several disparate fronts."

Wyatt nodded, like he'd expected as much, then leaned forward. "What do you really look like?" he asked flatly.

Gloom glanced over at Bo, questioning.

"Show him," Bo muttered.

Wyatt flinched backward as Gloom burst into his scuttling black motes. That might have given Bo some small bit of satisfaction, if he wasn't reflecting on what Wyatt had said. Even if they did rescue Lia and Violet and the others, it was only a matter of time before the door opened. The world was still going to end. In a way, it already had.

"What do you get out of all this?" Wyatt demanded, looking into the center of the swirling black with an almost enraptured expression. "Why are you trying to stop them?"

Gloom reformed, leaning back in his chair. "I do not know," he said sourly. "I am a saboteur. They are the enemy. They have always been the enemy."

Wyatt grinned so wide the cut on his lip reopened. "Enemy of my enemy is my friend," he said, thumbing away the blood. "Right, Bo?"

"Then what can we do?" Bo demanded, ignoring it. "If they're going to open the door eventually, what can we do?"

Wyatt shrugged. "We have to do something permanent," he said. He stared over Bo's head again, his gray eyes narrowed in thought.

Bo set his jaw and stared down at the dirty glass table, collecting thoughts of his own. Even if they couldn't stop the other ships from coming, they still had a chance of rescuing Lia and Violet. But was Wyatt going to help him? It would add more Lost Boys to the cause. They would have active Parasites, like Violet's. Would that be enough to persuade him? He opened his mouth to try.

Then Gloom leaned forward, steepling his pale hands on the table. "I have been thinking," he said. "Perhaps I could sabotage the machine."

Bo looked up sharply.

"Destroy it, you mean?" Wyatt asked. "That might work. Can they build another one?"

"Not destroy it," Gloom said. "It is possible I could reprogram it." His voice was tinged with excitement. "To bring the ships through, they will open the door in your atmosphere a safe distance from the surface. It will look, to you, like a tear in the sky. But it is possible I could reprogram the machine with new coordinates for where the door opens."

"So the other ships come out in a volcano, or something?" Bo asked.

"I do not know the coordinates of a volcano," Gloom said. "And the ship will not know them either. But the ship will know where it is now."

A beat passed, then Wyatt gave a wolfish grin. "The tear opens right where the ship is," he said. "Swallows it up. Sends it back to the other side. Is that right?"

"Yes," Gloom said. "The ship will be pulled through the door to the other side. It may even block the path of the other ships." His face was stretched out with a triumphant smile. "I can set the door to collapse. They will not have time to use their engines. When the door collapses, they will be trapped on the other side."

Bo's mind was racing. "But if we open the door, that means someone's going to have to be in the machine," he said. "They'll get pulled through too. All of us will. Anyone who's on the ship."

"The timing will be delicate," Gloom said. "I can ensure a delay. A small delay. A few minutes. Enough for us to leave the ship before it is pulled through."

Bo tried to picture it. How many kids had been floating in the tanks? Four. Minus whoever was in the machine, three. They would have to get all three of them out while Gloom rewired the machine, and Violet too. Then, once the machine was set, Gloom would have to drag whoever was inside of it out with him before the door opened and sucked the ship through.

Violet would say it was insane. Bo knew that much. They would have to be lucky, but they'd been lucky before.

"Alright," he said. "But how will we get back up there? And get everyone back off? Don't say you'll fly us."

Gloom's expression turned back to a frown. "I do not know," he said.

Wyatt was still staring over Bo's head, up at the sky. "I don't think going up will be a problem," he said. "They're landing. Look."

Bo spun up out of his seat. Wyatt was right. The massive black ship that had drifted over them like a shadow for the past four months was slowly sinking through the sky. Bo watched, his heart pounding his ribs. Scores of pods were circling around and underneath. Was something wrong with it? There was a rumbling like thunder and Bo realized the ship wasn't coming straight down. It was angled toward the docks. The warehouses.

If the ship set down on top of them, it would crush them and all the kids inside to dust. Bo felt his Parasite squirm at the thought. The ship passed out of sight, hidden by buildings, but Gloom turned to motes and slithered across the street, up the side of an apartment. Bo followed at a jog, careful to be aware of where Wyatt was behind him.

Gloom re-formed near the top of the building, clinging there like a lizard.

"Where's it landing?" Bo shouted up at him.

"The water," Gloom said. "It is going to set down in the harbor."

As he said it, the rumbling cut short, and a moment later Bo heard the distant thump of displaced water. He could imagine the waves of foam rippling out, the boats rocking on their lines. Off the docks, then, and behind the warehouses. Hard to get to, but not as hard to get to as it would've been in the sky.

"That's good, right?" Bo said. "That's good. We can get to it easier."

"It is not good, Bo," Gloom said, still looking out into the distance. "They are setting down to conserve power. They are conserving power because they are preparing to open the door. Another key must be tuned, or close to it."

He dropped down from the wall, splashed, and re-formed. His gaunt face was worried.

"How soon?" Bo asked, his mouth suddenly dry.

"They will have to test the machine first," Gloom said. "That should be visible. The testing might take a day. It might take only hours." An anxious ripple ran through him, his motes separating and melding again. "I do not know."

"Then we have to get ready," Bo said, looking to Wyatt now. "We have to tell everyone. Start making a plan."

Wyatt looked back at him, a smile playing around his lips. "So if Gloom can do what he says he can do, and it all works out, what happens? The aliens go home and everything goes back to how it was before, right?"

Bo knew it wouldn't be how it was before. Nothing would be. But he didn't know what Wyatt wanted to hear. He waited.

"What makes you think I want that?" Wyatt asked. "I'm thriving out here, Bo. I've kept the Lost Boys safe for this long. I'll keep them safe when the other ships come through. They'll have bigger problems than us, right? They'll be busy."

"But you wanted to beat them," Bo said. "That's what you

told me from the start. You hate them." He remembered back to the things he'd heard at knifepoint and took a careful step back before he spoke again. "Things won't be how they were before," he said, gathering his courage, wondering if he was making a mistake. "They won't take you back to the hospital."

"They wouldn't be able to," Wyatt said calmly.

The lack of reaction was almost more frightening than the outburst Bo'd been readying himself for. He racked his brain for the right thing to say. He wasn't like Wyatt. He didn't know how to make people do things. How to make people *want* to do things. But they needed Wyatt's help.

Wyatt was still standing there, arms folded, and Bo realized, with a jolt, that he was waiting for Bo to give him a reason. He could have walked away back to the theater already. Wyatt liked plans, he liked danger, he liked damage. He only needed a reason.

"You'll be a hero," Bo said, seizing on it at last. "You'll save the world. Not me." He clenched and unclenched his teeth. "I'll make sure everybody knows it," he said. "Everyone will know it was you. Everyone will love you. Nobody can ever think you're not good enough, because they'd all be dead if it wasn't for you."

Wyatt was still standing, still half smiling. Bo pushed on.

"Whatever you did before, they won't care about that," he said. "How could they, right? You saved the world. Just you. If it wasn't for you, I would've been back in the warehouses a day after I escaped. All of us would've been. You saved us. You can save the whole world."

Wyatt grinned. "I like the sound of that, Bo," he said. "Who wouldn't?" His eyes hardened. "But we're going to do it exactly how I say we do it. And before we do anything, we have to be on the same page about what happened the other night. About Violet and the pod and all that. I don't want anyone getting confused."

"Alright," Bo said, feeling queasy. "Alright. Whatever you say happened. That's what happened." It would mean lying: to Gilly, to Saif, to Jon. To all of them. It would mean making Violet out to be the villain. But if it gave him a chance to rescue her, and to rescue Lia, he had to do it.

Wyatt gave a satisfied nod, clapped him on the shoulder with his unbandaged hand. "Let's get to work, then," he said, and set off toward the theater. Bo followed after him, feeling static all through his body, equal parts fear and excitement and uncertainty. Gloom slithered down from his perch and followed along in his wake.

Bo felt a few motes creep along his shoulder as they walked.

"That was clever," Gloom's voice came in a whisper. "You are more clever than you seemed at first, Bo. Congratulations."

Bo swallowed. Shook his head. He didn't know if it was ever clever to make a deal with the devil.

26

Sometimes it was Stephen Fletcher, running circles around her, taunting her. Sometimes it was her dad, his nose all red with smashed capillaries, clutching an empty Heineken bottle. Sometimes it was Wyatt, torn between disgust and laughter. The worst was when it was her, but the perfect version of her, inhumanly beautiful and sneering at her through pale pink lips.

Violet fought them all. She hooked Stephen's legs out from under him, not caring how much smaller he was than her now. She shattered the bottle over her dad's head. She flung herself at Wyatt, hitting him over and over again, trying to break his white teeth. She chased the perfect Violet away.

They always came back, clambering through the windows, knocking on the front door, thumping up from the basement. And they never stopped talking. They said all the things Violet had thought about in the darkest parts of the nights she couldn't sleep. She clapped her hands over her ears, stumbling up and down the hall, trying to lock herself into one room and then another, but they always found a way inside and she couldn't stop them.

The kitchen knives were laid out on the counter instead of stuck in the block. Whenever she tried to step out the front door, she ended up back in the kitchen, looking down at them.

"Be nice to have it all over with, right?" Wyatt asked, smiling an innocent smile. "You can't handle this much longer. You're not strong enough for that."

Violet snatched up the butcher knife with a trembling hand. It looked like the one Wyatt had given her all those months ago, to kill her first othermother. She wanted to plunge it right into his chest.

"Or else it goes forever and ever and ever," Stephen said. "And ever, and ever, and ever, and ever, and ever..."

Violet stared at her reflected face in the flat of the blade, the ugly angles of it, the bristles on her chin. What would they do if she killed herself? Was that the way out they'd left for her? Would it shut off her brain in the real world too? Or maybe it would only start the whole thing over again.

Either way, she wasn't taking it. She'd always been stubborn. She was still stubborn. Violet laid the knife back on the counter and sat down. She closed her eyes.

They kept talking, crouching down around her, breathing hot air in her ears. It wasn't real. The aliens didn't know Stephen Fletcher. They didn't know Wyatt either, not really. They didn't know her parents or her life or anything about her. They hadn't made her own personal hell. She'd made it for them. This was just her, on a night she couldn't sleep, with her head so full of other people's bullshit that she wanted to take a drill to it.

But she'd always gotten through it. Violet inhaled, exhaled. She let the voices wash past her like white noise. She focused on syllables until the words didn't even sound like real words.

She tried to slow down her heart like she'd read Tibetan monks could, make it so she was pumping blood in a slow, strong tide, so she needed only a breath a minute.

She didn't know anything about meditation, but slowly, slowly, she felt something shift. She felt static, even though she didn't have a Parasite in here. Her breathing slowed down. Her hands stopped shaking. She could leave them slack instead of balled into fists. The voices were dimmer, duller.

Cold linoleum touched her arms and she realized she was sliding through the floor. Her lids twitched but she refused to open her eyes. The smell of the kitchen cut out. The voices cut out. She breathed. Breathed. When she finally opened her eyes, it was blank white space stretching endless in all directions.

She looked down at herself and felt relief ache her rib cage. She was herself again, or as close as she'd been to it in real life. Even her Parasite was back, sparking and wriggling. She stood up.

"You should not be able to do that." Her not-mom was standing in front of her, disapproving. "There is a flaw in the simulation."

Violet gave her a withering look. "Call the IT people," she said, then picked a direction at random and started walking off into the void.

There was no party when they got back to the theater. Wyatt called everyone into the auditorium—all of them cast Gloom odd looks on the way in—then got up onto the stage. Bo sat in the center of a row, expecting Gloom to sit beside him, but his new companion scuttled away toward a lamp in the corner instead. Gilly and Bree squeezed in.

With Bree jostling his elbow and Gilly leaning over her to

talk in his ear about the ship landing, it was easy to remember back to when he'd been so happy just to be alive and out of the warehouses. Back when Wyatt had been the tall boy with the scar who knew everything, who was stern but kind, who had always wanted a little brother.

Now Wyatt was the boy who'd straddled his stomach with the knife and nearly slit his throat. Wyatt the liar. The killer. It was hard to believe they were the same person.

"Listen up!" Wyatt shouted from the stage. "It's time to save the world."

That was enough for even Saif and Alberto to stop fidgeting. All the Lost Boys leaned forward to hear what came next, intent, and Bo leaned right with them.

"Bo came back to us," Wyatt said. "He brought us an ally. A friend. Gloom hates the aliens same as we do." He pointed to Gloom, who was squatting underneath one of the white solar lamps. The Lost Boys craned around to look at him. He raised one spidery hand. "And he brought us news too," Wyatt went on. "The aliens are scared of us."

Fierce nods, clenched jaws. Bree gave a loud whoop and thumped Bo's shoulder.

"We pissed them off," Wyatt said. "We got under their skin. We made that pod understand we're not to be fucked with. Right?"

"Right!" came back in a chorus, and even Bo mouthed it.

"So now they know they need help," Wyatt continued. "They're going to open up a portal in the sky to bring more ships. Hundreds of ships, as big as this one."

The news rippled through the Lost Boys; Bo saw Elliot shudder.

"But we're going to stop them," Wyatt said. "And our friend Gloom is going to send them right back through that portal. Send them home with their tails between their legs. We're going to save the world." His eyes were wide as he looked up and down the row. "They're scared of us. Are we scared of them?" He swung down off the stage and stalked to the end where Jon was sitting, his elbows resting on his thick knees. "Are you scared, Jon?" he demanded.

Jon looked him in the eye. "No," he said, his voice full of gravel.

Wyatt gave a sharp nod, turned to Bree. "You scared, Bree?" he asked.

"Fuck no," Bree snapped.

Wyatt skipped past Bo. "You scared, Saif?"

"No!"

"Scared, Gills?"

"No, never, never scared," Gilly said proudly.

Wyatt moved up and down the row with the same question, getting the same answer from each and every Lost Boy, and Bo could feel the adrenaline building like electric current. Like the static in his Parasite. Finally Wyatt stopped in front of him, his eyes shining.

"You scared, Bo?" he asked quietly.

Bo's heart pounded. "No," he said. And in his head he added, *Not of you either,* trying to think it hard enough to make it true. He stared right back into Wyatt's hard gray eyes.

"What's it take to be a Lost Boy, Bo?" Wyatt asked.

"Guts," Bo said.

"Guts," Wyatt echoed with something like relish. He hopped back up on the stage, careful with his bandaged hand.

"We're Lost Boys," he said, facing them again. "We've got guts. But this, this isn't going to be like killing the othermothers. It won't be like catching a pod. This is bigger than any of that. This is do or die." He paused, let the words sink. "Do or die," he repeated. "Do. Or. Die."

The chant caught. "Do or die," the Lost Boys echoed. "Do. Or. Die."

Bo knew it was only words now. He knew Wyatt was a liar. But even so he felt an ache in his throat, felt a deep burning pride to be here, to be one of them, to be about to save the world. He chanted with them. Gloom watched from the corner, his expression unreadable. Bo didn't care. They were going to save the world. They were going to save Violet and Lia.

Wyatt cut the chant short at its crescendo. "Jon, Bree, El, all of you to me," he said. He paused. "And Bo. With me. The rest of you, eat. We're going to need all our strength, right?"

Jenna took the under-tens out of the auditorium while the others went up to the stage. Bo made to follow, motioning for Gloom too, but Gilly stopped him with a tug on his arm. Her pointed face was serious.

"We buried him in the park," she said, her voice low and fierce.

Bo frowned. "What?"

"Quentin," she said. "We buried Quentin in the park."

Bo felt a wave of hot guilt. He'd known the numbers were off. He'd known someone was missing, and not just Violet. But he hadn't realized it was because of Quentin. Because Quentin was dead. His mind filled with the image of a limp body dangling off the pod's hooked proboscis. He'd been trying to erase it. Jenna had lost her brother, and there was no chance she'd get him back.

"Wyatt said he died trying to save you," Gilly whispered.

A shiver ran through him. He remembered Quentin's shaking hand holding the knife on him. But he hadn't been bad. Only scared. Scared of Wyatt, how any sane person would have been that night. Bo didn't reply for a minute. Jenna was waving impatiently for Gilly to follow her out of the auditorium. Wyatt was looking at him from the stage.

Whatever Wyatt said had happened, that was what had happened.

"Yeah," Bo lied. "He did. He died saving me."

Gilly nodded solemnly, then turned and darted off. Bo's stomach gave a guilty churn and his Parasite churned with it. He turned to the stage, where Elliot and Bree and Jon were already huddled up.

"We have to start getting ready," Wyatt was saying. "We need a watch on the ship and a watch on the warehouses. We need to send a forage for supplies." His smile was back in place, gleaming in his bruised face. "And we need gasoline."

Violet was still doing her best to walk in a straight line when her not-mom appeared beside her in mid-stride, like she'd been there all along.

"You are resilient," she said, falling into step. "Minds made of only meat are usually so fragile. We will use this data to adjust the positive simulations."

"So that was a beta, or something?" Violet snapped. "A test run?"

"We want to ensure the simulations are perfect," her not-mom said. "So your species will be happy until the very end. How you think of happy."

"Yeah, that's really thoughtful," Violet said bitterly. "Is that why you came all this way? Just to make sure we're all happy?"

"We came because it was necessary," her not-mom said. "That is all you need to know."

Violet paused. They were still in her head, but the not-mom wasn't anything she'd conjured up herself. She was some kind of avatar being controlled by the pods outside. With a sudden curiosity, with the static in her Parasite building, Violet reached for her.

"What are you doing?" her not-mom asked, suspicious, stepping backward.

Violet didn't answer. Instead, she lunged forward and plunged her hand into her not-mom's chest. The blank white space changed in an instant, full of whirling shapes, geometric symbols, some sort of machine code, and suddenly she was aware, dimly, of another mind on the other end. A pod's mind. She felt a wave of confusion, contempt, fear. Contempt for minds made of only flesh, and fear for a different kind of mind that had no flesh at all. Fear of the dark, but not the dark how Violet knew it.

She looked down and found herself floating over a seething black sea. Or she thought it was a sea: When she looked around she could see it carving into dunes and dips in the distance, rising into jagged black mountains. The sky was a hazy yellow around her. Violet stared down at the seething black surface again, and realized it was motes. Billions on billions of gleaming black motes.

The simulation flickered, and now she was out in space, looking down on the planet. Inky tendrils were spreading across it, wrapping it, embracing it. It was Gloom stretched out to cover an entire world. She saw the spiky black ships escaping the atmosphere, their burning blue engines carrying them away. As she watched the planet be covered over in shadow, she imagined the feel of Gloom's motes scurrying over her skin and shuddered. She felt the pod's fear, even more intense than before, and in the pod's mind she saw that the clamps had a second purpose. While the wasters stumbled around dreaming, the bulk of their brains were processing data, churning through possibilities, trying to solve the problem the pods couldn't solve themselves: how to stop the encroaching dark.

Violet didn't want to know any more. She reached out her hand and swiped it through the air, moving on instinct, not knowing why. White nothingness flowed out of her palm like paint. She waved her whole arm, washing away the doomed planet, the starry space, the drifting ships, until everything was white and void again.

They were still in her head. She called the shots in her head.

"You should not be able to do that," her not-mom said, reappearing. She sounded almost panicked.

And now Violet wanted out of her head. She wanted an exit. Her Parasite sparked.

"If you were adrift in the ocean with no home to return to, and you found the only island in that ocean that you could make into a home, what would you do?" her not-mom asked, voice grating. "If there were animals on the island, simple apes with simple tools, what would you do?"

Violet reached forward into the blank space and closed her hand around a doorknob. The cold metal stung her palm. She twisted.

"If there were animals on the island, would you sail past?"

her not-mom demanded. "Would you keep sailing and sailing until you were dead?"

Violet paused. Thought about it. "No," she said. "But when an ape bashed my head in with a rock, I'd know I had it coming."

She pushed the door open, carving a slice of the ship's dark interior onto the white void, and stepped through.

27

Violet's eyes flew open just as the dark blurred shape of a whirlybird descended on her. She saw the needle aiming for her neck, the one that put crying kids to sleep, and she tried to roll but found she was flat on her back and couldn't move at all. Panic kicked up through her. Her Parasite writhed to life. The needle swooped in, and as static ran through her body she tried desperately to shift the syringe, hoping it would break the way Wyatt's wrist had broken.

The static surged out of her in a wave, thicker and stronger than she'd ever felt it before, and the syringe vanished but so did the rest of the whirlybird, rippling and disappearing into thin air like it had never been there at all. Violet braced herself for it to pop back, to flicker into existence the way everything else always had. Maybe she was seeing in slow motion. Maybe they'd already given her drugs. She waited, senses straining, heart thumping.

But the whirlybird didn't come back. Violet tried to let her muscles unclench. Let herself relax. She really had vanished it, the way Bo did, and that could only mean one thing. Her Parasite was tuned. Violet swallowed spit. Took a deep breath. She still couldn't move, but she could twist her head enough to see she was in a small room, circular. The ceiling was a jagged mass of machinery and winking yellow lights. The air was filled with a deep hum that made her feel goose bumps on her skin.

She realized she wasn't being held down. She was splayed out on a soft black pad with her arms and legs spread-eagled, but only gravity was keeping them there. Gravity and whatever they'd drugged her with. She tried to move again and was relieved when she managed to wiggle her left arm back and forth. Then her right hand, then all of her toes. They were numb and tingling but not paralyzed. The back of her skull felt the same way. Hopefully it wore off fast.

She dragged her heavy head up and looked down the length of her body. Her Parasite was still rippling in her stomach, and she could see it. There was a hole cut through her shirt, exposing her belly, and her Parasite's dark red tendrils were pushing up at her pale skin like it was trying to escape. There were marks on top of her skin too. Small white scars in orderly rows. Tuned.

Violet cycled through her limbs again, wriggling her hands, her feet. The numbness was wearing off everywhere except the back of her head. She couldn't feel anything back there. Her mouth went dry. She'd been in their simulation without any black orb held to her eye. That meant they had gone straight to her brain.

The feeling was back in her fingers and she managed to flop them to her head, jam them underneath. They brushed something cold and metallic.

Her heart stopped. They'd clamped her. Her Parasite sensed her agitation, heaving and rippling more forcefully than usual. Clamp's in the head, better off dead—the rhyme bounced around her ears. She could practically hear Saif's reedy little voice repeating it. There was a flaw in the simulation, they'd said. But at any second, they might be able to drag her back to it. Back to her own little hell, but this time with no cracks to slip through.

Before she could worry about unplugging her brainstem and accidentally paralyzing herself, or worse, Violet closed her rubbery fingers around the clamp and pulled. She felt a distant pinch at the base of her neck, then a horrible rasping and sliding like she was yanking an impossibly long stitch. The white void flashed behind her eyes. She blinked. The clamp was moving, which was more than she'd expected. She'd always thought the whirlybirds drilled them in.

She gritted her teeth. Braced herself. Pulled again, as hard as she could.

The clamp came free, running a shudder all through her body. She gasped. Her vision swam for a second, then sharpened. She moved her legs. Her arms. Everything still worked. Slowly, she dragged her hand up and peered at the clamp.

It wasn't like the ones the wasters had. It was smaller, slimmer. Filaments nearly too thin to see trailed from the bottom of it, glistening wetly. She felt instantly sick knowing they'd gotten wet from sliding through her head. She dropped the clamp to the side and heard it clink onto the floor. She took a few deep breaths to gather herself, trying to think of her options.

She was somewhere on the ship. She wasn't clamped anymore, but she didn't know how long she'd been stuck inside the illusion. Her not-mom had said something, back at the very start, and it came back to her now: Another key was nearly ready. Maybe two, she'd said. Assuming Violet's Parasite was the maybe, that meant they were on track to open the door even if she escaped. And how was she supposed to escape? They were floating in the sky about a mile up.

Violet braced herself, then swung upright and off the platform. A little stiff, a little clumsy. The knee she'd skinned and the elbow she'd banged up following Gloom through the tunnels both smarted. But she could walk. She took a second to stomp down on the clamp; it rewarded her with a satisfying crunch.

She didn't know where she was, and she didn't know how to get off the ship, and she didn't know how close the aliens were to opening the door—and if they managed to do that, then escape was a moot point.

Violet walked a tight circle around the room as she thought, trailing her hand on the wall, looking for an exit but not finding one. The ship was massive, and she didn't have Mr. Gloomy to guide her around, but she reasoned she couldn't be far from the room with the tanks. If this was where they worked on tuning the Parasites, it would only make sense to keep the kids somewhere nearby. She didn't know if she would be able to find the tanks on her own, but she could try.

If Bo was alive, and if him and Gloom had found a way back aboard the ship—both were big ifs—they would head for the same place. To his sister and the other kids. And if Bo wasn't coming, then Violet would have to save the world herself.

Her Parasite wriggled and she gave up on finding an exit. She was tuned. Maybe even better than Bo was, because the Parasite was ready for action again. Static crackled up through her belly and she unleashed it at the smooth wall, ripping a chunk of it away and opening onto a corridor. The tiny hairs on her arms shivered. Her jaw was clenched tight, but she could feel a fierce kind of smile tugging at her lips as she set off down the corridor.

★   ★   ★

Bo was up on the theater roof. Night had already fallen, and
without the ship drifting overhead there was no light to illumi-
nate the city. No streetlamps, no lit windows. He could picture
the wasters all staggering through the dark, banging into doorways and corners, but it didn't seem funny how it might have
once.

  He was sitting in the dent of the electrical box, swinging his
legs so the heels of his sneakers thudded against the metal in
rhythm. A cold night breeze slipped over his shaved skull and
ruffled his clothes, but he didn't feel the chill. He was wired.
Everyone was. The air inside the theater seemed to buzz from
all the preparation, the anticipation. He'd disinfected all the
small cuts he'd sustained with rubbing alcohol, taken a few
Tylenol for his head. Then he'd come up to keep watch with
Gloom, who was standing very still and very straight in the
middle of the rooftop, neck craned back, eyes on the sky.

  "What'll it look like?" Bo asked. "The test."

  "I do not know," Gloom said. "But I will know it when I
see it."

  Bo nodded. He thought about the kids bobbing in the tanks
and how one of the tanks was maybe empty by now. Maybe
one of the kids was already in the machine.

  "It's going to be Lia," he said, without thinking. "Isn't it?"

  Gloom looked over at him.

  "You said it was in the genes," Bo said. "To be compatible,
or whatever. She has the same genes as I do."

  "Compatibility with the key is not entirely based on genet-
ics," Gloom said. "But it is likely that they will use her. Yes."

  Bo thought the words would hit him harder. Maybe he'd
known it all along, in the back of his head. Lia had always been

bigger than him. Smarter. No way would she end up with a worse Parasite than his.

But Bo had been luckier. He'd gotten out of the warehouse. He'd met Violet. He'd jumped off the ship and survived.

Now he only needed to be lucky one last time.

"Do you have a family, Gloom?" Bo asked, looking at the sky. "I didn't think about it before. Should've asked you."

"In a way," Gloom said. "Do you know about cells, Bo?"

"Sort of," Bo said. "We did diagrams last year."

"My motes are like my cells," Gloom said. "And I am like a cell of a larger Gloom. Larger than you can understand. Stretching through space. Burrowing into asteroids. Feeding off the stars." His face contorted, looking pained. "It is very beautiful, Bo," he said. "More beautiful than you can understand. But I am not a part of it anymore."

Bo tried to imagine it, but kept seeing Gloom in his human shape curling up around the sun, hanging his hat on the moon. He didn't think it looked like that. It would have to be more like a dark, living cloud so big it covered up the stars. Bo wondered what kind of war you could have against a cloud.

"You got sent away to sabotage the ship," he said. "Yeah?"

"I was cut off long before that," Gloom said sadly. "I was a deviation. My motes are corrupted. Mutated. Mutation is our greatest fear. So, I was cut away. They altered my replication drives, so I cannot create new motes on my own either." His lips formed a melancholy smile. "I was a deviation. Now I am a saboteur. They sent me away to be useful."

"Will they let you back?" Bo asked. "If we win, I mean. If you finish your mission."

"No," Gloom said. "I am too corrupted. I have become unique." His voice was still heavy, but Bo thought he detected a bit of pride in the last word. "Now I have only my own motes, and I will never connect to the whole again." Gloom paused. "But I will finish my mission. I am a saboteur."

Bo felt a spark of anger at the unfairness, at Gloom being cut off and sent away on a mission he wasn't supposed to come back from.

"You've got me now," he said fiercely. "And the other Lost Boys too, when they're not spooked of you anymore. Violet. Lia. If you can't go back to yours, you can be one of us."

Gloom stared at him for a long moment. "Thank you, Bo."

Bo shrugged. Gloom turned his attention back toward the dark sky, and Bo did the same. They watched in silence. Now that the ship was floating in the water off the docks, the sky seemed twice as big, a vast black dome. Even without the ship's pale yellow lights, and without the lights of the city, Bo couldn't see any stars. They were hidden the same way the sun was hidden during the day, cloaked by the thick banks of cloud.

Bo thought about Gloom's people, whatever they looked like, stretched far out in space. And there was a fleet of black ships waiting somewhere out there too, waiting for the door to open. It made him feel smaller than he'd ever felt. He didn't like it. He was about to go back down the stairs when the sky split in two.

At first he thought it was lightning, but no lightning had ever looked like this, a twisting pillar of violent greens and electric purples, so bright it stung his eyes as it streamed up into the darkness. Bo felt the hum of it in his jawbone, in his clenched teeth. Every hair on his body lifted at once; the fabric of his shirt rustled like a living thing. His Parasite crackled. Bo looked wide-eyed over at Gloom. His gaunt face seemed hollow in the stark light and his mouth was set, grim.

Then the pillar was gone, plunging them back into blackness. Bo blinked hard at the spots swimming past his eyes. The static slowly settled. He breathed in. Out.

Gloom was right. It didn't look anything like a door. Bo glanced over to him for confirmation. Gloom nodded his head. Adjusted his bowler hat.

"Time to go," he said.

28

Down in the theater lobby, everyone was gearing up, already dressed in their darkest clothes. Bo saw the old homemade blackjacks and police batons and some of the hooks they'd used on the pod. Elliot was passing out chunky neon water guns to the under-tens, canisters already sloshing full. Jon was pulling a camping backpack onto his broad shoulders to carry the other supplies. Nobody spoke. Everyone was focused and grim-faced.

Bo picked a collapsible baton and hooked it into the elastic of his waistband. His Parasite was on the move again, and he thought he could feel static off everyone else's too, even the inactive ones. His eyes trailed over the other Lost Boys. Gilly and Saif were helping Alberto fit a black bag over his water gun to hide the color. Bree was slapping a baton rhythmically into her palm, staring off into space. Elliot was testing his rigged lighters now with a *click-hiss, click-hiss.*

It seemed impossible that it was only a few days ago they'd set out like this to kill othermothers, to catch the pod. It felt like a lifetime.

Things would be different tonight. More dangerous. And he knew now that he couldn't trust Wyatt. He liked to think he could trust the other kids, but if it came down to picking Bo or picking the boy who'd cut out his own Parasite, the boy who'd been waiting for them with open arms when they escaped the warehouses, he didn't know what would happen.

His gaze fell on a familiar black duffel bag, sitting untouched in the corner of the lobby. Violet would pick him over Wyatt. He knew that. Once they found Violet, he would have someone he trusted with his life. Bo went over to the corner and unzipped the duffel. A few of the Lost Boys glanced over at the noise, but nobody said anything as he pulled the chrome baseball bat out.

"Ready, Bo?"

Bo flipped the bat up onto his shoulder and turned. Wyatt was dressed all in black, with his injured hand wrapped tight in sports tape and a crowbar clutched in the other. If he noticed Violet's bat he didn't show it. His gray eyes glinted and it looked like he was clamping down a grin.

"Yeah," Bo said. "Ready."

"Do or die," Wyatt said firmly, and clapped him on his arm, just above the elbow. He circulated through the others, doing the same thing, sometimes leaning in close to whisper a few words, sometimes just looking them in the eye. Gloom had slithered down the stairwell and was waiting by the door now, watching.

When Wyatt was finished, he walked past Gloom, out of the theater, and the Lost Boys all followed behind him for what Bo knew was maybe the last time. He brought up the rear with Gloom, last one out. When the doors screeched and thumped shut behind him, he swung the two-by-four back into place to keep them that way. It seemed like the right thing to do, even though they might never come back.

With no ship in the sky, the night was black as pitch. Wyatt and Jon led the way with their flashlights, carving up the dark. Normally the younger kids might have skipped ahead, chasing the beams of light, but not tonight. Tonight they marched. It was cold enough now that Bo could see the plumes of Jon's breath. The flashlight played over the husks of cars, the cracked tarmac, once a wandering waster, illuminating them for brief instants before the dark sucked them back again. The route back to the warehouses was dreamily familiar.

Bo couldn't help but think back to the night he'd escaped, how he ran and ran with no destination, feeling an increasing dread at the ruined buildings and the gaunt staggering adults who could no longer see him. They'd looked like something out of a nightmare then.

Now Gloom was stepping soundlessly beside him, his eyes turned to dark hollows under the brim of his hat, and Wyatt was leading the way with that feral grin on his face. Bo didn't know what nightmares were meant to look like anymore.

There was a click as Wyatt switched off his flashlight for the last stretch, and another when Jon followed suit. Bo blinked in the sudden dark. They were at the corner of a blackened apartment building.

"Hold up for a second," Wyatt's voice came, low but clear. "Let our eyes adjust."

They stayed for a ten-count, until Bo could mostly make out Gilly's grave face across from him, then Wyatt motioned them on. As they rounded the corner, the jagged shifting silhouette of the wormy wall came into view. It wasn't as high as Bo remembered it.

The others stopped and Bo stepped forward. The hole he'd ripped in it so long ago, back before he'd known what his Parasite was even capable of, was gone. He hadn't really expected it to still be there. If he'd left a mark or scar, it was invisible in the dark.

Wyatt gave a curt nod. Bo's Parasite was already turning, twisting, ready. The static crackled, enough so sparks ran up his body and one leapt to Wyatt. Wyatt didn't flinch. He had the greedy look on his face again, the same he'd had when he tried to take Bo's Parasite for his own. Bo was glad to see Gloom lurking behind him.

The wormy wall had noticed them, reaching out with its tendrils like a squid. Bo let the static go. It rippled the air and ripped a swathe out of the wall. A shudder went through the intact part of it, all the tendrils flailing madly. Bo looked through the hole he'd made and saw the bare black tarmac of the parking lot he'd sprinted through the night he escaped. Beyond it, the hulking outlines of the warehouses.

He'd daydreamed this, coming back to the warehouses to free everybody, coming back strong and sure. He knew it wasn't going to be like the daydreams, but he let the adrenaline carry him along with the other Lost Boys as they streamed through the shattered wormy wall. The nearest warehouse was Bo's. His legs carried him down the alley to the fire door almost on autopilot, remembering the mad chase, the pod huffing behind him.

At the fire door, Gilly screwed up her face and shifted the locking bar just long enough for Jenna and Elliot to haul the door open. She'd been practicing, and Wyatt thought it was better to conserve Bo's Parasite for the big vanishes. For a moment everyone stood still around the dark mouth of the warehouse door, all remembering the time they'd spent inside, the smelly cots and the whirlybirds and the needles.

Wyatt went first. But then, he'd never spent time in the warehouses—Bo knew that now. He followed a few steps behind. The familiar smell of dust and chemicals filled his nose. Wyatt's flashlight clicked to life and its beam raked over the stalled forklift, the piled crates, the powerjack, the high metal shelves and stacks of splintery wood pallets. The kids would all be in their beds by now. The whirlybirds would be drifting over them, watching them.

Bree found the light switches on the wall and toggled them up and down, but nothing happened. Maybe they were disconnected, or maybe the aliens had never bothered to get the electricity running again. Maybe the kids had been living in the dark ever since it went out. Bo grimaced at the thought. The rest of the Lost Boys were inside now, fingering their weapons, looking around. Gloom came in last, ducking to fit under the doorframe. The top of his hat splattered against it and re-formed on the other side.

"The diagnostic drones know we are here," he said tersely. "They are coming toward us from that direction." He pointed with one long finger, and a second later Bo could hear it too: the familiar high-pitched whine that still made him shiver.

"How many whirlys were in this building?" Wyatt asked, handing his flashlight off to Elliot and taking out the crowbar he'd tucked under his armpit. Bo racked his memory. He had never seen all the whirlybirds in one place, and it was impossible to tell them apart.

"Maybe ten, maybe twelve," he said.

Wyatt only grinned, spinning and catching the crowbar in his good hand, as the whine intensified. Everyone tensed, readied themselves. Jon turned his flashlight back on and pointed it toward the direction of the noise. Elliot's beam joined it just as the first whirlybirds appeared, humming forward, claws extended. Bo tightened his grip on Violet's bat.

Maybe it was the one that had done his Parasite. It didn't matter. Bo took a running start and swung as hard as he could. The impact jarred all the way to his shoulder, but he felt something crack apart inside the whirlybird and it dropped like a stone. Wyatt had the next one, the edge of his crowbar whistling as it came down, and then Bree was in the fray, and Jon swinging his blackjack. It was chaos. Elliot's roving flashlight put it into stop motion, all jerky silhouettes and faces frozen in frenzy. Gloom was threading through it all like a living shadow.

The whine had filled Bo's ears, rising and falling, and then all at once he couldn't hear it anymore. All he could hear was heavy breathing, Bree cursing, someone stomping on a fallen whirlybird over and over again, crunching it into the concrete.

"Everyone good?" Wyatt panted. "Bring the light, El."

Bo doubled over with the bat on his knees, breathing hard, then straightened. He wasn't sure how many he'd gotten. Maybe three. He wasn't sure how many were smashed onto the floor and how many might still be waiting in the sleeping rooms. Elliot shone the light around. Some scratches on Jon's arm that he only shrugged at, a swelling bruise where Alberto had accidentally elbowed Saif in the face. Nothing serious.

Everyone stood, collecting their breath, ears keen for the sound of more whirlybirds. Elliot was trying to take a count from the wreckage, but they were all tangled together or ripped apart and it was hard to tell. When he brought the light back up, pointing toward the other side of the room, Bo gave a start. Caught in the beam, blinking, wearing sleepy-curious expressions, were a handful of kids from the sleeping rooms. They were all soft and pale and wore the rags of the clothes they'd been captured in. He recognized a few of them.

"Are there any more whirlys back there?" Bo asked.

The kids stared. Bo could tell from their glazed eyes that they'd been drinking the water for a long time. Then one girl cut through from the back, pulling stringy blonde hair out of her face, and Bo recognized Ferris immediately. She wasn't dull or smiling.

"We trapped one in a closet," she said. "You got the rest. Is that you, Bo?"

Bo didn't have time to answer before Bree's baton clattered to the floor and she flew past him, wrapping up her cousin in a fierce hug. Ferris's eyes went wide, then she realized who it was and hugged back. Bree was sobbing, louder than Bo had ever heard her in the night, and Gilly was scampering around her anxiously, patting her back. Bree didn't push her away. She dragged her in too, holding her against her hip with one arm.

Bo looked away, feeling like he was watching something private and feeling a hard lump in his throat too. He wished Elliot would move the beam again. The other Lost Boys had a variety of expressions, from shocked to happy to jealous, but only Gloom and Wyatt were blank-faced, unmoved. Bo knew they were thinking of the time they didn't have to waste.

"Ferris, right?" Wyatt said loudly.

Bree's cousin disentangled herself, wiping her eyes with the heel of her hand. "Yeah."

"I need you to get the other kids out of bed," Wyatt said. "All of them. Bree, go with her."

Bo didn't think Wyatt could have kept them separate if he tried. They hurried away into the dark, leaving Gilly looking a little lost. Bo put a reassuring hand on her shoulder. All the Lost Boys stood in taut silence, waiting. Bo noticed the smashed whirlybirds had left some of their black fluids spattered on the chrome of Violet's baseball bat. He wiped it down with his sleeve, thinking, vaguely, that she would want it to be clean when he gave it back to her.

A minute later, the other kids were all assembled, dragged out of their cots. Most of them were blinking stupidly in the flashlight beam, too dull from the drugs to know they were being rescued. A few of them were clustered around Bree and Ferris, whispering and casting excited glances at the fallen whirlybirds. Those were the ones who had figured out how to get their water from other places.

Jon had taken his backpack off and was pulling out the extra blackjacks Elliot had made, laying them on the concrete floor.

Wyatt stepped forward.

"Who here is brave?" he asked. "Who's got guts?"

"Who are you?" one of the sharp-eyed kids demanded.

Bree cuffed him on the ear. "He's Wyatt," she snapped. "He saved your fat ass just now."

"Relax, Bree," Wyatt said, then turned his gaze to the other kids, hard as flint. "I think if any of you had guts, you would've gotten out by now. The rest of us did, right? But maybe you can prove me wrong. Tonight, we're busting the warehouses wide open. We're killing every last whirlybird. We're getting revenge."

Ferris was first, giving Bree's hand a last squeeze before she walked up to the line of blackjacks and picked one. She caught Bo's eye and he gave her a nod. He felt a trickle of guilt. Wyatt wasn't telling them everything. Freeing them was only a distraction. The warehouse revolt was supposed to draw the pods' attention, and the Lost Boys intended to be long gone by the time they showed up.

The boy Bree had slapped came up next, still rubbing his ear ruefully, and then the other whisperers and even some of the glazed-looking ones, maybe because Wyatt's words had gotten through or maybe just to do what everyone else was doing. Bo didn't think they had much chance of getting away themselves, never mind freeing the kids in the other warehouses.

Wyatt was opening his mouth to speak again, but his next words were cut off by the sound of shattering glass. Bo looked up and saw fragments raining down from the skylight, glittering in the beam of Elliot's flashlight. He recognized the dark shape an instant before it dropped into the warehouse. Long mechanical arms were already sliding out from its underbelly.

"Pod," Wyatt barked. "Gilly, Saif, Alberto—ready up. Everyone without a weapon, get out of the way."

Bo adjusted his grip on the bat, wondering if the pod had been drifting up there in the dark all along or if it had come all the way from the ship. They were fast when they wanted to be. Maybe the whirlybirds had sent some kind of signal. Maybe more were already on the way.

In the corner of his eye he saw Jon shove the fire door open and Jenna start herding the newly freed kids through. Some of them were crying, most of them just staring. The ones who'd picked weapons stayed where they were, but apart from Ferris, they looked ready to run at any second. Gilly and Saif and Alberto had the water guns out, pumping furiously. A plastic part had already snapped and fallen out of Saif's. He looked terrified.

The pod was descending. Its harsh yellow light flashed over the scene, over the huddled kids and metallic wreckage of the whirlys. Bo squinted hard against it. The pods knew who he was and they knew what he had in his stomach. Maybe they knew who Wyatt was by now too, because the pod dropped right at him.

Wyatt was ready, ducking under one arm and swinging at the other. The crowbar clanged and screeched, throwing sparks, then he jerked it free and drove it up into the pod's underside. A familiar low moan, and the pod's second arm came back to send Wyatt sprawling. Bo jumped in, and so did Bree and Ferris, battering the pod from its blindside until it retreated up into the air.

Gilly and Alberto darted underneath, spraying up at it with their water guns, dousing its slick black skin. It would've seemed funny if not for the pungent smell of gasoline filling the air, slicing at the back of Bo's nose and throat. He knew what was meant to happen next.

The pod was turning, still trying to track Wyatt and Wyatt's crowbar, when Elliot scampered in with one of the lighters. Bo heard the *click* and the *whoosh*, saw his pointed face illuminated in the blossom of flame, teeth biting down on his lip, concentrating. Then Elliot lobbed the lighter straight upward.

Elliot dove, Gilly dove, Wyatt dove, but Alberto only stood there, transfixed, as the lighter whirled through the dark, spinning like a tiny sun. Bo shot the gap, hooking Alberto under both armpits and sprawling him away. Both of them rolled across the concrete and Bo found himself looking straight up at the pod as it burst into flames.

There was a chemical roar as the pod's gasoline-soaked skin caught fire, then a sound Bo had never heard a pod make before, not even when he'd used the knife back in the storage unit. It was a raw panicked wailing that put goose bumps on his skin. The pod was a fireball now, invisible behind the unfurling tongues of hot orange flame. Black spatter struck and steamed on the concrete—melted flesh or metal, Bo didn't know—and then the pod fell, spun, plunging out of control into one of the shelves. Alberto gave a ragged shout of triumph from somewhere under Bo's arm.

The fire caught. Bo saw it lick from the pod to the crates, race up and down the shelves, springing from one to the next. Thick tarry smoke was billowing into the air. He scrambled to his feet, yanking Alberto upright on the way.

"That's our cue, right?" Wyatt had appeared through the smoke, the crowbar set jaunty on his shoulder, lips peeled back off a grin. "Let's get going."

Bo spun his head toward the exit; Jenna and Jon had it propped open and the other Lost Boys were hurrying through. Gilly stopped to unscrew her half-emptied canister and hurl it back toward the encroaching blaze. The inferno swelled.

"Is everyone out?" Bo demanded, shouting it over the roar and crackle of the fire.

Wyatt didn't answer. He made for the exit; Bree too, clipping Bo's elbow on the way past. Alberto was gone. Bo stayed where he was, spinning to see if all the rescued kids were out or not. The smoke billowed suddenly thick, stinging his eyes.

The acrid smell flung him back in time to his burning-down house and he didn't know if he was looking for the kids or looking for his mom in the blaze. Panic welled up in him, rooted him to the spot. The shelves were still toppling and in the middle of them he thought he could see the shape of the pod writhing, swelling like a balloon.

He felt Gloom wrap around him from behind. A cape of motes shielding him from the heat, nudging him toward the door.

"We need to leave, Bo," his tinny voice reverberated. "Fire is dangerous to humans."

Bo couldn't see anything more through the smoke. He dropped low and let Gloom guide him, holding his breath until he was outside on the tarmac. He saw Gilly, Alberto. Jon and Jenna. Elliot with Bree and Ferris and some of the new kids. More silhouettes up ahead that he could only see dimly. Everyone was staggering away from the blaze, trying to get distance from the heat. Bo looked back just in time to see the warehouse roof explode outward like a star going nova.

Whips of flame snapped up into the sky; shattered glass and superheated metal rained back down. A wall of rippling heat slammed over him, blistering his eyes dry. He kept moving. Gloom shielded him from the worst of it but he still covered his face with his sleeve too. Away from the warehouse and the wormy wall, toward the docks. Bo remembered the pod swelling and swelling, remembered what Wyatt had said about the gases inside them. Go off like a firework, he'd said. Bo had never seen a firework do this.

Through the roar of the fire he could hear someone laughing, and for a wild moment he thought it was himself, but then he pulled his arm away from his face and saw Wyatt, head thrown back as he jogged along, looking happier than Bo'd ever seen him. The other kids weren't laughing. Some of the Lost Boys were darting nervous looks at Wyatt and then each other. Bo saw fear on their faces, not admiration. For once, Alberto was nowhere near grinning. His eyes were glassed over with shock.

They didn't stop moving until they were on the pier, far

from the heat but still able to see the flickering orange light. His head was still a jumble and his throat still searing.

"It really fucking worked." Wyatt was grinning, gripping Alberto's shoulder. "Good shooting, man."

Alberto nodded numbly but didn't reply. The freed kids were huddled up in a group, smeared with soot, some of them coughing ragged coughs. Bo tried to headcount. He knew before he finished that they weren't all there. Not nearly. And if the fire spread to the other warehouses, to all those slow, dull-eyed kids sleeping inside...

"Where's Saif?" It was Jenna who asked it, her voice high and trembling. "Alberto, where's Saif?"

The words sent a jolt through Bo's whole body. He looked at Alberto.

Alberto looked back. "He said he was right behind me," he choked. "He said. But then I looked. And. He wasn't."

Bo's heart stopped. Saif, with his shy gappy grin. Saif, with his little rhymes and his plastic dinosaurs and his shaky hand-written notes. "We have to go back for him," he said. "We have to go back and look."

Wyatt shook his head. "Do or die," he said. "Saif knew that. He was a Lost Boy." He put his hand on Alberto's shaking arm. Lowered his voice. "I loved him too."

Bo sank to a crouch. He rubbed his stinging eyes and took a deep breath of the cold salt air coming in off the sea. Tried to clear his lungs and his head both. He looked out over the harbor, past the dark shapes of boats bobbing in their berths. Floating out on the black water like an enormous spiny sea creature, the eerie yellow glow from its underbelly illuminating the depths, was the ship. Their goal. He had to focus on their goal. Had to forget Saif.

The pods were swarming above the ship's hull, but as he watched, they started to break away. Wyatt ordered everyone down on their bellies as the pods flew toward the docks, toward the blaze. Bo saw some of them swooping down to skim the glossy black surface of the harbor. He realized they were scooping water to put out the fire. Pressed against the damp wood of the pier, Bo felt his heart thump hard against the beams. His Parasite squirmed as the pods passed overhead.

He knew now that Wyatt had always meant to set the warehouses on fire. Freeing the kids wouldn't have been enough to get the pods' attention. Bo rocked to his feet before Wyatt gave the order. He watched the pods circle over the blazing warehouse, long streams of water arcing out into the flames. He tried to tell himself that they were protecting their stock, and that was it. If something went wrong with the door, they might need more keys. More Parasites.

Violet's words echoed back to him. *Never think they care about you, Bo. They only care about what they put inside you.*

But it didn't look that way. It looked like they were trying to save the other kids from the spreading fire, and the Lost Boys were leaving them to burn the same way they'd left Saif.

"We have them looking the wrong way," Wyatt said. "We did good. Everyone did good. Now some of us go on, and some of us hide, right?" He jerked his head for Jon and Bree, the two he'd picked plus Bo to go to the ship. "No crying," he added. "We have a job to do, and we'll be back once it's done." He paused, looking at Alberto, who was still shaking. "Jenna, you're in charge of the Lost Boys. Ferris, you're in charge of yours."

Ferris's face was screwed up with tears, confused and angry, and Bo thought for a second she would protest. He knew what she was feeling. She'd been reunited with her cousin for only a few minutes and they were already being ordered apart. Gilly flung herself at Bree and wrapped around her, saying how she could come too, how she'd been practicing her shifts and she would be so, so useful.

Bree broke away from both of them. "Watch out for Gilly too," she murmured to Ferris.

Gloom had already picked a tiny yacht and slithered inside, making it rock back and forth. Jon shook Gilly off his back, then clambered in after him. Wyatt swung over the side next. Then Bree, and then Bo was the last one standing on the dock. Gilly and Jenna hugged him hard and Elliot nodded to him. Alberto didn't seem to see him.

If everything went wrong, and they were caught, and the other ships came through the door, Bo wondered if the four they were leaving behind could keep the Lost Boys going. Them plus the new kids who'd been freed. He wondered who would sleep in Saif's corner.

It was better not to think about it. Better to think about him and Lia and Violet coming back to the dock alive and well.

Bo hopped into the boat, steadying himself against the side. Everyone shifted around to even out the weight. Gloom was seated in the very back, at the rudder, and he made his fingers sharp to slice through the rope that held them tethered to the quay. They started to drift free. The other kids were moving back down the dock as scurrying shadows.

"He knows how to drive a boat?" Bree asked, shooting Bo a dubious look. Her voice was still thick from goodbyes.

In answer, Gloom eased himself off the back of the yacht, dipping his lower half into the water. A droplet splashed onto Bo's skin and he recoiled. It was cold as ice, but Gloom didn't seem to mind. Under the surface, Bo saw his trouser-clad legs meld together, then peel apart into a twist of thick tendrils that started to slowly churn like a rotor coming to life.

The boat pushed soundlessly into the harbor. More pods were flying overhead, toward the blaze, but Gloom steered well around. Nobody spoke. Bo couldn't properly see the shadowed faces of Bree and Wyatt across from him. He couldn't hear anything but the lap of water along the sides of the boat as they knifed through the dark toward the waiting ship.

29

Something was happening. Violet crouched low in the shadows as another pod rushed past her hiding place. Her Parasite twinged, still aching and throwing sparks from the surge, or whatever you wanted to call it. She'd barely been out of the tuning room when it hit. The bone-deep hum and the static, stronger than she'd felt it yet in her newly tuned Parasite, had seemed to fill the entire ship. She'd thought maybe the door was opening and it was already too late.

But the static storm had lasted only a few moments. Then she'd kept moving, eventually finding her way here, to a hall that looked dimly familiar. It was full of jagged black machinery and pale yellow tubes of light that seemed to swim across the ceiling like little glowworms. A pod had barreled right past her almost as soon as she'd entered, missing her in the dark.

Another had followed, and now Violet was hiding behind a bank of the whirring machinery, trying to figure out why, if the pods were trying to recapture her, they were heading away from the tuning room instead of toward it. Maybe something had gone wrong with the door. Maybe Bo had survived, found his way back onboard with Gloom's help, and was wreaking havoc on the other side of the ship.

She waited another minute, and when no more pods came, she stood up. Her Parasite wasn't sparking anymore, but it had settled into a strange steady rippling. As she walked down the hall, it intensified. She frowned, putting her hand to her stomach, trying to calm the Parasite down. It didn't help. When she steadied herself against the smooth black wall, the rippling grew even stronger.

Maybe being tuned wasn't all it was cracked up to be if it meant her Parasite was permanently caffeinated. She didn't think Bo's had ever been like this. Violet stared down at her pale stomach, at the tendrils moving underneath her skin. Suddenly she had a flash of Bo lifting up his shirt and showing her the same rippling motion, back when they'd been crouched inside Gloom's improvised tunnel. More Parasites up there, Bo'd said. Active ones. He could feel it.

Violet put both hands against the wall. The rippling turned urgent. She'd known the tank room had to be close. She hadn't expected it to be quite this close. Brushing back her hair, she put an ear to the wall to listen. Nothing she could detect. No whirlybird whine, no pods chugging for breath.

She drew the static up again and hoped she wasn't going to vanish any of the kids floating on the other side.

When they drew closer, Bo saw that only the very top of the ship extended above the surface, like the tip of an iceberg. The bulk of it, lit from below by the ghostly yellow glow, stretched down into the depths of the harbor. Bo had never realized how deep the water was until now. Deeper than any swimming pool. He tried to ignore it.

The ship's hull towered over them like a black wall by the time the boat knocked against it. It stretched up and away, curving slightly, not so high but too sheer to scale without help. They had Gloom, though. Jon and Wyatt wrestled the anchor over the side to make sure the boat didn't drift on them while they were gone. The chain clattered and scraped, oscillating like a snake as it rushed and splashed into the water. When it finally snapped taut the boat gave a lurch.

Gloom slopped his way back over the side, the water streaming off him in rivulets. "Now we climb, children," he said. "Hold onto me."

He sprang gracefully out of the boat, onto the hull, clinging to it like a gecko. They watched as his coattails twined together and stretched down to them in a thick black cable. Bo reached to grab it, but it had a mind of its own, wrapping around his waist instead. It looped Bree next. She stood stock-still and grimaced as the motes touched her. Then Wyatt. Jon and his backpack last; he gave the black tendril a suspicious look as it circled his thick waist.

Gloom started to climb, and Bo found himself jerked into the air. Bree, yanked forward, smacked against the side of the hull with a muffled curse. Gloom didn't seem to notice. He kept climbing, his hands and feet suctioning to the surface. Bo could imagine the individual motes digging into the sleek black hull. He tried to find handholds and footholds where he could, to take some of the weight off. Below him he could hear the others doing the same thing, scrabbling against the side.

Then they were over the edge, all five of them, and Gloom's cable loosened. Bo stood up. He rubbed the spot under his rib where it had knocked a bruise. The cable slithered back between Gloom's shoulder blades and disappeared.

Bo remembered back to the last time he'd stood on top of the ship, preparing to hurl himself off it. There was no howling wind this time, just the sea breeze, but the entire hull was moving slightly under their feet, rolling with the motion of the water. Bo bent his knees to stay balanced.

Gloom had steered the boat around to the side they'd jumped off, close as possible to the cargo elevator that had taken them up to the hull in the first place. Now the empty shaft was a massive square pit. Bree nearly stepped into it before Gloom yanked her back. Bo inched to the edge and looked down. Jon had his flashlight out, but the beam was swallowed up long before it touched the platform at the bottom.

"Again," Gloom said, sounding slightly strained as the cable sprouted from his back. "One at a time, please, children."

Bree grabbed hold first, maybe wanting to make up for her near slip. She squinted down into the shaft. "Like rappelling," she said. "Easy." She looked at Wyatt for permission.

"Go ahead," he said.

Bree nodded. Gloom's cable snaked around her while the rest of him hunkered down over the edge, anchoring himself there with his bony white hands. Then she slipped into the shaft and started her descent. Jon kept the flashlight trained on her from above as Gloom lowered her, bit by bit.

The cable stretched dangerously thin, and Bo thought of the black wings breaking apart in midair, how Gloom sometimes thought he could do things he couldn't, as Bree disappeared into the dark. They all waited in silence until they heard a distant thump and her *I'm okay* drifted up to them. The cable slithered back up the side of the shaft, reeling into Gloom's body.

Bo took next. As the cable looped around his waist, a

vibration shuddered through the ship's hull, almost taking him off his feet. He crouched to steady himself, shooting Gloom a questioning look. Before Gloom could speak, Bo's ears filled with the hum, the same he'd heard on the rooftop but louder now, deafening. The static leapt, and he squinted his eyes a split second before the pillar of light erupted skyward again.

It shot up from the dead center of the ship, so close it threw the hull into stark relief, showing all the pits and scars and clumps of machinery. The green and purple twisted together like a violent bruise, and this time Bo realized it was cutting a hole in the sky. The gash opened up like a hungry mouth, wide enough to envelop the entire ship, maybe the entire city. Bo couldn't see anything through it but blackness. It put a deep dread in every part of him.

Then it was gone, and Bo was left blinking watery eyes.

"Hurry, Bo," Gloom said. "I think they are ready."

Compared to jumping off the ship, scaling down an elevator shaft was nothing. He knew it in his head, but the vertigo still made him queasy. He tried to use the same trick he had before, pretending there was a swimming pool below him, pretending Lia was shouting for him to hurry up.

But it was harder and harder to imagine Lia anywhere but inside the machine, maybe with tubes running into her Parasite, maybe awake now, not knowing where she was or what was going on. Or worse, knowing exactly what was going on.

Bo didn't wait for his vision to clear before he slipped down over the edge, trusting Gloom to hold him. His gut gave a savage lurch. Then the cable sucked tight against his aching ribs, catching him, swinging him against the side of the shaft, and he started his descent.

* * *

Once the second surge ended and the hum cut out, Violet stepped through the fissure she'd carved in the wall. She immediately felt liquid lapping at the canvas of her sneakers. The tank room was how they'd left it. Nobody had replaced the glass Bo had vanished, and the tubes that had kept his sister suspended were dangling from the top of the tank, revolving slowly in the air like a mobile. She saw that the tank nearest it had sprung a leak too, adding to the thin layer of liquid slopping around under her feet. Some of it was still drizzling down into the hole Bo had torn in the floor to get them inside.

She made her way down the row. All the tanks were occupied except Lia's emptied one. She was somewhere else, then. Maybe wherever the pods had been rushing to.

Violet stood in the center of the room and tried to decide what to do. She couldn't leave the kids in the tanks, but she couldn't haul three unconscious bodies around with her either. And as soon as she busted one of the tanks, the alarm would start up again—though she suspected the aliens now had larger concerns. She chewed hard on her lip, looking from one drifting figure to the next, knowing the longer she stood here thinking the closer the aliens were to opening the door. Bringing the other ships.

A noise spun her around. Someone was climbing out of the floor, two hands gripping the smoothest edge, one of them wrapped in black tape. Wyatt raised his head out of the hole and Violet's heart stopped.

Surprise flashed over his bruised face for only a split second, then he gave a rueful smile. "Hey, Vi. This must feel a bit awkward, right?"

Violet realized she was still in the simulation. It made such perfect sense. They'd let her think she'd escaped. They'd let her think she was strong, that her tuned Parasite could do anything she wanted. And now it was going to start all over again. Wyatt first, but her other tormentors couldn't be far behind. As he clambered out of the hole, Violet brought the static up from her stomach. It was swirling, sparking.

She didn't know what would happen, didn't know if Wyatt would vanish and then reappear again behind her, or if he would stand there unharmed and laugh at her. The static tingled up and down her skin. She wanted him gone. Wanted him gone more than she'd ever wanted anyone gone. Violet focused.

Then Bo's head emerged from the hole. His eyes widened. "You got away?" he demanded. "You're okay?" An incredulous grin spread across his face, almost too big for it.

Violet faltered. She felt the static slipping. Was this part of the simulation? Was Bo the newest thing they'd come up with to hurt her? She watched as he hopped up and out, wiping his hands on his shirt. Bree came next, glowering as usual, then Jon, wrestling through the too-small hole. His brow was furrowed and he didn't look happy to see her. Last came Gloom, unfolding his long limbs like a spider.

"Hello, Violet," he said. "I see that you have been fully tuned. Congratulations, but please do not let yourself be recaptured. That would be disastrous."

Violet's gaze flicked from Gloom to Bo to Wyatt. Her heart was thudding hard.

"No hard feelings, Vi," Wyatt said, holding up his taped hand. "I hope you're not holding any grudges. That's what weak people—"

Violet's knuckles connected with the unbruised side of his face and the impact sang all the way up her arm. Wyatt staggered back. He ran his tongue around his teeth. His eyes narrowed as he stepped forward, and Violet readied herself to swing again, but Jon's bulk was suddenly between them.

"Out of the way, Jon," Wyatt said, sounding only faintly annoyed.

Jon didn't move. Through her rage, Violet felt a pang of gratefulness that Jon was still her friend and still on her side. Over his broad shoulder, Wyatt's face twisted livid for a second. Then he ran his tongue over his teeth again. Shrugged. His gray eyes suddenly went calm, which only made Violet want to claw them out even more.

"Good call," he said, stepping backward. "We don't really have time to waste, right, Gloom?"

Violet looked at Bo again. "I can't tell if you're real," she said, feeling crazy for saying it out loud. "They had me clamped."

She touched the back of her neck and felt the tiny puncture marks scabbing over. They felt real. But everything in the simulations had felt real, and it made sense, didn't it, that they would let her think she was free before they dragged her back to hell.

Bo's eyes were wide and worried. "We're real," he said. "I said I was coming back, remember?" The expression on his face reminded her of something. How he'd looked when he saw his sister in the tank, that expression Violet didn't think a simulation could get right. He took something from behind his back: her baseball bat.

"What the *fuck* is going on?" Bree demanded. "You're suddenly on our side again? Why are you even in here?"

"To me it seems Violet is trying to relocate these hosts and their keys," Gloom said. "Which is our aim as well. As the strategist says, we have no time to waste. We need to break the tanks open as quickly as possible. Disregard the alarm."

Gloom sounded like himself. So did Bree, so did Bo, so did Jon in his not-speaking. But there was no way to be sure. Maybe it would be like this for the rest of her life, however short that might end up being. She would always be wondering, in the back of her mind, if it was all a simulation.

Violet reached out and took the bat. The handle felt cold under her fingers. Solid. Real enough for now. She gave Bo a nod, mouthed a thank-you. The weight felt right. She tossed it up and down, then turned and swung, hitting the glass of the nearest tank with a resounding crack. Tiny fissures spider-webbed across the surface and the whole thing buckled.

It gave way on the third blow and Gloom rushed inside, unhooking the tubes, wrapping motes around the suspended sleeper. Violet took a breath. Shot another look at Wyatt. Then she moved on to the next tank. It helped to pretend she was swinging for his head.

30

Bo kept glancing over at Violet as they worked, pulling the sleepers out of their tanks and dressing them in the fleece sweatshirts he'd swiped off an XXL rack and asked Jon to put in the backpack. He'd figured it would keep them warm, and make them look more like real people. More dignified.

He was relieved they hadn't found Violet floating in a tank, but there was something unsettled about her that made him think that maybe whatever they'd done to her was worse. She was tuned, like Gloom had said. He could tell from the way his Parasite rippled back and forth with hers. But they'd had her clamped while they did it.

Bo remembered what Violet had said a long time ago, when he asked about what the wasters saw. Better than this, she'd said, meaning the ruined city, the empty streets. But Bo didn't think Violet had seen anything good. Her hand kept creeping to the back of her neck and she kept looking over at Wyatt, not with the sly longing glances he'd caught her at before, but the look you gave a wild animal. He wanted to explain why he'd had to bring Wyatt. How he'd needed his help to make a plan, how he still didn't trust him.

No time. Jon was pulling the last piece of equipment out of his backpack and assembling it with Bree's help—a stretcher, jerry-rigged from collapsible tent poles and a bedsheet stretched taut between them. Elliot had thought it up. It still wouldn't be easy to drag through the tunnel, but it would be easier than trying to carry the sleepers any other way.

Gloom wouldn't be there to make a scuttling body bag for them. Bo watched him tug the last tube free from the last sleeper, then stand up.

"Wait at the cargo elevator," Gloom said. "Then we will all go up together." His gaze circled the room and fell on Violet. "If you are followed, Violet is now fully tuned. She can use her key to defend you."

Violet blinked. "You're going after Lia?" she asked, her voice hoarse. "Where is she?"

Bo realized the question was directed at him. "They've got her in the machine," he said. "The machine they use to hold the door open. She's the battery for it. Gloom's going to reprogram it so the door opens up right here. So it vanishes the ship."

"I like that you are succinct, Bo," Gloom said. His gaunt face flashed an exaggerated smile before it turned grave again. "Yes. That is our strategy. You will take the other hosts to safety. Bo and the strategist called Wyatt will come with me to the machine."

Violet bristled. Bo could see a sudden tightness in her shoulders and her eyes were narrowed.

"The asshole called Wyatt can help carry the kids out," she said. "I'm coming to the machine with you and Bo."

A ripple passed through Gloom's body. He shook his head. "No. I may need help inside the machine. But I cannot take another key inside with me without risking interference."

"What do you mean?" Violet demanded.

"Between Lia's Parasite and mine," Bo interjected. "Or between hers and anyone else's. Gloom explained it back at the theater." He looked over sideways at Wyatt, who had dug his crowbar out of Jon's backpack again and had it dangling gripped loose in his good hand. Gloom had explained it, but that didn't mean he liked it.

"He needs someone without a Parasite to go inside with him," Wyatt finished. "Don't give me that look, Vi. We're all on the same side, right? We all want these fuckers gone. Whatever it takes."

"You are more valuable protecting the other hosts, Violet," Gloom said. "The diagnostic drones may attempt to retrieve them."

He was already at the broken wall Bo assumed was Violet's handiwork, waiting impatiently, his motes moving and blurring him. Wyatt crossed over to join him. Bo took the last fleece from Jon's outstretched hand, bundling it up under his shirt for Lia, then looked at Violet. She was stock-still, her hands clenched at her sides.

"Don't trust him," she said.

"I don't," Bo said.

Wyatt snorted.

"And if it's something where you have to pick," Violet said, looking over his head at Wyatt. "If it's either him or you." She looked straight at Bo. "Kill him. Make sure. Got it?" A muscle twitched in her cheek, but her eyes were dry as she leaned forward and wrapped him in a stiff hug. Her cold hand ran over his head. "Because if he comes back without you, I'm putting that brick where I should've," she whispered.

"I'll be okay," Bo said, feeling an ache in his chest that wasn't from Gloom's cable. "We'll all be okay. I think."

He pulled away, nodded to Jon and Bree. They already had the first kid loaded onto the stretcher and ready to lower down into the tunnel. Both of them nodded back, looking grim. Determined. They were Lost Boys, and maybe Violet wasn't anymore, technically, but she could still take care of herself easy. He hoped Lia would want to meet them all once she was awake. He figured she would.

He gave Violet one last look, then followed Gloom and Wyatt out into the hall. It was lit from above by wriggling yellow lights.

"The machine will be guarded," Gloom said. "Even if some of them have been diverted by the fire. Please be ready."

Bo pulled the baton from his waistband and flicked it out to full length. As for his Parasite, that was ready and waiting. He'd been full up with adrenaline from the moment they left the theater. It gave a twist in his stomach and he felt the static flare up.

He glanced over at Wyatt, remembering what Violet had said. Maybe the static wouldn't just be for whirlys. Even if Wyatt had given up his idea of taking Bo's Parasite, maybe he was lying about not holding grudges, lying the same way he lied about so many other things. If they were alone together for even an instant, Bo didn't know what he might do. But for now, Bo had to work together with him.

Gloom set off at speed, abandoning his human shape completely, flowing along the floor like shadow. Bo and Wyatt had to run to keep pace, shoes slapping against the metallic black floor. Bo kept one hand holding the fleece under his shirt and the other curled around the police baton. Wyatt was loping along easily beside him, his long legs doubling Bo's stride. Bo gritted his teeth and sped up, pushing through all his aches.

Gloom didn't scurry up onto the walls or run circles or switch back and forth with his human shape—he moved only forward, intent, focused. Fast. Bo and Wyatt pelted along behind him through the ship's dizzying architecture, through the cavernous spiky halls, sometimes past things Bo recognized. The bright silver pyramids, the blacklit pits full of tangled tendrils like the wormy wall. He couldn't be sure if they were the same rooms he'd seen before or just identical to them.

And there was nobody in their path. The ship seemed empty—maybe Wyatt's plan had worked even better than they'd hoped, maybe all the pods had flown to the warehouses. Bo had the fleece wrapped around his arm now, so he could pump both of them properly. He was still scared and strung but exhilarated too, in the way a good footrace always made him feel light as air, like he was flying through the dark. Faster than his own shadow.

They passed under an archway, and Bo was pushing his stride just a bit longer, feeling Wyatt slip a bit behind, when the ceiling opened up above him. Gloom came to an abrupt halt; Bo skidded into him and was caught, pushed back by a ripple of motes. He looked up.

It was the hugest room he'd ever seen, dwarfing the other halls, its black walls curving upward forever into a high-domed ceiling that reminded Bo of cathedrals but twice the size. And it wasn't empty. Dominating the space was a massive spiked tower that touched the vaulted ceiling, and Bo could guess extended through it too.

The entire thing was moving: revolving blocks shifted in its base, spars extended and retracted, strange bulbs expanded and emptied like gigantic black lungs. Arcs of pale green and purple sparked up and down its surface. Bo felt every hair on his body stand on end, felt his Parasite rippling hard. It was a machine, but not like any machine he'd seen before.

"The key is inside that structure," Gloom said, re-forming to point with one bony finger. Bo followed the motion and saw a black globe anchored into the base of the machine, unmoving. Lia was inside of it. He moved forward on instinct, forgetting all about his Parasite causing interference, about the plan to reprogram the machine. The only thought in his head was tearing the globe open and getting Lia out.

Then the pods descended on them, all of them harnessed with the gas guns, their proboscises extending, glinting scalpel-sharp. At least a dozen. More than Bo had ever seen in one place. Their low chugging sound filled the air and rumbled his chest. Gloom sank low to the floor—Bo remembered the horrible noise he'd made when the freezing gas had hit him last time.

But this time, Bo was ready. He dredged the static up from his Parasite and held it, let it swell and crackle, and as the pods dropped toward them he unleashed it. The first burst vanished an entire pod, ripping it out of the air. The others angled their blunt heads toward the empty space even as they streamed around it, still heading for them. One had its gas gun ready to fire, blue fog billowing from the tip, and Bo took that one next. The burst was misaimed, but it sheared half the pod's tail away and sent it crashing into its companion.

"Cover us," Wyatt said. Bo felt him take the fleece from his hands, then he was gone and there was no time to respond anyway. Not with his Parasite writhing, frantic, and the static racing through every part of his body like lightning as he turned it on the next pod, the next, the next.

Sometimes they vanished whole; sometimes the burst was less concentrated, scoring ragged holes in their slick black flesh. In the corner of his eye he saw Gloom make for the machine, darting and weaving with Wyatt close behind. The pods weren't coming for him anymore; they were jetting away, focused on Gloom or maybe on fleeing.

Bo kept at it, burst after burst, popping them out of the air. He was swaying where he stood, his Parasite nearly spent, his baton forgotten on the floor. He'd never used it like this, so much, so fast. Through the sheet of sweat in his eyes he saw Gloom and Wyatt disappear into a duct at the base of the machine.

One of his ears had popped and he didn't hear the pod behind him until it was too late. As he turned all he could see through the blur was a hooked proboscis bearing down on him, ready to spear him through. Bo reached deep and flung out whatever static was left, his Parasite's last gasp, and his eyes squeezed shut on instinct as—

He felt the proboscis slice through the air beside his head and heard it crunch against the floor. His eyes flew open to see the pod twist, curling reflexively around the hole Bo had punched straight through it. He rolled hard. Most of the pod's bulk slammed into the floor, but its tail came down on Bo's back, pinning him flat. It knocked the wind out of him and he gasped. His mouth fished open and shut as he waited for the next pod to come and finish him off.

The roaring in his ears subsided. He realized there were no more pods. All of them were gone or near to it, beached on the black metal floor, groaning and leaking their yellow fuel. Bo wriggled as far as he could, but his legs were still trapped. The pod's gas was escaping, turning it heavy. His exhausted Parasite was the same, sitting like lead in his gut.

Bo lay flat against the floor as his heartbeat slowed to normal. He'd destroyed the pods. He'd gotten Gloom and Wyatt safely inside the machine. Were they with Lia yet? Was Gloom already taking the tubes out of her? He braced himself to try getting his legs free again, thinking there might be more pods on the way, coming back from the warehouse.

"Man, Bo, that was impressive." Wyatt's voice came from somewhere behind him. "Really fucking impressive."

He stepped into view a few meters away and Bo's heart leapt. Lia was draped over his shoulder, wrapped in the oversized fleece. She was unconscious but even from a distance he could see her eyelids fluttering. Bo wriggled again, desperate to see her up close, to feel her pulse and be sure.

Still stuck. He ran his tongue around his dust-dry mouth, preparing to tell Wyatt that he was trapped, that he needed a hand. Violet's words came back to him. He shut his mouth and squirmed again, harder. He managed to loosen one leg. Barely.

Wyatt's eyes zeroed in on his motion. "Gloom's putting the new coordinates in," he said. "Says to make sure the pods are all dead, then head back to the boat. He told me how to work the elevator."

He set Lia down on the floor. Gently, but Bo didn't like him touching her at all, didn't like the smirking way he was looking at her. He knew Bo was stuck. Had to. Bo's gaze was glued to his sister as Wyatt stalked through the downed pods, finishing them off with sharp savage up-and-downs using the end of the crowbar, driving it into their heads. She was so close. Lying there just a meter away, breathing slow but alive.

The chemical smell Bo remembered from the storage unit was wafting into the air strong enough to sting his nose and throat.

"Help me out," he said. He licked his lips. "I'm stuck, help me out."

Wyatt nodded, started toward him, then stopped at the sound of a low groan. Bo saw one of the downed pods moving behind Wyatt's back. Its bright light flashed in the dark, scanning Wyatt up and down, turning him into a black silhouette. It moved again, rolling over so its damaged underside was exposed. Wyatt's eyes narrowed. He turned to it.

The pod's underbelly peeled open, and something pale and slimy slapped out onto the floor, something nearly human shaped, legless. Bo realized what it was just before she opened her red-pigmented mouth.

"Wyatt, my darling boy, my handsome boy, my darling boy, my handsome boy," the unfinished othermother sang, crawling toward them, leaving a slick on the floor beneath her.

Bo saw shock scrawl itself across Wyatt's face, saw Wyatt's knuckles throb white as they clutched even tighter around his crowbar. He remembered that Wyatt had never been inside the warehouses. He had never been hunted by his othermother or even seen her.

"So you do remember," Wyatt muttered. His expression shifted, a mixture of pride and fascination and, for some reason, relief. "Hey, Bo. You want to know why they put me in a hospital?" He asked it still looking at the othermother, transfixed.

Bo didn't want to know. He didn't want to be here, seeing this. He knew in his gut that it was dangerous to see this. The last time Wyatt had told him a secret, he'd been planning to cut him open. All Bo wanted was to get to his sister and get out. He gave up on the one leg and tried the other, jiggering it back and forth under the pod's dead weight.

Wyatt glanced at him over his shoulder. "It's because I saw this coming," he said. "All of this." He waved around with his taped-up hand, encompassing the othermother, the dead pods, the ship. "I saw it coming before anyone else did."

"My darling boy, my handsome boy, Wyatt, Wyatt, Wyatt!"

Bo watched him walk over to the unfinished othermother, stopping by her head. One of her hands gripped weakly at his ankle but he kicked it away, staring down at her with pure loathing. He toed up like he was taking a golf swing; Bo wanted to look away but didn't. The swing, the crack. Black fluid spattered up into the air and the othermother's smashed-in skull flopped to the floor with a dull crunch. Her shrill voice cut quiet.

"The first othermother is the hardest, right?" Wyatt asked, looking down at the ruined face. "After that, it's so easy." He turned back to Bo. "They sent mine early. Before the ship came down. She looked right. She looked human." He gave the othermother's body a contemptuous glance. "Not like the cheap ones they keep churning out now."

Nothing Wyatt was saying made sense. There had been no othermothers before the ship came down.

"We need to go," Bo said. "We need to hurry. Remember?"

But Wyatt ignored him. "I knew she wasn't my mother," he said softly. "She couldn't have been. A real mother wouldn't have done the things she did to me. She was an othermother, and my real one, well. Who knows what they did with her, right? Maybe I never really had one."

Bo realized he'd stopped kicking. He was paralyzed by knowing. He knew what Wyatt had done. There was only one way to become a Lost Boy.

"The first one is the hardest," Wyatt said, walking toward him now with the crowbar dangling from his good hand. "It was tough. I admit that, right? But I knew, deep down, no matter what she said, no matter how convincing she was, that she wasn't my mother. She wasn't human. I did her in with a kitchen knife."

Bo flinched as Wyatt dropped to a crouch right in front of him, resting the crowbar across his bony knees. His mouth was too dry to speak even if he'd wanted to, even if he'd thought Gloom could get out of the machine in time to help him. His Parasite was dead weight in his stomach like the pod was dead weight on his legs.

"I was confused for a while," Wyatt said. "I'll admit that too. No secrets between us, right, Bo? But then the ship came down, and everything made sense." He straightened up, gripping the crowbar tight. "I can make the tough decisions. The ones other people won't. I was *meant* to be here. Right here. Saving the world." He hefted the crowbar. "I think you've done your part already."

What kind of lies would he tell the others? What kind of lies would he tell Lia? Bo felt his heart ripped out thinking about it, felt sick and furious. *Made you a bit of a martyr.* That was what Wyatt had said. That was what he would do again. Violet would never believe him, Bo knew that much, and that meant he would find a way to kill her too. He locked his eyes on Lia's face and made one final thrashing bid to slip his legs free, but it wasn't enough, not nearly.

Wyatt jammed the crowbar underneath the pod's tail and

pushed. The rubbery flesh levered up off Bo's legs, freeing him. He was slow to slide out from underneath. He got to his feet, still stunned, nauseous. Wyatt let the tail drop down again, smacking the floor. The meaty noise echoed. All the pods were silent now. Dead.

Bo stumbled over to his sister. Her bare skin was cold and clammy against his, but she was alive. They were both alive.

"Let's get moving," Wyatt said. "Gloom can take care of himself."

Bo nodded, still unable to speak. He slung Lia onto his back, gripping her arms around his neck. She was lighter than she should've been, fed through tubes for too long. But she was alive, and they were nearly out.

"Alright," Bo said hoarsely. "I'm ready."

31

Violet helped Jon lower the last sleeper to the floor of the elevator platform lengthwise beside the other two. All three were still unconscious, breathing deep and slow. Peaceful-looking, apart from the Parasites rippling hard in their abdomens. Violet used her sleeve to wipe a long strand of drool off the red-haired girl's chin, then straightened up.

Her back and arms ached from the long crawl through the tunnel dragging the stretcher. Passing the kids up the metal ziggurat steps of the elevator hadn't been easy either. It didn't help that the entire time she'd been tensed, ready to fight or flee, ready for Jon and Bree to turn on her or for the simulation to dump her back in her kitchen.

But nothing had happened. Jon seemed like Jon and Bree, scowling, seemed like Bree. Despite Gloom's warning, they'd made it here unscathed, with no whirlybirds trying to stop them. Now all they needed was for Bo and his sister and Gloom to show up. And Wyatt. Jon had explained that they'd brought a boat, that the ship had touched down in the harbor.

Violet was glad she wouldn't be skydiving with Gloom even

if Bo seemed to have survived it alright. She flopped down onto the platform, massaging her sore wrists.

Jon sat down beside her. "I'm glad you're okay," he said. His voice sounded deeper than it had just a week ago. It startled her a bit. She tried not to think about her own.

"Me too," she said, putting her hand on his shoulder and squeezing. That felt real too.

Jon's black brows knit together, more expression than she'd ever seen on his face except at night, when he was dreaming bad dreams and speaking his foreign language.

"I thought Wyatt killed you," he said.

Bree, standing lookout, jerked her head up. She barked a laugh. "Why the fuck would you think that?" she demanded, not looking at Violet. "If she'd just stayed and taken the punishment, it would've been fine. Wyatt would've let her back."

Jon just shook his head. He looked at Violet. "He touches everyone on the same arm," he said.

Violet grimaced. "After tonight, we don't have to worry about Wyatt," she said. "We don't need him." She shot a hard look at Bree. "If you cared about Gilly, you'd get her the fuck away from him too."

Bree opened her mouth, red with anger, but cut short at the sound of echoing footsteps. Violet bolted upright. Wyatt and Bo appeared from the dark at the end of the hall, and Bo was bent over with someone clinging to his back. His sister. Violet felt a rush of relief. As they came closer she saw that Bo was exhausted, his face drawn and paler than normal, and she knew he'd been using his Parasite. She still couldn't blame him for wanting to carry Lia himself.

And exhausted as he looked, there was a brightness in his

eyes, something close to a smile on his mouth not quite daring to show itself, not yet. Violet clambered down the platform to help him lift his sister up.

"Where's Gloom?" she asked, keeping one eye on Wyatt even as she took Lia's legs.

"Finishing in the machine," Bo said. Worry flashed across his face. "He said to take the elevator up. Wait in the boat. He can climb it."

"What happens if he doesn't get out in time?" Violet demanded. "He'll go through the door with the ship, right? To wherever the aliens are waiting."

And maybe that was for the best. Violet remembered what she had seen in the simulation, the planet staining black with a spreading sea of motes, the ships fleeing. Maybe Gloom really was even more dangerous than they were.

"He'll make it," Wyatt said calmly, swinging himself up onto the platform. "Here." He reached down and helped them lift Lia up. Bo followed, looking scared to be even a hand's length apart from his sister now that they were together again. Violet felt a tiny churn of trepidation. Bo had his real family back, what was left of it, and whatever he'd said about her being his other sister, well, people forgot about things like that pretty fast.

She hauled herself back up onto the platform, ignoring Wyatt's offered hand. He shrugged and gave his innocent white grin, but it looked a lot uglier with his face all bruised up and something dark drying spattered across his cheek. Violet shot Bo a glance, but Bo's gaze was still glued to his sister. Wyatt stuck his good hand inside the broken-open panel.

They started to rise.

★   ★   ★

Getting back down to the boat was harder without Gloom. Bree went first, sliding down the curved hull, digging her heels in to slow herself. Then the rest of them made a human chain, Jon as the anchor, to pass the sleeping kids down one at a time. When it came time to pass Lia, Bo could barely make himself let go. He stretched as far as he possibly could, holding her under her armpits, then sucked in a deep breath and released. She slid the short distance to Bree, who grunted as she caught her. Bo didn't breathe until Lia was lying in the bottom of the boat with the others.

Bree started turning them all on their sides, in case they started to vomit up the drugs in their systems, while Jon clambered down. He helped Violet next. She wasn't touching the back of her neck anymore, but Bo could tell she was still on edge, tensed to breaking point. He didn't blame her. She dropped down into the boat, and then it was only him and Wyatt crouched up on the hull. Bo threw a glance toward the dark mouth of the elevator shaft, hoping to see Gloom slithering through.

"He'll make it," Wyatt repeated.

But Bo worried as a shuddering vibration ran through the ship's hull. The machine was warming up again. He judged the distance and slid down into the boat; Violet and Bree pulled him inside. He went to where Lia was stretched out and sat so he could cradle her head, so it wouldn't bang against the slick floor of the yacht.

Violet was looking up at Wyatt, now starting to descend, and Bo could tell she wished they could push off without him. But they didn't have a way to start the boat. They didn't even have paddles. The realization hit him in the gut.

"Gloom pushed us here," Bo said slowly. "We don't have a key for the ignition."

Violet's eyes widened. She had that look on her face that meant he'd done something incredibly stupid, but all she said was:

"Fuck."

Another vibration passed through the hull, rocking the boat. Bo gripped the edge with his free hand and his sister with the other. If Gloom didn't make it out, none of them would. They would be pulled right through the door along with the ship.

Wyatt hopped inside, making the boat bob. Jon was leaned over the side looking at the propeller; Bree and Violet were trying to take the panel off the ignition, but Bo didn't think even Elliot would know how to hotwire a boat engine. It was all on Gloom.

Bo knew he should be thinking, should be trying to find a solution, but he couldn't stop looking down into his sister's placid face. Whatever happened next, whether the door swallowed them up or not, they'd be together for it. He'd done that much. That was something.

Lia's eyes flicked open. Bo's heart leapt in his chest, then his shout of joy strangled off.

They weren't Lia's eyes. They were flat gleaming black.

"I am sorry, Bo," she said, in Gloom's tinny voice. "The key has to remain inside the machine while the door opens. There was no other way." Then she burst apart in his hands into cold black motes. They streamed around him like water, slipping through his fingers, and plunged over the side of the boat.

Bo was frozen, kneeling, his eyes still fixed where his sister's face had been a moment before. Lia was not in the boat. She'd never been in the boat. She was still in the machine.

"No, no, no, no!"

It was the only word he could form. Wyatt had unclipped the

anchor and the boat was moving, picking up speed as Gloom's tendrils churned the dark water, carrying them away. He shot to his feet, not caring if he unbalanced the boat, not caring if he capsized it. He tried to dive over the side but hands caught him, pulled him back. He thought it was Wyatt and curled his fist but ended up hitting Jon instead.

"It could have been me," Bo gasped. "I could have gone in the machine instead, if you told me, if I knew..."

Through the pounding in his head he heard Violet round on Wyatt, shouting, heard Wyatt's voice answering back clear and cold.

"It was the only way. You heard Gloom. She had to stay in the machine for the door to open."

Bo went slack in Jon's arms, letting all his limbs go limp. Jon loosened his hold for half a second. It was all Bo needed to wrench free and hurl himself into the water. The cold hit him like concrete, smashed the breath out of him. He felt bubbles swirling around his face as he fought his way up to the surface and started, desperately, to swim. He could see the yellow light of the ship's underbelly, see its dark crest emerging from the water. He pulled one stroke. Another.

Blood was rushing in his ears; his Parasite was kicking at him. He couldn't swim how Lia did. He was clumsy in the water. Slow. But he was going to make it to the ship. He was going to make it back inside. A swell caught him off guard and cold saltwater rushed up his nose. He choked but kept moving, stroke after stroke, dragging himself along the surface. From behind him he heard a dim splash.

"Bo!" It was Violet's voice, garbled by water. "It's too late, Bo. Come back."

But Bo knew he could make it. He just had to keep pushing.

Pods streamed overhead, racing back to the ship, knowing something was wrong. Bo's muscles were screaming and his breath was ragged, his chest stitched tight. He spat out another mouthful of seawater. Static was swirling all through him. His Parasite was going mad, spasming around in his gut. The dark wall of the ship was getting closer. Closer.

A blinding burst of light, electric green shot through with purple, stamped across his eyes. The hum was back, the deep hum that he could feel in his bones. Desperate, Bo threw himself into the next stroke, thrashing his way through the freezing water, losing any shred of technique. The ship was enveloped in the dancing light. The door was open.

And just as suddenly, it was shut and the ship was gone. Bo's anguished shout was lost in the roar of water rushing to fill the empty space. He was sucked under, tossed hard in the foam, losing up and down as he pinwheeled. Icy water filled his mouth and nose and he wondered if he was going to drown, after everything he'd survived, if he was going to drown right here in the city harbor. He was completely submerged and couldn't tell which way was up.

A hand grabbed the back of his shirt, then his arm. He felt Violet give two powerful kicks and they broke the surface. Bo choked out a stream of water and mucus. There was a sharp ache in the center of his chest and he could hear Violet gasping for breath beside him. She was treading water, still holding onto him, keeping him afloat.

"It's okay, Bo." He finally realized she was speaking, saying the same thing over and over. "It's okay. It's okay. It's okay."

But as the water turned his legs numb, as the dark shape of the boat circled back to retrieve them, he could tell from the ragged sound of her voice that she didn't believe it either.

32

The harbor was black as pitch and the inside of the boat was silent. A few pods that hadn't made it back to the ship before it vanished moved in the distance, making agitated circles over the water. Violet kept waiting for the door to reappear, for the green and purple light to split the sky again, but nothing happened. The ship was gone, and Bo's sister was gone with it.

Gloom was steering them back to the docks. "I know how it feels to lose motes," he finally said. "I know it is difficult."

Violet braced for Bo to explode, but his voice came small and shaky. "She's not a mote," he said. "Lia is not a mote. She's not a part of me." His eyes were shot through with pink, staring down between his feet. "She was a whole other person."

"I am sorry I deceived you," Gloom said. "There was no other way. The key must remain in the machine for the door to open." His expression morphed, turning from sadness to bewilderment. "I thought you would be happy, Bo. You and the other children are safe. Your world is safe. Your city is free."

"Shut your mouth, Gloom," Violet said.

He did, which surprised her a bit. The boat drew closer to the docks, and Violet realized the sky was clearing, the omnipresent gray clouds dissolving. Without any city lights to drown them, she could see the stars clearly for the first time since she'd gone camping as a kid. They looked like glittering glass shards strewn through the dark. It was so fucking beautiful she almost forgot to be sad.

Jon and Bree, who'd been respectively watching and trying not to watch Bo, looked up at them too. Wyatt had his eyes shut, his head tipped back, a smile curling his lips like he was basking in everything that had happened. He thought he'd saved the world. And if it really had been the only way, leaving Lia inside the machine, then maybe he and Gloom had made the right decision. In a tiny nasty part of her, Violet was even glad about it. Bo was starting over, the same way she was. Back to zero for each of them. No happy easy endings.

But she knew that Bo would never be able to look at a night sky without wondering where his sister had been disappeared to.

There was a crowd of kids waiting for them at the quay. Most of them Violet didn't recognize—the ones freed from the warehouses, she figured—but right at the front were the last of the Lost Boys. Everyone was whooping and hollering as the boat drew in, but when the Lost Boys caught sight of Violet they stared like she was a ghost. She waved to Elliot, and after a few stunned seconds got a shy wave back.

Wyatt swung out of the boat first, raising his arms all triumphant, and the Lost Boys swarmed him, some of the new kids from the warehouses too. They stared up at him like he was a god, or maybe a dad. Violet didn't know which was worse. Jon climbed out next, and then Bree. Gilly, followed by a blonde-haired girl Violet didn't recognize, hurled herself onto Bree's back, saying something about all the whirlybirds dropping dead at once.

Violet looked over at Bo, who still hadn't budged. He didn't look like he would ever be happy again. She thought about dragging him up into the celebration, knowing the rest of the day, maybe the rest of the week, would be a whirlwind that might take Lia off his mind. If Gloom was right and the fog at the city limits was clearing the same way the sky had, the rest of the world would be clamoring to know what had been going on for the past four months.

The thought of all the news crews and cameras made her feel slightly queasy. Now was the time to get one final supply run in, get new clothes, new pills, enough cash to be exactly who she wanted—there was nobody left to report thefts—and get out of the city for good. Start over somewhere new.

Her Parasite rippled in her stomach, a reminder that starting over was tough to do. She looked at Bo again, whose face was still so lost and so shocked. She looked up at the jetty, at Wyatt, remembering the static swirling around inside her as she'd stared at him back aboard the ship, preparing to make him disappear.

Gloom clambered up into the boat now, folding his long legs underneath himself. He stared guiltily at Bo.

"Gloom," Violet said. "What happens to a person if you vanish them?"

Bo's head jerked up.

Gloom opened his mouth. "They are not vanishing," he said. "They are passing through the door. Survival would depend on the conditions on the other side of the door. It would depend on if the other ships are in atmosphere or in vacuum, if they are near a gravity well or…" His face changed as he realized what she was thinking. "That is a very bad idea, Violet."

"Why?" Bo demanded, his voice strong again. "Why couldn't that work?"

"If you go through the door, there may not be any way of returning," Gloom said flatly. "Your keys were grown with exact coordinates embedded in them. They are intended to move matter through the door only to those coordinates. Only in one direction. Otherwise our enemy could reopen the door from the other side using your sister's key."

"He'd be trapped there," Violet surmised. "If I vanished him, he'd be trapped on the other side."

"That is likely," Gloom said, but she heard a bit of hesitation in his voice.

Bo had heard it too. "Likely," he echoed. "That's likely. So what's unlikely?"

"The keys are alive, as you know," Gloom said. "They can adapt. Mutate. Perhaps remember." He paused. "And I was not lying when I told you your key would have caused interference with your sister's. Both are powerful, both are tuned. They may interact in strange ways."

"To send us back here?" Bo demanded.

"It is possible," Gloom said. "But it is very unlikely."

Violet could tell Bo was already decided. He turned to her. His eyes were dry, all the tears poured out of them, but they were wide and pleading. "You have to try it," he said. "Please, Violet."

Violet realized her own eyes weren't dry. The saline stung and she wiped hard with the back of her hand. She tried to remind herself that Bo wouldn't be part of her fresh start anyway. That she'd known Bo for hardly any time at all. That he was just a little punk.

"If I mess it up, or if you don't come back, that means I'm killing you," she said. "Right now. I'd be killing you."

"Yeah," Bo said, with a helpless shrug. "I know."

If he didn't come back, she was killing him. If she didn't try, something else would be killing him all his life. She didn't think Bo was good at letting go. Violet remembered back to the parkade, to Bo's first othermother. She remembered the burned-down ruin of his house. She didn't know if he was strong enough to lose another person he loved. But Violet was.

Violet hoped she was.

"Do it now," Bo begged. "Before I get scared."

Violet took a deep breath, feeling the static, drawing it up. Her Parasite started to churn. She focused on the whole of Bo, on his hunched shoulders and scrawny arms and shaved head. She'd already had the gruesome cartoon in her mind of sending only half of him over.

"I advise against this, children," Gloom said, looking from her to Bo and back. "I advise against this, Bo and Violet."

Violet breathed again. She knew in a second the other Lost Boys would notice they hadn't joined in, would come and pull them out of the boat. It was now or never. "Good luck, Pooh Bear," she said, and she vanished him.

The static rippled out of her; Bo and a chunk of the wooden bench he'd been sitting on disappeared. The boat rocked. Settled. Then it was only her and Gloom staring at each other, wondering what she'd just done.

"He has been lucky before," Gloom finally said.

"Yeah." Violet swallowed. "He has."

* * *

Bo was floating, with light prying at his squeezed-shut eyelids. He opened them slowly and vertigo hit him. There was no up or down or sky or ground. Everything around him was the electric green that had shot up from the center of the ship, webbed with veins of pulsating purple. His eyes rolled around for something to fix on and found a vaguely familiar shape.

It was growing larger, rippling, waving its tendrils. The section of the wormy wall he'd ripped away not so long ago. Just hours ago. And it wasn't growing; he was moving toward it. Something like a current was carrying him along. Bo sucked in a deep breath and found he could breathe, or maybe that he didn't need to. He remembered what Gloom had said about alive and not alive. How people had a narrow definition for it.

Still, he hoped he was alive in the narrow definition way. The section of wormy wall slid past him, wriggling its tendrils like a goodbye wave. But there were other shapes approaching. He recognized the skeletal silhouette of the othermother he'd vanished with Violet, its legs all bashed in. Its mouth was open but he couldn't hear it, couldn't hear anything. He slid past her too, and then past the box trailer, orbited by chunks of tarmac, that he'd vanished at the end of the world.

He realized the piece of wormy wall was the one he'd sent away the night he escaped the warehouse. He was seeing everything he'd vanished, but it hadn't passed through the door how Gloom had said, not all the way. They were inside it still. Gloom was wrong. Bo's Parasite wasn't tuned all the way. Maybe Violet's wasn't either, and Bo wasn't going to get all the way through the door, leaving him stuck drifting here like everything else. He kicked hard with his legs and tried to swim with his arms, but it didn't seem to do anything. All he could do was keep floating forward and hope.

Next was a parade of little beetles, pop cans, crumpled bits of newspaper from his practicing in the theater. Then the spindly lamp he'd vanished inside the storage unit trying to get away from Wyatt's knife. A cylindrical plug of metal and meat, leaking viscera, from when he'd vanished his way through the dying pod up on the spar. More chunks of metal from moving around inside the ship, some close enough he could reach out and touch them.

He nearly missed the tiny black mote, thinking it was another beetle. On instinct he flung out a hand and caught it. The cold smooth feel of it in his palm was oddly comforting. If he made it back, he could return it to Gloom.

Another chunk of wormy wall, and then came what he'd been dreading most: the pods, or pieces of them. Their yellow fuel drifted in globules, and ropes of flesh and wire haloed around their sliced-up body parts. A few of the pods he'd vanished whole seemed to turn toward him as he passed. One of them reached with its long mechanical arm, maybe trying to take him with them, maybe just desperate to touch something, anything, in the empty space.

But the current carried Bo out of their reach, and suddenly the green-and-purple light was bleeding away. Bo felt his jaw drop. He was drifting toward a jagged tear in the glowing fabric, and through it he could see the ship, still lit up from its pale yellow underbelly. But that wasn't what made his mouth dry and his skin crawl all over. Beyond the ship, he could see more ships, hundreds more, how Gloom had said, drifting against the black void of space.

And they weren't alone. Bo saw what looked like blots of living ink jetting around them, darting and weaving in a way that reminded him of something. As he watched, one sharpened itself into a lance and drove through the hull of one of the ships. Another blot tried to follow, only to be incinerated by a blast of blue fire.

Bo realized he was watching a battle. The ships were maneuvering, sliding around each other, dispersing clouds of gas—the freezing gas—and destroying incoming blots with flickers of the same blue fire he remembered burning up his city. He'd wondered what it would look like, waging war against a living cloud, and now he knew. The shifting black blots were Gloom's people.

The light was bleeding off to gray and then black, and Bo was being pulled closer and closer to the tear. The ship was close, its hull rising up and blocking his view of everything going on behind it. Lia, inside it, was close. But between him and the ship and Lia, there was vacuum. Bo's chest tightened as he remembered what he'd imagined for the vanished othermother, head popped from the pressure, limbs coated in ice. He hoped his momentum would carry him all the way to the hull. He hoped he could use his Parasite to get inside and somehow plug up the hole behind him.

But he didn't know if momentum worked the same way inside the door. He didn't know how vacuum worked. For all he knew his eyeballs would explode in his head the instant he passed through. He braced himself, angled himself, tried to make sure he was pointing straight for the hull. The cold seared his skin.

He felt the door collapse around him—no, behind him—and

then he was through. His whole body tingled with it. Heat and cold raced through him; he felt sweat turning into ice, felt moisture whisking out of his mouth. Invisible hands were pressing at his head. He couldn't hear anything, but it didn't feel like his eardrums had ruptured. More pressure than pain.

Still moving forward. The hull was approaching, but it was farther than he'd judged. His tongue was swelling and freezing in his mouth. Blackness clamped the sides of his vision and started to squeeze. He knew his heart should be beating faster for how terrified he was, but it seemed to be doing the opposite, seemed to be slowing down.

Bo's head swam. He remembered what Violet had said: If you don't come back, that means I'm killing you right now. He couldn't die. Not if it meant Violet would think she'd killed him.

Not if it meant Lia would never know how hard he'd tried, how fucking hard he'd tried. The thought was stupid and selfish but he thought it anyway as he tried to kick again. His legs weren't listening anymore. His whole body was numb. All he managed was a twist of his head, and that set him in a lazy spin. He saw the blur of moving ships, the flickers of light, the distant stars. The door was long gone.

Then he couldn't see anything. Something blacker than space was swelling across his vision, blooming. Dying didn't feel so bad. Dying was like a warm cocoon. Wrapping him up, holding him, scuttling over his skin like a million tiny insects. Bo stiffened as the motes ran across him, into his mouth, down his arm. They slipped between his clenched knuckles. He remembered the lone mote still in his fist, the one he'd wanted to give back to Gloom.

As the motes touched it, a shudder passed through the cocoon, contracting it tight around him. Suddenly he could breathe again. He could feel his limbs, and the scalding pain spreading over his skin, under his muscles. But it was good. He knew it was good, but couldn't put his finger on why.

"Hello, Bo," came a tinny voice in his ear canal.

33

The warm walls of motes folded around him, bringing his circulation back, putting air back into his lungs, and Bo realized he was alive.

"Have we succeeded in our plan? Have we removed all of the keys from the ship?"

Bo blinked. It was Gloom, but it wasn't. It was the Gloom from back when he'd vanished the single mote, back in the room with the tanks. He remembered what Gloom had told him on the rooftop about being corrupted. Cut away. His single mote had taken over the others, or infected them, or something, with Gloom's personality. Bo moved his aching tongue around his mouth and felt more motes scurrying along it.

"Just one left," he whispered. "In the machine." He couldn't be sure, but it felt like they were starting to move. The motes swirled all around him, up and down his body, across his skin. The pain was slowly subsiding.

"Why are we on the other side of the door?" Gloom asked.

"Long story," Bo coughed. "You were only one mote. A second ago. You were only one mote that got sent through the door."

He felt a shudder go through the cocoon.

"Then I have caused another mutation," Gloom said, sounding almost bitter. "I have corrupted these motes and pulled them away from their purpose. They should be aiding in the assault."

Bo felt a stab of fear, wondering if Gloom might suddenly release them, might leave him adrift in vacuum again. "But they're you now," he said. "And you're... you know. You're a..."

"I am a saboteur," Gloom said gravely. "Yes. You are right. Perhaps we should sabotage the machine as well."

Wrapped in the blackness, Bo could hear nothing but his own lungs, his own heart, but he felt a change in pressure that made him think they were inside the ship. Heading toward the machine and toward Lia.

"Is there any way back?" Bo asked. "Is there any way me and Lia, me and the other host, can get back to our world?"

Gloom was silent for a long moment. "I do not know," he said. "You call your key a parasite. Parasites alter their hosts, but hosts also alter their parasites." He paused. "I can feel my other self. Dimly. Is he very different from me?"

"A day's worth, I guess," Bo said distractedly. "Not much."

They bumped against something, then Gloom started to come apart, motes streaming in all directions. Bo felt his feet touch floor. Gloom reassembled to his human shape, hands at his sides. They were facing the machine, but it was still now. There were no arcs of light, no revolving parts or swelling bulbs.

"The key is inside that structure," Gloom said, pointing to the same dark globe as he had an hour ago. "Shall I retrieve it?"

Bo inhaled. The air was thin, like he'd always imagined mountain air to be, not feeling like it filled his lungs all the way. He didn't think he would have been able to breathe properly anyway. Not right now.

"I'll come with you," he said. "Just lead the way."

"Very well," Gloom said, with no guile, no guilt. He slipped over to the duct at the base of the machine and motioned inside. Bo reminded himself that this wasn't the Gloom who'd left Lia behind, who'd made himself into a copy of her to fool him. It hadn't even occurred to this Gloom yet.

Bo crawled inside the machine and followed Gloom's lead, climbing then wriggling, sometimes pushing aside swatches of thick cable, once letting Gloom haul him up a sheer slippery surface. His heart was beating quicker and quicker and he had a strange floaty feeling all through his body. It didn't feel like this could be real after he'd been so close so many times. Then suddenly he was inside the globe, stepping into the curve of it, and he saw her.

She wasn't wired up, or full of tubes, or anything strange and horrible like he'd been dreading. Not even close. She had on the oversized fleece he'd handed to Wyatt so long ago. She was trying to walk, watching her feet, clinging with one hand to the circular black pad where she must have been laid out flat before.

Her head snapped up at his entrance. She pushed her hair out of her eyes. They were Lia's eyes.

"Bo?" she asked, her voice faint and rasping. "Is that you for real?"

Bo was swaying on his feet. It didn't feel like this could be real, after he'd imagined it so many times. "Hey," he said. "Hey. *Ina kwana?*"

Lia frowned. "What?"

"You know," Bo said, his heart pounding, thinking she had to remember or she wasn't Lia at all, it was another trick, another copy. "How Mom used to say to us in the mornings. *Ina kwana.*"

"Oh." Lia's mouth twitched toward a smile. "Yeah. *Lahiya lau.*"

Then Bo was flinging his arms around her and she was hugging back, harder than she had any right to be. Bo was crying and laughing at the same time and he didn't let her go until she wormed her finger under his rib and jabbed him where she'd left a bruise once. He yanked back.

"Hey!"

"You were crushing me." Lia wiped the tracks of tears down her cheeks. She shook her head. "I have no idea what's going on, Bo," she said. "My legs are jello. My head is like, whoa. They drugged me, I think." She plucked at the fabric of her fleece. "And left me this big-ass sweater, for some reason?"

Bo saw the Parasite undulating underneath and he remembered what came next. "I can tell you the whole story later," he said. "We have to use our Parasites right now. To get back to Earth. Do you got anything left?"

In answer, he felt a crackling surge of static from her abdomen. She wasn't looking at him, though. She was peering over his shoulder. "Who's that?" she demanded.

"He's a friend," Bo said, as Gloom slunk closer. He turned his head. "Do we do it at the same time, then?" he asked. "The vanish?"

"Yes," Gloom said, then he reached out with one long finger. His nail turned into a single black mote and dropped down onto Bo's shoulder. "Do you know about quantum entanglement, Bo?" he asked. "I can feel my other self. Motes are always drawn to their own. It might help you through the door."

The mote crawled down Bo's chest, onto his stomach, heating up against his wriggling Parasite. "What'll happen to you?" he asked.

"I have infected additional motes," Gloom said heavily. "I will be destroyed."

"Then you have to come with us," Bo said, shooting a look at Lia. "You can meet the other you."

"I will," Gloom said, pointing to the single mote. "If you successfully pass back through the door, of course." He paused, looking morose. "My other self succeeded in his mission, did he not?"

"Yeah," Bo said. "He was great. You were great."

Gloom was silent for a moment. "Good," he finally said. "Goodbye, children." He turned back into a mass of swirling motes and slid away before Bo could respond. He looked down at the single mote resting on his stomach. It was starting to spin.

"Have you vanished anything before?" Bo asked.

"A few times," Lia said. "Before they took me out of the warehouse. Never a person." She was sitting on the edge of the black pad now, holding her head. "Did that man really just dissolve? Was that real?"

"You'll get to meet him again," Bo said. "Maybe. Just focus on me. I'm going to focus on you. When the static is big, really big, we're going to let it go. Then..." He shrugged. "Think about home, I guess."

And if it didn't work, what then? Would they stay right where they were? Would they be spat out into space again? Would they end up stuck inside the door, drifting forever with everything else that Bo had vanished? A small part of him wanted to just wait here, just for a few minutes longer, just in case whatever they did next killed them.

"Same time, right?" Lia asked. "Count down from three?" Her face was already screwed up in concentration. The static was building between them, swelling. She reached out and grabbed his hand; he grabbed her other. His own Parasite was crackling now. His hairs were standing up.

"And go on the zero?" Bo asked.

"On the zero," Lia agreed. "But we don't say the zero."

Bo inhaled. Exhaled. His sister's hands were warm and dry against his, nothing like the cold clammy skin Gloom had made for himself. The mote was spinning between them now, suspended in the field of static. Whatever happened, wherever they ended up, they would be there together. That counted for something.

"Three," he said.

Violet was sitting on the jetty with Gloom standing beside her, hands at his sides, staring straight ahead in his unnerving way.

"You are a deviation," he said in a low voice.

Violet gave him a distracted glance. "What?"

Most of the other kids had bled away, with Wyatt leading them. Violet figured that was how he wanted the rest of the world to find him. Wyatt the savior, and his flock of Lost Boys. But Jon was still there, and so was Alberto, and Gilly, hugging herself against the chill. They had told Violet about Saif, and about the little note he had scrawled for her and left on her bed in the theater, the one in Arabic that nobody could read.

Up above them, dawn was streaking the sky with filaments of orange. But thinking about Saif, and about Bo, she couldn't enjoy it.

"You are a deviation," Gloom repeated. "You are not aligned with the animal binary of your people."

"Yeah," Violet said dryly. "I'm trying to get that fixed."

She didn't know where to watch. Didn't know if Bo and his sister would reappear in the boat, or out in the harbor, or somewhere else entirely. Or if they would reappear at all. But she didn't want to just leave, not yet.

"I am a deviation as well," Gloom said. "I was cut away from the whole. I cannot create new motes to replace the ones I lose. Sometimes it is very lonely."

Violet's jaw clenched. She thought about her parents. Gilly had joined them late, bringing news, like the fact that some of the wasters were waking up. Maybe her parents were among them, and Violet knew she would have to go and check. Go and see them one last time before she left. But if they were awake, she would do it from a distance. She wasn't going to let anything stop her from starting over.

"Yeah," she said. "It is sometimes."

"I would like to be friends," Gloom said. "Whether Bo returns or not. I prefer you to the strategist. I find him off-putting."

"Said the pot," Violet muttered. She didn't want to think about Wyatt. She didn't want to think about Bo not coming back. She didn't want to think at all.

"We are friends, then?" Gloom pressed.

She looked over at him again. His face was twisted up in one of his exaggerated frowns. Gloom needed to get out of the city too. It didn't sound like he had a home to go back to, and if people found out about him, he would end up locked away in Area 51 or some such shit. Besides, he would be useful to have along for whatever she did next. Maybe the bowler hat would grow on her eventually.

"Sure," she said. "Friends."

Gloom's gaunt face lit up in a smile, then turned suddenly serious. "I feel something," he said.

"Don't start crying," Violet warned.

Gloom turned his face up toward the sky. A ripple ran through his motes. Violet followed his gaze. The sun was rising a fiery orange, like smelted glass, shooting color through a blue-purple sky. She realized she hadn't seen a sunrise for months. But Gloom wasn't looking at the sun. Violet squinted. Up among the clouds, a tiny speck was falling toward Earth.

"You can fly, right?" she demanded.

Gloom's arms dissolved into thick black tendrils, swirled, re-formed into the giant moth wings Violet remembered from aboard the ship. He shot a worried glance at the sun. "The sunlight is not strong yet," he said. "Do you know about photovores, Violet?"

The other Lost Boys had caught sight of the speck; they were scrambling to their feet, Alberto with a yelp of surprise.

"Try, or I won't be your friend," Violet said hoarsely. She didn't take her eyes off the falling thing, or was it two things joined together? Her Parasite was starting to ripple. Gloom beat his wings once, twice, sending her hair whipping across her face.

By the time she'd raked it away from her eyes, he was airborne.

The door collapsed behind them and Bo and Lia were in free fall. His scream was ripped away but he could feel it in his chest; he tightened his grip on Lia's hands reflexively. The wind circled them, buffeted them. They were upside down; Bo saw a flash of his sister's open mouth, her eyes wide and terrified. They flipped again, falling on their stomachs, the ground hurtling up at them.

Through the chemical rush in his brain Bo recognized the downtown, maybe even the roof of the theater. They had made it back, but it didn't mean anything because they were plunging toward a sea of concrete and—

A dark shape swooped up underneath them. They bounced, tumbled, sank into something that was cool and slithering. Bo heard a gleeful warbling noise in his ears. He hauled his head up. Lia was across from him on Gloom's other wing, looking as shaken as Bo felt. The motes were clinging them in place.

Bo gave a yell that was triumph and elation and adrenaline all mixed. His hand was still locked tight to Lia's, and she looked at him now, with a grin growing across her face. She shouted something that might have been *Your friend?* but Bo couldn't quite hear it over the roaring in his ears. Gloom banked, then climbed higher.

The sky was clear. The ship, the ship that had loomed over his head for so many months, was gone forever. Pale purple clouds were rolling back in the far distance, and the sun was rising, hot and bright and clean. Gloom's motes were dancing with it underneath him. He could feel the sunshine on his face, bathing his skin.

He looked down over Gloom's shoulder and saw the ruined city in miniature, but with the sun lighting it, glimmering off all the smashed glass and water in the harbor, it was beautiful. The walls of fog that had kept them sealed off were gone, not even a wisp of them left. Bo could see a mass of tents set up outside the city, a whole camp of the people who he realized must have been watching, waiting, hoping for all those months. He could see a helicopter in the distance, humming across the harbor.

"The ship's gone," Lia shouted in his ear.

"You did that," Bo shouted back. "Sort of."

Lia raised her eyebrows, but she was still grinning. "You're welcome."

Gloom circled lower, and Bo felt the mote that had been clinging to his stomach melt away. A shudder went through the others. "Ah," he said. "You retrieved one of my motes. That was very thoughtful, Bo."

"What'll you do now?" Bo asked. "Now that your mission's over."

"Stay," Gloom said simply.

Bo was hit by a memory of the mote swarms tearing apart their enemy's ships, by the image Gloom had painted in his head of them stretching through space, wrapping around stars and draining them dark. Through all his joy, he felt a tremor of fear.

"Your people," he said. "Are they going to come here? Are they going to eat our sun?"

"Perhaps eventually," Gloom said. "Perhaps in a thousand years. Ten thousand. There are many suns." He paused. "But for now, things are well. Aren't they?"

Gloom swooped lower yet again, and now Bo could see they were heading toward a jetty. He saw Violet standing down there, and the other Lost Boys too, or at least some of them. He didn't see Wyatt's lanky frame, and that was a relief in itself.

"Who're they?" Lia asked, when they started to wave.

"You'll like them," Bo said. "They helped save the world."

A moment later they skidded into a landing on the wet wood. Bo and Lia got to their feet while Gloom re-formed, straightening the brim of his hat. Jon reached them first, tears rolling down his face how they did in the night, and pulled Bo into a fierce hug. Then Alberto and Gilly crowded in, half sobbing, half laughing—Bo tried to do the introductions even though he was crying too.

Violet was last, hanging back a bit. There was a smile playing on her lips, but it was small, almost sad. Bo reached forward and grabbed her hand.

"Violet, this is Lia," he said. "Lia, this is Violet." He gave her a bleary grin through his tears. "She's my other sister."

Lia looked her up and down for a moment, then slowly smiled. "I guess that makes us related, huh?"

Violet seemed surprised for a second, then she wiped her eyes with the heel of her hand and gave a shaky laugh. "Guess so. Yeah."

Bo hugged her hard as Jon and Alberto and Gilly crowded around again, everyone giddy from relief and exhaustion. He figured Gloom was right. For now, with Lia safe, with his family all around him, things were well.

For now, the sun was shining. Bo wasn't going to waste it.

Acknowledgments

The whole team at Orbit Books, without whom *Annex* wouldn't be the book it is today.

My sister, Heather Larson, who read each new scene as fast as I could write it and gave me feedback from start to finish.

Fellow writers Anthony Bell, Michael Hernshaw, Christopher Ruz, and Jeff Hemenway, who critiqued the shit out of the complete first draft.

The late Kit Reed, who was a mentor to me in my writing and introduced me to a terrific agent.

John Silbersack, the aforementioned agent, who sold *Annex* to the publisher with the help of his excellent assistant, Caitlin Meuser.

Samantha Riedel, whose insights were essential.

Cody Biberdorf, who called dibs on an acknowledgment way back in our soccer days.

My mom, who has listened to me brainstorm out loud for hours on end and is still my biggest fan.

All the other friends and family members who have either read my work, inspired it, or done both throughout the years. Thank you for getting me here, and please stick around for whatever comes next.

extras

meet the author

Photo Credit: Micaela Cockburn

RICH LARSON was born in Galmi, Niger, has studied in Rhode Island and worked in the south of Spain, and now lives in Ottawa, Canada. Since he began writing in 2011, he's sold over a hundred stories, the majority of them speculative fiction published in magazines such as *Analog*, *Asimov's*, *Clarkesworld*, *F&SF*, *Lightspeed*, and Tor.com.

His work also appears in numerous best-of-the-year anthologies and has been translated into Chinese, Vietnamese, Polish, Czech, and Italian. *Tomorrow Factory*, his debut collection, was released by Talos Press in October 2018. Besides writing, he enjoys traveling, learning languages, playing soccer, watching basketball, shooting pool, and dancing salsa and kizomba.

Find out more at richwlarson.tumblr.com and support his work via patreon.com/richlarson.

author interview

You've written short fiction for most of your career. What was it like transitioning to writing a full-length novel? Do you think your relationship with writing changes when writing short fiction versus a full-length novel?

Short stories provide that tight dopamine loop we all love so much: a little hit when you finish writing them, a bigger hit when you sell them, and successive hits when you get good reviews or reprint requests. Gratification comes fast and frequent, and the relative time commitment is small.

Full-length novels, on the other hand, take a long time to write, and if they turn out shitty nobody will ever read them—which makes you feel like you've wasted several months of your life. The three books I wrote before *Annex* are languishing in my Dropbox and will likely never see the light of day.

In that risk/reward way, writing novels is more stressful. The upside to writing novels, though, is that you can do things that are impossible in short fiction. You can create a really slow burn for certain character developments or layer small clues over an extended period of time before a big reveal. You can get deeper inside people's heads.

extras

Can you talk about how the idea for Annex developed?

Yes. I had the idea for Violet's character in 2012 and started writing a story that featured her as the lone survivor of a parasitic zombie outbreak. I never finished it.

In 2013, I wrote her into a short story called "Mother Mother," which was basically the scene where Bo and Violet hunt Bo's first othermother. All the editors I tried to sell to claimed that I had jammed too much backstory into too small a space, so I let it sit for a while.

Then, during the summer of 2015, I fleshed out "Mother Mother" into a novel with the working title *Mothership*. Several rounds of revision later, it was picked up by Orbit Books and became *Annex*.

How did you get started with writing speculative fiction? Why did it appeal to you as a writer?

When I was a kid I loved science fiction and fantasy books, so my first attempts at writing were speculative. There were a few years in college when I wrote realistic fiction about melancholy young Canadian men, but it was mostly to get published in trendy online lit mags.

Once I had crossed off most of the places on my little list, I switched over to speculative fiction and never looked back. It just affords me more options. I can use more of my creativity, and I've always loved thinking about the future. Oh, and it's more lucrative.

Having the novel unfold from Bo and Violet's perspectives is very moving. What did you hope to achieve by shifting the POV to children? How did it change the story being told?

I did the bulk of my reading when I was a kid, so my tastes sort of fossilized in YA. I'm very comfortable writing from younger perspectives, and it never occurred to me to write *Annex* from an adult POV—I always intended to write the sort of book I would have loved as a kid, one that features young protagonists but doesn't shy away from the dark. Sort of a tribute to Animorphs, *Shade's Children*, *The Thief Lord*, and other favorites of mine.

There are themes of belonging throughout Annex—belonging to the group, belonging to your family, belonging to yourself. Why did that subject appeal to you?

Belonging is a very personal theme for me, but it took me a long time to admit that. In 2014 I had a writing instructor (Charlie Jane Anders) point out to me that all the characters I wrote were outsiders. She asked me if that had something to do with how I grew up between cultures, moving between Niger, Canada, and the United States.

At first I felt sort of offended, as if she was questioning my ability to blend into new environments and build new relationships. Then I realized a lot of people don't have to measure their ability to blend into new environments and build new relationships. They don't even have to think about it.

So, yes. I struggle to feel like I belong in any particular place. I struggle to invest in people when I know so many relationships are temporary. My family is complicated. *Annex* let me engage with all that by exploring characters with similar struggles.

Diversity is a frequent conversation topic in publishing. Was it a conscious choice to include diverse characters in Annex or did it evolve on its own?

The idea for Violet as a trans teenager transitioning post-apocalypse has been with me since 2012, but Bo being Nigerian was a decision I made only when I actually started writing *Annex*. That was more of a personal thing for me, since I wanted to use some of my distinct memories from Niger in a character.

I do think writing diverse characters, particularly diverse young characters, is very important. I remember my aunt telling me about the first time she encountered a female Mennonite character in a novel, and what a big deal it was for her as a kid to read about a character that was *like her*.

I realized I had never had that revelatory experience, because practically all protagonists were superficially like me: white, male, often cerebral. So I guess I now want to give as many kids as possible that experience of finding characters who are in some way *like them*.

What was the most challenging moment of writing Annex?
The writing itself was relatively smooth. I wrote it while staying at my parents' place for a summer. Every morning I would walk to either a coffee shop or the library to work, and once I got into the flow of it I was breaking a thousand words a day. Revision is always the tricky part. When you change one thing in a novel, you have to change a dozen others. I hope to plan the next two out a little better to make that process easier, but probably won't.

Are there any authors who have particularly influenced how you see yourself as an author?
I still don't really see myself as an author. I'm way more likely to say "I write" than "I'm a writer." Writing is a thing that I do, and get paid for, but it's just a thing, not an identity. There are authors I consider important to what I write—Kenneth Oppel, Megan Whalen Turner, C. S. Lewis, M. T. Anderson, William Nicholson, K. A. Applegate,

Garth Nix—but it's for their specific works more than for their styles or personalities.

What do you want people to walk away with after reading Annex?

Nothing major: I just want them to have had a good time.

if you enjoyed
ANNEX

look out for

CYPHER

Book Two of the Violet Wars

by

Rich Larson

The invasion is over, but not all the aliens are gone. As the outside world learns what happened to their city, Violet and Bo struggle to keep Gloom hidden from prying eyes.

When those in power discover his capabilities, they realize Gloom may be the key to unlocking the mysteries behind the invaders and their technology. They'll stop at nothing until Gloom and his friends are captured and confined to a dissecting table ... or dead

"Remind me again." Violet tucked her hands beneath her head and looked down at her exposed stomach. Beneath her skin, the dull red shape of the Parasite bobbed up and down with the push-pull of her lungs. It was crackling with static, enough to make her arm hairs stand on end. "How much is this going to hurt?"

"I do not know, Violet." Her companion removed his black bowler hat and let it turn into a mass of seething black motes that coated his pale hands like gloves. "I am not familiar with the structure of its nervous system."

"I mean for me," Violet said. "How much is it going to hurt for me?"

A rippling shrug. "Vertebrates have a wide range of pain responses."

Violet snorted. "Bedside manner: five stars. Really great."

She tipped her head back and stared at the stucco ceiling, trying to slow her breathing and calm her Parasite. She couldn't rate the cleanliness of the surgical theater very highly either, since they were operating in a smoke-stained motel bedroom.

But she supposed she would cut her surgeon a break for his lack of interpersonal skills: Gloom wasn't a trained doctor or even a human being. As best she could figure, he was an insect colony of tiny intelligent machines that could do just about anything so long as there was enough sunlight.

Which made him a good choice to kill the alien organism in her stomach without killing her too.

"Okay, I'm ready," she said. "You ready?"

"I am always ready, Violet," Gloom said. "A saboteur..." He paused. "A surgeon must always be ready. I wonder, though, if you are making the correct decision." His black eyes fixed on the creature below Violet's skin. "The key has been very useful to you."

Violet knew that. In fact, she already felt a little bit guilty over it. Without the ability of the Parasite to shunt matter off to some other dimension, she and Bo and the other Lost Boys never would have been able to repel the alien invaders who had implanted them in the first place.

Sure, she still had nightmares every once in a while about the day they injected the Parasite through her belly button. But she figured the little monster hadn't had much of a choice either, and in the months since she had grown accustomed to its wriggles and churns and especially to the power it gave her to make things disappear. She would miss that.

On the other hand, her body chemistry was complex enough without an alien in her gut, and who knew what would happen if it kept growing? It was time to remove a variable.

"Yeah, it's been handy a few times," Violet admitted.

"But I've got you now, right? Friend?" As usual, the last word made Gloom's mouth twist up in a still vaguely creepy smile. He was like clockwork that way. "Yes. We are friends, Violet. We are the best of friends."

"Let's not go that far, Gloomy."

The lower half of Gloom's face dissolved and re-formed as a black surgical mask, but when he spoke his voice was unmuffled. "I do miss Bo, though. I like him better than you."

Violet's stomach gave a guilty twist that had nothing to do with the Parasite. "Yeah. He was a good kid. But he's happy. Safe. He's got his sister looking after him."

"Do you wish that we had stayed?" Gloom asked.

"I was born in that city and stuck there for fifteen fucking years," Violet said. "When the aliens showed up, I thought I was going to die there too. Now I'm going to see the world. So. No."

"I have seen many worlds," Gloom said solemnly. "Most were composed of gas."

"Yeah." Violet exhaled and nodded down at her stomach. "Let's kill this thing already."

Gloom nodded, then reached with both hands, his fingers unspooling into fine black tendrils. Violet squeezed her eyes shut as they slid through her skin.

if you enjoyed
ANNEX

look out for

ONE OF US

by

Craig DiLouie

They call him Dog.

Enoch is a teenage boy growing up in a rundown orphanage in Georgia during the 1980s. Abandoned from the moment they were born, Enoch and his friends are different. People in the nearby town whisper that the children from the orphanage are monsters.

The orphanage is not a happy home. Brutal teachers, farm labor, and communal living in a crumbling plantation house are Enoch's standard day-to-day. But he dreams of growing up to live among the normals as a respected man. He believes in a world less cruel, one where he can be loved.

extras

One night, Enoch and his friends share a campfire with a group of normal kids. As mutual fears subside, friendships form, and living together doesn't seem so out of reach.

But then a body is found, and it may be the spark that ignites revolution.

One

On the principal's desk, a copy of *Time*. A fourteen-year-old girl smiled on the cover. Pigtails tied in blue ribbon. Freckles and big white teeth. Rubbery, barbed appendages extending from her eye sockets.

Under that, a single word: WHY?

Why did this happen?

Or, maybe, why did the world allow a child like this to live?

What Dog wanted to know was why she smiled.

Maybe it was just reflex, seeing somebody pointing a camera at her. Maybe she liked the attention, even if it wasn't the nice kind.

Maybe, if only for a few seconds, she felt special.

The Georgia sun glared through filmy barred windows. A steel fan whirred in the corner, barely moving the warm, thick air. Out the window, Dog spied the old rusted pickup sunk in a riot of wildflowers. Somebody loved it once, then parked it here and left it to die. If Dog owned it, he would have kept driving and never stopped.

The door opened. The government man came in wearing a black suit, white shirt, and blue-and-yellow tie. His shiny shoes clicked across the grimy floor. He sat in Principal Willard's creaking chair and lit a cigarette. Dropped a file folder on the desk and studied Dog through a blue haze.

"They call you Dog," he said.

"Yes, sir, they do. The other kids, I mean."

Dog growled when he talked but took care to form each word right. The teachers made sure he spoke good and proper. Brain once told him these signs of humanity were the only thing keeping the children alive.

"Your Christian name is Enoch. Enoch Davis Bryant."

"Yes, sir."

Enoch was the name the teachers at the Home used. Brain said it was his slave name. Dog liked hearing it, though. He felt lucky to have one. His mama had loved him enough to at least do that for him. Many parents had named their kids XYZ before abandoning them to the Homes.

"I'm Agent Shackleton," the government man said through another cloud of smoke. "Bureau of Teratological Affairs. You know the drill, don't you, by now?"

Every year, the government sent somebody to ask the kids questions. Trying to find out if they were still human. Did they want to hurt people, ever have carnal thoughts about normal girls and boys, that sort of thing.

"I know the drill," Dog said.

"Not this year," the man told him. "This year is different. I'm here to find out if you're special."

"I don't quite follow, sir."

Agent Shackleton planted his elbows on the desk. "You're a ward of the state. More than a million of you. Living high on the hog for the past fourteen years in the Homes. Some of you are beginning to show certain capabilities."

"Like what kind?"

"I saw a kid once who had gills and could breathe underwater. Another who could hear somebody talking a mile away."

"No kidding," Dog said.

"That's right."

"You mean like a superhero."

"Yeah. Like Spider-Man, if Spider-Man half looked like a real spider."

"I never heard of such a thing," Dog said.

"If you, Enoch, have capabilities, you could prove you're worth the food you eat. This is your opportunity to pay it back. Do you follow me?"

"Sure, I guess."

Satisfied, Shackleton sat back in the chair and planted his feet on the desk. He set the file folder on his thighs, licked his finger, and flipped it open.

"Pretty good grades," the man said. "You got your math and spelling. You stay out of trouble. All right. Tell me what you can do. Better yet, show me something."

"What I can do, sir?"

"You do for me, I can do plenty for you. Take you to a special place."

Dog glanced at the red door at the side of the room before returning his gaze to Shackleton. Even looking at it was bad luck. The red door led downstairs to a basement room called Discipline, where the problem kids went.

He'd never been inside it, but he knew the stories. All the kids knew them. Principal Willard wanted them to know. It was part of their education.

He said, "What kind of place would that be?"

"A place with lots of food and TV. A place nobody can ever bother you."

Brain always said to play along with the normals so you didn't get caught up in their system. They wrote the rules in such a way to trick you into Discipline. More than that, though, Dog wanted to prove himself. He wanted to be special.

"Well, I'm a real fast runner. Ask anybody."

"That's your special talent. You can run fast."

"Real fast. Does that count?"

The agent smiled. "Running fast isn't special. It isn't special at all."

"Ask anybody how fast I run. Ask the—"

"You're not special. You'll never be special, Dog."

"I don't know what you want from me, sir."

Shackleton's smile disappeared along with Dog's file. "I want you to get the hell out of my sight. Send the next monster in on your way out."

Two

Pollution. Infections. Drugs. Radiation. All these things, Mr. Benson said from the chalkboard, can produce mutations in embryos.

A bacterium caused the plague generation. The other kids, the plague kids, who lived in the Homes.

Amy Green shifted in her desk chair. The top of her head was itching again. Mama said she'd worry it bald if she kept scratching at it. She settled on twirling her long, dark hair around her finger and tugging. Savored the needles of pain along her scalp.

"The plague is a sexually transmitted disease," Mr. Benson told the class.

She already knew part of the story from American History and from what Mama told her. The plague started in 1968, two years before she was born, back when love was still free. Then the disease named teratogenesis raced around the world, and the plague children came.

One out of ten thousand babies born in 1968 were monsters, and most died. One in six in 1969, and half of these died. One in three in 1970, the year scientists came up with a test to see if you had it. Most of them lived. After a neonatal nurse got arrested for killing thirty babies in Texas, the survival rate jumped.

More than a million monster babies screaming to be fed. By then, Congress had already funded the Home system.

Fourteen years later, and still no cure. If you caught the germ, the only surefire way to stop spreading it was abstinence, which they taught right here in health class. If you got pregnant with it, abortion was mandatory.

Amy flipped her textbook open and bent to sniff its cheesy new-book smell. Books, sharpened pencils, lined paper; she associated their bitter scents with school. The page showed a drawing of a woman's reproductive system. The baby comes out there. Sitting next to her, her boyfriend Jake glanced at the page and smiled, his face reddening. Like her, fascinated and embarrassed by it all.

In junior high, sex ed was mandatory, no ifs or buts. Amy and her friends were stumbling through puberty. Tampons, budding breasts, aching midnight thoughts, long conversations about what boys liked and what they wanted.

She already had a good idea what they wanted. Girls always complimented her about how pretty she was. Boys stared at her when she walked down the hall. Everybody so nice to her all the time. She didn't trust any of it.

When she stood naked in the mirror, she only saw flaws. Amy spotted a zit last week and stared at it for an hour, hating her ugliness. It took her over an hour every morning to get ready for school. She didn't leave the house until she looked perfect.

She flipped the page again. A monster grinned up at her. She slammed the book shut.

Mr. Benson asked if anybody in the class had actually seen a plague child. Not on TV or in a magazine, but up close and personal.

A few kids raised their hands. Amy kept hers planted on her desk.

"I have two big goals for you kids this year," the teacher said. "The main thing is teach you how to avoid spreading the disease. We'll be talking a lot about safe sex and all the regulations about whether and how you do it. How to get tested and how to access a safe abortion. I also aim to help you become accustomed to the plague children already born and who are now the same age as you."

For Amy's entire life, the plague children had lived in group homes out in the country, away from people. One was located just eight miles from Huntsville, though it might as well have been on the moon. The monsters never came to town. Out of sight meant out of mind, though one could never entirely forget them.

"Let's start with the plague kids," Mr. Benson said. "What do all y'all think about them? Tell the truth."

Rob Rowland raised his hand. "They ain't human. They're just animals."

"Is that right? Would you shoot one and eat it? Mount its head on your wall?"

The kids laughed as they pictured Rob so hungry he would eat a monster. Rob was obese, smart, and sweated a lot, one of the unpopular kids.

Amy shuddered with sudden loathing. "I hate them something awful."

The laughter died. Which was good, because the plague wasn't funny.

The teacher crossed his arms. "Go ahead, Amy. No need to holler, though. Why do you hate them?"

"They're monsters. I hate them because they're monsters."

Mr. Benson turned and hacked at the blackboard with a piece of chalk: MONSTRUM, a VIOLATION OF NATURE. From MONEO, which means TO WARN. In this case, a warning God is angry. Punishment for taboo.

"Teratogenesis is nature out of whack," he said. "It rewrote the body. Changed the rules. Monsters, maybe. But does a monster have to be evil? Is a human being what you look like, or what you do? What makes a man a man?"

Bonnie Fields raised her hand. "I saw one once. I couldn't even tell if it was a boy or girl. I didn't stick around to get to know it."

"But did you see it as evil?"

"I don't know about that, but looking the way some of them do, I can't imagine why the doctors let them all live. It would have been a mercy to let them die."

"Mercy on us," somebody behind Amy muttered.

The kids laughed again.

Sally Albod's hand shot up. "I'm surprised at all y'all being so scared. I see the kids all the time at my daddy's farm. They're weird, but there ain't nothing to them. They work hard and don't make trouble. They're fine."

"That's good, Sally," the teacher said. "I'd like to show all y'all something."

He opened a cabinet and pulled out a big glass jar. He set it on his desk. Inside, a baby floated in yellowish fluid. A tiny penis jutted between its legs. Its little arms grasped at nothing. It had a single slitted eye over a cleft where its nose should be.

The class sucked in its breath as one. Half the kids recoiled as the rest leaned forward for a better look. Fascination and revulsion. Amy alone didn't move. She sat frozen, shot through with the horror of it.

She hated the little thing. Even dead, she hated it.

"This is Tony," Mr. Benson said. "And guess what, he isn't one of the plague kids. Just some poor boy born with a birth defect. About three percent of newborns are born this way every year. It causes one out of five infant deaths."

Tony, some of the kids chuckled. They thought it weird it had a name.

"We used to believe embryos developed in isolation in the uterus," the teacher said. "Then back in the Sixties, a company sold thalidomide to pregnant women in Germany to help them with morning sickness. Ten thousand kids born with deformed limbs. Half died. What did scientists learn from that? Anybody?"

"A medicine a lady takes can hurt her baby even if it don't hurt her," Jake said.

"Bingo," Mr. Benson said. "Medicine, toxins, viruses, we call these things environmental factors. Most times, though, doctors have no idea why a baby like Tony is born. It just happens, like a dice roll. So is Tony a monster? What about a kid who's retarded, or born with legs that don't work? Is a kid in a wheelchair a monster too? A baby born deaf or blind?"

He got no takers. The class sat quiet and thoughtful. Satisfied, Mr. Benson carried the jar back to the cabinet. More gasps as baby Tony bobbed in the fluid, like he was trying to get out.

The teacher frowned as he returned the jar to its shelf. "I'm surprised just this upsets you. If this gets you so worked up, how will you live with the plague children? When they're adults, they'll have the same rights as you. They'll live among you."

Amy stiffened at her desk, neck clenched with tension at the idea. A question formed in her mind. "What if we don't want to live with them?"

Mr. Benson pointed at the jar. "This baby is you. And something not you. If Tony had survived, he would be different, yes. But he would be you."

"I think we have a responsibility to them," Jake said.

"Who's we?" Amy said.

His contradicting her had stung a little, but she knew how Jake had his own mind and liked to argue. He wore leather jackets, black T-shirts advertising obscure bands, ripped jeans. Troy and Michelle, his best friends, were Black.

He was popular because being unpopular didn't scare him. Amy liked him for that, the way he flouted junior high's iron rules. The way he refused to suck up to her like the other boys all did.

"You know who I mean," he said. "The human race. We made them, and that gives us responsibility. It's that simple."

"I didn't make anything. The older generation did. Why are they my problem?"

"Because they have it bad. We all know they do. Imagine being one of them."

"I don't want things to be bad for them," Amy said. "I really don't. I just don't want them around me. Why does that make me a bad person?"

"I never said it makes you a bad person," Jake said.

Archie Gaines raised his hand. "Amy has a good point, Mr. Benson. They're a mess to stomach, looking at them. I mean, I can live with it, I guess. But all this love and understanding is a lot to ask."

"Fair enough," Mr. Benson said.

Archie turned to look back at Amy. She nodded her thanks. His face lit up with a leering smile. He believed he'd rescued her and now she owed him.

She gave him a practiced frown to shut down his hopes. He turned away as if slapped.

"I'm just curious about them," Jake said. "More curious than scared. It's like you said, Mr. Benson. However they look, they're still our brothers. I wouldn't refuse help to a blind man, I guess I wouldn't to a plague kid neither."

The teacher nodded. "Okay. Good. That's enough discussion for today. We're getting somewhere, don't you think? Again, my goal for you kids this year is two things. One is to get used to the plague children. Distinguishing between a book and its cover. The other is to learn how to avoid making more of them."

Jake turned to Amy and winked. Her cheeks burned, all her annoyance with him forgotten.

She hoped there was a lot more sex ed and a lot less monster talk in her future. While Mr. Benson droned on, she glanced through the first few pages of her book. A chapter headline caught her eye: KISSING.

She already knew the law regarding sex. Germ or no germ, the legal age of consent was still fourteen in the State of Georgia. But another law said if you wanted to have sex, you had to get tested for the germ first. If you were under eighteen, your parents had to give written consent for the testing.

Kissing, though, that you could do without any fuss. It said so right here in black and white. You could do it all you wanted. Her scalp tingled at the thought. She tugged at her hair and savored the stabbing needles.

She risked a hungering glance at Jake's handsome profile. Though she hoped one day to go further than that, she could never do more than kissing. She could never know what it'd be like to scratch the real itch.

Nobody but her mama knew Amy was a plague child.

if you enjoyed
ANNEX
look out for

ROSEWATER

by

Tade Thompson

Rosewater is a town on the edge. A community formed around the edges of a mysterious alien biodome, its residents comprise the hopeful, the hungry and the helpless—people eager for a glimpse inside the dome or a taste of its rumored healing powers.

Kaaro is a government agent with a criminal past. He has seen inside the biodome, and doesn't care to again. But he is a sensitive, able to access the minds of others through the "xenosphere"—a shared unconsciousness the aliens brought to Earth—and something is killing off others of his kind. He must defy his masters to search for an answer, facing his dark history and coming to a realization about a horrifying future.

Chapter One

Rosewater: Opening Day 2066
Now

I'm at the Integrity Bank job for forty minutes before the anxieties kick in. It's how I usually start my day. This time it's because of a wedding and a final exam, though not my wedding and not my exam. In my seat by the window I can see, but not hear, the city. This high above Rosewater everything seems orderly. Blocks, roads, streets, traffic curving sluggishly around the dome. I can even see the cathedral from here. The window is to my left, and I'm at one end of an oval table with four other contractors. We are on the fifteenth floor, the top. A skylight is open above us, three foot square, a security grid being the only thing between us and the morning sky. Blue, with flecks of white cloud. No blazing sun yet, but that will come later. The climate in the room is controlled despite the open skylight, a waste of energy for which Integrity Bank is fined weekly. They are willing to take the expense.

Next to me on the right, Bola yawns. She is pregnant and gets very tired these days. She also eats a lot, but I suppose that's to be expected. I've known her two years and she has been pregnant in each of them. I do not fully understand pregnancy. I am an only child and I never grew up around pets or livestock. My education was peripatetic; biology was never a strong interest, except for microbiology, which I had to master later.

I try to relax and concentrate on the bank customers. The wedding anxiety comes again.

Rising from the centre of the table is a holographic tele-prompter. It consists of random swirls of light right now, but within a few minutes it will come alive with text. There is a room adjacent to ours in which the night shift is winding down.

"I hear they read Dumas last night," says Bola.

She's just making conversation. It is irrelevant what the other shift reads. I smile and say nothing.

The wedding I sense is due in three months. The bride has put on a few pounds and does not know if she should alter the dress or get liposuction. Bola is prettier when she is pregnant.

"Sixty seconds," says a voice on the tannoy.

I take a sip of water from the tumbler on the table. The other contractors are new. They don't dress formally like Bola and me. They wear tank tops and T-shirts and metal in their hair. They have phone implants.

I hate implants of all kinds. I have one. Standard locator with no add-ons. Boring, really, but my employer demands it.

The exam anxiety dies down before I can isolate and explore the source. Fine by me.

The bits of metal these young ones have in their hair come from plane crashes. Lagos, Abuja, Jos, Kano and all points in between, there have been downed aircraft on every domestic route in Nigeria since the early 2000s. They wear bits of fuse-lage as protective charms.

Bola catches me staring at her and winks. Now she opens her snack, a few wraps of cold moin-moin, the orange bean curds nested in leaves, the old style. I look away.

"Go," says the tannoy.

extras

The text of Plato's *Republic* scrolls slowly and steadily in ghostly holographic figures on the cylindrical display. I start to read, as do the others, some silently, others out loud. We enter the xenosphere and set up the bank's firewall. I feel the familiar brief dizziness; the text eddies and becomes transparent.

Every day about five hundred customers carry out financial transactions at these premises, and every night staffers make deals around the world, making this a twenty-four-hour job. Wild sensitives probe and push, criminals trying to pick personal data out of the air. I'm talking about dates-of-birth, PINs, mothers' maiden names, past transactions, all of them lying docile in each customer's forebrain, in the working memory, waiting to be plucked out by the hungry, untrained and freebooting sensitives.

Contractors like myself, Bola Martinez and the metalheads are trained to repel these. And we do. We read classics to flood the xenosphere with irrelevant words and thoughts, a firewall of knowledge that even makes its way to the subconscious of the customer. A professor did a study of it once. He found a correlation between the material used for firewalling and the activities of the customer for the rest of the year. A person who had never read Shakespeare would suddenly find snatches of *King Lear* coming to mind for no apparent reason.

We can trace the intrusions if we want, but Integrity isn't interested. It's difficult and expensive to prosecute crimes perpetuated in the xenosphere. If no life is lost, the courts aren't interested.

The queues for cash machines, so many people, so many cares and wants and passions. I am tired of filtering the lives of others through my mind.

I went down yesterday to the Piraeus with Glaucon the son of Ariston, that I might offer up my prayers to the goddess; and also because I wanted to see in what manner they would celebrate the festival, which was a new thing. I was delighted with the procession of the inhabitants; but that of the Thracians was equally, if not more, beautiful. When we had finished our prayers and viewed the spectacle, we turned in the direction of the city...

On entering the xenosphere, there is a projected self-image. The untrained wild sensitives project their true selves, but professionals like me are trained to create a controlled, chosen self-image. Mine is a gryphon.

My first attack of the day comes from a middle-aged man from a town house in Yola. He looks reedy and very dark-skinned. I warn him and he backs off. A teenager takes his place quickly enough that I think they are in the same physical location as part of a hack farm. Criminal cabals sometimes round up sensitives and yoke them together in a "Mumbai combo"—a call-centre model with serial black hats.

I've seen it all before. There aren't as many such attacks now as there were when I started in this business, and a part of me wonders if they are discouraged by how effective we are. Either way, I am already bored.

During the lunch break, one of the metalheads comes in and sits by me. He starts to talk shop, telling me of a near-miss intrusion. He looks to be in his twenties, still excited about being a sensitive, finding everything new and fresh and interesting, the opposite of cynical, the opposite of me.

He must be in love. His self-image shows propinquity. He is good enough to mask the other person, but not good enough to mask the fact of his closeness. I see the shadow, the ghost beside him. Out of respect I don't mention this.

The metal he carries is twisted into crucifixes and attached to a single braid on otherwise short hair, which leaves his head on the left temple and coils around his neck, disappearing into the collar of his shirt.

"I'm Clement," he says. "I notice you don't use my name."

This is true. I was introduced to him by an executive two weeks back, but I forgot his name instantly and have been using pronouns ever since.

"My name—"

"You're Kaaro. I know. Everybody knows you. Excuse me for this, but I have to ask. Is it true that you've been inside the dome?"

"That's a rumour," I say.

"Yes, but is the rumour true?" asks Clement.

Outside the window, the sun is far too slow in its journey across the sky. Why am I here? What am I doing?

"I'd rather not discuss it."

"Are you going tonight?" he asks.

I know what night it is. I have no interest in going.

"Perhaps," I say. "I might be busy."

"Doing what?"

This boy is rather nosy. I had hoped for a brief, polite exchange, but now I find myself having to concentrate on him, on my answers. He is smiling, being friendly, sociable. I should reciprocate.

"I'm going with my family," says Clement. "Why don't you come with us? I'm sending my number to your phone. All of Rosewater will be there."

That is the part that bothers me, but I say nothing to Clement. I accept his number, and text mine to his phone implant out of politeness, but I do not commit.

Before the end of the working day, I get four other invitations to the Opening. I decline most of them, but Bola is not a person I can refuse.

"My husband has rented a flat for the evening, with a view," she says, handing me a slip of paper with the address. Her look of disdain tells me that if I had the proper implant we would not need to kill trees. "Don't eat. I'll cook."

By eighteen hundred hours the last customer has left and we're all typing at terminals, logging the intrusion attempts, cross-referencing to see if there are any hits, and too tired to joke. We never get feedback on the incident reports. There's no pattern analysis or trend graph. The data is sucked into a bureaucratic black hole. It's just getting dark, and we're all in our own heads now, but passively connected to the xenosphere. There's light background music—"Blue Alien" by Jos. It's not unpleasant, but my tastes run to much older fare. I'm vaguely aware that a chess game is going on, but I don't care between whom. I don't play so I don't understand the progress.

"Hello, Gryphon," someone says.

I focus, but it's gone. She's gone. Definitely female. I get a wispy impression of a flower in bloom, something blue, but that's it. I'm too tired or lazy to follow it up, so I punch in my documentation and fill out the electronic time sheet.

I ride the elevator to street level. I have never seen much of the bank. The contractors have access to the express elevator. It's unmarked and operated by a security guard, who sees us even though we do not see him or his camera. This may as well be magic. The elevator seems like a rather elegant wooden box. There are no buttons and it is unwise to have confidential conversations in there. This time as I leave, the operator says, "Happy Opening." I nod, unsure of which direction to respond in.

The lobby is empty, dark. Columns stand inert like Victorian dead posed for pictures. The place is usually staffed when I go home, but I expect the staff have been allowed to leave early for the Opening.

It's full night now. The blue glow from the dome is omni-present, though not bright enough to read by. The skyline around me blocks direct view, but the light frames every high-rise to my left like a rising sun, and is reflected off the ones to my right. This is the reason there are no street lights in Rosewa-ter. I make for Alaba Station, the clockwise platform, to travel around the edge of the dome. The streets are empty save the constable who walks past swinging her baton. I am wearing a suit so she does not care to harass me. A mosquito whines past my ear but does not appear to be interested in tasting my blood. By the time I reach the concourse, there is a patch of light sweat in each of my armpits. It's a warm night. I text my flat to reduce internal temperature one degree lower than external.

Alaba Station is crowded with commercial-district workers and the queues snake out to the street, but they are almost all going anticlockwise to Kehinde Station, which is closest to the Open-ing. I hesitate briefly before I buy my ticket. I plan to go home and change, but I wonder if it will be difficult to meet up with Bola and her husband. I have a brief involuntary connection to the xenosphere and a hot, moist surge of anger from a cuckolded husband lances through me. I disconnect and breathe deeply.

I go home. Even though I have a window seat and the dome is visible, I do not look at it. When I notice the reflected light on the faces of other passengers, I close my eyes, though this does not keep out the savoury smell of akara or the sound of their triv-ial conversation. There's a saying that everybody in Rosewater dreams of the dome at least once every night, however briefly. I know this is not true because I have never dreamed of the place.

That I have somewhere to sit on this train is evidence of the draw of the Opening. The carriages are usually full to bursting, and hot, not from heaters, but from body heat and exhalations and despair.

I come off at Atewo after a delay of twenty-five minutes due to a power failure from the North Ganglion. I look around for Yaro, but he's nowhere to be found. Yaro's a friendly stray dog who sometimes follows me home and to whom I feed scraps. I walk from the station to my block, which takes ten minutes. When I get signal again, my phone has four messages. Three of them are jobs. The fourth is from my most demanding employer.

Call now. And get a newer phone implant. This is prehistoric.

I do not call her. She can wait.

I live in a two-bed partially automated flat. Working two jobs, I could get a better place with fully humanised AI if I wanted. I have the funds, but not the inclination. I strip, leaving my clothes where they lie, and pick out something casual. I stare at my gun holster, undecided. I do not like guns. I cross the room to the wall safe, which appears in response to signals from my ID implant. I open it and consider taking my gun. There are two magazines of ammo beside it, along with a bronze mask and a clear cylinder. The fluid in the cylinder is at rest. I pick it up and shake it, but the liquid is too viscous and it stays in place. I put it back and decide against a weapon.

I shower briefly and head out to the Opening.

How to talk about the Opening?

It is the formation of a pore in the biodome. Rosewater is a doughnut-shaped city that surrounds the dome. In the early days we actually called it the Doughnut. I was there. I saw it grow from a frontier town of tents and clots of sick people huddling together for warmth into a kind of shanty town of hopefuls and from there into an actual municipality. In its eleven years of existence the dome has not taken in a single outsider. I was the last person to traverse it and there will not be another. Rosewater, on the other hand, is the same age and grows constantly.

Every year, though, the biodome opens for twenty or thirty minutes in the south, in the Kehinde area. Everyone in the vicinity of the opening is cured of all physical and some mental ailments. It is also well known and documented that the outcome is not always good, even if diseases are abolished. There are reconstructions that go wrong, as if the blueprints are warped. Nobody knows why this happens, but there are also people who deliberately injure themselves for the sole purpose of getting "reconstructive surgery."

Trains are out of the question at this time, on this night. I take a taxi, which drives in the opposite direction first, then describes a wide southbound arc, taking a circuitous route through the back roads and against the flow of traffic. This works until it doesn't. Too many cars and motorbikes and bicycles, too many people walking, too many street performers and preachers and out-of-towners. I pay the driver and walk the rest of the way to Bola's temporary address. This is easy as my path is perpendicular to the crush of pilgrims.

Oshodi Street is far enough from the biodome that the crowd is not so dense as to impede my progress. Number 51 is a tall, narrow four-storey building. The first door is propped open with an empty wooden beer crate. I walk into a hallway that leads to two flats and an elevator. On the top floor, I knock, and Bola lets me in.

One thing hits me immediately: the aroma and heat blast of hot food, which triggers immediate salivation and the drums of hunger in my stomach. Bola hands me field glasses and leads me into the living room. There is a similar pair dangling on a strap around her neck. She wears a shirt with the lower buttons open so that her bare gravid belly pokes out. Two children, male and female, about eight or nine, run around, frenetic, giggling, happy.

"Wait," says Bola. She makes me stand in the middle of the

room and returns with a paper plate filled with akara, dodo and dundu, the delicious street-food triad of fried beans, fried plantain and fried yam. She leads me by the free hand to the veranda, where there are four deckchairs facing the dome. Her husband, Dele, is in one, the next is empty, the third is occupied by a woman I don't know, and the fourth is for me.

Dele Martinez is rotund, jolly but quiet. I've met him many times before and we get along well. Bola introduces the woman as Aminat, a sister, although the way she emphasises the word, this could mean an old friend who is as close as family rather than a biological sibling. She's pleasant enough, smiles with her eyes, has her hair drawn back into a bun and is casually dressed in jeans. She is perhaps my age or younger. Bola knows I am single and has made it her mission to find me a mate. I don't like this because… well, when people matchmake, they introduce people to you whom they think are sufficiently like you. Each person they offer is a commentary on how they see you. If I've never liked anyone Bola has introduced me to, does that mean she doesn't know me well enough, or that she does know me but I hate myself?

I sit down and avoid talking by eating. I avoid eye contact by using the binoculars.

The crowd is contained in Sanni Square—usually a wide-open space framed by shops that exist only to exploit visitors to the city, cafés that usually cater to tired old men, and travel agents—behind which Oshodi Street lurks. A firework goes off, premature, a mistake. Most leave the celebrations till afterwards. Oshodi Street is a good spot. It's bright from the dome and we are all covered in that creamy blue electric light. The shield is not dazzling, and up close you can see a fluid that ebbs and flows just beneath the surface.

The binoculars are high-end, with infrared sensitivity and a kind of optional implant hack that brings up individual detail about whoever I focus on, tag information travelling by laser dot and information downloading from satellite. It is a bit like being in the xenosphere; I turn it off because it reminds me of work.

Music wafts up, carried in the night but unpleasant and cacophonous because it comes from competing religious factions, bombastic individuals and the dome tourists. It is mostly percussion-accompanied chanting.

There are, by my estimate, thousands of people. They are of all colours and creeds: black Nigerians, Arabs, Japanese, Pakistani, Persians, white Europeans and a mishmash of others. All hope to be healed or changed in some specific way. They sing and pray to facilitate the Opening. The dome is, as always, indifferent to their reverence or sacrilege.

Some hold a rapt, religious awe on their faces and cannot bring themselves to talk, while others shout in a continuous, sustained manner. An imam has suspended himself from a roof in a harness that looks homemade, and is preaching through a bullhorn. His words are lost in the din, which swallows meaning and nuance and shits out a homogenous roar. Fights break out but are quashed in seconds because nobody knows if you have to be "good" to deserve the blessings from the biodome.

A barricade blocks access to the dome and armed constables form up in front of it. The first civilians are one hundred metres away, held back by an invisible stanchion. The officers look like they will shoot to kill. This is something they have done in the past, the latest incident being three years back, when the crowd showed unprecedented rowdiness. Seventeen dead, although the victims rose during that year's Opening. They were...destroyed two weeks later as they clearly were not themselves any more. This happens. The alien can restore the body, but not the soul, something Anthony told me back in '55, eleven years ago.

I cough from the peppery heat of the akara. The fit drives

my vision briefly to the sky and I see a waning gibbous, battling bravely to be noticed against the light pollution.

I see the press, filming, correspondents talking into microphones. Here and there are lay scientists with big scanners pointed finger-like towards the dome. Sceptics, true believers, in-between, all represented, all busy. Apart from the classified stuff about sensitives and the xenosphere, most information about the dome is in the public domain, but it is amazing that the fringe press and conspiracy theorists have different ideas. A large segment of the news-reading population, for example, believes that the alien is entirely terrestrial, a result of human biological experimentation. There is "proof" of this on Nimbus, of course. There are scientists who don't believe, but they take observations and collate data for ever, refusing to come to conclusions. There are those who believe the dome is a magical phenomenon. I won't get started on the quasi-religious set.

I feel a gentle tap on my left shoulder and emerge from the vision. Aminat is looking at me. Bola and her husband have shifted out of earshot.

"What do you see?" she asks. She smiles as if she is in on some joke but unsure if it's at my expense.

"People desperate for healing," I say. "What do you see?"

"Poverty," says Aminat. "Spiritual poverty."

"What do you mean?"

"Nothing. Maybe humankind was meant to be sick from time to time. Maybe there is something to be learned from illness."

"Are you politically inclined against the alien?"

"No, hardly. I don't have politics. I just like to examine all angles of an issue. Do you care?"

I shake my head. I don't want to be here, and if not for Bola's invitation I would be home contemplating my cholesterol levels. I am intrigued by Aminat, but not enough to want to access her thoughts. She is trying to make conversation, but I don't like talking about the dome. Why then do I live in Rosewater? I should move to Lagos, Abuja, Accra, anywhere but here.

"I don't want to be here either," says Aminat.

I wonder for a moment if she has read my thoughts, if Bola matched us because she is also a sensitive. That would be irritating.

"Let's just go through the motions to keep Bola happy. We can exchange numbers at the end of the evening and never call each other again. I will tell her tomorrow, when she asks, that you were interesting and attentive, but there was no chemistry. And you will say...?"

"That I enjoyed my evening, and I like you, but we didn't quite click."

"You will also say that I had wonderful shoes and magnificent breasts."

"Er...okay."

"Good. We have a deal. Shake on it?"

Except we cannot shake hands because there is oil on mine from the akara, but we touch the backs of our hands together, co-conspirators. I find myself smiling at her.

A horn blows and we see a dim spot on the dome, the first sign. The dark spot grows into a patch. I have not seen this as often as I should. I saw it the first few times but stopped bothering after five years.

The patch is roughly circular, with a diameter of six or seven feet. Black as night, as charcoal, as pitch. It looks like those dark bits on the surface of the sun. This is the boring part. It will take half an hour for the first healing to manifest. Right now, all is invisible. Microbes flying into the air. The scientists are frenzied now. They take samples and will try to grow cultures on blood agar. Futile. The xenoforms do not grow on artificial media.

In the balcony everyone except me takes a deep breath, trying to get as many microbes inside their lungs as possible. Aminat breaks her gaze from the dome, twists in her seat and kisses me on the lips. It lasts seconds and nobody else sees it, intent as they are upon the patch. After a while, I am not sure it happened at all. I don't know what to make of it. I can read minds but I still don't understand women. Or men. Humans. I don't understand humans.

Down below, it begins, the first cries of rapture. It is impossible to confirm or know what ailments are taken care of at first. If there is no obvious deformity or stigmata, like jaundice, pallor or a broken bone, there is no visible change except the emotional state of the healed. Already, down at the front, younger pilgrims are doing cartwheels and crying with gratitude.

A man brought in on a stretcher gets up. He is wobbly at first, but then walks confidently. Even from this distance I can see the wideness and wildness of his eyes and the rapid flapping of his lips. Newcomers experience disbelief.

This continues in spurts and sometimes ripples that flow through the gathered people. The trivial and the titanic are equally healed.

The patch is shrinking now. At first the scientists and I are the only ones to notice. Their activities become more agitated. One of them shouts at the others, though I cannot tell why.

I hear a tinkle of laughter from beside me. Aminat is laughing with delight, her hands held half an inch from her face and both cheeks moist. She is sniffing. That's when it occurs to me that she might be here for healing as well.

At that moment, I get a text. I look at my palm to read the message off the flexible subcutaneous polymer. My boss again.

Call right now, Kaaro. I am not kidding.

orbit

Follow us:

/orbitbooksUS

/orbitbooks

/orbitbooks

Join our mailing list
to receive alerts on our
latest releases and deals.

orbitbooks.net

Enter our monthly
giveaway for the chance
to win some epic prizes.

orbitloot.com